*Praise for Henning Mankell and*

# Kennedy's Brain

"Henning Mankell is crime fiction's master juggler. Few of this genre's writers—few of any genre's writers—have been able to balance the ordinary and the grotesque with such literary dash and page-turning brio. . . . Mankell's atmospherics . . . give you metaphysical goose bumps." —*Boston Herald*

"Henning Mankell is an addictive writer."
—*Los Angeles Times Book Review*

"A cautionary tale, an exploration of family relationships, a provocative portrayal of grief and an indictment of worldwide ignorance. . . . Mankell's poetic style . . . will move readers of all kinds of literature." —*Bookreporter*

"Gruesome enough to satisfy any gore-loving mystery reader. . . . [Mankell] has emerged as the natural heir to the great Swedish crime novelists Maj Sjöwall and Per Wahlöö."
—*The New York Times*

"Bracing. . . . A moving tale of loss."
—*Booklist* (starred review)

Also by Henning Mankell

Henning Mankell

# Kennedy's Brain

Internationally bestselling novelist and playwright
Henning Mankell has received the German Tolerance
Prize and the U.K.'s Golden Dagger Award and has been
nominated for a *Los Angeles Times* Book Prize three
times. His Kurt Wallander mysteries have been published
in thirty-three countries and consistently top the best-
seller lists in Europe. He divides his time between Sweden
and Maputo, Mozambique, where he has worked as the
director of Teatro Avenida since 1985.

www.henningmankell.com

# Henning Mankell

# Kennedy's Brain

TRANSLATED FROM
THE SWEDISH
BY

Laurie Thompson

*Vintage Crime/Black Lizard*
Vintage Books
A Division of Random House, Inc.
New York

To Ellen and Ingmar

FIRST VINTAGE CRIME/BLACK LIZARD EDITION, NOVEMBER 2008

*English translation copyright © 2007 by Laurie Thompson*

All rights reserved. Published in the United States by Vintage Books, a division of Random House, Inc., New York. Originally published in Sweden as *Kennedys Hjärna* by Leopard Förlag, Stockholm, in 2005. Copyright © 2005 by Henning Mankell. This translation originally published in hardcover in Great Britain by Harvill Secker, London, and subsequently published in hardcover in the United States by The New Press, New York, in 2007.

Vintage is a registered trademark and Vintage Crime/Black Lizard and colophon are trademarks of Random House, Inc.

This is a work of fiction. Names, characters, places, and incidents either are the product of the author's imagination or are used fictitiously. Any resemblance to actual persons, living or dead, events, or locales is entirely coincidental.

Library of Congress Cataloging-in-Publication Data:
Mankell, Henning, 1948–
[Kennedys hjärna. English]
Kennedy's brain / by Henning Mankell ; translated from the Swedish by Laurie Thompson.
—1st Vintage Crime/Black Lizard ed.
p. cm.
Originally published under title Kennedy's hjärna: Stockholm : Leopard, 2005.
ISBN 978-0-307-38591-8
1. Archaeologists—Fiction. 2. AIDS (Disease)—Patients—Fiction.
3. Children—Death—Fiction. I. Thompson, Laurie. II. Title.
PT9876.23.A49K4613 2008
839.7'374—dc22
2008028027

www.vintagebooks.com

Printed in the United States of America
10  9  8  7  6  5

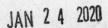

# CONTENTS

# PART 1

## Christ's Cul-de-sac

'Defeats should be out in the open, they shouldn't be hidden away, for it is defeats that make one a human being. A man who never understands his defeats takes nothing with him into the future.'

*Aksel Sandemose*

# CHAPTER 1

The catastrophe happened in the autumn. She had no idea what was coming, no warning. No shadow was cast; it struck without a sound.

It was like being waylaid in a dark alley. But the fact was that it forced her away from her ruins, into a reality that she had never really concerned herself with. She was hurled with immense force into a world where the excavation of Greek Bronze Age graves was irrelevant.

She had been living deep down in her dusty trenches, or hunched over shattered vases that she was trying to piece together. She had loved her ruins, and failed to notice that the world around her was starting to collapse. She was an archaeologist forced to leave the past and stand next to a grave she had never imagined possible.

There were no portents. The tragedy had been robbed of its voice. It was unable to shout out a warning to her.

The evening before Louise Cantor travelled to Sweden to take part in a conference on current archaeological excavations of Bronze Age graves, she stood on a ceramic fragment in the bathroom and suffered a deep wound in her left foot. It bled copiously over the floor, making her feel sick. The shard dated from the fifth century BC.

She was in Argolis on Peloponnisos, 137 kilometres outside Athens, it was September and the year's excavations were coming to a close. She could already feel a chill in the wind that presaged the coming winter. The dry heat with its scent of rosemary and thyme was beginning to fade.

She stemmed the flow of blood and applied a plaster. A memory came storming into her mind.

A rusty nail that had gone right through her foot – not the one she had cut now, but the other one, her right foot. She must have been five or six years old. The brown nail had penetrated her heel, forced its way through skin and flesh and impaled her as if on a pole. She had howled with pain, and thought that she was undergoing the same kind of torture experienced by the man crucified on the cross at the front of the church where she sometimes played her lonely horror games.

We are pierced over and over again by these barbs, she thought as she wiped the blood off the cracked floor tiles. A woman spends all her life in the proximity of these sharp edges out to penetrate what she is trying to protect.

She limped to the part of the house that doubled as her workplace and bedroom. In one corner was a creaky rocking chair and a CD player. She had been given the CD player by old Leandros, the caretaker. Leandros had been around as a poverty-stricken but curious child when the Swedish excavations at Argolis began in the 1930s. Nowadays he spent his nights fast asleep while on caretaking duty at the Mastos hill. But everybody on the project supported him. Leandros was an essential cog in the wheel. Without him, all future grants to enable the continuation of the excavations would be under threat. Exercising the prerogative of old age, Leandros had become a toothless and often noticeably filthy guardian angel.

Louise Cantor sat down on the rocking chair and examined her wounded foot. She smiled at the thought of Leandros. Most Swedish archaeologists she knew were aggressively impious, and refused to accept various authorities as anything other than obstacles in the way of the continued dig. A few gods who had lost all significance a very long time ago could hardly affect the distant Swedish authorities when it came to approving or rejecting expenditure on archaeological ventures. Swedish bureaucracy was a sort of tunnel world with entrances and exits, but nothing in between; and the decisions that eventually found their way to the sweltering Greek burial vaults were often extremely difficult to understand.

An archaeologist always needs to be doubly blessed, she thought. We never know if we are going to find what we are looking for, or if we are looking for what we want to find. If we get it right, we are greatly blessed. But at the same time we never know if we are going to be given permission and sufficient money to dig deeper into the marvellous ruined worlds, or if the milch cow's udders will suddenly dry up. This was Louise's contribution to archaeological jargon: to describe the funding authorities as milch cows with capricious udders.

She looked at the clock. It was a quarter past eight, an hour earlier in Sweden. She reached for the telephone and dialled the number of her son in Stockholm.

She could hear the ringing, but nobody answered. When the answering machine cut in, she listened to his voice with her eyes closed.

It was a voice that calmed her down. '*Det här är en telefonsvarare och du vet vad du ska göra. I'll repeat that in English. This is an answering machine and you know what to do. Henrik.*'

She left her message. '*Don't forget that I'm coming home. I shall be in Visby for two days, discussing the Bronze Age. Then I'll go to Stockholm. I love you. See you soon. I might ring you later. If not, I'll be in touch from Visby.*'

She fetched the ceramic fragment that had injured her foot. One of her closest colleagues, a very keen female student from Lund, had found it. It was a shard like millions of others, a piece of Attic pottery that she guessed came from a pot or jar made just before the colour red started to dominate.

She enjoyed piecing together ceramic fragments, imagining the original object that she would probably be unable to reconstruct. She would give this one to Henrik as a present. She put it on top of her packed suitcase that was waiting for the lid to be closed.

As usual, she was feeling restless before leaving. She was finding it hard to curb her increasing impatience, and decided to change her plans for the evening. Until she had cut her foot, she had intended to spend a few hours on the paper she was writing about Attic pottery. Instead, she turned off her desk lamp, switched on the CD player and sank back in the rocking chair.

As usual when she was listening to music, the dogs started barking in the darkness outside. They belonged to her nearest neighbour, Mitsos, who was part-owner of an excavator. He was also the owner of the little house she rented. Most of her colleagues lived in Argolis, but she had preferred to stay close to the dig.

She had almost dozed off when she sat up with a start. It had struck her that she did not want to spend the night on her own. She turned down the volume and phoned Vassilis. He had promised to take her to the airport in Athens the next morning. As the Lufthansa flight to Frankfurt left very early, they would need to set off at five o'clock. She'd rather have company when she knew she would not be able to sleep soundly anyway.

She looked at the clock and realised that Vassilis was probably still at the office. One of their rare quarrels had concerned his job. She thought she had been a bit insensitive in saying that the accounting profession must be the most combustible in existence. She could still recall her exact words, which sounded much nastier than she had intended.

'The most combustible profession there is. So dry and lifeless that it could burst into flames at any minute.'

He had been surprised, perhaps saddened, but most of all angry. At that moment it dawned on her there was more to their relationship than just sex. She enjoyed his company despite the fact – or because of it – that he had no interest whatsoever in archaeology. She had been afraid that he would be so offended that he would break off their affair on the spot. But she had managed to convince him that she was only joking.

'The world is driven by cash books,' she had said. 'Cash books are the liturgy of our time, and accountants are our high priests.'

Louise dialled the number. Engaged. She rocked gently back and forth in the chair. She had met Vassilis by chance. But aren't all important meetings in this life chance happenings?

Her first love, the ginger-haired man who hunted bears, built houses and could sink into long periods of depression, had once given her a lift when she'd been to visit a friend in Hede and missed the train back to Sveg. Emil had stopped his old lorry for her. She was seventeen at the time and still not worldly wise. He drove her home. That was in the late autumn of 1967. They were together for six months before she could summon up the strength to escape from his bear-like embrace. She then moved from Sveg to Östersund, started at college and one day decided to become an archaeologist. There were other men at university in Uppsala, and she simply happened to bump into them in various circumstances. Aron, the man she married and the father of Henrik, the reason why she changed her name from Lindblom to Cantor, was somebody she happened to sit next to on a flight between London and Edinburgh. She had received a scholarship from Uppsala University to attend a conference on classical archaeology, Aron was on his way to Scotland to go fishing, and up in the air, high above the clouds, they had fallen into conversation.

She forced herself not to think about Aron, not wanting to grow angry, and rang the number again. Still engaged.

She always used to compare the men she met after her divorce – it was not a conscious process, but she had a ranking scale deep down in her mind on which Aron was registered as the norm, and everybody else she went with was too short or too tall, too boring, too untalented. In other words, Aron always won. She still had not met anybody who could match his memory. That could make her both disconsolate and furious; it seemed that he still dictated the course of her life even though it was nothing to do with him any more. He had betrayed her, he had deceived her, and when the truth started to come out he simply disappeared – just as a spy about to be exposed flees to his controller. It had come as a terrible shock to her: she had no idea that he had been seeing other women. To make matters worse, one of them was a close friend of hers, a fellow archaeologist who had devoted her life to excavations on Thassos, in search of a Dionysos temple. Henrik was still very young at the time. She had taken a temporary post as a university lecturer while trying to survive what had happened and patching together her wrecked life.

Aron had shattered her like a sudden volcanic eruption can shatter a settlement, a person or a vase. When she sat with her ceramic fragments, trying to envisage the whole that she would never be able to reconstruct, she often thought of her own predicament. Aron had not only smashed her to pieces, he had also hidden some of the fragments in order to make it more difficult for her to recreate her identity, as a human being, a woman and an archaeologist.

Following Aron's disappearance she had found a letter a mere three or four lines long, carelessly written, announcing that their marriage was at an end, he simply couldn't go on any longer, he begged her pardon and he hoped that she wouldn't turn their son against him.

Then she heard nothing more from him for seven months. In the end she received a letter posted in Venice. She could tell from his handwriting that he had been drunk at the time, one of the staggering Aron benders he not infrequently indulged in, a constant state of intoxication dotted with peaks and troughs that could last for over a week. At last he had written to her, his tone was maudlin and oozing with self-pity, and he wondered if she could consider having him back. It was only then, as she sat there with the wine-stained letter in her hand, that it dawned on her that her marriage was over. She both wanted and didn't want to have him back, but she didn't dare risk it because she knew that he could well destroy her life again. A human being can be wrecked and then resurrected and restored once in this life, she thought – but not twice. That would be too much. So she replied and informed Aron that their marriage was finished. Henrik existed and lived with his mother, it was up to him and his father to work out what sort of a relationship they wanted to have: she would not intervene.

Almost a year passed before he was in touch again. This time it was by means of a dodgy telephone connection from Newfoundland, where he and several like-minded computer experts had assembled to form a network that was reminiscent of a sect. He explained somewhat vaguely that they were investigating the future of archives, now that all human experience could be reduced to a combination of ones and zeros. Microfilm and underground libraries were no longer of significance for the recording of human experience. Now it was computers that would guarantee that mankind living at a specific time would not leave behind a vacuum. But was there any guarantee that in the magical demiworld in which he was living, computers would not be able to create their own experiences and record them as well? The line was poor and she couldn't understand a lot of what he said: but at least he was not drunk and self-pitying.

He wanted her to send him a lithograph of a hawk pouncing on a dove, a picture they had bought shortly after they were married, when they happened to visit an art gallery. A week or so later, she sent him the picture. It was about then she realised that he had started to contact his son again, albeit secretly.

Aron continued to appear on the horizon. She sometimes wondered if she would ever be able to erase his features and discard the assessment table she used to measure other men with – and which sooner or later led to their being condemned, rejected.

She phoned Henrik again. Every time the old wounds from her relationship with Aron were opened up, she needed to hear Henrik's voice in order to avoid being overwhelmed by bitterness. But once again her only response was the answering machine, and she left a message to the effect that she wouldn't phone again until she arrived in Visby.

Every time he failed to answer, she felt a twinge of childish unrest. For a second or two she imagined accidents, fires, illnesses. Then she calmed down again. Henrik was very careful, never took unnecessary risks, even if he did a lot of travelling and liked to probe the unknown.

She went outside the back door to smoke a cigarette. She could hear the sound of laughter from Mitsos's house. The man laughing was Panayiotis, Mitsos's elder brother. To the mortification of his family Panayiotis had won a fortune on the lottery and hence created the financial foundation for a life of idleness. Louise smiled at the thought, inhaled deeply and made a mental note that she would give up smoking on her sixtieth birthday.

She was alone in the darkness. The sky was full of stars, the evening warm, and there were no chilly breezes. So this is where I've ended up, she thought. From the melancholy northern wastelands of Sveg and Härjedalen to Greece and Bronze Age graves. From snow and ice to the warm, dry olive groves.

She stubbed out her cigarette and went back indoors. Her foot was hurting. She paused, uncertain of what to do next. Then she phoned Vassilis's number again. It was no longer engaged, but nobody answered.

At that moment Vassilis's face merged in her mind with that of Aron.

Vassilis was cheating her, he was treating her as a part of his life he could do without.

Feeling jealous, she phoned his mobile. No reply. A Greek female voice asked her to leave a message. She gritted her teeth and said nothing.

Then she closed her suitcase and made up her mind at the same moment to put an end to her relationship with Vassilis. She would wind up the cash book, close it down, just as she had closed her suitcase.

She lay down on her bed and stared up at the stationary ceiling fan. How on earth could she have entered into a relationship with Vassilis? It suddenly seemed incomprehensible, she felt that the whole business was distasteful. Not so much from his point of view, but from hers.

The fan was motionless, her jealousy had faded away, and the dogs out there in the darkness were no longer barking. As usual when faced with an important decision, she addressed herself in the third person.

*Louise Cantor here, autumn 2004. This is where she leads her life, black on white – or rather, red on black, which is the usual colour combination on the fragments of urns we dig up from the Greek earth. Louise Cantor is fifty-four years old, she is not scared when she looks at her face or her body in a mirror. She is still attractive, not yet old; men notice her even if they don't turn round to look at her. What about her? Who does she turn round to look at? Or does she only look back in time to see the faces and traces of the past? Louise Cantor has just closed a book entitled Vassilis. She will never open it again. He will not even be allowed to drive Louise Cantor to the airport in Athens tomorrow morning.*

She got up from the bed and looked up the number of a local taxi firm. The woman she spoke to was hard of hearing, but she managed to shout loud enough to make herself understood. She could only hope that the taxi she had ordered really would turn up on time. As Vassilis had arranged to pick her up at five, she ordered a taxi for half past four.

She sat down at her desk and wrote a letter to Vassilis. *This is it, it's all over. All good things come to an end. I can feel that I'm on my way to somewhere else. I'm sorry that you came to pick me up in vain. I did try to ring you. Louise.*

She read through the letter. Did she have second thoughts? She often did – she had written so many farewell letters in her life that had never been sent. But not this one. She put the letter into an envelope, sealed it, and braved the darkness to fasten it to the letter box by her gate with a clothes peg.

She dozed for a few hours on top of her bed, drank a glass of wine and stared at a pack of sleeping pills without being able to make up her mind.

The taxi turned up a few minutes early, and it was pitch black. She was waiting for it, by the gate. Mitsos's dogs were barking. She slumped down into the back seat and closed her eyes. She couldn't sleep until her journey had started.

It was dawn when she arrived at the airport.

# CHAPTER 2

When she had checked in her suitcase with one of Lufthansa's half-asleep staff and was on her way to the security barrier, something happened that made a very deep impression on her.

Looking back, she would think that she ought to have taken it as an omen, a warning. But she didn't. All she saw was a solitary woman sitting on the stone floor with her bundles and ancient suitcases held together by the string tied round them. The woman was crying. She was totally immobile, completely self-absorbed. She was old, her sunken cheeks indicating that many teeth were missing. Louise thought she might well be from Albania. There were a lot of Albanian women looking for work in Greece, they are prepared to do anything at all since a little is better than nothing, and Albania is a desperately poor country. She had a scarf round her head, the scarf of a decent elderly lady, she was not a Muslim; but she was sitting on the floor, crying. The woman was on her own, it looked as if she had been washed ashore in this airport, surrounded by her bundles, her life in tatters, and all she had left was this heap of worthless flotsam.

Louise paused, people in a hurry barged into her, but she stood firm as if bracing herself against a strong wind. The woman on the floor surrounded by the bundles had a brown, furrowed face, her skin was like a petrified lava landscape. There is a special sort of beauty in the faces of old women, where everything has been reduced to a thin film stretched over bare bones, where all the events of her life are registered. Two parched furrows had been excavated from her eyes down towards her cheeks, and they were now filled with the woman's tears.

She is watering a pain I know nothing about, Louise thought. But something inside her is also inside me.

The woman suddenly raised her head, her eyes met Louise's briefly, and she slowly shook her head. Louise took it as an indication that her assistance, whatever that might have involved, was not needed. She hurried on towards the security check, elbowing her way through the teeming crowd, through a haze smelling of garlic and olives. When she turned round to look, it was as if a human curtain had closed and the woman was no longer visible.

Louise had kept a diary since she was very young in which she used to record incidents that she thought she would never forget. This was one of them. She thought about what she would write as she placed her handbag on the moving belt, her mobile phone in a small blue plastic box, and passed through the magic barrier that separated bad from good.

She bought a bottle of Tullamore Dew for herself and two bottles of retsina for Henrik. Then she sat down outside the exit and found to her annoyance that she had left her diary behind in Argolis. She could see it in her mind's eye, on the table next to the green lamp. She took the conference programme from her bag and wrote down on the back of it: '*Old woman weeping at Athens airport. A face of human ruin, dug up after thousands of years by a curious and intrusive archaeologist. Why was she crying? That universal question. Why does a person cry?*'

She closed her eyes and tried to imagine what must have been inside those bundles and the battered suitcases.

Emptiness, she decided. Empty suitcases, or perhaps filled with ash from fires long since extinguished.

When it was announced that her flight was boarding, she woke up with a start. She went to her aisle seat and sat down next to a man who gave the impression of being terrified of flying. She decided to sleep as far as Frankfurt, and to delay breakfast until the flight from Frankfurt to Stockholm.

When she got to Arlanda and had retrieved her suitcase, she still felt tired. She always looked forward to a trip, but not the journey itself. She suspected that one of these days she would suffer a panic attack in mid-flight. So for many years now, she had always taken with her a pack of tranquillisers, in readiness for when the attack took place.

Louice made her way to the domestic terminal, handed over her suitcase to a woman who was rather more awake than the one in Athens, and sat down to wait. A door opened and she was hit by a blast of Swedish autumn wind. She shuddered, and made a mental note to buy a jumper knitted from the local Gotland wool while she was in Visby. Gotland and Greece have sheep in common, she thought. If Gotland had olive groves, there would not be much difference between the places.

She wondered if she ought to ring Henrik. But he might be asleep: his day was often the night, and he preferred to work by starlight rather than sunshine. Instead she dialled the number of her father up in Ulvkälla, just outside Sveg, on the southern side of the River Ljusnan. He never slept, she could phone him at any time of day or night. She had never managed to catch him asleep, no matter when she rang. That's how she remembered him from her childhood as well. She had a father who had banished the Sandman, a giant of a man whose eyes were always open, who was always alert, always ready to protect his daughter.

She dialled the number, but hung up the moment she heard it ringing. She had nothing to say to him just now. She put the phone into her suitcase and thought of Vassilis. He had not left a message on her mobile. But why should he? She felt a pang of disappointment. She suppressed it immediately, regret was not on the agenda. Louise Cantor came from a family that did not reflect on a decision once it had been made, even if it had been totally wrong. The rule was to grin and bear it, no matter what.

A cold wind was blowing in from the sea as the aeroplane thudded down onto the runway at Visby. The wind played havoc with her overcoat as she crouched down and hurried into the terminal. A man was holding up a card with her name on it. As they drove to the town centre, she watched the trees; the wind was so strong, they would lose most of their leaves. There's a battle going on between the seasons, she thought. A battle whose outcome is a foregone conclusion, from the very start.

She was staying at the Strand hotel, which was on the hill running down to the harbour. Her room did not have a view of the square, and she begged the receptionist to give her one that did. She was in luck. The new room was smaller, but it faced in the right direction and the first thing she did when she entered her room was to look out of the window. What can I see? she thought. What am I hoping is going to happen out there?

She had an incantation that kept running through her mind. *I'm fifty-four years old. I'm here now, where am I heading for, when will I get there?*

She watched an old lady struggling with her dog on the windswept hill. She felt more in sympathy with the dog than with the lady in the lurid red coat.

Shortly before four that afternoon she went to the college, which was situated on the water's edge. It was not far, and she had time to stroll round the deserted harbour. Water was being hurled at the stone quays. The colour was different from the Aegean surrounding the Greek mainland and islands. It's wilder here, she thought. More primitive, a young tearaway sea that launches an attack on the first vessel or quay that it comes across.

The wind was still strong, but perhaps more squally now. A ferry was on its way out from the harbour to the open sea. Louise was a punctual person. As far as she was concerned it was just as important not to arrive too early as it was not to arrive late. A friendly man with a scar where his hare lip had been operated on welcomed her at the entrance. He was one of the organisers, introduced himself, and said that they had met once before, many years ago; but she could not remember him. Recalling other people is one of the most difficult of social skills, she knew that. Faces change, and often become unrecognisable. But she smiled at him and said she remembered him, remembered him very well.

All twenty-two of them assembled in an impersonal conference room. They pinned on their name tags, drank coffee and tea, then listened to a Dr Stefanis from Latvia who started proceedings in faltering English with a paper on recent discoveries of Minoan ceramics that presented classification difficulties. She could not understand what was so difficult to classify: Minoan ceramics were Minoan ceramics, full stop.

She soon realised that she was not listening. In spirit she was still in Argolis, breathing in the smell of thyme and rosemary. She studied the other people sitting round the oval-shaped table. Which of them were listening, which of them were like her, transported of their own volition into another reality? She knew none of the others round the table, apart from the man who claimed he had met her on some occasion in the past. They were all from the Nordic and Baltic countries, some of them field archaeologists like herself.

Dr Stefanis stopped abruptly, as if he could no longer cope with his bad English. After the polite applause came a brief and decidedly subdued discussion. Some announcements regarding practical arrangements for the next day were made, and the opening session of the conference came to an end. On her way out of the building she was asked to wait behind for a moment, because a photographer from a local newspaper wanted to take a picture of as many of the archaeologists attending the conference as he could fit in. He noted her name, and afterwards she surrendered herself to the tender mercies of the stormy wind.

Louise fell asleep on her bed, and when she woke up was not at all sure where she was. Her mobile was on the table. She ought to phone Henrik, but decided to wait until she'd eaten. She went to the square, took pot luck and ended up in a basement restaurant that had few diners but served good food. She drank several glasses of wine, again regretted that she had broken off her relationship with Vassilis, but tried to concentrate on the lecture she would deliver the following day. She drank another glass of wine and ran through in her mind what she was going to say. She had it written down, but as she had given it before, she could almost remember it off by heart.

*I shall talk about the colours red and black in the clay. The reddish colour of the clay is caused by ferric oxide: during the firing process, the iron in the ferric oxide is separated from the oxygen and the clay turns black. As the pottery cools, the iron and the oxygen bond again if oxygen is present in the kiln, and the clay regains its red hues. If no oxygen is present, the clay remains black. So although the finished pot might be either red or black, the colours originate from the same raw material.*

The wine was taking effect, her body felt warm, her head was filled with waves flowing back and forth. She paid her bill, emerged into the gusting wind and told herself that she was already longing for tomorrow to come.

She phoned the flat in Stockholm. Still the answering machine. Sometimes Henrik would make a special recording just for her if something important had happened, a private message she shared with the whole world. She said that she was in Visby, that she was on her way. Then she rang his mobile. No answer.

She felt uneasy, a feeling so slight that she was barely aware of it.

She slept that night with the window open. She woke up once, around midnight. Some young drunks were shouting about a girl who was an easy lay, but evidently she wouldn't have them.

At ten o'clock the next morning she delivered her paper on Attic clay and its consistency. She talked about the high iron content and contrasted the red colour of the ferric oxide with the lime-rich clay from Corinth that produced white or even green ceramics. After a hesitant start – several of her audience had evidently had a long and late dinner the previous evening, washed down with copious amounts of wine – she managed to capture their interest. She spoke for exactly forty-five minutes, and received an enthusiastic round of applause when she finished. During the subsequent discussion she did not have to field any awkward questions, and when they broke up for coffee, she felt she had justified her coming here.

The wind had eased off. She took her coffee into the courtyard and balanced it on her knee when she sat down on a bench. Her mobile rang. She was sure it would be Henrik, but the call came from Greece and was from Vassilis. She hesitated, and decided not to answer. Soon enough she would return to Argolis and go to see him then.

She put her mobile back in her handbag, drank her coffee, then decided that she had had enough. The speakers scheduled for the rest of the day would no doubt have very interesting things to say, but she did not want to hang around any longer. She returned her coffee cup and went to see the man with the hare lip. She told him that a friend had unexpectedly fallen ill – it wasn't life-threatening, but serious enough for her to feel that she ought to return home immediately.

She would regret those words. They would return to haunt her. She had cried wolf, and the wolf had come.

But just then Visby was bathed in autumn sunshine. She went back to her hotel, was helped by the receptionist to change her air ticket and was lucky enough to find a seat on a flight leaving at three o'clock. That gave her time to take a walk round the city walls, and she called in at two shops to try on knitted jumpers made from local wool but failed to find one that fitted her. She had lunch at a Chinese restaurant and decided not to phone Henrik, but to surprise him. She had a key to his flat, and he had told her that she could go in at any time – he had no secrets from her.

She arrived at the airport in good time, and saw the photograph taken the previous day in a local newspaper. She tore the page out and put it in her handbag. Then came an announcement that the aircraft she was due to fly on had developed a technical fault, and she would have to wait for a replacement plane that was already on its way from Stockholm.

She was not annoyed, but could feel her impatience growing. As there was no alternative flight, she sat in the sun outside the terminal building and smoked a cigarette. She was sorry now that she hadn't spoken to Vassilis: it would have been as well to get it over with and weather the furious outburst of a man whose vanity had been wounded and who could not accept a no for what it was.

But she did not phone him. Her flight eventually left after a two-hour delay, and it was nearly six by the time she was back in Stockholm. She took a taxi to Henrik's flat on Söder. They were caught in a traffic jam caused by a road accident – it was as if invisible forces were combining to hold her back, to spare her what was in store. But she knew nothing of that, of course, and merely felt her impatience increasing. It seemed that in many ways Sweden had started to become more like Greece, with gridlocked traffic and constant delays.

Henrik lived in Tavastgatan, a quiet street set back from the busiest roads on Söder. She tried the entry code, hoping it had not been changed. It was easy to remember: the Battle of Hastings, 1066. The door opened. Henrik lived on the top floor, with a view over rooftops and church towers. He had also told her, to her horror, that if he stood on the narrow railing outside one of his windows, he could just glimpse the water at Strömmen.

She rang the bell twice, then unlocked the door. She noticed immediately that the air in the flat smelled stale.

She suddenly felt scared. Something was wrong. She held her breath and listened. She could see into the kitchen from the entrance hall. There's nobody here, she thought. She shouted that she had arrived, but there was no reply. She felt better. She hung up her coat and kicked off her shoes. There was no post or junk mail on the doormat. So Henrik was not away, at least. She went into the kitchen. No dirty crockery in the sink. The living room was unusually tidy, the desk empty. She opened the bedroom door.

Henrik was under the covers. His head lay heavily on the pillow. He was lying on his back, one hand hanging down towards the floor, the other open over his chest.

She realised immediately that he was dead. In a desperate attempt to banish the thought, she screamed out loud, but he did not move, he just lay in his bed but was no longer there.

It was Friday, 17 September. Louise Cantor fell into an abyss.

Then she ran out of the flat, still screaming. Those who heard her said afterwards that she sounded like an animal howling in pain.

# CHAPTER 3

A single tangible thought emerged from the chaos. Aron. Where was he? Did he still exist? Why was he not here by her side? Henrik was their joint creation, and that was not something he could run away from. But needless to say, Aron did not appear, he was absent just as he had always been absent, like a thin column of smoke that she could neither grasp hold of nor lean on for support.

Afterwards, she had no clear memory of the next few hours: all she knew was what others had told her. A neighbour had opened his door and found her lying on the stairs. In due course a constant stream of people turned up, police officers and ambulance men. She had been taken back to the flat, despite her resistance. She had no desire to go back in there, she had not seen what she had seen, Henrik had just slipped out, he would soon be home again. A woman police officer with a childlike face had patted her arm, like a friendly old aunt trying to console a little girl who had fallen and grazed her knee.

But Louise had not grazed her knee, she had been shattered by the realisation that her son was dead. The woman police officer kept repeating her name – Emma. Emma was an old-fashioned name that had recently become popular again, she thought confusedly. Everything came back eventually, even her own name which in the old days had been used mainly by the rich and high-born: now it had slipped down through the joists of the class system and become available to all. Her father, Artur, had been responsible for choosing the name, and she had been teased at school. At the time there was a Queen Louise in Sweden, an ancient old crone looking like a withered tree trunk. She had hated the name all the time she was growing up, until the end of her relationship with Emil when she had wriggled free of his bear hug and been able to move away. Then the name of Louise suddenly became a significant advantage.

Such thoughts whirled around inside her head as Emma sat patting her arm, as if beating time to the tragedy, or as if it were time itself ticking by.

One thing she could remember, one of the few things she did not need to be reminded of or to have explained to her: *time was like a ship sailing into the distance.* She was standing on the quay and the clocks of life were ticking away more and more slowly. She had been left behind, she was no longer involved in the course of events. It was not Henrik who was dead, it was her.

She occasionally tried to run away, to drag herself away from the policewoman sympathetically patting her arm. They said later that Louise's screams had been heart-rending; eventually somebody had forced a tablet down her throat, making her even more confused and sleepy. She recalled how all the people crammed into the little flat had started to move at snail's pace, as if in a slow-motion film.

As she fell into the abyss she had also had confused thoughts about God. She had never conducted a real conversation with God before, or at least not since her teens when she had gone through a phase of persistent religious brooding. One snowy morning in early December, shortly before the traditional processions to celebrate St Lucia, one of her classmates had been run over and killed by a snowplough on her way to school. It was the first time death had affected her personally. It was a death smelling of wet wool, a death enveloped by wintry cold and heavy snow. Her teacher had wept – that in itself had been a ghastly attack on her child-hood idyll, seeing her strict class teacher burst into tears like a terrified and abandoned child. A candle was burning on the desk where the dead child used to sit. It happened to be the desk next to her own, and now her friend had gone away: that is what death meant, *going away,* no more than that. What was so frightening, and eventually horrific, was the realisation that *death struck at random.* She started to wonder how that could be, and it suddenly dawned on her that the question may well have been addressed to what was known as God.

But He did not reply. She tried every trick she could think of to attract His attention, she made a little altar in a corner of the wood-shed, but no inner voice answered her questions. God was an absent adult who only spoke to a child when it suited Him. She eventually discovered that she did not really believe in God: perhaps at most she had fallen in love with Him, a secret passion, rather like one for an inaccessible boy several years older than herself.

From then on there had never been a God in her life, not until now; but He did not speak to her on this occasion either. She was alone. There was only herself plus the policewoman patting her arm and all the other people speaking in low voices, moving slowly and apparently looking for something that had been lost.

There was a sudden stillness, like when a recorded tape snaps. The voices all around her were no longer there. Instead she could hear whispers inside her head, saying over and over again that it wasn't true. Henrik was merely asleep, he was not dead. He could not possibly be dead. After all, she had come to visit him.

A police officer, in plain clothes, with tired eyes, asked her gently to go to the kitchen with him. She realised afterwards it was so that she did not have to watch Henrik being taken away. They sat down at the kitchen table, and she could feel the breadcrumbs against the palm of her hand.

*Henrik couldn't possibly be dead, the breadcrumbs were still there!*

The policeman had to repeat his name before she caught on. Göran Wrath. I shall feel boundless anger if what I refuse to believe eventually turns out to be true, she thought.

She answered his questions with questions of her own, which he replied to in turn. It was as if they were circling round each other.

The only certainty was that Henrik had died. Göran Wrath said there was nothing to suggest foul play. Had he been ill? She said he had never been seriously ill, the usual childhood ailments had come and gone without leaving any trace, and he had never been prone to infections. Wrath wrote down her replies in a little notebook. She looked at his chubby fingers and wondered if they were sensitive enough to seek out the truth.

'Somebody must have killed him,' she said.

'There are no signs of his having been assaulted.'

She wanted to protest, but lacked the strength. They were still sitting in the kitchen. Wrath asked if there was anybody she would like to phone. He gave her a mobile, and she rang her father. If Aron no longer existed and was unable to accept his responsibilities, her father would have to step in. She could hear the phone ringing, but there was no reply. Perhaps he was out in the forest, making his wood sculptures? Somewhere where there was no signal. But if she shouted loudly enough, would he hear her then? At that moment, he answered.

She started crying the moment she heard his voice. It was as if she had flown backwards through time and returned to the helpless creature she had once been.

'Henrik is dead.'

She could hear him breathing. To fill his enormous lungs required vast amounts of oxygen.

'Henrik is dead,' she said again.

She heard him spit something out, perhaps he said 'Good God', or maybe he swore.

'What's happened?'

'I'm sitting in his kitchen. I came here. He was asleep in bed. But he was dead.'

She was lost for words and handed the mobile to Wrath, who stood up, as if to demonstrate his sympathy. It was when she heard him tell her father that it hit her: Henrik really was dead. It was not just words and imagination, a macabre game involving visual impressions and her own horror. *He really was dead.*

Wrath hung up.

'He said he'd been drinking and was unable to drive. But he would take a taxi. Where does he live?'

'In Härjedalen.'

'What? A taxi from Härjedalen?! That's three hundred miles!'

'He'll take a taxi. He loved Henrik.'


She was driven to a hotel where somebody had booked a room for her. While she waited for Artur to arrive, she was never left alone.

Most of her companions were in uniform. She was given some more tranquillisers, she may have slept – she was not sure about that afterwards. Henrik's death was shrouded in mist for those first few hours.

The only thought she could recall from that evening when she was waiting for Artur's taxi to arrive was that Henrik had once constructed a mechanical hell. Why she recalled that very thing, she had no idea. It was as if all the shelves containing memories inside her brain had collapsed, and all the contents had ended up in the wrong place. No matter what thought or memory she tried to summon up, what actually came to mind was something unexpected.

Henrik had been fifteen or sixteen at the time. She had just been putting the finishing touches to her doctoral thesis on the difference between Attic Bronze Age graves and burial customs in northern Greece. It had been a time of worry – would her dissertation stand up to intense scrutiny? – and sleepless nights. Henrik had been restless and irritable, the rebellious feelings he would normally have directed at his father had been channelled towards her instead, and she was afraid that he was drifting into company where drugs and antisocial feelings were the norm. But everything had blown over, and one day he had shown her a picture of a mechanical hell that was displayed in a Copenhagen museum. He said he would like to see it, and it was obvious that he could not be put off. So she suggested they should go there together. It was early spring, and she was due to be examined for her doctorate in May – she needed a few days of relaxation.

The trip brought them closer together. For the first time they outgrew the mummy-child relationship. He was on the verge of manhood, and wanted her to treat him like an adult. He started asking questions about Aron, and she had finally told him in all seriousness about their intense mutual passion, the only positive outcome of which was Henrik's conception. She tried to avoid talking ill of Aron, she did not want to reveal her husband's lies and his constant efforts to avoid responsibility for the child she was expecting. Henrik listened attentively, and it was clear from his questions that they had been prepared well in advance.

24

They spent two windy days in Copenhagen, sliding around on the slushy pavements, but they duly found the mechanical hell, and it seemed to be the triumphal climax of their expedition. The hell had been created by an unknown master (or perhaps rather a lunatic) in the early eighteenth century, and was no bigger than a puppet theatre. You could wind up springs and then watch devils made out of tinplate gobbling up desperate human beings who fell down from a rod at the top level of hell. Flames had been cut out of yellow-coloured metal, and there was a chief devil with a long tail who moved rhythmically until the power generated by the clockwork mechanisms wore out. They managed to persuade one of the museum staff to wind up the springs again even though it was not officially permitted: the mechanical hell was very fragile and extremely valuable. There was nothing else like it in the world.

It was then that Henrik made up his mind to create a hell of his own. She did not believe he was serious. And in addition, she doubted if he had sufficient technical skill to construct the necessary mechanisms. But three months later he invited her into his room and showed her an almost exact copy of the hell in Copenhagen. She had been most surprised, and felt very bitter towards Aron who was not interested in what his son was capable of achieving.

Why did she think of that now, as she sat with her police companions, waiting for Artur? Perhaps because on that occasion she had felt great satisfaction deep down for the fact that Henrik gave her life a meaning far beyond any satisfaction she could derive from doctoral dissertations or archaeological digs. If there is a meaning in life it must be centred upon a person, she thought, nothing else. It had to be a person.

Now he was dead. And she was dead as well. She cried in waves; tears came like showers that squeezed out their contents then vanished again. Time had ceased to be of any significance at all. She had no idea how long she waited. Shortly before Artur arrived the thought struck her that Henrik would never deliberately expose her to the slightest pain, no matter how much difficulty life was causing him. She was the guarantee that he would never take his own life.

What was the alternative? Somebody must have killed him. She tried to tell that to the policewoman guarding her. Soon afterwards Göran Wrath came into her hotel room. He flopped down onto a chair in front of her and asked her why. Why what?

'What makes you think that he was murdered?'

'There is no other explanation.'

'Did he have any enemies? Had something happened?'

'I don't know. But why else should he die? He's twenty-five years old.'

'We don't know. There's no sign of any assault.'

'He must have been murdered.'

'There's no indication of that.'

She continued to insist. Somebody must have killed her son. It was a crude, brutal murder. Göran Wrath listened, notebook in hand. But he wrote nothing down, and that annoyed her.

'Why aren't you writing anything?' she suddenly yelled in frustration. 'I'm telling you, something must have happened!'

He opened his notebook, but still wrote nothing down.

At that very moment Artur came into the room. He was dressed as if he had just come home after being out hunting in heavy rain and trudging for ages through endless swamps. He was wearing wellington boots and the old leather jacket she could remember from her childhood, the one that smelled so pungently of tobacco and oil and goodness knows what else. His face was pale, his hair tousled. She leapt to her feet and clung tightly onto him. He would be able to help her out of this nightmare, just like he did when she was little and crept into his bed after waking up in the middle of the night. She told him everything. There was a brief moment when she was convinced that everything had been a figment of her imagination. Then she noticed that he had started crying, and Henrik died for the second time. Now she knew that he would never wake up again.

Nobody could console her any longer, the catastrophe was total. But Artur forced her to carry on telling him, he was determined in his despair. He wanted to know. Göran Wrath appeared once again. His eyes were red, and this time he did not even take his notebook out of his pocket. Artur wanted to know what had happened, and it seemed that now he was present, Louise dared to listen to what the police officer had to say.

Göran Wrath repeated what he had said before. Henrik had been lying under the covers, wearing a pair of blue pyjamas, and had probably been dead for at least ten hours before Louise discovered him.

The most obvious thing was that nothing appeared to be unusual. There was no sign of a crime, no sign of a struggle, no break-in, or a sudden attack or anything else to suggest that anybody had been in the flat while Henrik had gone to bed and passed away. There was no farewell letter to indicate suicide. The probability was that something had burst inside him, a blood vessel in his brain, a hereditary weakness in his heart that had never been discovered. It was the medical experts who would be able to discover the truth once the police had handed the case over to them.

Louise registered what he was saying, but something immediately started to nag away inside her. There was something wrong. Henrik was talking to her, even though he was dead. He was urging her to be careful and watchful.


It was dawn by the time Göran Wrath stood up and left. Artur had asked to be left alone with Louise. He lifted his daughter onto the bed, then lay down beside her and held her hand.

She suddenly sat up. Now she had understood what Henrik had been trying to tell her.

'He never slept in pyjamas.'

Artur got off the bed and stood beside it.

'I don't follow you.'

'The police said that Henrik was wearing pyjamas. I know that he never wore pyjamas. He owned a few pairs, but he never wore them.'

Artur stared uncomprehendingly at her.

'He always slept naked,' she said. 'I'm certain. He told me that he always slept with nothing on. It started when he used to sleep in front of an open window, in order to toughen himself up.'

'I don't think I understand what you're getting at.'

'Somebody must have killed him.'

She could see that Artur didn't believe her. There was no point in going on. She didn't have the strength. She would have to wait.

Artur sat down on the edge of the bed.

'We must get in touch with Aron,' he said.

'Why do we have to talk to him?'

'He was Henrik's father.'

'Aron has never bothered about him. He's gone away. This has nothing to do with him.'

'But he has to know, even so.'

'Why?'

'It's just the way it is.'

She wanted to protest, but he took her by the arm.

'Did you really have no contact with each other?'

'No.'

'None at all?'

'He rang occasionally. And wrote the odd letter.'

'You must know where he lives, roughly?'

'Australia.'

'Is that all you know? Where in Australia?'

'I don't even know for sure if it is Australia. He was always digging new burrows, which he abandoned when he felt threatened. He was like a fox that never left a forwarding address.'

'It must be possible to find him. Don't you know whereabouts in Australia?'

'No. He wrote once that he wanted to live close to the sea.'

'Australia is surrounded by sea.'

He said nothing more about Aron. But she knew that Artur would never give up until he had done everything possible to find him.


She occasionally dozed off, and when she woke up he was always by her side. Sometimes he made a phone call, or spoke quietly to one of the police officers. She was no longer listening, exhaustion had reduced her consciousness to a point where she could no longer distinguish any details. The only thing that existed now was pain, and the never-ending nightmare that refused to release its grip on her.

She had no idea how much time had passed when Artur said they ought to go up to Härjedalen. In any case, she offered no resistance but accompanied him to the car he had rented. They drove north in silence. He had chosen to take the coastal road, not the meandering inland route he usually preferred. They passed by Ljusdal, Järvsö and Ljusnan. As they passed Kolsätt, he suddenly informed her that there used to be a ferry there. Before the bridges were built, you had to take a ferry over the mighty river in order to reach Härjedalen.

The autumn colours were sharp. She sat in the back seat, staring at the display of colour. She was asleep when they reached their destination, and he carried her into the house and laid her down.

He sat beside where she was lying on the red sofa that was patched and mended and had always been in that very spot.

'I know,' she said. 'I've known all along. I'm certain. Somebody killed him. Somebody killed him, and me as well.'

'You are alive,' Artur said. 'You are very much alive.'

She shook her head.

'No,' she said. 'I'm not alive. I'm also dead. The person you see is not me. I don't know yet who it is. But everything is different now. And Henrik did not die a natural death.'

She stood up and walked over to the window. It was dark. The street light outside the gate shone dully and was swinging back and forth in the wind. She could see her face mirrored in the window. She had always looked like that. Dark, medium-length hair, centre parting. Blue eyes, narrow lips. Even if everything inside her had changed, her face was the same.

She gazed into her own eyes.

Inside her, time had started to pass once more.

# CHAPTER 4

As dawn broke, Artur took her out into the woods with him. The air was filled with the smell of moss and damp bark, the sky hidden by mist. The first frost had arrived, the ground creaked under their feet.

During the night Louise had woken up and gone to the toilet. As she passed a half-open door she saw Artur in his old armchair, its springs almost touching the floor. He had an unlit pipe in his hand – he had stopped smoking some years previously, abruptly, as if it had struck him that he had used up his lifetime ration of tobacco. She paused and observed him, and it seemed to her that this was how she had always experienced him. No matter what her age, she had always stood outside a half-open door and observed him, assuring herself that he was there, standing guard over her.

He had woken her up early, gave her no chance to protest but insisted that she should dress for a walk in the forest. They drove over the bridge in silence and turned northwards, following the river towards the mountains. The tyres produced a crackling noise, the forest was motionless. He stopped on a logging road and put his arm round her shoulders. Barely visible paths meandered in all directions into the trees. He chose one of them, and they entered the vast silence. They came to an area where the ground was uneven, covered in pine trees. This was his gallery. They were surrounded by his sculptures. Carved out of the trunks were faces, bodies, trying to release themselves from the hard timber. Some trees had many bodies and faces intertwined, others had only one small face, often several metres above the ground. He created his works of art both on his knees and perched on primitive stepladders he had cobbled together. Some of the sculptures were very old. He had made those over forty years ago, when he was young. As the trees grew, they had distorted the images, changed bodies and faces, just as people change as they grow older. Some sculptures had burst, heads were shattered, as if they had been crushed or decapitated. He told her that sometimes people would come here during the night, saw out his sculptures and take them away with them. Once, a whole tree had vanished. But he did not worry, he owned twenty hectares of pine forest and that would be enough for his life and quite a lot more besides. Nobody would be able to steal everything he carved for his own pleasure, and for those who wanted to see them.

He eyed her surreptitiously, looking for any signs that she was disintegrating. But she was still drowsy from the strong tablets, he was not even sure that she noticed the faces peering at her from the tree trunks.

He took her to his holy of holies, three big pine trees growing close together. Brothers, he had thought; brothers or sisters who could not be separated. He had spent a long time contemplating these trees, hesitating for many years. Every sculpture existed inside the trunk, but he had to wait for the moment when he saw the invisible. Then he could sharpen his knives and chisels and start work, exposing what already existed. But those three mighty pines had remained silent. Sometimes he thought he might have caught a glimpse of what was hidden under the bark. But then he hesitated, it wasn't quite right, he needed to look deeper. One night he had dreamed about solitary dogs, and when he came back to the forest he had realised that it was animals inside those pine trunks – not really dogs, but something between a dog and a wolf, or perhaps a lynx. He had started carving, he no longer had any doubts, and now there were three animals there, each of them both dog and cat, seeming to climb up the massive trunks, as if they were climbing out of themselves.

She had never seen the animals before. He watched her, saw her searching for the story. His sculptures were not images but stories, voices whispering and shouting and urging her to listen. His gallery and her archaeological digs had the same roots. They were voices that had disappeared, and she was the one who had to interpret the silence they emitted.

'Silence has the loveliest voice,' he had said once. She had never forgotten those words.

'Do they have names, these dogcats of yours, or catdogs?'

'The only name I'm satisfied with is yours.'

They penetrated deeper into the forest, paths criss-crossed, birds took off and fluttered away. Suddenly – it was not his intention – they found themselves in the hollow where he had carved Heidi's face. The sorrow he still felt weighed heavily down on him. Every year he carved her face and his sorrow anew. Her face became more and more frail, more elusive. The sorrow delved deeper and deeper into the trunk as he dug his chisel into himself as much as into the tree.

Louise caressed her mother's face with the tips of her fingers. *Heidi, Artur's wife and Louise's mother.* She continued stroking the damp tree. A strip of resin had stiffened over her eyebrows, as if Heidi had a scar on her face.

He knew that Louise wanted him to speak. So much had remained unsaid about Heidi. They had pussyfooted around each other all these years, and he had never been able to bring himself to tell her what he knew, and at least some of what he didn't know, but suspected.

It was forty-seven years since Heidi had died. Louise was six at the time, and Artur had been up in the forest logging, at the foot of the mountains. Nobody could know what Heidi had been thinking, but she was certainly unaware she was about to die when she had asked her neighbour, Rut, if the girl could spend the night at her place while she went out to do what she loved doing more than anything else: skating. The fact that it was minus nineteen degrees did not worry her: she set off with her kick-sledge without telling Rut that she was going to the tarn known as Undertjärn.

What happened next could only be surmised. Having arrived at the tarn with her sledge, she strapped on her skates and ventured out onto the black ice. It was almost full moon, otherwise it would have been too dark for skating. Somewhere out there on the darkness she had fallen and broken her leg. When they found her two days later, she was curled up in the foetal position. The sharp blades of her skates looked like strange talons on her feet, and they had considerable difficulty in working her cheek free from the ice.

There had been many unanswered questions. Had she cried for

help? What had she shouted? To whom? Had she appealed to some god or other when it became clear that she was going to freeze to death?

Nobody could be blamed, apart from herself who had not said that she was going to Undertjärn. The locals had searched the Vändsjön lake, but it was not until they had contacted Artur and he had come home that he suggested she might have gone to the tarn where she used to go swimming in the summer.

Artur did everything he could to protect Louise from the horror of it all when she was a child. Everybody in the village had done their bit to help, but nobody could keep the sorrow at bay. It was like wisps of smoke, or little mice seeking refuge in the autumn: it penetrated everywhere, no matter how well protected a space might be.

Sorrow was like mice, it always found a way in.


For a year she had slept in his bed every night – that was the only way she could cope with the dark. They had looked at photographs of Heidi, laid a place for her at table, and sworn that they would always be a threesome, even if only two of them turned up for meals. Artur had tried to learn how to cook like Heidi: he had never managed it, but young though she was, Louise thought she had understood what Artur was trying to do for her.

They grew up together over subsequent years. He continued his work as a lumberjack, devoting the little time he had over to his sculptures. There were those who thought he was mad, and unsuitable for taking care of the girl. But as he was polite and never got into fights or swore, he was allowed to keep her.

But now Heidi, the German, was by their side once more. And Henrik had passed away, the grandchild Heidi had never seen.

One death was linked with the other. Did it help, did anything become comprehensible by staring into one black mirror in the hope of seeing something constructive in the other?

Death was darkness, there was no light to be found there. Death was attics and cellars, it smelled raw, of mice and soil, and loneliness.

'I don't really know anything at all about her,' said Louise, shuddering in the early-morning air.

'It was a sort of fairy tale,' he said. 'Fate steered her into my path.'

'Didn't it have something to do with America? Something I've never really understood? Something you've never told me?'

They began walking along the path. The faces carved in the tree trunks kept watch over them. He started talking, and he tried to present himself as Artur, not as her father. He was the narrator now, and he would try to tell the story as accurately as he possibly could. If he could divert her attention from Henrik, even for a short time, he would have achieved something worthwhile.

Heidi had come to Härjedalen after the war, 1946 or 1947. She was only seventeen, despite the fact that everybody thought she was older. She had found work at the Vemdalskalet mountain hotel for the winter season, and cleaned rooms and changed bed linen for the tourists. He had met her as a result of his work as a lumberjack, delivering logs. He was intrigued by her peculiar Swedish accent, and they married in 1948, even though she was only eighteen. A lot of documentation was required because she was a German citizen and nobody really knew what Germany was any more – did it really exist, or was it only a sort of no-man's-land under military supervision, devastated by fire and bomb sites? But she had never been involved in the horrors of the Nazi period – indeed, she was a victim herself. Heidi had never said anything much about her origins, only that her grandmother on her mother's side had been Swedish, called Sara Fredrika and emigrated to America around the time of the First World War. She had arrived in America with her daughter, Laura, and had been forced to live in very harsh conditions. In the late 1920s they had lived on the outskirts of Chicago, and Laura had met a cattle dealer of German descent and accompanied him back to Europe. They married, and in 1930 celebrated the birth of their daughter Heidi, despite the fact that Laura was so young. Both her parents had died during the war, victims of nocturnal bombing raids, and she had been a wandering refugee until the war was over and purely by accident had hit upon the idea of emigrating to Sweden, which had not been involved in the war.

'A Swedish girl goes to America? Then her daughter emigrates to Germany before the circle is closed by her grandchild? Who returns to Sweden?'

'She thought that her background wasn't all that unusual.'

'Where did her grandmother come from? Did she ever meet her?'

'I don't know. But she used to go on about the sea and an island, an archipelago somewhere or other. She suspected that there was some complicated reason why her grandmother left Sweden.'

'Aren't there any relatives still in America?'

'Heidi didn't have any documents, no addresses. She used to say that she had survived the war. But that was about all. She had no possessions. No memories. The whole of her past had been bombed out, and had been consumed by the flames.'

They had returned to the logging track.

'Are you going to carve Henrik's face?'

The thought caused them both to weep. The gallery closed down on the spot. They sat in the car. He was about to start the engine when she put her hand on his arm.

'What has happened? He can't possibly have taken his own life.'

'He might have been ill. He used to travel to dangerous places.'

'I don't believe that. Something doesn't add up.'

They drove back home through the forest. The mist had lifted, it was a bright autumn day, the air clear. She made no objections when Artur sat down at the telephone with grim determination, refusing to give up until he had tracked down Aron.

He is like his old hunting dogs, she thought. All the Norwegian elkhounds and spitzes that came and went, hunted in the forest, grew old and died. Now he has turned into a dog himself. His chin and cheeks are covered in shaggy fur.

It took all of twenty-four hours, involving desperate attempts to work out time differences and opening times of the Swedish Embassy in

Canberra, and countless calls trying to pin down some official of the Swedish-Australian Society, which turned out to have an incredible number of members. But there was no trace of Aron Cantor. He was not registered with the embassy, nor was he a member of the society. Not even an old head gardener in Perth by the name of Karl-Håkan Wester, who was reputed to know every Swede in Australia, could provide any information.

They discussed the possibility of placing advertisements, or hiring somebody to find him. But Louise argued that Aron was so elusive that he could vanish at will. He could confuse anybody trying to follow him by turning into his own shadow.

They would not be able to find Aron. Perhaps that was what she really wanted, deep down? Did she want to rob him of the right to accompany his own son to the grave? In revenge for all the hurt he had caused her?

Artur asked her point-blank that very question and she told him the truth; she did not know.

She spent most of those September days crying. Artur sat at the kitchen table in silence. He could do nothing to console her, all he could offer her was silence. But the silence was cold, it merely increased her desperation.

One night she went to his room and snuggled down beside him in his bed, just as she had done for years after Heidi's death. She lay quite still, her head on his arm. Neither of them slept, neither spoke. The lack of sleep was like waiting for the waiting to come to an end.

But when dawn came, Louise could remain inert no longer. Even if it was going to be impossible, she had to begin to try to understand what dark forces had robbed her of her only child.


They had got up early and were sitting at the kitchen table. They could see the rain through the window, and autumn drizzle. The rowan berries were bright red. She asked to borrow his car, as she wanted to return to Stockholm that very morning. He seemed worried, but she reassured him. She would not drive too fast, nor would she drive over a cliff.

Nobody else was going to die. But she must go back to Henrik's flat. She was convinced that he had left behind some clue or other. There had not been a letter. But Henrik never wrote letters, he left other kinds of message that only she would be able to interpret.

'I have no option,' she said. 'I have to do this. Then I'll come back here.'

He hesitated before saying what had to be said. What about the funeral?

'It must take place here. Where else could he be buried? But that can wait.'

She left an hour later. His car smelled of hard work, hunting, oil and tools. A ragged dog blanket was still in the boot. She drove slowly through the endless forests, thought she had glimpsed an elk on a hillock near the Dalarna border. It was late afternoon by the time she reached Stockholm. She had slithered around on the cold, slippery roads, tried hard to concentrate on her driving and told herself that she owed it to Henrik. It was her duty to stay alive. Nobody else would be able to find out what had really happened. His death made it imperative for her to live.

She checked into a hotel at Slussen that was far too expensive. She left the car in an underground car park, and returned to Tavastgatan as dusk fell. To help give her the required strength, she opened the bottle of whisky she had bought at Athens airport.

Like Aron, she thought. I always used to be annoyed when he drank straight from the bottle. Now I am doing it myself.

She opened the door. The police had not sealed it.

On the mat was some junk mail, but no letters. Only a postcard from somebody called Vilgot, with enthusiastic descriptions of stone walls in Ireland. The card was green and depicted a slope down to a grey sea, but oddly enough without any stone walls. She paused motionless in the hall, holding her breath until she was able to control her panic and an instinctive urge to run away. Then she hung up her coat and took off her shoes. She worked her way slowly through the flat. There were no sheets on the bed. When she came back to the hall, she sat down on the stool by the telephone. The light on the answering machine was flashing. She pressed the appropriate button. The first message was from somebody called Hans who wondered if Henrik had time to go to the Ethnographical Museum to see an exhibition of Peruvian mummies. Then came a click, and a call but no message. The tape kept running. Now it was her calling from Mitsos's house. She could hear the enthusiasm in her voice, looking forward to the reunion that never took place. Then it was her again, this time from Visby. She pressed the repeat button and listened to the messages again. First Hans, then an unknown person, and herself. She remained sitting by the telephone. The light had stopped flashing. Instead she felt something go off inside herself, a warning light, just like the one on the answering machine. It was as if she'd received an incoming message. She held her breath and tried to isolate her thoughts. It happens all the time that somebody phones, says nothing although the sound of breathing can be heard, then hangs up. She did it herself sometimes, no doubt Henrik did as well. But what troubled her was her own messages. Had Henrik heard them at all?

Suddenly she was certain. He had never heard them. The sound of the telephone ringing had echoed round the flat but no contact had been made.

She felt scared. But she needed all her strength now in order to look for clues. Henrik must have left something for her. She went to the room he used as a study, where he also had a hi-fi system and a television. She stood in the middle of the room and looked slowly round.

Nothing appeared to be missing. It's too tidy, she thought. Henrik was not into tidiness. We sometimes used to quarrel about what was reasonable and what was pedantic. She went round the flat again. Had the police cleared up? She needed to know. She called Göran Wrath. She could hear that he was busy, so only asked him about the state of the flat.

'We don't do that,' said Wrath. 'Obviously, if we've disturbed something we try to put it right again.'

'The sheets have been taken from his bed.'

'That can't have been us. There was no reason to take anything away as there was no sign of a crime having been committed.'

He apologised for having to cut short the conversation and gave her a time when she could phone him the following day. She stood in the middle of the room again and looked round once more. Then she investigated the linen basket in the bathroom. There were no sheets, only a pair of jeans. She searched methodically through the flat, but could find no trace of any dirty sheets. She sat down on his sofa and looked at the room from a different angle. There was something odd about how neat and tidy everything looked. But she couldn't put her finger on anything specific. She went to the kitchen and opened the refrigerator. It was almost empty, but that was what she had expected.

Then she turned her attention to his desk. She opened all the drawers. Papers, photographs, old boarding cards. She picked one out at random. On 12 August 1999 Henrik had flown to Singapore with Qantas. His seat number had been 37G. He had made a note on the reverse side: '*N.B. Phone call.*' That was all.

She continued cautiously to become better acquainted with her son's life, the parts of it she did not know about. She lifted up the mouse pad with a picture of cacti in a desert: there was a letter underneath. She could see immediately that it was from Aron. She recognised his sprawling handwriting, always scribbled in a great hurry. She hesitated before reading it. Did she really want to know what kind of a relationship the two of them had? She picked up the envelope and turned it over. There was something that could have been an undecipherable address.

She stood by the kitchen window and tried to imagine how he would react. Aron, who never wore his heart on his sleeve, who always tried to keep a stiff upper lip when faced with the realities of life and everything it could throw at him.

You need me, she thought. In the same way that both I and Henrik needed you. But you never came when we appealed to you. Not when I did, at least.

She went back to the desk and looked at the letter. Instead of reading it she put it in her pocket.

She found Henrik's journals and diaries in a box under the desk. She knew that he kept an account of his activities. But she did not want to find anything in the diaries about her son that she had never suspected. She would save those for later. She also found several CDs, which according to what was written on them were copies of material from his computer hard drive. She looked but failed to find a computer. She put the CDs in her handbag.

She picked out his diary for 2004 and looked up the latest entry. It was dated two days before she had left Greece. *Monday, 13 September. Try to understand.* That was all. Try to understand what? She looked at previous entries, but there were not many for the last few months. She looked into the future, at the days Henrik would never experience. She found only one note: *10 October. To B.*

I can't find you, she thought. I still can't interpret the clues you have left for me. What happened in this flat? Inside you?

Then it dawned on her. Somebody had been in the flat after Henrik's body had been taken away. Somebody had been here, just as she was here now.

It was not Henrik's movements she was having difficulty in tracking. She was being thrown by a trail left by somebody else. The compass was whirling round.

She searched methodically through the desk and all the drawers and shelves. All she found was that letter from Aron.

She suddenly felt very tired. *He must have left a clue.* Once again, the feeling came sneaking up on her. Somebody else had been in the flat. But who would take it upon his or herself to tidy up, and take away the bed sheets? Something else must be missing, something she had not been able to identify. But why the sheets? Who had taken them?

She started searching the wardrobes. In one of them she found several fat files bound together by an old belt. Henrik had written *JFK* on the cover, in Indian ink. She took out the individual files and laid them out on the desk in front of her. The first one was full of computer printouts and photocopies. The text was in English. The subject matter astonished her. They were about the brain of the American president, John F. Kennedy. She frowned more and more intensively as she read, then started again from the beginning and read more carefully.

When she closed the last of the files several hours later, she was convinced. Henrik had not died of natural causes. This catastrophe was caused by some external means.

She stood by the window and looked down into the dark street, into the shadows.

Something or someone out there killed my son.

For one brief moment she thought she had noticed somebody slinking into the darkness. Then all was still again.

It was midnight when she left the flat and returned to her hotel. She kept turning round checking her back. But nobody was following her.

# CHAPTER 5

Her hotel room enveloped her in silence. Rooms occupied by people constantly moving in and out collected no memories. She stood in the window and contemplated the Old Town, watched the traffic flowing past and noted that no sound penetrated the thick glass. The soundtrack of reality had been switched off.

She had taken with her some of the fattest folders. The desk in her room was very small, so she spread the papers out on her bed and started reading again. She spent nearly the whole night reading. At some point between half past three and a quarter past four she nodded off, afloat on the sea of paper oozing out of the folders. Then she woke up with a start, and continued reading. Sorting out the information about Henrik she had in front of her seemed to be similar to the problems she faced as an archaeologist. Why had Henrik devoted so much time and energy to something that had happened to an American president over forty years ago? What had he been looking for? What information was buried there? How do you look for something that somebody else has been looking for? It was like one of the many shattered Grecian urns she had faced during her life. A pile of tiny pieces, and her task was to produce a phoenix rising from the ashes of a vase smashed a thousand years ago. She needed knowledge and patience in order to succeed, and not be too frustrated by the recalcitrant bits that refused to fit into the puzzle. But what should she do now? How would she be able to glue together the shards Henrik had left behind?

Over and over again during the night she burst out crying. Or was it that she had been crying all the time, without noticing that the tears occasionally dried up? She read through all the confusing documents that Henrik had collected, most of them in English, some of them photocopies of extracts from books or archives, others emails from university libraries or private foundations.

As dawn broke and she felt incapable of reading any more, she stretched out on the bed and tried to sum up the most important things she had read.

In November 1963, round about midday, Central Time, President John Fitzgerald Kennedy had been shot while travelling with his wife in a motorcade through the centre of Dallas. Three shots were fired from a rifle. Bullets had hurtled forth at mind-boggling speed and transformed everything in their path into a bloody mash of flesh and sinew and bone. The first shot hit the president in his throat, the second one missed, but the third hit him in the head and created a large hole through which lumps of his brain were blown out with enormous force. The president's body was flown back to Washington that same day in Air Force One. On board the flight, Lyndon Johnson was sworn in as president: by his side was Jackie, still in her bloodstained clothes. A post-mortem examination of the president was carried out at an air force base. The whole procedure was veiled in secrecy, and nobody knows what actually happened. Many years later, it was established that what remained of Kennedy's brain after the shot and the subsequent post-mortem had disappeared. Several investigations attempted to find out what had happened to the missing organ, but it proved impossible to establish the facts. The probability was that Robert Kennedy, the dead president's brother, had the remains buried. But nobody knew for sure. And a few years later, Robert Kennedy was also murdered.

President J. F. Kennedy's brain disappeared, and its location is still unknown.

Louise lay in her bed with her eyes closed and tried to understand. *What had Henrik been looking for?* She thought through the marginal notes he had made in the various documents.

The dead president's brain is like a hard drive. Was somebody afraid that it would become possible to decode the brain, just as it is possible to dig down into the cellars of a hard drive and retrieve imprints of texts that really ought to have been erased?

Henrik did not answer his own question.

She lay on her side in bed and studied a painting on the wall next to the bathroom door. Three tulips in a beige vase. The table dark brown, the cloth white. A bad painting, she thought. It doesn't breathe, the flowers don't produce any perfume.

In one of the files Henrik had inserted a full page torn out of a notebook on which he had tried to answer the question about why the brain might have disappeared.

Fear of what it contains, of the possibility that it might become possible to extract the innermost thoughts of a dead man. Like safe cracking or stealing diaries from somebody's most intimate hiding place. Is it possible to penetrate any deeper into a person's private world than by stealing his thoughts?

Louise could not understand who was afraid, or of what. What does Henrik think the dead president can tell him? A story that came to an end a long time ago? What exactly is this story Henrik is searching for?

I must be on the wrong track, she thought. She sat up in bed and felt for the piece of paper on which he had made notes. She could see he had been writing quickly. The wording was careless, the punctuation haphazard, and there were a lot of crossings-out. She also thought she could detect that he had not been resting the paper on something solid, possibly just his knee. He had written down the word *trophy*. He continued: *A scalp can be the ultimate prize, just like the antlers of a deer or the skin of a lion. So why couldn't a brain be a trophy? In that case, who is the hunter?* Then came Robert Kennedy's name, with a question mark after it.

The third motive was *the unknown alternative, something that it is impossible to imagine. As long as the brain is missing, this unknown alternative has to be a possibility. I cannot afford to overlook the unknown aspect.*

It was still dark, but she got out of bed and stood by the window again. It was raining, car headlights were glistening. She was forced to lean against the wall so as not to fall down. *What was he looking for?* She felt sick and could stay in the room no longer.

By soon after seven she had packed up Henrik's papers, paid her hotel bill and was sitting in the breakfast room with a cup of coffee.

At a nearby table a man and a woman were reading lines from a play. The man was very old. He was peering short-sightedly at the script and his hands were shaking. The woman was wearing a red over-coat and read in a monotonous tone of voice. The play was about a separation, and the scene was set in a hallway, or possibly in a stairwell. Louise was unable to work out if he was leaving her, or if it was the other way round. She finished her coffee and left the hotel. It had stopped raining. She walked up the hill to Henrik's flat. She was exhausted, her mind was swimming. *I shall think no further ahead than my next step. One step at a time, no more.*

She sat down at the kitchen table and avoided looking at the bread-crumbs still on its surface. She thumbed through his diary one more time. The letter 'B' kept recurring. She tried to think of a possible name that it stood for: Birgitta, Barbara, Berit. There was no clue anywhere to be found. Why was Henrik so interested in President Kennedy and his brain? Something had taken possession of him. But was what he was looking for something real, or merely a symbol? Did the shattered vase actually exist in the real world, or was it only a mirage?

She forced herself to open his wardrobe door, and go through his pockets. All she found was small change, most of the coins Swedish, but there were a couple of euros. In the pocket of one of Henrik's jackets she found a dirty bus ticket, or it might have been for the under-ground. She went into the kitchen and examined it under the table lamp. *Madrid.* So Henrik had been in Spain. He had not mentioned anything about that, she would have remembered if he had. Often all he said about his travels was where he had been. He never said why he had gone to a particular place, just the name of it.

She went back to the wardrobe. In one trouser pocket she found the remains of a dried flower that crumbled into powder when she took it out. Nothing else.

She started to go through his shirts. There was a ring at the door. She gave a start. The shrill bell sound cut into her like a knife. Her heart was beating frenetically as she went to the hall and opened the door. It was not Henrik standing there, but a short girl with dark hair and eyes to match, wearing an overcoat buttoned high up at the neck.

The girl looked expectantly at Louise.

'Is Henrik in?'

Louise burst into tears. The girl backed away almost imperceptibly.

'What are you doing here?' she asked. She sounded frightened.

Louise was unable to reply. She turned and went back to the kitchen. She could hear the girl coming in and closing the door quietly behind her.

'What are you doing here?' she asked again.

'Henrik is dead.'


The girl stood motionless, staring at Louise.

'Who are you?' Louise asked.

'My name's Nazrin and I was in a relationship with Henrik. Perhaps we still are a couple. We are friends in any case. He is the best friend you could ask for.'

'He's dead.'


Louise drew up a chair for the girl to sit on. Her overcoat was still buttoned up at the neck. When Louise told her what had happened, Nazrin shook her head slowly.

'Henrik can't possibly be dead,' she said when Louise had finished.

'No. I agree. He can't be . . .'

Louise waited for Nazrin's reaction. But she waited in vain, there was no reaction. Then Nazrin started asking tentative questions. Louise thought the truth had still not struck home.

'Was he ill?'

'He was never ill. He'd had a few of the usual childhood illnesses, such as measles, without our really noticing there was anything wrong with him. He had a phase as a teenager when he kept getting nosebleeds. But that passed. He always used to say he was so fit because life passed by so slowly.'

'What did he mean by that?'

'I've no idea.'

'But he can't have just died, surely, without warning? That doesn't happen.'

'It doesn't happen. But it happens even so. What doesn't happen is the worst that can happen.'

Louise suddenly felt furious over the fact that Nazrin had not started to cry. It was as if she were desecrating his memory.

'I want you to leave now,' she said.

'Why should I leave?'

'You came to see Henrik. He doesn't exist any more. So you should leave.'

'I don't want to leave.'

'I don't even know who you are. He's never said anything about you.'

'He told me he'd never mentioned me to you. "*You can't live without secrets*".'

'Is that what he said?'

'He said it was you who had taught him that.'

Louise's anger faded. She felt embarrassed.

'I'm afraid,' she said. 'I'm shaking. I've lost my only child. I've lost my own life. I'm sitting here waiting to fall to pieces.'

Nazrin stood up and went to the other room. Louise could hear her sobbing. She was away for some considerable time. When she came back, she had unbuttoned her coat and her dark eyes were red.

'We had decided to "go for the long walk". That's what we used to call it. We'd follow the river and head out of town for as long as we could manage. The rule was that we shouldn't say a word on the way out, but we could talk on the way back.'

'How come that you are called Nazrin but don't speak Swedish with a foreign accent?'

47

'I was born at Arlanda airport. We'd been hanging around there for two days, waiting to be allocated to some refugee camp or other. Mum gave birth to me on the floor next to passport control. It all went very quickly. I was born at the precise spot where Sweden begins. Neither Mum nor Dad had a passport, but as I was born on the floor there, I was awarded Swedish citizenship right away. An old passport officer still keeps in touch.'

'How did you and Henrik meet?'

'On a bus. We were sitting next to each other. He started laughing and pointed to something somebody had written in Indian ink next to the window. I didn't think it was funny at all.'

'What did it say?'

'I can't remember. Then he called on me at work. I'm a dental nurse. He'd stuffed cotton wool into his mouth and claimed that he had toothache.'

Nazrin took off her coat. Louise eyed her up and down and imagined her naked lying next to Henrik.

She reached out over the table and grasped Nazrin's arm.

'You must know something. I was in Greece. You were here. Did something happen? Did he change?'

'He was happy, happier than ever these last few weeks. I've never seen him so elated.'

'What had happened?'

'I don't know.'

Louise could tell that Nazrin was telling the truth. It's like digging down into complex strata, she thought. It can take even an experienced archaeologist some time to realise that they have come to a new cultural horizon. You can dig through these complex remains and only through analysis later can you realise the significance of what has been found.

'When did you notice this happiness?'

Nazrin's reply surprised her.

'When he came back home after a trip.'

'Where to?'

'I don't know.'

'Didn't he tell you where he was going to?'

'Not always. On this occasion he didn't say anything at all. I met him at the airport. He'd come from Frankfurt. But he'd started off from much further away than that. I don't know where.'

Louise felt a shooting pain, as if from a damaged tooth. Henrik had transferred in Frankfurt, just as she had done only the other day. She had come from Athens. Where had his aeroplane started from, before descending through the clouds over Germany?

'He must have said something. You must have noticed something. Was he tanned? Did he bring any gifts?'

'He said nothing at all. He has a more or less permanent tan. He was much happier than when he left. He never used to give me presents.'

'How long had he been away?'

'Three weeks.'

'But he didn't say where he'd been?'

'No.'

'When did this trip take place?'

'About two months ago.'

'Did he explain why he hadn't said anything about it?'

'He spoke about his "little secret".'

'Is that what he called it?'

'That's exactly what he said.'

'And he didn't have anything for you?'

'As I said, he never used to buy me presents. But he did write poems.'

'What about?'

'Darkness.'

Louise looked at Nazrin in astonishment.

'Are you saying he gave you some poems about darkness that he'd written on his journey?'

'There were seven poems, one written every third day throughout the trip. They were about remarkable people who lived in constant darkness. People who had given up looking for a way out.'

'That sounds pretty grim.'

'They were horrible.'

'Do you still have them?'

'He wanted me to burn them after I'd read them.'

'Why?'

'I asked the same question. He said they weren't needed any longer.'

'Was that usual? For him to ask you to burn what he's written?'

'It had never happened before. This was the only time.'

'Did he ever talk to you about a brain that had disappeared?'

Nazrin stared uncomprehendingly at her.

'John Kennedy was murdered in Dallas in 1963. After the post-mortem, his brain disappeared.'

Nazrin shook her head.

'I've no idea what you're talking about. I wasn't even born in 1963.'

'But you must have heard of President Kennedy?'

'I might have done.'

'Did Henrik ever talk about him?'

'Why should he?'

'I'm only asking. I've found lots of papers here about President Kennedy. And his missing brain.'

'Why should Henrik have been interested in that?'

'I don't know. It's just that I think it's important.'

There was a clatter from post dropping onto the doormat. Both of them gave a start. Nazrin went to the door and returned with advertising leaflets about special offers on pork loin and computers. She put them on the kitchen table, but did not sit down again.

'I can't stay here. I feel as if I'm suffocating.'

She burst out sobbing. Louise stood up and embraced her.

'What happened to bring things to an end?' she asked when Nazrin had calmed down. 'When love turned into friendship?'

'That only applied to him. I still loved him. I hoped everything would get back to normal.'

'Why was he so happy? Had he found another woman?'

Nazrin answered without hesitation. Louise realised that this was a question Nazrin had asked herself.

'There was no other woman.'

'Help me to understand. You saw him from a different point of view.

For me, he was my son. You never see your own children clearly. There's always an expectation or a worry that distorts the picture.'

Nazrin sat down again. Louise could see that Nazrin's eyes were flitting back and forth over the kitchen walls, as if seeking a point of reference to hang on to.

'Maybe I'm using the wrong words,' Nazrin said. 'Maybe I ought to be talking about a sorrow that had suddenly disappeared, rather than unexpected happiness.'

'Henrik was never depressed.'

'Perhaps he didn't show it when you were there? You said it yourself. You never see your own children clearly. Parents don't. When I met Henrik on that bus, he was laughing. But the Henrik I got to know was a very serious person. He was like me. He regarded the world as a mess that was only getting worse and heading for the ultimate catastrophe. He used to get animated when he talked about poverty. He tried to express his anger, but he always found it easier to express his sorrow. He was too soft-hearted, I think. Or it may be that I could never quite make him out. I regarded him as a failed idealist. But perhaps the truth was different. He was planning something, he wanted to resist. I remember once we were sitting at this very table, he was sitting where you are now, and he said that "every human being has to be his own resistance movement. We can never wait for others to act. This frightful world needs every single one of us to make an effort. When there's a fire, nobody asks where the water is going to come from. That fire simply has to be put out." I remember thinking that he could sometimes sound a bit high-flown. Like a priest. Perhaps all priests are romantics? I could get fed up of his seriousness. His anguish was like a barrier I kept thumping on. He was a social reformer, but he felt most sorry for himself. Nevertheless, there was a distinct seriousness under the surface that I could never ignore. A seriousness, a sorrow, a failed attempt to express anger. When he tried to be angry, he was more like a scared little boy. But everything had changed when he came back from that trip.'

Nazrin dried up. Louise could see that she was trying hard to remember.

'I noticed right away that something had happened. When he came from airside into the terminal he was walking slowly, almost as if he hesitated to go any further. He smiled when he saw me, but I remember thinking he looked as if he'd hoped nobody would be there to meet him. He was the same as usual, or at least he tried to be the same as usual. He was miles away mentally, even when we made love. I didn't know whether or not to be jealous. But he would have told me if he'd met another woman. I tried to find out where he'd been, but he just shook his head. When he unpacked his bags I noticed that there was red sand on the soles of one pair of shoes. I asked him about that, but he didn't answer, just seemed annoyed. Then all of a sudden, he changed completely again. His mind was no longer miles away, he became more cheerful, more at ease, as if he'd thrown off some invisible burden. I noticed that he was often tired when I came to visit him in the afternoons: he'd been up all night, but I could never get him to tell me what he'd been doing. He was writing something, I noticed more and more new files around the flat. All the time he used to talk about the anger that needed to be vented, about everything that was being hushed up, everything that ought to be exposed. It sometimes sounded as if he was quoting the Bible, as if he were turning into some kind of a prophet. I tried to make a joke about it once, but he was furious. It was the only time I've ever seen him really angry. I thought he was going to hit me. He raised his fist, tightly clenched – if I hadn't shouted he'd have punched me. I was scared. He apologised, but I didn't believe him.'

Nazrin dried up again. Noises from the flat next door could be heard through the kitchen wall. Louise recognised the music, it was the theme tune of a film, but she couldn't remember its name.

Nazrin buried her face in her hands. Louise sat motionless, waiting. What was she waiting for? She had no idea.

Nazrin stood up.

'I must go now. I haven't the strength to go on.'

'Where can I get in touch with you?'

Nazrin wrote her telephone number on one of the advertising leaflets. Then she picked up her coat, turned and left. Louise could hear the echo of her footsteps going down the stairs, then the sound of the front door closing.

A few minutes later she left the flat herself. She walked towards Slussen, turning into side streets at random and keeping close to the walls of buildings, afraid of suddenly suffering a panic attack. When she came to Slussen she hailed a taxi and went to Djurgården. The wind had eased off, the air felt milder. She wandered through the trees dressed in their autumn colours, and thought back to what Nazrin had said.

*Sorrow that had suddenly disappeared, rather than unexpected happiness. A journey he did not want to talk about.*

An obsession? All those files? Louise was convinced the ones Nazrin had referred to were the ones she had read herself, about the assassinated president. Those were the ones Nazrin had seen. So Henrik's interest in the dead president's brain was not something long-term. It was something new.

She strolled around the trees and meandered through the many thoughts running across her mind. Sometimes she was unsure if the autumn leaves were rustling in her head or under her feet.

She suddenly remembered the letter from Aron she had found. She took it out of her pocket and opened it.

It was brief.

*Still no icebergs. But I'm not giving up. Aron.*

What did it mean? Icebergs? Was it a code? A game? She put the letter back into her pocket and carried on walking.


It was late afternoon when she returned to Henrik's flat. Somebody had left a message on the answering machine. *Hi, it's Ivan. I'll try again later.* Who was Ivan? Nazrin might know. She was about to call her, but changed her mind. She went into Henrik's bedroom and sat down on the mattress. She felt dizzy, but forced herself to remain seated.

There was a photograph on a shelf of the two of them together.

They had been to Madeira when Henrik was seventeen. They had spent a week on the island, and after visiting the Valley of the Nuns, they had decided to return in ten years' time. That was going to be the destination of their own very special pilgrimage. She suddenly felt very angry at the thought that somebody had robbed them of their journey. Death was so damnably long, she thought. So eternal. We shall never return to *Correia des fuentes*. Never.

She looked around the room. Something had attracted her attention, but she was unsure what. She looked around again. A pair of bookshelves made her pause. At first she did not know why. Then she noticed that one of the books on the lower shelf was jutting out. She got up from the bed and ran her hand behind the books. She could feel two thin notebooks. She eased them out and took them to the kitchen. They were very simple notebooks, containing bits of handwriting in pencil, ink, Indian ink, and with lots of blots. The text was in English. On the cover of one it said: *Memory Book for my mother Paula.*

Louise leafed through the thin book. It contained a few paragraphs, some dried flowers, the shrivelled skin of a little lizard, a few faded photographs, and a crayon drawing of a child's face. She read the text and gathered it was about a woman who would soon be dead, was suffering from Aids, and had written this little book for her children, something for them to remember her by when she was no longer with them. '*Don't cry too much, just cry enough to water the flowers you plant on my grave. Study and make use of your lives. Make use of your time.*'

Louise looked at the black woman's face that could just about be discerned in a faded photograph. She was smiling straight at the camera lens, straight at Louise's sorrow and feeling of hopelessness.

She read the other book. *Miriam's Memory Book for her daughter Ricki.* There were no photographs here, the texts were short, the handwriting cramped. No dried flowers, a few empty pages. The book was not finished, it stopped in the middle of a sentence. '*There are so many things I would –*'

Louise tried to complete the sentence. In the same way that Miriam would have liked to say. Or do.

*There are so many things I would like to say to you, Henrik. Or do. But you have vanished, you have hidden yourself away from me. Above*

*all you have left me with a terrible agony. I don't know why you vanished.*
*I don't know what you were looking for and what drove you to what*
*happened. You were alive, you didn't want to die. But now you are dead*
*even so. I don't understand why.*

Louise looked at the notebooks lying on the kitchen table.

*I don't understand why you have these memory books about two women*
*who died from Aids. Nor why you had hidden them behind other books*
*on your shelves.*

She slowly spread out the shards inside her head. She picked out
the biggest fragments. She hoped they would act like magnets and
attract other shards until it became possible to discern a whole.

*The red soil under his shoes. Where had he been to?*

She held her breath and tried to make out a pattern.

*I must have patience. In the same way that archaeology has taught me*
*that you can only find your way through all the earth layers of history*
*by using energy and gentleness. But never by hurrying.*


It was late when Louise left the flat that evening. She took a room in
a different hotel. She phoned Artur and told him she would be back
soon. Then she took out Göran Wrath's business card and rang him
at home. He sounded half asleep when he answered. They agreed to
meet in his office at nine o'clock the next morning.

She emptied several of the little bottles of spirits in her minibar.
Then she slept uneasily until about one in the morning.

She lay awake for the rest of the night.

The shards had still not spoken.

# CHAPTER 6

Göran Wrath met her in the foyer of police headquarters. He smelled of tobacco, and on the way up to his office he told her that in his youth he had dreamed of searching for bones. She wasn't sure what he meant – it was only when they had sat down at his cluttered desk that she received an explanation. As a student he had been fascinated by the Leakey family who devoted their time to digging for human fossils, and if they sometimes failed to find humans, at least they discovered hominids in the deep canyons in East Africa known as the Rift Valley.

Wrath removed a mountain of documents from his desk and keyed a number into his telephone that would block incoming calls.

'I used to dream about it. Deep down I knew I would become a police officer. But, nevertheless, I used to dream about finding what was then called "the missing link". When did apes become humans? Or perhaps one ought to rephrase that and ask: when did humans stop being apes? Now and then when I get time, I try to read up on all the latest discoveries that have been made in recent years. But it becomes increasingly obvious to me that the only missing links I'm going to find are to do with my police work.'

He stopped abruptly, as if he had let slip a secret by mistake. Louise observed him with a vague feeling of sadness. She was sitting opposite a man with an unfulfilled dream. The world was full of middle-aged men like Göran Wrath. In the end, the dream became no more than a pale reflection of what had once been a burning passion.

What had her dream been? Nothing at all, really. Archaeology had been her first passion after the giant-like Emil had let her go and she had travelled a couple of hundred miles north in order to shake him off and become a normal person again. It often seemed to her that her life had taken shape when the little train stopped at Rätansbyn, halfway between Östersund and Sveg, where they were due to meet their south-bound counterpart. There was a hot-dog stall at the side of the station building. Everybody seemed to be overcome by extreme pangs of hunger when the train came to a halt. Whoever was last in the queue might have to go hungry – either because the stall had run out of sausages, or because the train was about to leave.

She had not joined in the mad rush for the hot-dog stall. She had remained in her seat, and it was then she had resolved to become an archaeologist. She had considered taking the long course to become a doctor: specialising in children's illnesses was also a tempting possi-bility. But as darkness fell, she had made up her mind that night at Rätansbyn. It seemed an obvious choice to make, there was no longer any doubt about it. She would devote her life to hunting down the past. She pictured herself working on the front line, doing the actual digging; but she also had a vague idea that her future might just as well lie in searching for secrets in old manuscripts, reinterpreting the facts that had been established by previous generations of archaeolo-gists.

On all sides she was surrounded by people chewing away at sausages with mustard and ketchup, and a strange feeling of peace enveloped her. She knew.

Göran Wrath had left the room and returned with a cup of coffee. She had declined his offer to bring one for her. She settled down on her chair with the feeling that she would need to put up a fight.

He spoke to her in a friendly tone of voice, as if she were a close friend of his.

'There is nothing to suggest that your son was murdered.'

'I want to know every detail.'

'We don't know every detail yet. It takes time to root out everything that has occurred when a person dies unexpectedly. Death is a compli-cated business. Probably the most complicated and hard to grasp process that life has to offer. We know a lot more about how a human being is created than we know about how life comes to an end.'

'I'm talking about my son! Not some foetus or other, or an old man in a care home!'

Afterwards, she wondered if Göran Wrath had expected her outburst. He must have been in this position many times before – faced with desperate parents who could not have their child back but nevertheless wanted some form of redress, no matter how pointless it might seem. Not wanting to be classified as a bad parent, not wanting to be accused of being remiss.

Wrath opened a plastic folder on the desk in front of him.

'There is no answer,' he said. 'There ought to have been. I can only apologise. Due to a series of unfortunate circumstances, the test results have been destroyed and have to be done again. Doctors and lab technicians are hard at work. They are meticulous, they need time. But the first thing we need to do, of course, is to establish that no outside party was involved. And there wasn't.'

'Henrik was not the suicidal type.'

Wrath looked at her hard and long before answering.

'My father was called Hugo Wrath. Everybody considered him to be the most cheerful person in the world. He was always laughing, he loved his family. Every morning he would set off for his job as a typographer for *Dagens Nyheter* in a cheerful mood. Nevertheless he unexpectedly committed suicide at the age of forty-nine. He had seen the birth of his first grandchild, and he had received a pay rise. He had just concluded a long-running dispute with his sisters and hence was the sole owner of a holiday home on Utö. I was eleven at the time, still a little boy. He always used to come in and give me a hug before I fell asleep. One Tuesday morning he got up as usual, had breakfast, read the morning paper, was in a good mood as usual, hummed a tune as he fastened his shoes, and gave my mum a kiss before leaving. Then he set off on his bike. The same route as usual. But just before he came to Torsgatan, he turned off. He didn't go to work at all. He left town altogether. Somewhere in Sollentuna he branched off into country lanes that led into the forest. There's a scrapyard there that you can see clearly as you approach Arlanda airport. He parked his bicycle and disappeared into the scrap metal. They eventually found him on the back seat of an old Dodge. He had lain down there, taken a huge overdose of sleeping tablets, and died. I can remember the funeral. Obviously, the shock over his death was immense. But the most painful aspect nevertheless was not knowing why. The whole funeral was dominated by that mysterious, painful 'why'. Nobody said a word at the gathering for coffee afterwards.'

Louise felt provoked. Her son had nothing to do with Göran Wrath's father.

Wrath understood her reaction. He leafed through the file on the desk in front of him, although he already knew what was in it.

'There is no explanation for why Henrik died. The only thing we are certain of is that there was no obvious physical violence.'

'I could see that myself.'

'There's nothing to suggest that another person caused his death.'

'What do the doctors have to say?'

'That there is no simple explanation. Which shouldn't surprise anybody. When a young, healthy person dies suddenly, there has to be something unexpected behind what happened. We'll find out eventually.'

'What?'

Wrath shook his head.

'Some little part stops working. When some minor connection or other is broken it can cause just as much damage as when a dam wall collapses or when a volcano erupts without warning. The medics are looking for clues.'

'Something odd must have happened. Something unnatural.'

'Why do you think that? Explain to me.'

Wrath's voice had changed. She could detect a trace of impatience in his question.

'I knew my son. He was a happy person.'

'What is a happy person?'

'I don't want to talk about your father. I'm talking about Henrik. He did not die willingly.'

'But nobody killed him. Either he died of natural causes, or he took his own life. Our pathologists are very thorough. We shall know the answer before long.'

'And then?'

'What do you mean?'

'When they have failed to find an explanation?'

The silence bounced back and forth between them.

'I'm sorry that I can't help you any more just now.'

'Nobody can help me.'

Louise stood up abruptly.

'There is no explanation. There is no missing link, no faulty connection. Henrik died because somebody else wanted him to die, not himself.'

Göran Wrath accompanied her to the entrance. They parted without saying a word.


Louise went to the car and drove out of Stockholm. Just before reaching Sala she stopped in a lay-by, tipped back her seat and fell asleep.

Vassilis appeared in her dreams. He insisted that he had nothing to do with Henrik's death.

Louise woke up and continued her journey northwards. That dream was a message, she thought. I dreamed about Vassilis, but in fact I was dreaming about myself. I was trying to convince myself that I hadn't abandoned Henrik. But I didn't listen to him as much as I ought to have done.

She stopped at Orsa for something to eat. A group of young men wearing football shirts – or maybe they were ice-hockey shirts – were laughing and shouting at a nearby table. She felt an urge to tell them about Henrik and ask them to be quiet. Then she started crying. A pot-bellied lorry driver stared at her. Louise shook her head and he looked away. She saw that he was carefully filling in some kind of betting slip or football coupon, and she hoped he would win.

It was evening by the time she came to the never-ending forests. She thought she caught a glimpse of an elk in a clear-felled patch. She stopped and got out of the car. She thought hard in an attempt to find something she had overlooked.

*Henrik did not die a natural death. Somebody killed him. The red soil under his shoes, the memory books, his sudden happiness. What is it that I can't see? Perhaps the shards fit together, even if I can't see how.*

She stopped again in Noppikoski, when she felt so tired, she could not possibly drive any further.

She dreamed about Greece again, but this time Vassilis only appeared as a shadowy figure on the periphery. She was at the site of a dig when there was a sudden landslide. She was buried underneath the rubble, she was terrified and just as she found herself unable to breathe any more, she woke up.

She carried on driving north. This last dream had an obvious explanation.

It was late at night by the time she reached Sveg. She could see a light in the kitchen as she turned into the forecourt. Her father was still up, as usual. As she had done so many times before, she wondered how he had managed to survive all these years despite having so little sleep.

He was sitting at the kitchen table, greasing some of his carving tools. He did not seem surprised at her coming home in the middle of the night.

'Are you hungry?'

'I had a meal in Orsa.'

'That's a long way away.'

'I'm not hungry.'

'OK, I won't mention it again.'

She sat down on her usual chair, smoothed out the tablecloth and reported on what had happened. When she had finished, neither spoke for a long time.

'Perhaps Wrath is right,' he said eventually. 'Let's see if they can come up with an explanation.'

'I don't think they're doing everything they could do. They're not really interested in Henrik. One young man among thousands who's suddenly discovered dead in his bed.'

'You're being unfair.'

'I know I'm being unfair. But that's how I feel.'

'I suppose we'll have to wait and see what they say, anyway.'

Louise knew he was right. The truth about what had happened, about what had caused Henrik's death, would never be discovered if they refused to consider the post-mortem examination.

Louise was tired. She was about to stand up and go to bed when Artur held her back.

'I've had another go at finding Aron.'

'Have you traced him?'

'No. But I've made an effort, at least. I've been in touch with our embassy in Canberra again, and talked to a few people at the friendship society. But nobody has ever heard of Aron Cantor. Are you sure he's living in Australia?'

'Nobody can be sure of anything as far as Aron is concerned.'

'It would be sad if he didn't find out what had happened and hence couldn't be present at the funeral.'

'Maybe he doesn't want to be there? Maybe he doesn't want us to find him at all?'

'Surely he would want to be there?'

'You don't know Aron.'

'You could be right about that. You hardly gave me a chance to meet him.'

'What do you mean by that?'

'There's no need to get het up. You know I'm right.'

'You're not right at all. I never got in the way of you and Aron.'

'It's too late at night for an argument like this.'

'It isn't an argument. It's a pointless conversation. Thank you for taking the trouble, but Aron won't be coming to the funeral.'

'Nevertheless, I think we ought to keep on looking.'

Louise made no reply. And Artur stopped talking about Aron.


Aron was not present at the funeral of his son, Henrik Cantor, in the Lutheran church in Sveg two weeks later. After the notice of Henrik's death had appeared, a lot of people contacted Nazrin, who was a big help to Louise during those difficult weeks. Many of Henrik's friends, most of whom Louise had never heard of, had said they would like to be present at the funeral. But Härjedalen was too far away. Nazrin had suggested a memorial service in Stockholm after the burial. Louise realised that she ought to meet Henrik's friends, who might be able to help her find an explanation of his death; but she did not feel up to anything more than the funeral. She asked Nazrin to keep a record of everybody who made enquiries.

The funeral took place on Wednesday, 20 October, at one o'clock. Nazrin arrived the day before, accompanied by another girl by the name of Vera who, if Louise understood the situation correctly, had also had a relationship with Henrik. There would be very few people present at the funeral. It seemed like a huge betrayal of Henrik and all the people he had known during his life. But there was no possible alternative to the arrangements they had made.

Louise and Artur had quarrelled vehemently over who should conduct the funeral. Louise had insisted that Henrik would not have wanted the ceremony to be carried out by a vicar, but Artur thought that his grandson may have been interested in spiritual matters. Who was there in Sveg who could carry off a worthy ceremony for Henrik? Nyblom, the vicar, was not an overzealous preacher of God's word and usually expressed himself in simple, everyday terms. He could be persuaded to omit God and sanctity from the funeral service.

Louise gave way. She lacked the strength to fight a battle. She felt weaker for each day that passed.


Göran Wrath phoned on Tuesday, 19 October. He informed Louise that the post-mortem had established that the cause of death had been barbiturate poisoning, a big overdose of sleeping tablets. He apologised once more for the length of time it had taken. Louise listened to what he had to say in a sort of trance. She knew that he would not dream of giving her this information unless it was a clear and incontestable outcome. He promised to send her all the documentation, expressed his sympathy once more, and told her that the investigation was now at an end. The police had nothing more to say, no prosecutor would need to be consulted as suicide had been confirmed.

When Louise told Artur what Wrath had said, he commented: 'Well, that's it confirmed.'

Louise knew that Artur did not believe this. He would worry about it endlessly. Why had Henrik decided to take his own life? Assuming that really was what had happened.

Nazrin and Vera could not believe either that what Wrath had told them was the truth. Nazrin said: 'If he was going to commit suicide he would have done it in some other way. Not in his bed, with sleeping tablets. That would have been too wimpish for Henrik.'


Louise awoke on the morning of 20 October and saw that there had been a frost during the night. She went down to the railway bridge and stood for ages leaning over the rail, staring into the black water below, just as black as the earth into which Henrik's coffin would shortly be lowered. Louise had been adamant on that point. Henrik should not be cremated, his body should be delivered into the ground. She stared down into the river and remembered standing at the very same spot when she had been young and unhappy, and perhaps even thought of taking her own life. It was as if Henrik were standing by her side. He would not have jumped either. He would have clung on to life, he would not have let go.

She stood on the bridge for a long time in the early-morning hours. *Today I am about to bury my only child. I shall never have another child. Henrik's coffin contains a vital part of my life. A part that will never return.*

The coffin was brown, decked with roses, no wreaths. The organist played Bach, and a piece by Scarlatti that he had suggested himself. The vicar spoke calmly, without fuss, and God was not present in the church. Louise sat beside Artur; on the other side of the coffin were Nazrin and Vera. Louise appeared to observe the whole funeral ceremony from a great distance. Nevertheless, she was the one that it was for. You could not feel sorry for the deceased. The dead cry no more.

But Louise? She was a ruin. However, some arches inside her remained undamaged, and she was determined to preserve them.

Nazrin and Vera left early to begin their long bus ride back to Stockholm. But Nazrin promised to keep in touch, and said that when Louise felt up to emptying Henrik's flat in Stockholm, she would be pleased to help.

That evening Louise sat in the kitchen with Artur and a bottle of vodka. He drank it to accompany his coffee, Louise watered it down with lemonade. As if by silent agreement, they both drank themselves silly. By about ten o'clock they were slumped hollow-eyed over the kitchen table.

'I'm leaving tomorrow.'

'Going back?'

'Isn't everybody always going back to somewhere? I'm going to Greece. I must finish my work there. What happens after that, I have no idea.'

The next day, well before dawn, he drove her to Östersund airport. The ground had a thin covering of powdery snow. Artur took her hand and urged her to be careful. She could see he was trying to think of something else to say, but couldn't. As she sat back on the flight to Arlanda, she thought he would doubtless start work later that day on carving Henrik's face into one of his trees.

She caught the 7.55 flight from Arlanda to Frankfurt, intending to continue from there to Athens. But when she arrived in Frankfurt it seemed that all the decisions she had made collapsed. She cancelled her flight to Athens.

She knew now what she had to do. Artur had been neither right nor wrong, her concession had nothing to do with him. It was her own decision, her own insight into the reality of the situation.

Aron. He existed. He must exist.

* * *

65

She managed to catch the 9.50 Qantas flight to Sydney. The last thing she did before leaving was to ring one of her colleagues in Greece and say that she was not in a position to return there yet.

Another journey, another meeting would have to take place first.

Sitting next to her on the flight was an unaccompanied child, a little girl oblivious to everything around her. The only thing she had eyes for was her doll, a strange mixture of an elephant and an old lady.

Louise Cantor gazed out of the window.

Aron. He existed. He must exist.

# CHAPTER 7

When they made a refuelling stop in Singapore, Louise left the plane and strolled in the damp heat through the long corridors with yellowish-brown carpets that only seemed to lead to new, distant terminals.

She paused at a shop selling stationary, and bought a diary with birds embroidered on the violet-coloured covers. The girl who served her smiled at her with eyes full of warmth. Louise immediately felt the tears welling up inside her. She turned on her heel and left.

On the way back she was afraid of being overcome with panic. She walked close to the walls, increased her pace and tried to concentrate on breathing. She was convinced that at any moment everything would go black and she would fall over. But she had no desire to wake up on that yellowish-brown carpet. She did not want to fall. Not now when she had made the vital decision to go and look for Aron.

The plane took off for Sydney soon before midnight. Even before she left Frankfurt she had lost count of the time zones she would pass through. She was travelling in a weightless and timeless state. Perhaps that was the best way of approaching Aron? During the years they had lived together he had always had a strange ability to be aware of when she was on her way home, when she was approaching him. On many an occasion when she was annoyed by something he had said or done, it had struck her that she would never be able to surprise him if he was unfaithful to her.

She had an aisle seat, 26D. Fast asleep in the seat next to her was a friendly man who had introduced himself as a retired group captain in the Australian air force. He had made no attempt to converse with her, and she was relieved about that. She sat in the dimly lit aircraft and accepted a series of glasses of water that the silent cabin crew carried round on trays at regular intervals. On the other side of the aisle was a woman about her own age, listening to one of the radio channels.

Louise took out her newly acquired diary, switched on her reading light, found a pencil and started writing.

*Red soil.* Those were her first words. Why was that the first thing to come to her mind? Was that the most important clue she had? The key piece that all the other fragments would eventually fit around?

In her mind's eye she leafed through the two memory books about the dead or dying women.

How had Henrik come across them? He was not a child who needed to have something to remember his parents by. He knew a lot, albeit not everything, about his mother. And Aron was somebody he was in regular contact with, even if his father was mostly absent. Where had he got those books from? Who had given them to him?

She wrote down a question. *Where does the red soil come from?* That was as far as she could get. She put away the diary, switched off the reading light and closed her eyes. *I need Aron in order to think.* In his best moments he was not only a good lover, he also understood the art of listening. He was one of those rare creatures who could give advice without taking into account what advantages he could gain for himself.

She opened her eyes in the darkness. Perhaps that was the aspect of Aron and their life together that she missed most of all? The listening and sometimes immensely clever man she had fallen in love with, and had a son with?

That's the Aron I'm looking for, she thought. Without his help I shall never be able to understand what has happened. I'll never be able to find my way back into my own life without his support.

She dozed through the rest of the night, hopping around the radio channels, occasionally disturbed by music that seemed unsuitable for the darkness of the night. I'm in a cage, she thought. A cage with thin walls that nevertheless can withstand the intense cold and the high speed. Inside this cage I'm being hurled towards a continent I never

imagined I would ever visit. A continent I have never had any desire
to go to.

A couple of hours before landing in Sydney she had the feeling that
the decision she had made in Frankfurt was pointless. She would never
be able to find Aron. All on her own at the far edge of the world she
would merely be overcome by sorrow and increasing desperation.

But she had no power to turn the cage round and hurl it back at
Frankfurt. Soon after breakfast the aircraft touched down in Sydney
airport. Half asleep, she re-emerged into the world. A friendly customs
officer removed an apple from her hand luggage and threw it into a
rubbish bin. She found her way to an information desk and reserved
a room at the Hilton. She had a nasty shock when she realised how
much it would cost, but did not have the strength to cancel it. She
changed some money then took a taxi to her hotel. She observed the
city in the morning light and thought about the fact that Aron must
once have taken the same route, along the same motorways, over the
same bridges.

She had been allocated a room with windows that would not open.
If she had not been so tired she would have left the hotel and looked
for another one. The room felt suffocating, but she forced herself to
take a shower, then crept naked between the sheets. I sleep like Henrik
used to do, she thought. I sleep naked. Why was he wearing pyjamas
that last night of his life?

She fell asleep without finding an answer to the question, and woke
up at noon. She went out, found her way to the harbour, walked to
the Opera House and installed herself in an Italian restaurant for a
meal. The air was chilly, but the sunshine was warm. She drank a glass
of wine and tried to think about what to do next. Artur had spoken
to the embassy. He had also been in contact with members of an asso-
ciation that apparently kept tabs on immigrant Swedes. But Aron is
not an immigrant. He would never allow himself be put on a register.
He is a man who always has at least two routes in and out of his hiding
places.

She forced herself not to feel too downhearted. It must be possible to find Aron, always assuming he really was in Australia. He was the kind of person who always made an impression on people. They would never forget Aron.

She was about to leave the restaurant when she heard a man at the next table speaking Swedish on a mobile phone. He was talking to a woman, she could make that out, about a car that needed repairing. He hung up and smiled at her.

'There's always problems with cars,' he said in English. 'Always.'

'I speak Swedish. But you're right, cars are nothing but trouble.'

The man stood up, came over to her table and introduced himself. His name was Oskar Lundin, and his handshake was firm.

'Louise Cantor. A pretty name. Are you a casual visitor or resident?'

'A very casual visitor. I haven't even been here for a full day yet.'

He gestured towards a chair, asking permission to sit down. A waiter moved his coffee to Louise's table.

'It's a lovely spring day,' he said. 'There's still a bit of a nip in the air, but spring is on the way. I never cease to be surprised by this world, where spring and autumn can be companions even if they are separated by continents and oceans.'

'Have you lived here long?'

'I came to Australia in 1949. I was nineteen then. I was convinced that I would be able to whittle gold using my trusty sheath knife. I'd made a mess of my school studies, but I had a bent for gardening, for plants. I knew I would always be able to make a living trimming hedges or pruning fruit trees.'

'Why did you come here?'

'I had such lousy parents. Excuse me for saying so, but it's the truth. My father was a vicar and hated everybody who didn't believe in the same God as he did. I didn't believe in anything at all and hence was a heathen: he used to beat me whenever he could until I became old enough to defend myself. Then he stopped speaking to me. My mother always used to mediate. She was a Good Samaritan, but unfortunately

70

she kept a running tally and never did anything to make my life easier without demanding something in return. She forced out all my emotions, my bad conscience, my guilt feeling over all the sacrifices she made, just as you squeeze out a lemon in a fruit press. So I did the only thing open to me. I ran away. That was more than fifty years ago. I never went back. Not even to their funerals. I have a sister over there and talk to her every Christmas. But basically, I'm here. And I became a master gardener. With a firm of my own that doesn't only trim hedges and prune fruit trees, but creates whole gardens for anybody who's prepared to pay.'

He drank his coffee and adjusted his chair so that his face was in the sun. It seemed to Louise that she had nothing to lose.

'I'm looking for a man,' she said. 'His name is Aron Cantor. We used to be married. I think he's here in Australia.'

'You think?'

'I'm not sure. I've asked the embassy and the friendship society.'

Lundin pulled a dismissive face.

'They haven't a clue about the Swedes living in Australia. It'll be like looking for a needle in a haystack. The society has no idea.'

'What are you suggesting? That people come here in order to hide?'

'Just as many people from here go to a country like Sweden where they can conceal their sins. I don't think there are all that many Swedish crooks hiding in Australia, but I've no doubt there are a few. Ten years ago there was a man here from Ånge who had committed murder. The Swedish authorities never tracked him down. He's dead now and has his own gravestone in Adelaide. But I take it the man you used to be married to isn't wanted for some crime or other?'

'No. But I need to find him.'

'We all do. Need to find the people we are looking for.'

'What would you do if you were me?'

Oskar Lundin stirred his half-empty cup of coffee as if deep in thought.

'I suppose I'd ask me to help you,' he said eventually. 'I've got vast numbers of contacts in this country. Australia is a continent where most things still happen by personal contact. We shout and we whisper to one another, and we generally find out what we want to know. Where can I get in touch with you?'

'I'm staying at the Hilton. But it's really too expensive for me.'

'Stay there for two days, if you can afford it. I won't need any longer than that. If your husband's here, I'll find him. If I don't find him, you can look somewhere else. New Zealand is often the next place to go.'

'I can't believe that I was lucky enough to bump into you. And that you are prepared to help somebody you don't know at all.'

'Maybe I try to do the good that my father only pretended to do.'

Lundin waved to the waiter and paid his bill. He raised his hat when he left.

'I'll be in touch within forty-eight hours. With good news, I hope. But I'm already beginning to worry that I might have promised too much. Sometimes I promise my clients too much fruit on the apple trees I plant for them. I always feel guilty about that afterwards.'

She watched him walk straight out into the sun and stride along the quay as far as the ferry terminal, which nestled at the foot of a line of sky-scrapers. She was often wrong when it came to judging people's character; but she had no doubt at all that Oskar Lundin would try to help her.

Twenty-three hours later the telephone rang in her room. She had just come back from a long walk. She had been trying to think about what she would do if Oskar Lundin was not able to give her any informa-tion, or if he had tricked her and would never be heard of again. Earlier she had spoken to her father and also rung Greece to tell them she would be away in mourning for another week, possibly even two. They were as understanding as they had been earlier, but she knew that she would have to put in an appearance at the dig if people were not to start feeling impatient with her before long.

Lundin's voice was exactly as she had remembered it: normal Swedish but lacking lots of words that had come into fashion during the long years he had been away. That's how they used to speak Swedish when I was a child, she had thought after their first meeting.

Lundin did not beat about the bush.

'I think I've found your missing husband,' he said. 'Unless there are several Swedes in Australia by the name of Aron Cantor.'

'There can only be one.'

'Do you have a map of Australia in front of you?'

Louise had bought one. She spread it out over the bed.

'Put your finger on Sydney. Then follow the road south to Melbourne. Continue from there along the south coast until you come to a place called Apollo Bay. Have you found it?'

She could see the name.

'According to what I've managed to find out, a man called Aron Cantor has been living there for several years. My informant couldn't give an exact address, but he was pretty sure that you'll find the man you're looking for in Apollo Bay.'

'Who was this informant of yours?'

'An old trawler captain who grew so fed up with the North Sea that he moved to the other side of the globe. He spends some of his time on the south coast. He's a very nosy person and he never forgets a name. I think you'll find Aron Cantor in Apollo Bay. It's a tiny little place that only livens up in summer. There won't be many people there at this time of year.'

'I don't know how to thank you.'

'Why do Swedes spend so much bloody time saying thank you? Why can't somebody be helpful without keeping an invisible cash book? But I'll give you my phone number as I'd like to know if you find him in the end.'

She noted down Oskar Lundin's number on the map. When he said goodbye and hung up, it was like when he raised his hat. She stood there motionless and could feel her heart pounding heavily.

Aron was alive. She had not done the wrong thing by interrupting her journey back to Greece. By pure chance she had found herself sitting next to a good fairy in a summer hat at a restaurant table.

Oskar Lundin could well be my father's brother, she thought. Two elderly men who would never hesitate to help.

A dam inside her burst, and all the energy that had been harnessed was suddenly released. In no time at all she had rented a car that was delivered to her hotel, and paid her bill. She left Sydney, entered the network of motorways and headed for Melbourne. She was in a hurry now. Aron might be in the place called Apollo Bay, but there was always a risk that he would get it into his head to do a vanishing trick. If he caught the scent of somebody on his trail, he would run away. She planned to stay the night in Melbourne, then follow the coast road to Apollo Bay.

She found a station playing classical music. It was almost midnight when she found herself in central Melbourne. She had a vague memory of the Olympic Games being held there when she was very small. A name came to mind: a high-jumper called Nilsson that her father had rated. Artur had made a mark on the outside wall of their house the height of the jump that had won him the gold medal. Nilsson – but what was his first name? Rickard, she thought. But she was not sure. Perhaps she was mixing up two different people, or even two different competitions. She would have to ask her father.

She took a room in a hotel not far from the parliament building – much too expensive again. But she was tired, and lacked the strength to go hunting for a cheaper room. A few blocks away she discovered a miniature Chinatown. The restaurant was half empty and most of the waiters were gaping at a television screen; but she ate bamboo shoots and rice. She drank several glasses of wine and became tipsy. She was thinking about Aron all the time. Would she find him the next day? Or would he have fled?

She went for a walk after her meal, to clear her head. She found a park with well-lit paths. If she had not drunk a fair amount of wine she might very well have decided to continue her journey now: her bag was still unpacked, and she could have carried it straight down to the car. But she needed some sleep. The wine would help.

She lay down on top of the bed and wrapped the quilt round her. She slept fitfully, avoiding a mass of faces in her dreams until dawn broke.


By half past six she had finished her breakfast and left Melbourne. It was raining, and the wind blowing off the sea was squally and cold. She was shivering as she settled down in the car.

Somewhere out there in the rain was Aron.

*He's not expecting me, nor is he expecting to hear about the tragedy that has befallen him. But soon reality will catch up.*


She arrived at her destination at about eleven. It had rained incessantly all the way. Apollo Bay was a narrow strip of houses along the shore of a bay. There was a pier keeping the waves away from a small armada of fishing boats. She parked next to a café, stayed in the car and gazed out into the rain as the windscreen wipers cleared the screen every few seconds.

*Somewhere out there in the rain is Aron. But where will I find him?*

For a moment she had the feeling that the task she had set herself was beyond her. But she had no intention of giving up, not now when she had travelled to the other side of the globe. She got out of the car and ran across the road to a shop selling sports clothes. She selected a rainproof windcheater and a peaked cap. The shop assistant was a young girl, overweight and pregnant. It seemed to Louise that she had nothing to lose by asking.

'Do you know Aron Cantor? A man from Sweden. He speaks good English, but with a foreign accent. I've been told he lives here in Apollo Bay. Do you know who I mean? Do you know where he lives? If you don't, could you suggest somebody who might?'

Louise was not convinced that the girl had made much of an effort when she replied: 'I don't know any Swedes.'

'Not Aron Cantor? It's an unusual name.'

The girl handed over Louise's change and shook her head nonchalantly.

'We see so many people here, coming and going.'

Louise put on the jacket and left the shop. The rain had eased off. She walked along the road in front of the row of houses, and realised that this was the whole of Apollo Bay. A road following the curve of the bay, a row of houses, nothing else. The sea was grey. She went into a café, ordered a pot of tea and tried to think. Where could Aron be if he really did live here? *He liked to go out when it was wet and blustery. He liked fishing.*

The man who had served her was walking around the room, wiping down the tables.

'Where do people go fishing here in Apollo Bay if they don't have a boat?'

'They usually stand at the end of the pier. Some people fish in the dock.'

She asked him if he knew anybody visiting here called Aron Cantor. The man shook his head and carried on wiping the tables.

'Maybe he's staying at the hotel? That's on the road down to the harbour. You could ask there.'

Louise knew that Aron would never stand living in a hotel for more than a few days.


The rain had stopped, the clouds were starting to disperse. She went back to the car and drove to the harbour, not bothering to stop at the hotel, which was called Eagle's Inn.

She parked at the entrance to the harbour and started walking along the quay. The water was oily and dirty. A barge laden with wet sand was chafing against the old tractor tyres hanging along the quay wall. A fishing boat piled up with lobster pots was called *Pietà*, and she wondered in passing if the name gave promise of good catches. She walked to the edge of the inner mole. A few boys were busy fishing, concentrating so hard on their floats that they did not even cast a glance at her. She looked at where the outer jetty projected from the inner basin a long way out to sea. Somebody was standing there, fishing, or perhaps there was more than just one person. She retraced her steps then turned onto the outer jetty. The wind was stronger now, and blustery, whistling between the large blocks of stone that formed the outer wall of the jetty. It was so high that she could not see the sea beyond it, only hear it.

There was only one man standing out there fishing, she could see that now. His movements were jerky, as if he had suddenly become impatient.

She felt a mixture of joy and horror. It was Aron, nobody else moved as awkwardly as he did. But finding him had been too easy, too quick.

It occurred to her that she did not have the slightest idea about what kind of a life he led now. He could well have remarried, and maybe even had more children. The Aron she had known and loved did not exist any more. The man standing a hundred metres away from her in the bitterly cold wind, with a fishing rod in his hand, could turn out to be a man she no longer knew. Perhaps she ought to go back to the car, and then follow him when he had finished fishing?

Then she felt angry at being so indecisive. As soon as she came into close proximity with Aron, she lost her usual resolve. He still had a hold on her.

She made up her mind to confront him here, on the pier.

*He has no escape route, unless he jumps into the icy water. This pier is a cul-de-sac. He can't run away. This time he's forgotten to allow himself a secret exit.*

When she reached the end of the pier he was facing away from her. She could see the back of his head; his bald patch had grown bigger. He seemed to have shrunk, his figure gave an impression of weakness she had never associated with him before.

Next to him was a square of plastic sheeting, held in place with a stone on each corner, weighing it down. He had caught three fish. She thought they looked like a sort of cross between a cod and a pike, if such a cross was conceivable.

She was about to call his name when he turned round. It was a quick movement, as if he suspected he was about to be attacked. He looked hard at her, but she had the hood of her windcheater up and tightly fastened around her face, so that he did not recognise her at first. When it did dawn on him who it was, she could see that he looked afraid. That had never happened during the time they had lived together: Aron had never seemed insecure, never mind frightened.

It only took him a couple of seconds to regain his composure. He jammed the rod between some stones.

'I didn't expect this. You finding me here.'

'You'd never expect me to come looking for you.'

He looked serious, waited, was afraid of what might come next.

During the long hours on board the plane and during the car journey she had told herself she must be gentle with him, wait for the least hurtful moment to tell him about Henrik. It was now clear to her that it would be impossible.

It had started raining again, the wind was more blustery than ever. He turned his back on the wind, and came towards her. His face was pale. His eyes were red, as if he had been drinking, his lips were chapped. *Lips that don't kiss split and crumble away*, he used to say.

'Henrik is dead. I've tried everything I could think of to make contact with you. In the end this was the only possibility left, so I came here and looked for you.'

He looked at her, his face expressionless, as if he had failed to understand. But she knew that she had stuck a knife into him, and that he was feeling the pain.

'I found Henrik dead in his flat. He was in bed, as if he were asleep. We buried him in the cemetery in Sveg.'

Aron swayed and looked as if he were about to fall over. He leaned against the stone wall, and held out his hands. She took hold of them.

'It can't be true.'

'I don't think it can be true either. But it is.'

'Why did he die?'

'We don't know. The police and the pathologist say that he took his own life.'

Aron stared at her, his eyes popping.

'They say the lad committed suicide? I can't believe that for one moment.'

'Nor can I. But his body contained a large dose of sleeping pills.'

Aron gave a roar, threw the fish into the water, then hurled the bucket and the fishing rod over the pier wall. He took firm hold of Louise's arm and led her away. He told her to follow his rusty old Volkswagen campervan. They left Apollo Bay, taking the road she had used to get here. Then Aron turned off onto a road that twisted steeply

78

up into the hills that tumbled down into the sea. He drove fast and unsteadily, as if he were drunk. Louise followed close behind him. In among the hills they turned off onto a road that was barely more than a path, climbing steeply upwards all the time, and eventually stopped at a wooden house perched on the very edge of a cliff. Louise got out of the car, thinking that this was exactly the sort of place she would have imagined Aron choosing as a hideaway. The view was boundless, the sea stretched as far as the horizon.

Aron flung open the door, grabbed a bottle of whisky from a table next to the open fire and filled a glass. He looked enquiringly at her, but she shook her head. She needed to be sober. It was enough for Aron to go overboard and when he drank he could become violent. She had seen too many broken windows and smashed chairs and had no desire to experience anything like that again.

There was a big wooden table outside the large picture window facing the sea. She could see colourful parrots landing on it and pecking at crumbs of bread. *Aron had moved to the land of parrots. I would never have imagined he would do that.*

She sat on a chair opposite him. He was slumped on a grey sofa, holding his glass in both hands.

'I refuse to believe this is true.'

'It happened six weeks ago.'

He flared up.

'Why did nobody tell me?'

She made no reply, but turned away to look at the red and light blue parrots.

'I'm sorry, I didn't mean that. I realise that you have been looking for me. You would never have left me in ignorance if you could have avoided it.'

'It's not so easy to find somebody who's hidden himself away.'


She remained there, sitting opposite him, all night. Conversation was spasmodic, with long, silent intervals. Both she and Aron were skilled at allowing silence to roam. That was also a sort of conversation, she

79

had discovered that during the early part of their life together. Artur was another person who never spoke unnecessarily. But Aron's silence sounded different.

For a long time afterwards Louise would remember that night with Aron as being like returning to the time before Henrik was born. Of course, he was the one they were talking about. Their sorrow was one long scream. But even so, they remained sufficiently far apart to prevent her moving to the sofa beside Aron. It was as if she could not rely on his sorrow being as intense as it ought to have been in somebody who has lost their only child. And that made her bitter.

Shortly before dawn she asked him if he had fathered any more children. He made no reply, merely stared at her in astonishment: that told her all she needed to know.


The red parrots returned at dawn. Aron put birdseed out on the table. Louise went outside with him. She shivered. The sea way down below them was grey, the waves foaming.

'I dream about seeing an iceberg out there one of these days,' he said without warning. 'An iceberg that's drifted all the way from the South Pole.'

Louise remembered that letter he had written.

'That must be an impressive sight.'

'The most remarkable thing is that a gigantic iceberg melts away without our being able to see it happening. I've always thought of myself like that, melting away, vanishing bit by bit. My death will be the result of slow warming.'

She observed him in profile.

He's changed, but he's still the same, she thought.

They had been talking all night.

She took his hand. They stared out to sea together, looking for an iceberg that would never come.

# CHAPTER 8

Three days after the meeting on the pier, amid all the wind and the rain and the hurt Louise sent a postcard to her father. She had already phoned him and explained how she had found Aron. The line to Sveg had been surprisingly clear, her father seemed to be very close, and he had asked her to send his best. She had described the colourful parrots that gathered on Aron's table, and promised to send him a card. She had discovered a shop next to the harbour that sold everything from eggs to hand-knitted jumpers and picture postcards. The picture she chose was a flock of red parrots. Aron was waiting for her in the café where he regularly started and finished his fishing expeditions. She wrote the card while still in the shop and posted it in a box next to the hotel she would have booked into if she had not found Aron on the pier so quickly.

What did she write to her father? That Aron was living the life of a comfortable hermit in a wooden cabin in the forest, that he had lost weight, and above all that he was heartbroken. *You were right. It would have been irresponsible not to track him down. You were right and I was wrong. The parrots are not only red, but also blue – or perhaps turquoise. I don't know how long I shall stay here.*

She posted the card, then went down to the beach. It was a cold day with a clear sky and virtually no wind. A few children were playing with an old football, an elderly couple were walking their black dogs. Louise walked along the beach, just above the waterline.

She had been together with Aron for three days. At dawn, after that first long night, when she had taken hold of his hand, he had asked her if she had anywhere to stay. His house had two bedrooms, and she could use the spare one if she wished. What were her plans? Had the tragedy of Henrik's death hit her hard? She did not reply, merely accepted the offer of the bedroom, collected her bag and slept until late in the afternoon. When she woke up Aron had left. He had left a message on the sofa, in his usual impatient and scrawling handwriting. He had gone to work. '*I look after some trees in a little rainforest. There is food. The house is yours. My grief is unbearable.*'

She prepared a simple meal, put on her warmest clothes and took her plate to the table outside the window. Before long the tame parrots were perched all around her, waiting for their share of the food. She counted the birds. There were twelve of them. It's the Last Supper, she thought. The last meal before the crucifixion. She felt a moment of peace, for the first time since she had crossed the threshold to Henrik's flat. She had somebody else besides Artur with whom she could share her sorrow. She could tell Aron all about the worries and fears that were plaguing her. Henrik's death was not natural. Nobody could explain the sleeping tablets. But nevertheless there must be a reason. He had committed suicide without being responsible for it.

*There is something else, something to do with President Kennedy and his missing brain. If anybody can help me to find that truth, it's Aron.*

When Aron came back home it was already dark. He took off his boots, gave her a furtive glance and disappeared into the bathroom. When he came out, he sat next to her on the sofa.

'Did you find my note? Have you eaten?'

'With the parrots. How did you manage to make them so tame?'

'They're not frightened of humans. They've never been hunted or trapped. I've got used to sharing my food with them.'

'You wrote that you were looking after some trees. Is that what you do? How you earn your living?'

'I thought I'd show you tomorrow. I look after trees, go fishing, and I keep out of the way. The latter is my biggest job. You have dealt me a major blow, simply by finding me. Naturally I am grateful that you were the one who came with the awful news. Perhaps I would have wondered why Henrik stopped writing to me. I would have found out sooner or later. Possibly by chance. I would never have survived a shock like that. But you were the messenger.'

'What happened to all your computers? You were the one who was going to prevent the world from losing all the memories created in our age. You once said that the "ones and zeros" in the world's computers were demons that could trick the human race into losing all its history.'

'I believed that for a long time. We felt that we were saving the world from a devastating epidemic caused by the virus of vacuity, the ultimate death that blank pieces of paper represent. All the empty archives stripped of all their contents by a cancer that was incurable would make our day and age an insoluble riddle for people who live in the future. We really did believe we were on the way to finding an alternative archive system that would preserve our time for generations to come. We were looking for an alternative to the "ones and zeros". Or, rather, we were trying to create an elixir which would guarantee that one day computers would refuse to allow data inside them to be removed. We created a formula, an unprotected source code, that we later sold to a consortium in the USA. We received huge amounts of money for it. We had also made a contract guaranteeing that within twenty-five years the patent would become available to all countries of the world to use without their needing to pay for a licence. One day I stood in a New York street with a cheque for five million dollars in my hand. I kept one of those millions and gave away the rest. Do you understand what I'm saying?'

'Some . . . Not everything.'

'I can explain in detail.'

'Not now. Did you give anything to Henrik?'

Aron gave a start and looked at her in astonishment.

'Why should I have given him any money?'

'It wouldn't have been entirely unreasonable to give one's own son a contribution towards his living expenses.'

'I never received any money from my parents. I still thank them for that even today. Nothing can spoil children more than giving them something they ought to earn for themselves.'

'Who did you give the money to?'

'There were so many possibilities to choose from. I gave it all to a foundation here in Australia that works to preserve the dignity of the Aborigines. Their life and their culture, to put it another way. I could have given the money to cancer research, to the preservation of rain-forests, to the fight against locust plagues in East Africa. I put thousands of bits of paper in a hat and pulled out one that said Australia. I gave away the money, then I came here. Nobody knows it was me who donated the money. That's the most satisfying part of all.'

Aron stood up.

'I need to get a few hours' sleep. My tiredness is getting to me.'

She remained on the sofa, and soon heard him snoring. The snores rolled through her consciousness like waves. She remembered them from the old days.

In the evening he took her to a restaurant that clung on to a mountain ledge like an eagle's nest. There were few other diners. Aron seemed to know the waiter well, and went out into the kitchen with him.

The meal served as another reminder of the time when she and Aron had lived together. Poached fish and wine. That had always been their celebratory menu. She remembered an odd camping holiday when they had eaten pike caught by Aron in dark forest tarns. But they had also eaten cod and whiting in northern Norway, and sole in France.

He spoke to her through the choice of menu. That was his way of becoming familiar with her, making a cautious attempt to find out if she had forgotten what had once existed, or if it was still a reality for her.

A feeling of melancholy overcame her. Love could not be reawakened, just as it was impossible for them to get back their dead son.

That night they both slept soundly. She woke up once with the feeling that he had come to her room. But there was nobody there.

The next day she got up early to accompany him to the small patch of rainforest he was responsible for. It was still dark when they left the house. There was no sign of the red parrots.

'I see you've learned how to get up early in the morning,' she said.

'Nowadays I don't understand how I could live for so many years and hate early mornings.'

They drove through Apollo Bay. The forest was in a valley that sloped down to the sea. Aron told her it was the remains of an ancient rainforest that once covered all the southern area of Australia. Now it was owned by a private foundation which was financed by one of the men who, like Aron, had been paid millions of dollars for the unprotected source code they had sold.

They parked the car on a gravelled plot at the edge of the forest. The tall eucalyptus trees formed a wall in front of them. A path meandered down a slope before disappearing from view.

They started walking, him first.

'I take care of the forest, make sure there are no fires, and prevent the visitors from leaving a mess. It takes half an hour to walk through the forest and back to the starting point. I like to watch the people who undertake that walk. Many of them look exactly the same when they get back, but others have changed. There is a large part of our soul in a rainforest.'

The path sloped steeply down. Aron stopped occasionally to point something out. The trees, their names, their ages, the narrow streams deep down under their feet bubbling with the same water as had flowed there millions of years ago. Louise had the impression that what he was really showing her was his own life, how he had changed.

At the very bottom of the valley, in the depths of the rainforest, there was a bench. Aron wiped it with the sleeve of his jacket. Water was dripping down everywhere. They sat down. The forest was silent, damp, cold. Louise had fallen in love with it, just as she was in love with the endless forests back home in Härjedalen.

'I came here to get away from it all,' said Aron.

'You never used to be able to function unless you were surrounded by people. Surely you couldn't become a recluse, just like that?'

'Something happened.'

'What?'

'You're not going to believe this.'

There was a fluttering noise among the trees and lianas. She glimpsed a bird flying upwards, towards the distant sunlight.

'I lost something when I realised that I could no longer live with you. I let you and Henrik down, but I let myself down just as much.'

'That doesn't explain anything.'

'There's nothing to explain. I don't understand myself. That's the absolute truth.'

'I think that's an excuse. Why can't you be honest with me?'

'I can't explain it. Something broke. I had to get away. I spent a year drinking heavily, wandering around, burning bridges, using up money. Then I landed up with that bunch of loonies who had made up their minds to save the memory of the world. That's what we called ourselves: 'Protectors of the Memory'. I've tried to drink myself to death, work myself to death, laze myself to death, fish myself to death, feed red parrots until I eventually drop dead. But I've survived.'

'I need your help to find out what really happened. Henrik's death is my death as well. I can't bring myself back to life until I understand why he died. What was he doing shortly before he died? Where did he travel to? What people did he meet? What happened? Did he speak to you?'

'He suddenly stopped writing three months ago. Before that I often received a letter a week.'

'Do you still have the letters?'

'I saved all his letters.'

Louise stood up.

'I need your help. I want you to go through several disks I have with me. They are copies of the data inside his computer that I haven't managed to access. I want you to do everything you can, to dig down into "the ones and zeros" and reveal what's hidden there.'

They continued along the path that now sloped upwards until they came back to their starting point. A bus full of schoolchildren had just arrived, the kids came swarming out in their brightly coloured anoraks.

'Children cheer me up,' said Aron. 'Children love tall trees, mysterious ravines, streams you can hear but can't see.'

They got into the car. Aron's hand was on the ignition key.

'What I said about the children applies to grown men as well. I can also love a stream you can only hear but can't see.'

On the way back to the house with the parrots Aron stopped at a shop to buy food. Louise went in with him. He seemed to know everybody, something that surprised her. How did that fit in with his desire to be invisible, unknown? As they drove up the steep mountain road, she put the question to him.

'They don't know what my name is, or where I live. There's a difference between knowing somebody, and recognising somebody. They're at ease because my face isn't that of a stranger. I belong here. They don't want to know any more than that, really. It's enough for me to be somebody who keeps calling in at the shop, doesn't cause trouble and pays his bills.'

That day Aron cooked lunch. Fish again. He seemed to be more approachable when they were eating, Louise thought. As if a burden had been lifted from his shoulders – not his sorrow over Henrik's death, but something to do with her.

When they had finished, he asked her to tell him again about the funeral, and about the girl Nazrin.

'Did he never mention her in his letters?'

'Never. If he referred to girls, they were always nameless. He could give them faces and bodies, but not names. He was remarkable in many ways.'

'He was like you. When he was little and in his teens, I always used to think he was like me. But now I know he took after you. I thought that if he lived long enough he would have completed the circle and come back to me.'

She burst into tears. He went out to scatter birdseed over the table.

Later that afternoon he put two bundles of letters on the table in front of her.

'I'll be away for a few hours,' he said. 'But I'll be back.'

'Yes,' she said. 'You won't do the vanishing trick this time.'

Without asking, she knew that he would be going to the harbour to fish. She started reading the letters, and it occurred to her that he had gone away in order to leave her on her own. He had always understood the value of being alone. For himself, first and foremost; but perhaps he had now learned to respect the needs of others as well.

It took her two hours to read the letters. It was a painful journey into an unknown world. Henrik's world. The more she discovered, the more she realised she had never really known much about it. She had never been able to understand Aron. Now she realised that her son had been just as impenetrable. The Henrik she had known was his superficial self. His feelings for her had been genuine, he had loved her. But on the whole he had kept his thoughts concealed. This worried her as she read the letters, it was a sort of nagging jealousy that she could not shake off. Why had he not spoken to her in the way he spoke to Aron? After all, she was the one who had brought him up and taken responsibility for him while Aron had immersed himself in his computers or his drunken orgies.

She was forced to accept this as fact. The letters annoyed her, made her feel angry with her dead son.

Henrik spoke to Aron in a foreign language. He would present arguments, something he never did in letters to Louise; he described emotions, ideas.

She put the letters on one side and went out. The grey sea was dancing way down below her, the parrots were hovering in the eucalyptus trees.

*I am also a split personality. To a man like Vassilis I was one person, another one to Henrik, a third one to my father, and God only knows what I have been to Aron. Slender threads hold me together. But everything is as fragile as a door suspended on rusty hinges.*

She returned to the letters. They covered a period of nine years. Occasional letters at first, then periods when they were more frequent. Henrik described his travels. He did the famous walk along the beach at Shanghai, and was fascinated by the Chinese silhouettists and their amazing skills. *They somehow manage to cut out their silhouettes so that something of their subject's inner personality becomes visible. I wonder how that is possible.* In November 1999 he was in Phnom Penh, on the way to Angkor Wat. Louise tried hard to remember. He had never told her about details of that journey, merely said that he had been to various places in Asia with a girlfriend. In two letters to Aron he described the girl as *pretty, silent and very thin.* They travelled together round the country, and were scared by *the big silence after all the horrors that had taken place. I've begun to realise what I want to do with my life. I want to reduce the pain, to make my little contribution, to comprehend the big picture in the small one I see.* He sometimes became emotional, almost pathetic in his great anguish over the state of the world.

But nowhere in the letters to Aron did he refer to Kennedy's missing brain. And none of the girls or women he described corresponded to Nazrin.

What was most striking, and what hurt her most, was that Henrik never referred to her in his letters. Not a word about his mother digging away in the hot sun of Greece. No indication of their relationship, their intimacy. He renounced her through his silence. She realised that he might have avoided mentioning her out of consideration for the circumstances, but nevertheless, it felt like a betrayal. The silence tormented her.

She forced herself to read on, keeping all her senses on the alert when she came to the last few letters. Then came what she might have been expecting subconsciously: a letter with a legible postmark. *Lilongwe, Malawi, May 2004.* He wrote about a shattering experience he had had in Mozambique, a visit to a place where the sick and dying were taken care of. *The catastrophe is so overwhelming that one is lost for words. But most of all it is frightening. People in the Western world have no idea about what is going on. They have abandoned the last outposts of humanity without making the slightest attempt to help to protect these people, to prevent them from being infected, or to help the dying to live a dignified life, no matter how long or short it turns out to be.*

There were two more letters, both of them without envelopes. Louise assumed Henrik was back in Europe. The letters were posted on 12 and

14 June. He gave the impression of being extremely unstable: in one letter he was depressed, in the other he was in high spirits. In one letter he had given up, in the other he wrote: *I have made an horrific discovery which nevertheless inspires me to act. But it also scares me.*

She read those sentences several times. What did he mean? A discovery, inspiration to act, but scared? How had Aron reacted to this letter?

She read the letters again, tried to discover meanings between the lines, but found nothing. In the last letter, sent on 14 June, he returned one last time to his fear: *I'm scared, but I shall do what I have to do.*

She stretched out on the sofa. The letters were drumming away at her temples like agitated blood.

*I only knew a small part of him. Perhaps Aron knew him better than I did. But in any case, he knew him in a totally different way.*


It was dark when Aron came back, bringing freshly caught fish. When she stood beside him in the kitchen to brush the potatoes, he suddenly took hold of her and tried to kiss her. She pulled back. It was completely unexpected, she could never have imagined that he would try to make a pass at her.

'I thought you wanted to.'

'Wanted to what?'

He shrugged.

'I don't know. I didn't mean it. I apologise.'

'Of course you meant it. But there's no longer anything like that between us. Not on my part, at least.'

'It won't happen again.'

'No. It won't happen again. I haven't come here to find a man.'

'Do you have somebody else?'

'I think it's best if we leave our private lives out of this. Isn't that what you always used to say? That we should avoid digging too deeply into each other's souls?'

'I did say that, and I still think it's true. Just tell me if there's somebody in your life who's there to stay.'

'No. There is nobody.'

'There's nobody in my life either.'

'You don't need to answer questions I haven't asked.'

He looked quizzically at her. Her voice was becoming shrill, accusing.

They ate in silence. The radio was on, broadcasting an Australian news bulletin. A train crash in Darwin, a murder in Sydney.

They drank coffee after the meal. Louise fetched the disks and the documents she had brought with her, and put them on the table in front of Aron. He looked at what she had given him, without touching it.

He went out again, she heard the car start, and he did not return until after midnight. She had fallen asleep by then, but was woken up by the car door slamming. She heard him moving quietly around the house. She thought he had gone to bed, but then she heard the sound of the computer being switched on, and him tapping at the keyboard. She got up cautiously and peered at him through the half-open door. He had adjusted a lamp and was studying the screen. She recognised the man she used to live with. The intense concentration that made his face totally motionless. For the first time since she had met him on the pier in the rain, she felt a wave of gratitude flowing through her.

*Now he's helping me. Now I'm not on my own any more.*

She slept restlessly. She occasionally got out of bed and observed him through the half-open door. He was working at the computer, or reading Henrik's papers that she had brought with her. By four in the morning he was lying on the sofa, with his eyes open.

Shortly before six she heard faint noises coming from the kitchen, and got up. He was standing over the cooker, making coffee.

'Did I wake you up?'

'No. Have you slept at all?'

'A little bit. Enough, anyway. You know I've never needed much sleep.'

'As I remember it you could sleep in until ten or eleven.'

'Only when I'd been working very hard for a long time at a stretch.'

She noticed a hint of impatience in his voice, and back-pedalled immediately.

'How did it go?'

'It has been a very strange experience, trying to enter into his world. I felt like a burglar. He'd erected some pretty efficient fences to keep unwanted visitors out, and I couldn't get through them. It felt like fighting a duel with my own son.'

'What have you found out?'

'I must have a cup of coffee first. So must you. When we lived together we had an unwritten rule, never to discuss anything seriously until we'd had a cup of coffee in dignified silence. Have you forgotten that?'

Louise had not forgotten. Locked away in her memory was a whole rosary of silent breakfasts they had endured together.

They drank their coffee. The parrots circled round and round over the wooden table in a shiny red swarm.

They cleared away their cups and sat down on the sofa. She was expecting him to clasp hold of her at any moment. But he switched on the computer and waited for the screen to light up. It eventually did so to the accompaniment of a furious drum roll.

'He's made this music himself. It's not too difficult to do if you are a computer professional, but it's pretty hard for a normal computer user. Did Henrik have any IT tuition?'

*You don't know because you were never there. In his letters to you he never wrote about what he was working on, or what he was studying. He knew that you weren't really interested.*

'Not as far as I know.'

'What did he do? He wrote that he was studying, but he never said what.'

'He read theology in Lund for one term. Then he got bored. After that he qualified as a taxi driver, and earned his living by erecting venetian blinds.'

'Could he really make a living out of that?'

'He was very thrifty, even when he was on his travels. He used to say that he didn't want to make up his mind what work he was going to take up until he was absolutely certain. In any case, he didn't work with computers, although he did use them, of course. What have you found?'

'Nothing at all, really.'

'But you were up all night?'

He glanced at her.

'I thought I could hear that you were awake sometimes.'

'Of course I was awake. But I didn't want to disturb you. What did you find?'

'I got a feeling for how he used his computer. The stuff I couldn't open, all those closed doors, the high walls and cul-de-sacs he built up – it all indicates what lay behind it.'

'And what was that?'

Aron suddenly seemed to be uneasy.

'Fear. It was as if he'd erected every possible barrier to prevent anybody discovering what he had hidden in his computer. These disks are a safety valve, deep down in Henrik's private underworld. I know how I used to conceal the contents of my computer, but I never did it like this. It's very skilfully done. I'm a pretty good burglar, I can usually find loopholes if I really apply myself to it. But not in this case.'

*Fear. It's coming back now. Nazrin talked about happiness. But Henrik himself talked about the last few weeks of his life in terms of fear. And Aron has discovered that straight away.*

'The files that I can open don't contain anything of interest. He keeps track of his poor financial state, he is in contact with several Internet auction sites, mainly for books and films. I've spent all night banging my head against locked doors.'

'And you haven't come across anything unexpected?'

'I did find one thing, in fact. Something filed in the wrong place, in among the system files. I stumbled upon it by pure chance! Look!'

Louise leaned towards the screen. Aron pointed.

'A little file that has nothing to do with the system. The interesting thing is that he's made no attempt to hide it. There are no blocks at all.'

'Why do you think he did that?'

'There can only be one reason. Why does anybody leave one file accessible but hides all the rest?'

'Because he wanted it to be found?'

Aron nodded.

'That's one possibility, at least. The file reveals that Henrik has a flat in Barcelona. Did you know about that?'

'No.'

Louise thought about the letter 'B' that kept cropping up in Henrik's diaries. Could it stand for a city rather than a person?

'He has a little flat in a street that's called, believe it or not, "Christ's Cul-de-sac". It's in the very centre of Barcelona. He's noted down the name of the caretaker, Mrs Roig, and the amount of rent he pays. If I understand his notes correctly, he's had this flat for about five years, since December 1999. It looks as if he signed the contract on the final day of the last century. Was Henrik keen on rituals? New Year's Eve? Did he send messages over the sea in bottles? Was it important for him to sign a contract on a particular day?'

'I've never thought about that. But he does like to go back to places he's been to before.'

'That's something that splits humanity into two groups – those who hate going back, and those who love it. You know where I belong. What about you?'

Louise did not answer. She pulled the computer closer to her and read what it said on the screen. Aron went out to feed his birds. Instinctively, Louise worried that he might pull a fast one.

She put on her overcoat and followed him. The birds took off and fled to the safety of their trees. Louise and Aron stood side by side, gazing out to sea.

'One of these days I'll get to see an iceberg. I'm quite certain about that.'

'I couldn't care less about your icebergs. I'd like you to come to Barcelona with me, and help me to understand what happened to Henrik.'

He did not answer, but she knew that, this time, he would do as she wished.

'I'm going to the harbour, fishing,' he said eventually.

'Do that. But make sure you see somebody about looking after your trees while you're away.'


Two days later they left the red parrots behind and drove to Melbourne. Aron was wearing a crumpled brown suit. Louise had bought the tickets, but did not protest when Aron gave her the money. At a quarter past ten they boarded the Lufthansa flight that would take them to Barcelona, via Bangkok and Frankfurt.

They discussed what they would do when they got there. They did not have a key to the flat, and they had no idea of how the caretaker would react. What if she refused to allow them in? Did Sweden have a consulate in Barcelona? They were unable to foresee what might happen, but Louise insisted that they would have to ask questions. Keeping silent would neither allow them to make any progress, nor get them any closer to Henrik. They would have to continue searching for him among the shadows.

When Aron fell asleep with his head on her shoulder, she grew tense. But she did not move him.


They arrived in Barcelona twenty-seven hours later. In the evening of the third day since leaving the red parrots behind them, they found themselves standing outside the block of flats in the narrow alley that bore the name of Christ.

Aron took hold of her hand, and they went in together.

# PART 2

# The Lantern-Bearer

'Better to light a candle than to rant against darkness.'

*Confucius*

# CHAPTER 9

The caretaker, Mrs Roig, lived on the ground floor to the left of the stairs. The light came on to the accompaniment of a rattling noise, presumably from the automatically timed switching-off device.

They had decided to tell the truth. Henrik was dead and they were his parents. Louise imagined the caretaker would look like the one she got to know when she spent six months in Paris in the mid-1970s. Powerfully built, an aggressive hairstyle, a few rotten teeth. A television set blaring away in the background, and a glimpse of what might have been her husband's naked feet resting on a table.

The door was opened by a woman of about twenty-five. Louise noticed that Aron gave a little start when he saw how good-looking she was. Aron spoke pigeon Spanish. He had spent six months, in Las Palmas in his younger days, working in various bars.

Mrs Roig's first name was Blanca, and she gave a friendly nod when Aron explained that he was Henrik's father, and the woman by his side was Henrik's mother.

Blanca smiled, but had no idea of what was coming next. Louise was horrified, thinking that Aron was saying everything in the wrong order. Aron realised his error, and turned to her for help: but Louise looked away.

'Henrik is dead,' he said. 'That's why we're here. To take a look at his flat and collect his belongings.'

Blanca appeared not to understand at first, as if Aron's halting Spanish had suddenly become totally incomprehensible.

'Henrik is dead,' he said again.

Blanca turned pale. She crossed her arms tightly.

'Is Henrik dead? What happened?'

Aron glanced at Louise again.

'A car accident.'

Louise was not prepared to let Henrik die in a car accident.

'He fell ill,' she said in English. 'Do you speak English?'

Blanca nodded.

'He fell ill and collapsed.'

Blanca took a step backwards and invited them in. The flat was small: two little rooms, an even smaller kitchen, and a plastic curtain in front of a tiny bathroom. To her surprise, Louise noted two large coloured posters with classical Greek motifs on one wall. Blanca seemed to live alone in the flat, Louise could see no trace of a man or any children. Blanca invited them to sit down. Louise could see that she was shaken. Had Henrik been a routine tenant, or something more than that? They were about the same age.

Blanca had tears in her eyes. It seemed to Louise that she was very like Nazrin – they could have been sisters.

'When was he last here, in his flat?'

'In August. He arrived late at night. I was asleep, and he was always very quiet. The next day he knocked on my door. He gave me some flower seeds. He always used to do that when he'd been off on his travels.'

'How long did he stay?'

'A week. Maybe ten days. I didn't see much of him. I don't know what he was up to, but whatever it was, he did it at night. He slept during the day.'

'So you have no idea at all what he was doing?'

'He said he was writing newspaper articles. He was always short of time.'

Louise and Aron exchanged glances. Be careful now, Louise thought. Don't go barging in like a bull in a china shop.

'You're always short of time when you work for a newspaper. Do you know what he was writing about?'

'He used to say he was part of a resistance movement.'

'Is that the phrase he used?'

'I didn't really understand what he meant. But he said it was a bit like Spain during the Civil War, and the side he was on would have been fighting against Franco. But we didn't often talk about what he was doing. It was mostly practical matters. I did his washing for him. And the cleaning. He paid well.'

'Did he have plenty of money?'

Blanca frowned.

'You ought to know about that if you're his parents.'

Louise could see that she needed to intervene.

'He was at the age when young men don't tell their parents everything.'

'He never mentioned you at all, in fact. But I suppose I shouldn't have said that?'

'We were very close. He was our only child,' said Aron.

Louise was aghast, and wondered how he was able to lie so convincingly. Had Henrik inherited that ability from his father? Had he also been as convincing as that when he was not speaking the truth?

Blanca stood up and left the room. Louise was about to say something, but Aron shook his head and mouthed the word 'wait'. Blanca came back with a bunch of keys.

'He lived on the top floor.'

'Who did he rent the flat from?'

'A retired colonel who lives in Madrid. It's actually his wife's house, but Colonel Mendez sees to all the practical details.'

'Do you know how he found the flat?'

'No. He just turned up one day with a tenancy agreement. Before him the flat had been occupied by two problematic American students who spent most of their time playing very loud music and bringing home girls. I never liked them. Things were much better when Henrik came.'

Blanca led them out into the stairwell and opened the lift doors. Louise paused.

'Has anybody been here during the last few weeks, asking after him?'

'No.'

Louise was on edge. She could sense that something was wrong. The answer had come too quickly, and seemed too well rehearsed. Blanca Roig had been expecting that question. Somebody had been there, but

101

she did not want to admit to it. Louise looked at Aron as they squeezed into the little lift, but he did not seem to have noticed anything.

The lift clattered its way up.

'Did Henrik often have visitors?'

'Never. Or at least, very rarely.'

'That sounds odd. Henrik always liked to be surrounded by people.'

'In that case he must have met them somewhere else, not here.'

'Did he receive many letters?' Aron asked.

The lift came to a stop. When Blanca unlocked the door to Henrik's flat, Louise noticed that there were three locks. At least one of them seemed to have been added recently.

Blanca opened the door and stepped to one side.

'His mail is on the kitchen table,' she said. 'I'll be downstairs if you need me. I still can't believe he's dead. You must be very upset. I'll never dare to have any children, I'd be too frightened they would die.'

She handed the keys to Aron. Louise felt slightly irritated: Aron always seemed to be the most important person in other people's eyes.

Blanca set off downstairs. They waited until they heard the sound of her door closing before entering the flat. Music could be heard from somewhere or other. The landing light switched itself off. Louise gave a start.

*For the second time I'm about to enter a flat in which Henrik is lying dead. He's not here, he's in his grave. But he's here even so.*

They stepped into the hall and closed the door behind them. It was a small, cramped flat that had originally been a part of the attic space. There was a skylight, exposed beams, a sloping ceiling. One room, a little kitchen, a bathroom with a toilet. They could see the whole of the flat from the hall.

The mail was on the kitchen table. Louise looked through the heap: several advertising leaflets, an electricity bill and an invitation to change to a different telephone company. Aron had gone into the main room, and was standing in the middle of the floor when she joined him. She saw the same as he could see: a room with naked walls, no decorations of any kind. A bed with a red cover, a desk, a computer and a shelf containing books and files. That was all.

*Henrik lived here in secret. He didn't tell either of us about this flat. It seems that he'd inherited from Aron the ability to set up various hiding places.*

They said nothing, merely wandered about the flat. Louise pulled back a curtain in front of a recess acting as a wardrobe. Shirts, trousers, a jacket, a basket of underwear, some shoes. She picked up a pair of heavy boots and held them up to the light. There was red soil on the rubber soles. Aron had sat down at the desk and opened the only drawer. She put the shoes back and went to peer over his shoulder. She felt a brief impulse to stroke his thinning hair. The drawer was empty.

Louise sat down on a stool at the side of the desk.

'Blanca wasn't telling the truth.'

Aron looked at her in surprise.

'When I asked if anybody had been here, she replied too quickly. It didn't feel right.'

'Why should she lie?'

'In the old days you used to say that you respected my intuition.'

'I said a lot of things in the old days that I wouldn't say now. I'm going to switch his computer on now.'

'Not yet! Wait! Can you imagine Henrik in this flat?'

Aron rotated his chair and looked around the room.

'Not really. But then, I hardly knew him. You're the one who can answer that question, not me.'

'We know for certain that he lived here. He's been renting this flat in secret for five years. But I can't imagine him being here.'

'Are you saying that it was a different Henrik who lived here?'

Louise nodded.

*Aron had always found it easy to follow her train of thought. In the days when they had been close to each other, they used to play at guessing the other's reactions. Even if their love had died, they might still be able to play that game successfully.*

'A different Henrik, one he wanted to keep hidden.'

'But why?'

'Aren't you the one best qualified to answer that question?'

Aron pulled a face.

'I was a drunken lout who ran away from everything and everybody, from responsibility for others, and most of all from myself. I can't imagine that Henrik could have been like that.'

'How do you know? He was your son, after all.'

'You would never have allowed him to become so like me.'

'How can you be so sure that you're right?'

'I've never been sure about anything in my life, apart from the fact that uncertainty and despair have been my constant companions.'

Aron checked the plug on the computer and lifted the lid. He rubbed the tips of his fingers together, as if he were wearing invisible rubber gloves and was about to start an operation.

He looked at her.

'There is a letter from Henrik that I have not shown you. It was as if he were telling me something in confidence that he didn't want me to share with anybody else. Maybe that wasn't what he intended, but what he told me was of such significance that I didn't want to tell anybody else about it, not even you.'

'You've never wanted to share anything with me.'

Her comment annoyed him.

'I shall tell you.'


It was one of the last letters Aron had received before he made the break from computing and decided to have nothing more to do with his electronic archive. He had just been to New York and collected the big cheque, the thing that would enable him to do whatever he liked for the rest of his life, and he returned to Newfoundland to gather together his belongings, most of which he burned – for him, burning an old sofa or a bed was just as significant as burning a bridge. That was when the letter arrived from Henrik. It was postmarked in Paris. One of Henrik's friends, a young cellist from Bosnia – it was not clear how they had become friends, nor even if it was a male or a female friend – had won a competition for young soloists and the prize was to play with one of the finest orchestras in Paris. At an early rehearsal, Henrik had been given the opportunity to sit in the middle of the orchestra, behind the strings and in front of the brass. It had been a staggering experience: the loud noise had shot through him like an agonising pain. But Henrik had described that moment as one he would always think back to in order to confirm *the strange power that pain confers upon you.* He had never mentioned the occasion again.

'We had a son who once sat in the middle of an orchestra and learned something about pain,' Aron said. 'He was a remarkable person.'

'Switch the computer on,' she said. 'Carry on searching.'

She took some of the files from the shelf and went into the kitchen. There was a pounding in her temples, as if she had taken over the pain Henrik had written about in his letter. Why had he never mentioned it to her? Why had he chosen to tell the story of the orchestra to Aron, the father who had never bothered about his son?

She gazed out over the dark rooftops. The thought upset her. She was weighed down with painful grief, and now Henrik had caused her more pain, something she was ashamed of.

She brushed the thought aside.

*There is something else more troubling.*

*Blanca was not telling the truth. I have found a new fragment that I must piece together with other shards in order to create a context. I don't know if her lie is the beginning of a story, or its end. Did she lie because Henrik had asked her to? Or was there somebody else who had insisted she should lie?*

She started leafing through the files. Every page was a new fragment, broken off an unknown whole. Henrik had lived a double life, he had a flat of his own in Barcelona *that nobody knew about.* Where did he get the money from? A flat in the centre of Barcelona couldn't be cheap. I shall follow in his footsteps, every page is like a new crossroads.

She soon realised that she was not coming across anything about Kennedy, neither photocopies of archive material and articles, nor his own notes. On the other hand Henrik had collected material about the biggest pharmaceutical companies in the world. Most of it was critical articles and statements by organisations such as Médecins Sans Frontières and the Third World Academy of Sciences. He had marked and underlined passages. He had drawn a red rectangle around a heading saying that nowadays nobody needed to die from malaria, and written exclamation marks in the margin. In another file he had collected articles and extracts from books about the history of plagues.

*Fragment after fragment. Still no whole. How was all this connected with Kennedy and his brain? Was there any connection at all?*

She could hear Aron clearing his throat in the other room. Occasionally he would tap away at the keyboard.

*We so often used to sit like this when we lived together. He in one room, I in another, but always with an open door between us. One day he closed it. When I opened it again, he had gone.*

Aron came into the kitchen for a drink of water. He looked tired. She asked if he had found anything, but he shook his head.

'Not yet.'

'How much do you think he paid for this flat? It can't have been exactly cheap.'

'We'll have to ask Blanca. What have you found in his files?'

'He's collected a lot of material on illness and disease. Malaria, the plague, Aids. But there's nothing about you, nothing about me. He sometimes marks certain sections or sentences, or even individual words, with red lines and exclamation marks.'

'Then you should look closely at the sections he's underlined. Or perhaps even more closely at those he hasn't.'

Aron went back to the computer. Louise opened the refrigerator. It was almost empty.

Midnight came and passed. Louise was sitting at the kitchen table, leafing slowly through one of the last of the files. Yet again press cuttings, mainly from British and American newspapers, but also a series of articles from *Le Monde*.

*Kennedy's brain. There must be a connection somewhere between your obsession with the dead president's brain and the material I have in front of me now. I'm trying to see it through your eyes, to handle the files with your hands. What were you looking for? What was it that killed you?*

She gave a start. Aron had come into the kitchen without her noticing. She could see straight away that he had found something.

'What is it?'

He sat down opposite her. He was obviously upset, perhaps frightened. That scared her more than anything else. One of the reasons why she had once fallen for him was that she was convinced he would protect her from every danger that threatened her.

'I found a secret file inside another one. Like those Russian dolls you take out from inside another.'

He fell silent. Louise waited for him to go on, but Aron said nothing. In the end she went into the living room, sat down at the computer and read what it said. There were not many words. When she thought about it afterwards she could not imagine what she had expected to find. Anything at all, but not that.

And so I also have death inside me. That knowledge makes everything unbearable. I may be robbed of my life before I reach 30. Now I have to be strong, and turn the whole business into its opposite. The unbearable must be turned into a weapon. I must not allow anything to scare me. Not even the fact that I am HIV-positive.

Louise could feel her heart pounding. In her confusion, she thought that she must phone Artur and tell him. At the same time she wondered what Nazrin knew. *Was she also infected? Had he infected her? Was that why he no longer had the strength to live?*

The questions were buzzing around inside her head. She was forced to hold onto the desk, in order not to fall over. She could hear vaguely that Aron had come into the room.

He caught her as she fell.

# CHAPTER 10

Several hours later they locked the door of the flat and went out to get some fresh air, and some breakfast. Blanca was asleep – or at least showed no sign of life when they left the building.

The early morning surprised them with the mildness of its air.

'If you want to sleep you can go the hotel. I need some air, but I can wander around on my own.'

'At this time in Barcelona? You'll attract all sorts, a solitary woman strolling the streets – everybody would draw the obvious conclusion.'

'I'm used to looking after myself. I've learned how to shake off importunate men with their cock in one hand and their wallet in the other. Although they don't show you the latter.'

Aron could not conceal his astonishment.

'I've never heard you talk like that before.'

'There's a lot you don't know about me. And how I choose my words.'

'If you want to be alone, think of me as an extra shadow. A sort of jacket you take with you over your arm when you're not sure if it's going to rain or not.'


They stuck to the main streets sloping down towards a square. There was very little traffic, the restaurants were empty. A single police car glided slowly past.

Louise was very tired. Aron walked by her side without speaking, as always hiding what he really thought or felt. Her mind was in chaos following their discovery that Henrik was HIV-positive. Now he was dead, inaccessible to the infection that had invaded him. But had it caused his death even so? Had he been unable to bear the burden he had suddenly found himself laden with?

'How come the post-mortem didn't reveal the state of Henrik's blood?' Aron suddenly exclaimed. 'Was it too soon? Had he been infected so recently that the antibodies hadn't had time to form? If so, how could he be sure that he really was infected?'

Aron broke down. It came suddenly, without warning. He was sobbing violently. Louise could not recall ever having seen him cry, apart from when he was drunk and maudlin and assuring her of his boundless love. As far as she was concerned, Aron's tears were always associated with the stench of strong drink or a hangover. But there was no trace of that now. His tears expressed only deep sorrow.

They were standing in a street in Barcelona. It was dawn, and Aron was sobbing. When he regained control of himself, they looked for a café where they could have breakfast, and then they returned to the flat.

As soon as they opened the door Aron disappeared into the bathroom. When he emerged, he had combed his hair and had clearly been rubbing his eyes.

'I apologise for my lack of dignity.'

'Why does such a lot of shit always come out of your mouth?'

Aron did not respond. He merely raised his hands defensively.

They continued searching through Henrik's computer with Aron as the determined pathfinder.

'Uncas,' she said. 'Do you remember him?'

'*The Last of the Mohicans*. James Fennimore Cooper. I was fascinated by it as a child. I dreamed of being the last of my tribe, the Aron tribe. Did girls really read that book?'

'Artur read it aloud to me. I don't think it ever occurred to him that it wasn't suitable for girls. He only used to read to me books that he wanted to listen to himself. I suppose I had read to me the occasional detective story when I was about seven or eight, but the book I remember best is the one about Uncas.'

'What's the incident you always remember most?'

'When one of the daughters of Colonel Monroe steps over the edge of the cliff and chooses death in preference to the bloodthirsty Indian. That was me, brave to the very end. I decided to devote my life to stepping off cliffs.'


Aron spent that day in Barcelona forcing his way into Henrik's life, with Louise as a spectator. He worked feverishly at breaking into various rooms Henrik had tried to lock. Some doors were dragged off their hinges, others had their locks picked, but all they found in the rooms were new questions, seldom any answers. How long had Henrik been ill? How long had he been infected? Who had infected him? Did he know who had infected him? He noted that he was ill in July 2004: *the infection is inside me – I have been afraid that was the case, but now I know for certain. With today's antiretroviral drugs I could live for another ten years, and given tomorrow's drugs, no doubt longer. Nevertheless, it's a death sentence. That will be the most difficult thing to shake off.* Not a word about how it had happened, where, who, in what circumstances. They tried going back in time, leafing through his fragmentary and chaotically disorganised diaries, found details of various journeys, but nothing was quite clear, there was always something elusive about it all. Louise tried to find old air tickets, without success.

Aron found his way into a file in which Henrik made regular attempts to account for his income and outgoings. Both of them reacted to one particular entry: in August 1998, Henrik had listed a significant item of income, 100,000 dollars.

'Over 800,000 kronor,' said Aron. 'Where in God's name did he get that from?'

'Doesn't it say?'

'All it says is the number of his account here in Spain.'

Aron continued searching, and they continued to be amazed. In December of the same year, 25,000 dollars suddenly cropped up out of nowhere. The amount simply appeared in Henrik's account, and he noted the payment without saying where it had come from. Payment for what? Aron looked questioningly at Louise, but she had no answer. And there were further surprises. Large amounts had been paid into

Henrik's account during the spring of 2000. Aron worked out that, in all, Henrik had acquired 250,000 dollars.

'He's had access to considerable amounts of money. He's spent most of it. We don't know on what, but he could have afforded this flat many times over. And he'd have been able to travel to wherever he wanted.'

Louise realised the further Aron dug the deeper his concern.

*Perhaps he sees it more clearly than I do. It's far too much money which has simply appeared out of nowhere.*

Aron kept on searching and muttering about culs-de-sac.

'Just like the address of this place. Christ's Cul-de-sac.'

'Henrik often used to say that he didn't believe in coincidences.'

'With that amount of money at his disposal, he could have chosen any address he wanted, of course.'

Aron continued tapping away at the keyboard. He suddenly stopped. Louise was squatting in front of a bookcase.

'What's the matter?'

'Something's opening. I don't know what it is.'

There was a crackling sound and what appeared to be a heavy snowfall on the screen. Then the picture became clear. They both leaned forward, Louise close to Aron's cheek.

A text appeared:

The lantern in the hand of Diogenes. I now realise that I'm living in an age where the concealment of truths has been elevated to an art as well as a science. Truths that always used to be allowed to emerge as a matter of course are nowadays being kept secret. Without a lantern in your hand, it is practically impossible to find somebody you're looking for. Cold gusts of wind extinguish the lantern's flame. You then have a choice: let it stay out, or light it again. And carry on looking for people.

'What does he mean?' Aron wondered.

'Diogenes asked Alexander to move because he was blocking the sunlight,' Louise told him. 'Diogenes wandered around with a lantern, looking for somebody. A consummate human being, a moral person.

He despised greed and stupidity. I've heard about security companies and detective agencies that use his name as their symbol. *Lantern-Bearers*, the ones who resist darkness.'

They continued to read the manifesto Henrik had set himself:

Of all the trolls that the valiant Bruse goats fight against, there are three that scare me more than any others. 'Winkelman and Harrison', with their secret gene research in their giant complex in Virginia, remarkably enough not far from the CIA headquarters in Langley. Nobody knows what really goes on behind those grey walls, but English headhunters who track down illegal money made from dealing in drugs and arms, not to mention excessive profits from trading in sex slaves in Europe and South America, have discovered fruitful channels in 'Winkelman and Harrison'. The ultimate owner is an insignificant man by the name of Riverton, who is said to live in the Cayman Islands, but nobody is sure. The second troll is the Swiss company Balco: at first sight they appear to be conducting research into new antibiotics effective against resistant strains of bacteria. But behind the scenes, something rather different is going on. Rumour suggests that there are secret research outposts in Malawi and Tanzania where new drugs against Aids are being tested, but nobody is clear about what really happens there. The third and last troll doesn't even have a name. But there is a group of researchers in South Africa working on Aids in conditions of extreme secrecy. One hears of mysterious deaths, and people who simply disappear. Nobody knows, but if the lanterns are extinguished they have to be relit.

Aron leaned back in his chair.

'At first he talks about a single lantern. Then there are suddenly several. What does that mean? Is there a group of people trying to dig under the skin of these pharmaceutical companies?'

'This could well be Henrik. Even if I thought I had made him immune to any thought of digging down into the earth to discover secrets.'

'Did he never want to follow in your footsteps?

'Become an archaeologist, you mean? Never. He even hated digging in sandpits when he was a child.'

Aron pointed at the screen.

'He must have been pretty well up in IT. There again, the programs he uses are not the very latest ones. That also gives food for thought. Given the amount of money he had, why didn't he acquire the very latest, state-of-the-art technology? I can only think of one explanation.'

'That he wanted to use the money for something else?'

'Every penny was important. For something else. The question is: what?'

Aron opened a new seam in the computer's underworld, and called up another of Henrik's secrets. It was a series of newspaper articles that had been scanned directly into the computer.

'He didn't do this here,' said Aron. 'There is no scanner in this flat. Was there one in his Stockholm flat?'

'I didn't see one.'

'Do you know what a scanner is?'

'We're hardly likely to dig them up out of the ground as ancient relics, but we do use them occasionally.'

They read the articles. Two were from the English newspaper the *Guardian*, two from the *New York Times* and two from the *Washington Post*. The articles were about health-care workers who had been bribed to leak case notes on two different people, one man who wanted to remain anonymous, and another, Steve Nichols, who allowed a photograph of his face to be used. Both men had been blackmailed and forced to pay huge amounts of money because they were HIV-positive.

Henrik had made no notes or comments. The articles were silent signposts in a room where Henrik was not present. Could Henrik's large income come from blackmail? Could he be a blackmailer? Louise was sure Aron was thinking the same thing. The thought was so repulsive and impossible that she banished it. But Aron said nothing, simply sat in front of the computer, stroking a finger over the keyboard. Could it be that Henrik found himself in a dark tunnel leading into an even darker room?

They did not know. And that is where they left matters. They locked up and left the building without Blanca having put in an appearance. They went for a walk through the town, and when they finally got back to their hotel Aron asked if he could sleep in her room.

'I can't face up to being on my own.'

'Bring your own pillow,' she said. 'And don't wake me up if I'm asleep when you arrive.'


After a few hours of sleep Louise was woken up by Aron moving around the room. He was wearing trousers, but no shirt. She watched him through half-closed eyes and noticed a scar running across his left shoulder blade. It looked as if it had been caused by a knife. In the days, now long ago, when she had often rested her head on his back, there had been no such scar. When had he acquired it? Possibly in one of all those drunken brawls he had always been keen to take part in, disregarding the danger – most of them started by himself. He put on a shirt and sat down on her bed.

'I see you're awake.'

'Where are you going?'

'Nowhere. Out. Coffee. I can't sleep. I might go to a church.'

'Since when did you start going to church?'

'I still haven't lit a candle for Henrik. That's something it's best to do on one's own.'

Aron picked up his jacket, gave her a nod and disappeared through the door.


She got up and hung the 'Do Not Disturb' notice on the door handle. On the way back to bed she paused by the wall mirror and examined her face. *Which face is it that Aron sees? I've always been told that my face keeps changing. My colleagues, the ones who are close to me and dare to say what they think, maintain that I wear a different face every morning. I'm not like Janus with only two faces: I have ten or fifteen masks that are always changing. Unseen hands place a mask over my face as dawn breaks, and I have no idea what expression I'm wearing on that particular day.*

That is an image that frequently crops up in her dreams.

Louise Cantor, archaeologist, bent over an excavation with a classic Hellenic mask covering her face.

She went back to bed, but was unable to go back to sleep. The nagging feeling of despair refused to go away. She phoned Artur. There was no reply. On the spur of the moment, she looked up Nazrin's telephone number, but there was no reply there either. She left a message on the answering machine and said that she would be in touch later, although it was rather difficult as she was on a journey.

When she was about to leave the room and find somewhere serving coffee, she noticed that Aron had left his room key on the table.

*During the time of suspicion, when I thought he was being unfaithful, the years before our marriage collapsed, I used to search through his bags and pockets in secret. I would read his diary, and always try to be first to collect the post as it dropped through the letter box. If now had been then, I would have taken the key and unlocked his door.*

She was embarrassed by the thought. When she was in Australia, in the house with the red parrots, she had never had the feeling that there was a woman in Aron's life, somebody he was hiding away because Louise had turned up. Even if there had been another woman, it was nothing to do with her. The love she had once felt for him was not something that could be dug up out of the ground and restored once more.

She had coffee and then went for a walk. It occurred to her that she ought to phone Greece and talk to her colleagues. But what could she say?

She paused in the middle of the pavement and realised that she may never return to Greece to work, just for a few days to fetch her belongings and shut up the house. The future was a blank page. She turned round and went back to the hotel. A chambermaid was busy in her room. Louise went down to reception to wait. A beautiful woman was stroking a dog, a man was reading a newspaper with a magnifying glass. She returned to her room. The key was still on the table, Aron still hadn't come back. She pictured him inside a church, with a candle in his hand.

She knew nothing about his pain. One of these days he would be transformed into a volcanic eruption. The hot lava compressed inside him would force its way out through cracks in his body. He would die like a dragon spitting fire.

She rang Artur again. This time he answered. It had snowed during the night. Artur loved snow, it made him feel secure, she knew that. She told him that she was in Barcelona with Aron, and that they had discovered a flat belonging to Henrik that nobody knew about. But she did not say that Henrik was HIV-positive. She was unsure how Artur would react. It was a brief call, Artur never liked talking on the telephone. He always held the receiver some way from his ear, forcing her to shout.

She hung up, then made a call to Greece. She was lucky and spoke to the person who had replaced her in charge of the dig, a colleague from Uppsala. Louise asked how the work was going, and heard that the autumn excavations were coming to an end before everything closed down for the winter. Everything was going according to plan. She had decided to be very clear about her own role. She simply did not know when she would be in a position to take up her duties again. It was not all that important just now, winter was approaching and fieldwork would be suspended. Nobody knew what would happen next year, if the necessary grants to continue the work would be approved.

She was cut off. When she tried the number again, she heard a female voice speaking Greek. Louise understood that fate had ordained that she should try again later.

She lay down on the bed and went to sleep. It was half past twelve when she woke up. Aron had still not returned.

For the first time she started to feel uneasy. Four hours in which to have coffee and light a candle in church? Had he run away again? Could he not face any more? Would she have to wait six months yet again before he rang her, drunk and maudlin, from some far distant haven? She took the key and went to his room. His case was lying open on the bench provided: clothes in a mess, and an electric razor in a shabby case. She felt among the clothes, and found a plastic pouch containing a very large sum of money. She transferred the notes into her own purse, to ensure that they wouldn't be stolen. At the very bottom of the case she discovered a book by Bill Gates, meditating on computers and the future. She thumbed through it and found a few pages where Aron had highlighted certain extracts and made notes in the margin. Just like Henrik, she thought. They were two of a kind. She never made marginal notes in books. She replaced it, and picked up another one. It was a study of unresolved mathematical problems. The corner of one page was folded over, to mark where Aron had got to. The next chapter would deal with Fermat's riddle.

Louise replaced the book, and looked round the room. She investigated the waste-paper basket: an empty vodka bottle. He had not smelled of strong drink in the morning since they had met on the pier in Australia. Nevertheless, since they arrived in Barcelona he had evidently emptied a whole bottle. There was no sign of any glasses, and so he had drunk straight from the bottle. But when? He and Louise had been together almost all the time.

Louise returned to her room, and it occurred to her that all she was doing now was waiting for Aron. I come to a stop when the pathfinder stops, she thought, and felt annoyed. Why don't I do my own thing?

She left a message on the table. She had lunch in a little restaurant not far from the hotel. When she paid her bill she noticed that it was three o'clock: surely Aron would be back at the hotel by now. She checked her mobile, but he had not rung and left a message.

It started to rain. She hurried back with her jacket over her head. The man in reception shook his head. *Mr Cantor hasn't come back. Has he phoned? We don't have a message for Mrs Cantor.*

Now she was seriously worried. But it was a different kind of worry – she was not afraid that Aron might have run away from her again. Something had happened. She rang his mobile, but there was no reply.


She stayed in her room until evening. Still no Aron. She had tried his mobile number several times, but it was switched off. At about seven she went down to reception. She sat down in an armchair and watched the people circulating between the exit, reception, the bar and the newspaper stand. There was a man on a chair, studying a map in a corner next to the bar entrance. She looked at him surreptitiously. Something had attracted her attention. Did she recognise him? Had she seen him before? She went to the bar and drank a glass of wine. And another. When she returned to the lobby the man with the map had gone. There was a woman sitting there now. On the phone. The woman was so far away that Louise could not even hear what language was being spoken, never mind what was being said.

At eight thirty Louis drank another glass of wine. Then she left the hotel. Aron had taken the keys to Henrik's flat with him. That was where he had been all day, of course, at Henrik's computer. She walked quickly and turned into Christ's Cul-de-sac. When she came to the entrance door she checked her back. Was that a shadowy figure lurking in the darkness just outside where the street lamp reached? Once again she was enveloped by a mysterious fear emanating from somewhere she was unable to pin down.

*Was this the fear Henrik had referred to in his conversations with Nazrin, and in his notes?*

Louise rang Blanca's bell. There was a pause before she answered.

'Sorry, I was on the phone, my father's ill.'

'Have you seen my husband here today?'

Blanca shook her head.

'Are you absolutely sure?'

'He's not been, and he's not left.'

'He's got the keys. We must have misunderstood each other.'

'I can open up for you. You just need to slam the door when you leave.'

It occurred to Louise that she ought to ask Blanca why she was not telling the truth. But something got in the way. Her main task for the moment was to find out where Aron was.

Blanca opened the door to Henrik's flat, then vanished down the stairs. Louise stood still in the semi-darkness, listening. Then she switched on the lights, one after the other, and walked round the flat.

All of a sudden, it seemed to her that several of the wayward pieces had just found their places in the puzzle, and that an unexpected pattern was emerging.

*Somebody wanted Aron out of the way. It was something to do with Henrik, something to do with Kennedy's brain, with Henrik's journeys, his illness and his death. Aron was the pathfinder. He was the most dangerous person, the one who had to be disposed of first, so that the path would not be discovered.*

Louise turned cold with fear. She edged cautiously closer to the window, and looked down at the street.

Though there was nobody there, she had the impression that somebody had just left.

# CHAPTER 11

Louise Cantor was plagued by insomnia when she returned to the hotel. She reminded herself of what it had been like when things were at their worst. When Aron had left her. When he started sending his tearful, drunken letters from various drinking dens all over the world. Now he had vanished again. And she was waiting, on guard.

In an attempt to appeal to whatever forces were keeping him away, she went to his room and snuggled down in the bed he had never used. But still she was unable to sleep. Her thoughts went into free fall: she had to catch them before they crashed into the ground. What had happened? Could she have misread the situation after all? Had he run away, abandoned her and Henrik yet again? Simply sneaked off, for the second time? Could he really have been so brutal that he had pretended to be in mourning and going to a church to light a candle for his dead son when in fact he had already made up his mind to disappear?

She got up and took some miniatures from the minibar. She paid no attention to what she was drinking. She poured into herself a mixture of vodka, Tia Maria and cognac. The spirits induced in her a sort of calm, but needless to say, it was deceptive. She went back to bed, and could hear Aron's voice:

*No human being can paint a wave. A person's movements, a smile, a wink can be captured on canvas by a skilful artist. So can pain, Angst, as in the case of Goya, his man stretching out his arms in desperation to the firing squad. All these things can be depicted, I've seen all of them reproduced in a convincing way. But never a wave. The sea is always elusive, waves will elude anybody who tries to capture them.*

She remembered the trip to Normandy. It was the first one they had made together. Aron was due to lecture on his view of future developments in telephony and computers. She had taken study leave from her lecturing post at Uppsala University, and accompanied him. They had spent a night in a Paris hotel where the sound of oriental music penetrated the walls of their room.

Early the next morning they had taken a train to Caen. Their passion had been intense. They had made love in the cramped toilet: never in her wildest dreams could she have imagined anything so blissful.

They had spent several hours in the beautiful cathedral in Caen. She had observed Aron from a distance and thought: there stands the man with whom I shall spend the rest of my life.

That same evening, after he had delivered his lecture and received a standing ovation, she told him about her thoughts in the cathedral. He had looked at her, embraced her and said that he had thought exactly the same thing. Their destiny was to live together for the rest of time.

The next day, very early, in pouring rain, they had hired a car and driven to the beaches where the invasion took place in June 1944. A relative of Aron's, from a branch of the family now in the USA, one Private Lucas Cantor, had died on Omaha Beach, before he had reached dry land. They found a parking place, then braved the wind and the rain and wandered along the deserted sands. Aron had been very intro-verted and silent, and Louise thought it best not to disturb him. She thought he was moved emotionally, but a long time afterwards he told her he had just felt freezing cold in the damp, driving wind. What did he care about Lucas Cantor? When you're dead, you're dead, especially after thirty-five years.

But it was out there on the beaches of Normandy that he had finally stopped, broken his silence, pointed at the sea and said that there was no artist who could paint a wave in a convincing way. Not even Michelangelo could have painted a wave, not even Phidias could have sculpted one. Waves bring home to human beings their limitations, he had said.

She had tried to protest, to give examples. Surely Hägg, the seascape specialist, had been able to depict waves? All those biblical motifs with empty rafts being battered in a storm, or the sea in Japanese wood-cuts? But Aron had insisted, he even raised his voice – which surprised her as he had never done so before.

It was not possible for a human being to paint a wave in a way that the wave would approve of, said Aron, and therefore it must be true.

They had never talked about waves again, just that one time on the freezing cold beach where Lucas Cantor had died before reaching dry land. Why had she thought about that now? Was there a message in it, a message about Aron's disappearance she was sending to herself?

She got out of his bed and went over to the open window. It was dark, a warm breeze wafted into the room. There was a hum of distant traffic, and a clattering from a nearby restaurant kitchen.

It dawned on her out of the blue: the warm night was deceptive. Aron would never return. All those shadows in the darkness that she had been vaguely aware of, Blanca's lie, Henrik's pyjamas, they all combined to tell her that she too could be in danger. She moved away from the window and checked that the door was locked. Her heart was pounding. She could not control her thoughts.

She opened the minibar again, and took out the remaining bottles. Vodka, gin, whisky. She got dressed. It was a quarter past four and she took a deep breath before daring to open the door. The corridor was deserted. Even so, she thought she could detect a shadow by the lift. She stood motionless. It was her imagination playing tricks on her, she was creating shadows herself.

She took the lift down to the empty reception area.

She could see the blue glow from a television set in a back room. The sound was barely audible. An old film, she guessed. The night porter had heard her footsteps and come out to the desk. He was young, not much older than Henrik. He had a name tag on his lapel: Xavier.

'You're up early, Mrs Cantor. It's a warm night, but it's raining. I hope nothing has woken you up?'

'I haven't slept. My husband has disappeared.'

Xavier checked the key cupboard.

'I have his key. He's not in his room. He's been missing since yesterday morning, almost twenty-four hours.'

Xavier was unaffected by her concern.

'Are his belongings still in his room?'

'Nothing has been disturbed.'

'Then he'll be back, for sure. I expect it was just a misunderstanding?'

He thinks we've quarrelled, Louise thought, and felt annoyed.

'There's no question of a misunderstanding. My husband has vanished. I suspect something serious has happened. I need help.'

Xavier eyed her doubtfully. Louise looked him in the eye.

Xavier nodded and picked up the telephone. He said something in Catalan. Replaced the receiver carefully, as if not to wake up the rest of the hotel.

'Our head of security, Señor Castells, lives next door. He'll be here in ten minutes.'

'Thank you for your help.'

*Thirty years ago I'd have fallen for him*, she thought. *Just as I fell for a man in an aeroplane on the way to Scotland. But not any more. I wouldn't fall for him nor for Aron, whom I dug up in Australia and has now disappeared again.*

She waited. Xavier served her a cup of coffee. Fear was digging deep down inside her. An old man in cleaner's overalls padded past.

Señor Castells was in his sixties. He came in without a sound, wearing a long overcoat and with a Borsalino hat on his head. Xavier nodded in the direction of Louise.

'Mrs Cantor, room 533. She's lost her husband.'

She thought that sounded like a line from a film. Señor Castells removed his hat, eyed her up and down, then led her into a room off reception. It was small, with no windows, but was comfortably furnished. He invited her to sit down, and took off his overcoat.

'Tell me about it. Leave nothing out. Take as much time as you need.'

She spoke slowly, summarising as much for herself as for Señor Castells, who made a few notes. He seemed to become more attentive every time she mentioned Henrik and his death. She said all that she had to say without a single interruption from his side. He paused for a few moments and seemed lost in thought, then he sat up straight on his chair.

'So you can see no obvious reason why he should hide himself away?'

'He's not hiding himself away.'

'I realise that you are very upset about the death of your son. But if I understand the matter correctly, there is no reason to suspect that it was caused by anything other than his own hand. The Swedish police have stated their position. Is it possible that your husband has simply been overcome by grief? Perhaps he feels the need to be alone?'

'I know something terrible has happened. But I can't prove it. That's why I need help.'

'Maybe, despite everything, the sensible thing to do would be to remain patient and wait?'

Louise stood up, angry.

'I don't think you understand,' she said. 'I'll create merry hell for this hotel if you don't help me. I want to talk to the police.'

'Of course you can speak to a police officer. But I suggest that you sit down again.'

He seemed undeterred by her outburst, picked up the telephone and dialled a number. There ensued a brief conversation. Señor Castells replaced the receiver.

'Two English-speaking police officers are on their way here. They will hear your story, and ensure that a search for your husband is launched immediately. Between now and their arrival, I suggest that you and I have a cup of coffee.'


One of the police officers was middle-aged, the other younger. They all sat down in the empty bar. She repeated her story, the younger officer made notes, there were not many questions. When they had finished talking, the older officer asked for a photograph of Aron.

She had removed his passport from the room. They asked for permission to take the passport with them in order to make copies of the photograph, and to make various notes. She would get it back in an hour or so.


It was dawn by the time the police officers left. The security chief had vanished, the door of his office was closed and locked. There was no sign of Xavier in reception.

She went up to her room, lay down on the bed and closed her eyes.

*Aron had gone to a church, he had lit a candle. And then something had happened.*

She sat up. Had he ever arrived at the church? She stood up and unfolded a map of central Barcelona.

Which church was nearest to the hotel or the street in which Henrik had lived? It was not clear from the map, she could not be certain which church Aron would have chosen. But he would surely have picked one in the vicinity. Aron was not the type to make unnecessary detours when he had a specific goal in mind.

When the passport was returned a couple of hours later, she took her jacket and handbag and left the room.


Blanca was cleaning the glass panels in the front door when she arrived.

'I need to talk to you. Now, straight away.'

Her voice was shrill, as if she were castigating some unusually incompetent student who was making a mess of his task at an archaeological dig. Blanca was wearing yellow rubber gloves. Louise took hold of her arm.

'Aron went to a church last night. He hasn't come back. Which church would he have chosen? It must have been one not far from here.'

Blanca shook her head. Louise repeated her question.

'A church or a chapel?'

'Somewhere where the door would not be locked. Where he could light a candle.'

Blanca thought for a moment. Louise was irritated by the yellow rubber gloves, and had to force herself not to rip them off.

'There are lots of churches in Barcelona, big and small. The nearest to here is Iglesia de San Felip Neri,' she said.

'Come on,' said Louise. 'We're going there.'

'We?'

'You and me. Take those gloves off.'


The façade of the church was criss-crossed with cracks, but the dark wooden door was standing ajar. The inside was in semi-darkness. Louise paused while her eyes got used to the light. Blanca crossed herself, curtsied and crossed herself again. Right at the front, by the altar, a woman was busy dusting.

Louise gave Blanca Aron's passport.

'Show her the photograph,' she whispered. 'Ask her if she recognises Aron.'

Louise kept in the background while Blanca showed the woman the photo. She studied it in a beam of light from a pretty stained-glass window. *Mary with her dead son on the cross. Magdalena with her face averted.* A shimmering blue beam of light from the sky.

*You can paint a sky. But not a wave.*

Blanca turned to Louise.

'She recognises him. He was here yesterday.'

'Ask her when.'

Questions and answers. Blanca, the woman, Louise.

'She doesn't remember.'

'She must remember. Pay her to remember!'

'I don't think she wants money.'

Louise realised that she had offended Blanca who was representing the whole of Catalonian womanhood. But just now she paid no attention. She insisted on Blanca repeating the question.

Blanca said: 'It might have been between one and two. Father Ramon called in shortly beforehand and told her that his brother had broken a leg.'

'What did the man in the photograph do when he came here?'

'He sat down in the front pew.'

'Did he light a candle?'

'She didn't notice that. He looked at the windows. Examined his hands. Or he simply sat there with his eyes closed. She only glanced at him occasionally. Like you look at people you don't really see.'

'Ask her if there was anybody else in the church. Did he come on his own?'

'She doesn't know if he was alone when he came, but there was nobody sitting next to him in the pew.'

'Did anybody come in while he was here?'

126

'Only the two Perez sisters who come here every day. They light candles for their parents then leave right away.'

'Nobody else?'

'Not as far as she can remember.'

Although Louise could not understand what the woman with the duster was saying in Catalan, she could hear a degree of uncertainty in her voice.

'Ask again. Explain to her that it's extremely important to me for her to remember. Say it has to do with my dead son.'

Blanca shook her head.

'It will make no difference. She's answering the best she can.'

The woman was hitting the duster against her leg without speaking.

'Can she point out exactly where Aron sat?'

The woman seemed surprised, but did as she was asked. Louise sat down.

'Where was she?'

The woman pointed towards the altar and the side of an arch. Louise turned round. From where she was sitting she could only see a half of the entrance door. It was still standing ajar. *Somebody could have come in without Aron hearing them, or perhaps been lying in wait outside?*

'When did he leave?'

'She doesn't know. She went to fetch a new duster.'

'How long was she away?'

'About ten minutes.'

'And when she came back, he'd left?'

'Yes.'

Louise realised something very important. Aron had left no trace behind because he had had no idea that something was going to happen. But something did.

'Thank her and tell her she has been of great help.'


They walked back to Blanca's flat. Louise thought carefully. Should she tell Blanca outright that she suspected her of lying about Henrik not having had visitors? Or should she try to win her confidence and wait for her to volunteer the truth? Was Blanca scared? Or was there some other explanation?

They sat down in the living room.

'I'll be frank with you. Aron has vanished, and I'm afraid something has happened to him.'

'What could have happened?'

'I don't know. But Henrik did not die a natural death. Perhaps he found something out he shouldn't have.'

'What could that have been?'

'I don't know. Do you?'

'He never told me what he was busy with.'

'You said last time that he told you about his newspaper articles. Did he show them to you?'

'Never.'

Once again Louise detected a slight tremor in Blanca's voice. She had considered her answer.

'Never at all?'

'Not that I can remember.'

'And you have a good memory?'

'No worse than anybody else's, I would say.'

'I'd like to go back to something you've already answered. Just to make sure that I've understood you correctly.'

'I've got work I must be getting on with.'

'This won't take long. You said nobody had been to visit Henrik recently, is that right?'

'That is correct, yes.'

'Could anybody have been without you noticing?'

'It hardly ever happens that somebody comes or goes without me seeing or hearing them.'

'But you must go out shopping sometimes?'

'When I go out my sister is here in the flat. She tells me what's happened when I get back. If Henrik had had any visitors or anybody asking for him, I'd have known about it.'

'When Aron and I left the building in the middle of the night, did you hear us?'

'Yes.'

'How could you be sure it was us?'

'I always listen out for footsteps. Everyone, footsteps are different.'

I'm not getting through to her, Louise thought. She's not scared, but there is something preventing her from telling me the whole truth. What is she holding back?

Blanca looked at her watch. Her impatience seemed to be genuine. Louise decided to raise the stakes and risk shutting Blanca up completely.

'Henrik wrote about you in several of his letters.'

Once again a sudden reaction, this time in Bianca's body language. Barely discernible, but Louise noticed it.

'He referred to you as his landlady,' she said. 'I thought you were the owner of the house. He never mentioned a retired colonel.'

'I hope he didn't say bad things about me.'

'Not at all. On the contrary.'

'What do you mean by that?'

She had committed herself now. There could be no going back.

'I think he was fond of you. In secret. I think he was in love.'

Blanca looked away. Louise was just about to continue when Blanca held up her hand.

'I had a mother who blackmailed me. She played havoc with my emotions ever since I was twelve years old and fell in love for the first time. As far as she was concerned, any love I felt for a man was nothing more than a betrayal of her love for me. If I loved a man, I hated her. If I wanted to be with a man, I was abandoning her. She was horrible. She's still alive, but she no longer remembers who I am. I think it's wonderful visiting her now, when she doesn't recognise me. I know that sounds brutal, and perhaps it is. But I'm telling you the truth. I can stroke her cheek and tell her that I've always hated her, and she has no idea what I'm talking about. But she did teach me one thing: never beat about the bush, never go round and round in circles unnecessarily. Never do what you are doing now. If you have questions, ask them.'

'I think he was in love with you, but I don't know.'

'He was in love with me. When he was here, we made love almost every day. Never during the night, he wanted to be alone then.'

Louise could feel an ache growing inside her. Had Henrik infected Blanca? Was she carrying the deadly virus in her bloodstream without knowing it?

'Did you love him?'

'He's not dead for me. I desired him, but I don't think I loved him.'

'Then you must know a lot more about him than you have told me?'

'What do you want me to tell you? How he made love, what positions he preferred, if he wanted to do things people don't talk about?'

Louise felt offended.

'I don't want to know anything about that sort of thing.'

'And I'm not going to tell you. But nobody was here visiting him.'

'Something in your voice prevents me from believing you.'

'You can please yourself what you believe or don't believe. Why should I lie about that?'

'That's exactly what I'm wondering. Why?'

'When you asked if he'd had visitors, I thought you were referring to me. An odd way of asking about something you wanted to know but didn't dare ask about.'

'I wasn't thinking about you. Henrik never wrote about you. That was just a guess.'

'Let's conclude this conversation by telling the truth. Have you any more questions?'

'Did Henrik ever have any visitors?'

What happened next astonished Louise, and changed completely the way she searched for the answer to what had caused Henrik's death. Blanca suddenly stood up, opened a drawer in a little desk and took out an envelope.

'Henrik gave me this the last time he came here. He said he wanted me to look after it for him. I don't know why.'

'What's inside the envelope?'

'It's sealed. I haven't opened it.'

'Why have you waited until now before showing me it?'

'Because it was for me. He never mentioned you or your husband when he gave it to me.'

Louise turned the envelope over. Had Blanca in fact opened it? Or was she telling the truth? Was it of any significance? She opened the envelope. It contained a letter and a photograph. Blanca leaned forward over the table in order to see. Her curiosity was genuine.

The photograph was black and white, square, an enlargement of what could have been a passport photo. The picture was grainy, the face looking straight at Louise was slightly blurred. A black face, a pretty young woman, smiling. Her white teeth gleamed between her lips, her hair was plaited ingeniously, tight against her head.

Louise turned the picture over. Henrik had written a name and a date. *Lucinda, 12 April 2003.*

Blanca looked at Louise.

'I recognise her. She's been here.'

'When?'

Blanca thought for a moment.

'After a rainstorm.'

'What do you mean by that?'

'A cloudburst that soaked the whole of the city centre. Water came flooding in over the threshold. She came the next day. Henrik must have collected her from the airport. In June 2003, the beginning of June. She stayed for two weeks.'

'Where did she come from?'

'I don't know.'

'Who was she?'

Blanca looked at Louise with a strange expression on her face.

'I think Henrik was very much in love with her. He was always very reserved when I met the two of them together.'

'Did Henrik say anything about her after she'd left?'

'Never.'

'What effect did it have on your relationship?'

'One day he came down and invited me for dinner. I accepted. The food was not good, but I stayed the night with him. It was as if he'd decided that everything should go back to what it had been before the girl's visit.'

Louise picked up the letter and started to read it. Henrik's handwriting when he was in a hurry, lots of wild flourishes, occasional sentences in barely legible English. No mention of Blanca, no introductory greeting, the letter started immediately, as if it had been taken out of an unknown context.

Through Lucinda I'm starting to see more and more clearly what it is I'm trying to understand. She tells me of a shameless suffering I didn't think was possible. All in the name of greed. Though I still have difficulty imagining a world worse than I imagine it to be in my darkest moments. Lucinda can tell me about a different kind of darkness, a darkness that is as hard and impenetrable as iron. In it lurk the reptiles who have pawned their hearts, who dance on the graves of all those who have died unnecessarily. Lucinda will be my guide: if I'm away for a long time, I shall be with her. She lives in a hovel made of concrete and corrugated-iron sheets behind the ruined houses in the Avenida Samora Machel number 10, Maputo. If she's not at home, she can be found in the bar Malocura in Feira Popular in the centre of town. She works as a barmaid from 11 p.m. onwards.

Louise handed the letter to Blanca who read it slowly, forming each word with her lips. Then she folded the letter and put it on the table.

'What does he mean when he says that she will be his guide?' Louise asked.

Blanca shook her head.

'I don't know. But she must have been important to him.'

Blanca put the letter and the photograph back in the envelope, and gave it to Louise.

'It's yours. Take it.'

Louise put the envelope in her handbag.

'How did Henrik pay his rent?'

'He gave the money to me. Three times a year. There's no rent due until the new year.'

Blanca accompanied her out. Louise looked down the street. There was a stone bench on the pavement opposite, were a man sat reading a book. Only when he slowly turned a page did she take her eyes off him.

'What happens now?' asked Blanca.

'I don't know. But I'll be in touch.'

Blanca gently stroked Louise's cheek and said: 'People always run away when things get too much to bear. Aron will come back, I'm sure.'

Louise turned away quickly and set off walking, so as not to burst into tears.

When she got back to the hotel she found the two police officers waiting for her. They all sat down in a corner of the big lobby.

It was the younger of the two officers who did the talking. He read from his notes, and his English was sometimes difficult to understand.

'Unfortunately we have been unable to find your husband, Mr Aron Cantor. He is not in any of the local hospitals or mortuaries. Nor is he in any of our police cells. His details are now on the police computer. All we can do is wait.'

She found it difficult to breathe, she lacked the strength now.

'Thank you for your help. You have my telephone number, and there's a Swedish Embassy in Madrid.'

The police officers saluted and left. She sank back into the soft armchair, and it struck her that she had lost everything. She had nothing left any more.

Exhaustion hit her like an attack of cramp. I must get some sleep, she thought. Nothing else. Now I can see nothing clearly. I'll leave here tomorrow.

She stood up and walked towards the lifts. She took another good look round the lobby, but there was nobody there.

# CHAPTER 12

When the aircraft took off from Madrid airport late in the evening, Louise felt as if the thrust generated from the four engines was emanating from herself. She had a window seat, 27A, and sat with her cheek pressed against the pane, forcing the aeroplane to rise. She was rather drunk. On the flight from Barcelona to Madrid she had already downed several glasses of vodka and red wine on an empty stomach. She had carried on drinking while waiting for her connection in Madrid. Only when she began to feel sick was she able to force down an omelette. The rest of the time she had spent wandering impatiently around the airport. She thought she might find a face she recognised. She was uneasy and becoming increasingly convinced that she was being kept under constant observation.

She rang both Nazrin and her father from Madrid airport. Nazrin was in a street somewhere in Stockholm, the line was bad, and Louise was not at all sure that Nazrin had grasped what she told her about Henrik's flat in Barcelona. The call was cut off, as if somebody had sliced through the signal. Louise tried again four more times, but all she heard was a voice telling her to try again later.

Artur was in the kitchen when she rang. He's speaking in his coffee voice, she thought. I remember playing that game when I had moved to Östersund and phoned home. I used to guess if he was drinking coffee, or if he was sitting reading, or even preparing a meal. He kept a record of the scores. Once a year he used to give me the result for the previous twelve months. I always scored most points for guessing right when he was drinking coffee.

She tried to pull herself together and speak slowly, but he saw through her immediately.

'What time is it in Madrid?'

'The same as in Sweden. Possibly an hour ahead or behind. Why do you ask?'

'So it's not evening?'

'It's afternoon. It's raining.'

'Why are you drunk in the middle of the day?'

'I'm not drunk.'

Silence. Artur had backed off immediately. Lies always affected him like a punch in the solar plexus. She felt ashamed.

'I've had a drop of wine. Is there anything wrong with that? I'm afraid of flying.'

'You never have been in the past.'

'I'm not afraid of flying. I've lost my son, my only child. And now Aron has vanished.'

'You'll never survive this business if you can't keep sober.'

'Go to hell!'

'Go to hell yourself!'

'Aron has vanished.'

'He's done a runner before. He always runs off with his tail between his legs when it suits him or when the pressure becomes too great. He disappears through one of his escape routes.'

'It's not a question of tails or escape routes this time.'

She told him what had happened. He asked no questions. The only thing she could hear in the receiver was his breathing. *The greatest feeling of security I felt as a child was seeing and hearing him breathe.* When she had finished, the silence wandered back and forth between them, from Härjedalen to Madrid and back.

'I'm going to follow Henrik's trail. The letter and the photograph of the girl called Lucinda.'

'What do you know about Africa? You can't go there on your own.'

'Who would come with me? You?'

'I don't want you to go there.'

'You taught me how to look after myself. My fear will guarantee that I don't do anything silly.'

'You're drunk.'

'It'll pass.'

'Have you any money?'

'I have Aron's money.'

'Are you sure you know what you're doing?'

'No. But I have to go.'

Artur said nothing for a long time.

'It's raining here,' he said in the end. 'But soon it'll be snowing. You can see it over the mountains, the clouds are getting heavier. It will be snowing before long.'

'I have to do what I'm doing. I have to know what happened,' she said.

When the call ended she stood under some stairs, hiding among a collection of abandoned luggage trolleys. It was as if somebody had taken a hammer and smashed the pile of fragments she had so carefully gathered together. Now they were smaller than ever, even harder to match with one another.

I'm the pattern, she thought. Just now the pieces are combining to form my face. Nothing else.


As she was about to board the flight for Johannesburg shortly before eleven, she hesitated. *What I'm doing is madness. I'm travelling into the fog instead of out of it.*

She continued drinking during the night. Sitting next to her was a black woman who appeared to be afflicted with stomach pains. They did not speak to each other, merely exchanged looks.

Even as she had been waiting to board the flight in Madrid, it had struck Louise that there was nothing to indicate that they were about to travel to an African country. There were few black or coloured passengers, most of them were Europeans.

What did she know about the Dark Continent? Where was Africa in her consciousness? While she was a student in Uppsala, the struggle against apartheid had been an important part of the so-called solidarity movement. She had taken part in various demonstrations, without really having put her heart into it. As far as she was concerned Nelson

Mandela was an enigmatic person who possessed almost superhuman abilities, like the Greek philosophers she read about in her course books. Africa did not really exist. It was a continent made up of blurred images, many of them unbearable. Flies swarming over the eyes of starving children, apathetic mothers with pendulous dugs. She recalled photographs of Idi Amin and his son, dressed up like tin soldiers in their grotesque uniforms. She had always thought that she could detect hatred in the eyes of Africans, but was that in fact her own fear reflected in dark mirrors?

During the night they flew over the Sahara. She was travelling to a continent that was for her as blank and unexplored as it had been for the Europeans who ventured there hundreds of years previously. It suddenly struck her that she had forgotten all about the possible need of injections. Would the authorities allow her into the country? Would she fall ill? Should she not have taken tablets against malaria? She had no idea.

She tried to watch a film during the night when all the lights had been turned off, but she was constantly being distracted. She pulled the blanket up to her chin, tilted her seat backwards and closed her eyes.

Almost immediately she gave a start and opened them again in the darkness. What was it she had asked herself? *How do you search for something somebody else has been searching for?* She was incapable of thinking the question through, it eluded her. She closed her eyes again. She occasionally dozed off, but twice clambered over the sleeping woman by her side to fetch a glass of water.

Over the tropics they hit a patch of turbulence, the whole aeroplane shuddered, the seat belt light came on. She looked out of the window and saw that they were passing over a violent thunderstorm. Flashes of lightning bored holes through the darkness, as if somebody were holding a giant welding gun in his hands. Vulcan, she thought, in his smithy, hammering away at his anvil.

As dawn broke she saw the first faint strips of light on the horizon. She had breakfast, felt her angst clenching its fist in her stomach, and was eventually able to make out the brownish-grey countryside down below. But wasn't Africa supposed to be lush green? What she could see looked more like a desert, or fields of burnt stubble.

She hated landing, it always scared her. She closed her eyes and took tight hold of the armrests. The aircraft thudded down onto the tarmac, slowed down, swung round towards one of the terminal buildings and came to a halt. She remained seated, preferring not to jostle with the rest of the passengers who seemed in a tremendous hurry to get out of their cage. The African heat with all its strange smells filtered slowly through the sterile air-conditioning system. She started to breathe again. The heat and the smells reminded her of Greece, even though the details were different. This was not thyme and rosemary. Different spices, perhaps pepper or cinnamon, she thought. The smoke from wood fires.


She left the aircraft, followed the transfer signs and had her ticket checked. The man behind the desk asked for her passport. He thumbed through it, then looked at her.

'You don't seem to have a visa?'

'I was told that I could buy one at the airport in Maputo.'

'Sometimes you can, sometimes you can't.'

'What happens if I can't?'

The man behind the desk shrugged. His black face was dripping with sweat.

'In that case you are welcome to spend your time here in South Africa. As far as I know there isn't a single lion or leopard or even a hippo in Mozambique for you to see.'

'I haven't come here to look at animals!'

I'm screeching, she thought with a sigh. I'm using my tired and shrill voice. I'm exhausted, I'm sweaty, my son is dead. How will he be able to understand that?

'My son is dead,' she said out of the blue, an unexpected piece of information that nobody had asked for.

The man behind the desk frowned.

'You're bound to get your visa in Maputo,' he said. 'Especially if your son is dead. I'm sorry to hear about that.'

She went to the large departure lounge, exchanged some money for South African rands, and drank a cup of coffee. Looking back, she would recall the hours she spent at the airport in Johannesburg as one long wait, shut inside a vacuum. She could remember no sounds, no music from invisible loudspeakers, no announcements about impending departures or safety regulations. Nothing but unbroken silence, and a vague glimmer of colours.

Least of all could she remember any people. It was only when she heard the announcement: 'South African Airways flight 143 to Maputo', that she was hurled back into the real world.

She fell asleep from sheer exhaustion and woke up with a start when they landed in Maputo. She could see through the window that it was greener here. But still pale, shabby, a desert scantily covered by sparse grass.

The landscape reminded her of Aron's thinning hair on the crown of his head.

The heat hit her like a clenched fist as she left the aeroplane and walked to the terminal. The bright sunlight forced her to screw up her eyes. What the hell am I doing here? she thought. I'm going to look for a girl called Lucinda. But why?

She was able to purchase a visa with no problems, although she had a strong suspicion that she had been charged far too much for the stamp in her passport. Sweat was pouring off her as she stood beside her suitcase. I must make a plan, she thought. I need a car and I need a hotel, most of all a hotel.

A black man in a uniform was standing next to her. He had a badge saying Hotel Polana. He saw that she was looking at him.

'Hotel Polana?'

'Yes.'

'Your name?'

'I haven't booked a room.'

By then she had managed to read his name: Rogerio Mandlate.

'Do you think there might be a room for me even so, Mr Mandlate?'

'I can't promise anything.'

She was driven off in a minibus together with four white South African men and women. The city was frazzling in the heat. They passed through extremely deprived areas. People everywhere, children, mainly children.

It occurred to her that Henrik must have travelled along this road as well. He had seen the same sights as she was seeing. But had he thought the same thoughts? There was no way of knowing. She would never have an answer.

The sun was directly overhead when she arrived at the white, palatial hotel. She was given a room with a view over the Indian Ocean. She adjusted the air conditioning in an attempt to cool the room down, and thought about the bitterly cold mornings in Härjedalen. Extreme heat and extreme cold balance each other out, she thought. I learned in Greece that I could tolerate the extreme heat because my body was used to the other extreme. Both Härjedalen and Greece have conditioned me to survive this ridiculously hot climate.

She undressed, stood naked in the cold air coming from the contraption on the wall, then stepped into the shower. She slowly washed away that long flight.

Then she sat down on the bed, switched on her mobile and rang Aron. There was no reply, just a voice requesting her to try again later. She stretched out on the bed, pulled the thin cover over her body and fell asleep.

When she woke up she had no idea where she was. The room was distinctly cool, the clock showed ten minutes to one. She had slept for over three hours, deeply, dreamlessly. She got up, dressed, and could feel that she was hungry. She locked away her and Aron's passports plus most of her money in the safe and tapped in a code, the first four numbers of Artur's telephone number, 8854. She ought to ring him and tell him where she was, but first she needed to have something to eat, and find out what it was like to be in a country she knew absolutely nothing about.

The only thing in the attractive lobby that reminded her that she was in Africa was several black women shuffling around, dusting. Nearly all the guests were Europeans. She went to the dining room and ordered a salad. She looked round. Black waiters and waitresses, white customers. She found a bank where she could change some money. She explored the hotel. There was a news-stand where she could buy a map of Maputo and a guidebook to Mozambique. In another part of the hotel she discovered a casino. She did not go in, merely peered in at the solitary overweight men operating the one-armed bandits. She walked round the rear of the hotel, past the large swimming pool, down towards the railings marking the limit of the hotel grounds that sloped down towards the beach and the sea. She stood in the shade of an awning. The sea reminded her of the Aegean, the same shade of turquoise, glinting in similar fashion in the bright sun.

A waiter appeared at her side, and asked if she wanted anything. My son, she thought. I want Henrik alive, and Aron's voice on the telephone, telling me that all is well.

She shook her head. The waiter had broken her train of thought.

She walked to the front of the hotel, which faced a car park. Street vendors were flocking outside the hotel entrance. She hesitated for a moment, then continued onto the pavement, past the street vendors with their sculptures made of aromatic sandalwood, their giraffes, playful elephants, little storage boxes, chairs and carved statuettes of people with grotesque faces. She crossed over the street, noted that there was an Avis office on the corner, then walked down a wide avenue named, to her surprise, after Mao Tse-tung.

A group of street children sat round a fire of burning rubbish. One of them came rushing up to her, his hand outstretched. She shook her head and increased her pace. The boy was an old hand: he did not follow her, but gave up immediately. It's too soon, she thought. I'll cope with the beggars later.

She turned off into a street with less traffic, then into another one with high walls on each side and behind them dogs barking angrily. The street was deserted, it was the hottest part of the day, siesta time. She was very careful about where she stepped – the paving stones were cracked and potholed. She wondered if it would be possible to walk along these streets after dark.

Then she was mugged. There were two of them, and they crept up on her from behind. Without a sound one of the men wrapped his arms around her and restricted her movements, the other one pressed a knife against her cheek. She noticed that his eyes were red, his pupils dilated, he was drugged up to the eyeballs. His English consisted mainly of the word *fuck*. The man pinning her arms to her side, whose face she could not see, shouted into her ear: 'Give me money.'

A cold shiver ran through her, but she managed to keep the shock at bay. She replied slowly: 'Take whatever you want. I shall not resist.'

The man behind her snatched her handbag from her left shoulder, and started running away. She never saw his face, gathered only that he was barefooted, his clothes were in rags and he ran very fast. The man in front of her with the dilated pupils stabbed her under the eye, then ran off. He was also barefoot.

They were both about Henrik's age.

Then she started screaming. But nobody seemed to hear her, the only sign of life was the invisible dogs behind the high walls. A car approached. She stood in front of it, waving her arms. Blood was pouring from underneath her eye, dripping down onto her white blouse. The car stopped, apparently hesitantly: she saw that the driver was a white man. She continued screaming and ran towards the car. It backed away at racing speed, turned on a sixpence and vanished. She started to feel dizzy, could no longer repress the shock.

*This was something that Aron could have prevented, damn him. He ought to have been here, protecting me. But he's gone, everybody's gone.*

She slumped down onto the pavement and breathed deeply in order not to faint. When a hand touched her shoulder she screamed loudly. It was a black woman. She was holding a basket of peanuts in her hands, smelled strongly of sweat, her blouse was ragged, the length of fabric wrapped round her body filthy.

Louise tried to explain that she had been mugged. The woman obviously did not understand, she said something in her own language and then in Portuguese.

The woman helped Louise to her feet. She came out with the word 'hospital', but Louise insisted 'Polana, Hotel Polana'. The woman nodded, took a firm hold of Louise's arm, balanced the basket of peanuts on her head, and supported the invalid as they started walking. Louise staunched the flow of blood with a handkerchief. The wound was not deep, not really much more than a scratch. But she felt as if the knife had penetrated deep into her heart.

The woman by her side smiled encouragingly. They came to the hotel entrance. Louise had no money, what she had was in the handbag the muggers had stolen. She opened her arms wide, and the woman shook her head. She was smiling all the time, her teeth were white and even, and she walked off down the street. Louise watched her disappear into the sun-drenched haze.

When she had got as far as her room and washed her face, everything collapsed. She fainted and fell onto the bathroom floor. She had no idea how long she had been unconscious when she eventually came to. Perhaps only a couple of seconds.

She lay motionless on the tiled floor. From somewhere or other came the sound of a man laughing, then shortly afterwards a woman squealing in delight. Louise stayed on the floor, thanking her lucky stars that she had not been seriously injured.

Once, when she was very young and been on a visit to London for a few days, a man had approached her one evening, grabbed hold of her and tried to force her into a doorway. She had kicked and screamed and bitten her way free. That was the last time she had been exposed to violence.

Was it her own fault? Ought she to have established if it was safe to wander along the streets, even in daylight? No, it was not her fault.

She refused to accept responsibility for it. The fact that her attackers had been barefoot and dressed in rags was no excuse for stabbing her in the face and stealing her handbag.

She sat up. Then got to her feet slowly, and lay down on the bed. She shuddered. She was like a fragile vase that had shattered; the pieces whirling all round her. She realised that Henrik's death had caught up with her. Now she was facing collapse, there was nothing that could keep her in one piece. She sat up in bed in a vain attempt to offer resistance, but then lay down again and just let it hit her.

The tidal wave she had heard about, the wave that nobody could depict, the wave that developed into a fury that nobody could imagine. *I have tried to catch up with him. Now I'm in Africa. But he's dead, and I don't know why I'm here.*

First came the wave, and then impotence. She stayed in bed for more than twenty-four hours. When the chambermaid unlocked the door in the morning, Louise raised her hand and rejected service. There was water in bottles on the bedside table. All she ate was an apple she had taken with her from Madrid.

At some point during the night she got up, walked to the window and looked out over the illuminated garden with the glittering swimming pool. Beyond that was the bay, a lighthouse flashing through the darkness, and lanterns swaying on invisible fishing boats. A solitary security guard was patrolling in the garden. Something reminded her of Argolis, of the excavations in Greece. But she was a long way away from there, and she wondered if she would ever return. In fact, was there any possibility of her continuing her life as an archaeologist?

*I am as dead as Henrik. A human being can be turned into a ruin once during his or her life, but not twice. Is that why Aron vanished? Because he was afraid of being changed again into a hammer with the task of annihilating me?*

She went back to bed. She occasionally dozed off. It was afternoon before she began to feel that her strength was coming back. She took a bath, then went downstairs to eat. She sat outside, under an awning.

It was hot, but there was a cooling breeze off the sea. She studied the local map she had bought. She soon found her hotel, but it took her much longer to locate the district known as Feira Popular.

When she had finished her meal she sat down on a bench in the shade cast by a tree and watched some children playing in the swimming pool. She had her mobile in her hand, and eventually made up her mind to call Artur.

His voice came from another world. There was a time lag between what they said. They collided, and started speaking simultaneously.

'Odd that I can hear you so well when you are so far away.'

'Australia was even further away.'

'Is everything OK?'

She was on the point of telling him that she had been mugged, and for a brief moment she felt the urge to lean on his shoulder and cry. But she restrained herself, and said nothing.

'The hotel I'm staying at is like a palace.'

'I thought Mozambique was a poor country.'

'Not for everybody. Being rich opens your eyes to all those who have nothing.'

'I still don't understand what you are intending to do.'

'Like I said. I'm going to look for Henrik's girlfriend, a girl called Lucinda.'

'Have you heard anything from Aron?'

'I've heard nothing from him nor about him. He's still missing. I think he's been killed.'

'Why would anybody want to kill Aron?'

'I don't know. But I'm trying to find out.'

'You are all I have. I'm scared when you are so far away.'

'I'm always careful.'

'Sometimes that's not enough.'

'I'll get back to you. Have you had snow yet?'

'It came last night. Just a few flakes at first, but then it grew thicker. I was sitting here in the kitchen, watching. It's like a white silence falling down to embrace the ground.'

*A white silence falling down to embrace the ground. Two men who*

*attacked me. Had they followed me from the hotel? Or had they been*
*lurking in the shadows, without my seeing them?*

She hated them. She wanted to see them whipped, bleeding, screaming.


It was eleven when she went down to reception and asked for a taxi to take her to Feira Popular. The man at the information counter looked surprised, but then smiled.

'The porter will help you. It's only a ten-minute walk.'

'Is it dangerous there?'

She was surprised by her question, that just came out unexpectedly. But she was well aware that the muggers would resurface in her consciousness, no matter where she was. Even the man who had attacked her in London all those years ago still turned up to haunt her occasionally.

'Why should it be dangerous?'

'I don't know. That's why I'm asking you.'

'I suppose it might be dangerous for some, but they won't be interested in you.'

Prostitutes, she thought. But you find them everywhere, surely?


The taxi smelled of fish. The man behind the wheel drove fast and seemed not to notice the absence of a rear-view mirror. In the darkness the ride seemed to be like a descent into the underworld. He dropped her at what appeared to be the entrance to a fairground. She paid the entry fee, suspecting that she was being overcharged, then found herself in a conglomeration of little restaurants and bars. In the centre there was a dilapidated and forgotten carousel, on which many of the horses were headless, and an equally abandoned big wheel that had long since ceased to turn. Music from all sides, shadows, dimly lit rooms where men and women hunched over bottles and glasses. Young black girls in miniskirts, their breasts barely covered, swished past in their high-heeled shoes. Dangerous women hunting for harmless men.

Louise was looking for the bar named Malocura. She kept losing her way in the labyrinth, repeatedly finding herself back where she had started from. Occasionally she would give a start, as if she had been attacked yet again by muggers. She imagined knives glinting on all sides. She ventured into a bar that was distinguished from all the others by being brightly lit. She drank a beer and a glass of vodka. To her surprise she saw that two of the South Africans who had shared her minibus from the airport were sitting in a corner. Both the man and the woman were drunk. He kept tapping her shoulder, over and over again, as if he were trying to knock her over.

It was past midnight now. Louise continued her search for Malocura. She found it in the end. It really was called Malocura – the name was written on a piece of cardboard – and was tucked into a corner next to the outer wall. Louise peered into the dimly lit premises, and found an empty table.

Lucinda was standing by the bar, loading a tray with bottles and glasses. She was thinner than Louise had expected, but there was no doubt about who she was.

Lucinda went to a table and unloaded her tray.

Then she noticed Louise, who raised her hand. Lucinda came to her table.

'Would you like something to eat?'

'I just want a glass of wine.'

'We don't serve wine. Only beer.'

'Coffee?'

'Nobody ever asks for coffee.'

'Then I'll have a beer.'

Lucinda returned with a glass and a brown bottle.

'I know your name is Lucinda.'

'Who are you?'

'I'm Henrik's mother.'

Then it dawned on her that Lucinda could not possibly know that Henrik was dead. But it was too late now, it was impossible for her to withdraw that remark, there was no possibility of retreat.

'I've come to tell you that Henrik is dead. I've come to ask if you know why.'

Lucinda was motionless. Her eyes were very deep, her lips tightly closed.

'My name's Louise. Maybe he's told you about me?'

*Did he ever mention his mother? Did he say anything about me? Or am I as unknown to you as you are to me?*

# CHAPTER 13

Lucinda took off her apron, exchanged a few words with the man behind the bar who appeared to be in charge, then led Louise to another dimly lit, out-of-the-way bar where young women were sitting along the walls. They sat down at a table and Lucinda ordered beer for them both without asking. It was totally silent in the room. There was no radio, no canned music. The heavily made-up women did not speak to one another. They either sat in silence, smoking, or looking at their lifeless faces in pocket mirrors, or swinging their legs restlessly back and forth. Louise noted that some of them were very young, thirteen or perhaps fourteen, no more. Their skirts were extremely short, hiding practically nothing, the heels of their shoes high and pointed, their breasts almost bare. They are made up like dead bodies, Louise thought. Bodies waiting to be buried, perhaps mummified. But no prostitute is preserved for generations to come. They just rot away behind their heavily painted faces.

Two bottles were brought to their table, glasses and paper serviettes. Lucinda leaned forward towards Louise. Her eyes were red.

'Say it again. Slowly. Tell me what has happened.'

Louise could detect no trace of dissimulation in Lucinda. Her face, covered in beads of sweat, was an open book. Lucinda's horror at what she had been forced to listen to was obvious.

'I found Henrik dead in his flat in Stockholm. Have you visited him there?'

'I have never been to Sweden.'

'He was lying in bed. His body was full of barbiturates. That's what caused his death. But why had he taken his own life?'

One of the young women came over to their table and asked for a light. Lucinda lit her cigarette. In the light from the match Louise could see the young woman's emaciated face.

*Black patches on her cheeks, badly smeared over with make-up, powdered. Symptoms of Aids that I've read about. The black marks of death, wounds that refuse to heal.*

Lucinda sat motionless.

'I can't understand it.'

'Nobody can understand it. But you might be able to help me. What could have happened? Might it have had something to do with Africa? He was here in early summer. What happened then?'

'Nothing that could have made him want to kill himself.'

'I have to know what happened. What state was he in when he arrived, who did he meet? How was he when he left?'

'Henrik was always the same.'

I must give her time, Louise thought. She has been shocked by what I've told her. At least now I know that Henrik meant something to her.

'He was my only child. He was all I had, there was nobody else.'

Louise noticed a sudden glint in Lucinda's eye, surprise, perhaps worry.

'Didn't he have any brothers and sisters?'

'No, he was an only child.'

'He told me he had a sister. He was the youngest.'

'It's not true. I'm his mother. I ought to know.'

'How do I know you're telling me the truth?'

Louise was furious.

'I'm his mother, and I'm totally devastated by his death. You hurt me deeply if you question who I am.'

'I didn't mean to offend you. But Henrik was always talking about his sister.'

'He didn't have a sister. Perhaps he would have liked one.'


The girls lined up along the walls left the bar one after the other. Soon Louise and Lucinda were alone in the silence and darkness, apart from the barman, busy filing away at a thumbnail.

'They are so young, the girls who were sitting here.'

'The youngest are the most sought-after. South African men who come here like to go with twelve-and thirteen-year-olds.'

'Aren't they carrying infections?'

'You mean Aids? The one whose cigarette I lit is ill. But not all of them are. Unlike many of their age, these girls know the score. They look after themselves. They are not the ones who die or pass the infection on.'

But you do, Louise thought. You passed it on to him, you opened the door and allowed death to enter his bloodstream.

'The girls hate what they do. But they only have white men as clients. That means they can tell their boyfriends that they haven't been unfaithful. They've only had sex with white men. That doesn't count.'

'Is that really the case?'

'Why shouldn't it be?'

Louise wanted to ask the question right out, no beating about the bush. Did you infect him? Didn't you know you had the virus? How could you do that?

But she said nothing.

'I have to know what happened,' she said after a while.

'Nothing happened while he was here. Was he alone when he died?'

'Yes, he was alone.'

I don't actually know that, Louise thought. There could have been somebody with him.

She suddenly thought of an explanation for the pyjamas. Henrik did not die in his bed. Only after he had lost consciousness or could no longer offer any resistance had he been undressed and the pyjamas put on him. Whoever was with him in the flat had not known that Henrik always slept naked.

Lucinda suddenly burst into tears. The whole of her body was shaking. The man behind the bar studying his thumbnail raised an eyebrow in the direction of Louise. She shook her head, she did not need any help.

Louise took hold of her hand. It was hot and sweaty. She held hard onto it. Lucinda calmed down, wiped her face with a serviette.

151

'How did you manage to find me?'

'Henrik left a letter in Barcelona. He wrote about you.'

'What did he say?'

'That you would know if something happened to him.'

'Know what?'

'I don't have the slightest idea.'

'And you've come all the way here, just to talk to me?'

'I have to try to understand what happened. Did he know anybody else here, apart from you?'

'Henrik knew lots of people.'

'That's not the same as having friends.'

'He had me. And Eusebio.'

'Who?'

'That's what he called him. Eusebio. A civil servant at the Swedish Embassy who used to be one of the gang that played football on the beach every Sunday. A very awkward person who was nothing like the footballer of that name. Henrik sometimes used to stay at his place.'

'I thought he stayed with you?'

'I live with my parents and the rest of the family. He couldn't sleep there. Sometimes he would borrow a flat from somebody at the embassy who was away on business. Eusebio used to help him.'

'Do you know his real name?'

'Lars Håkansson. I'm not sure if I'm pronouncing it right.'

'So you lived there with Henrik?'

'I was in love with him. I dreamed of marrying him. But I never lived with him in Eusebio's house.'

'Did you discuss that? Getting married?'

'Never. It was just a dream I had.'

'How did you meet?'

'The way you always meet – by chance. You walk down a street and turn a corner. Everything in life is about what's in store for you round the corner.'

'Which corner was it where you bumped into each other?'

Lucinda shook her head. Louise could see that she was worried.

'I must get back to the bar. We can talk tomorrow. Where are you staying?'

'At the Hotel Polana.'

Lucinda pulled a face.

'Henrik would never have stayed there. He didn't have enough money.'

Oh yes he did, Louise thought. So he didn't tell Lucinda the whole truth either.

'It's expensive,' she said. 'But my journey was unplanned, as you can probably understand. I'll change hotels.'

'How long is it since he died?'

'A few weeks.'

'I must know the exact date.'

'September 17.'

Lucinda stood up.

'Not yet,' said Louise, holding her back. 'There's something else I haven't told you yet.'

Lucinda sat down again. The man from behind the bar came to their table. Lucinda paid for the drinks. Louise took money from her jacket pocket, but Lucinda shook her head, almost aggressively. The man returned to the bar and his thumbnail. Louise braced herself to say what had to be said.

'Henrik was ill. He was HIV-positive.'

Lucinda was unmoved. She waited for what Louise was going to say next.

'Do you understand what I've just said?'

'I heard what you said.'

'Was it you who infected him?'

Lucinda's face went blank. She looked at Louise, as if from a distance.

'Before I can talk about anything else, I have to have an answer to that question.'

Lucinda's face was still expressionless. Her eyes were in partial shade. Her voice was steady when she replied. But Louise had learned from Aron that fury could be concealed just under the surface, especially in people of whom you would least expect it.

'It was not my intention to hurt you.'

'I never found in Henrik what I can see in you – your contempt. You despise black people. Maybe not consciously, but it's there even so. You think it's our own weaknesses that have made the agonies of Africa so devastating. Just like nearly all other white people, you think the most important thing is to know how we die. You couldn't care less about how we live. The miserable life an African leads is no more significant than a slight shift in the wind direction.'

'You can't accuse me of being racist.'

'You can decide for yourself if that's a justified accusation or not. If you must know, it wasn't me who infected Henrik.'

'How did he get the virus, then?'

'He put himself about. A lot of the girls you saw here not long ago could well have been to bed with him.'

'But you said a few minutes ago that they weren't carriers?'

'There only needs to be one. He was careless. He didn't always use a condom.'

'Good God!'

'When he was drunk he would become careless and went from woman to woman. When he came crawling back to me after his jaunts, he was full of remorse. But he soon forgot.'

'I don't believe you. Henrik wasn't like that.'

'What he was like is not something you and I are going to agree about. I loved him, you were his mother.'

'But he didn't infect you?'

'No.'

'I apologise for the accusation. But I find it hard to believe that he lived as you say he did.'

'He's not the first white man who's come to a poverty-stricken African country and taken advantage of black women. Nothing is as important for a white man as getting in between the legs of a black woman. It's just as important for a black man to bed a white woman. If you wander around this city you'll find a thousand or more black men willing to sacrifice everything in order to get you into their beds.'

'You're exaggerating.'

'Sometimes the truth can be found in exaggerations.'

'It's late. I'm tired.'

'It's early for me. I can't go home until tomorrow morning.'

Lucinda stood up.

'I'll accompany you to the exit and make sure you get a taxi. Go back to your hotel and get a good night's sleep. I'll see you again tomorrow.'

Lucinda escorted Louise to one of the gates, said a few words to the attendant. A man with car keys in his hand emerged from the shadows.

'He'll take you home.'

'What time tomorrow?'

But Lucinda was already walking away. Louise watched her disappearing into the shadows.

The taxi stank of petrol. Louise tried not to imagine Henrik putting himself about among the thin African girls with their short skirts and hard faces.

When she reached the hotel she drank two glasses of wine in the bar. Once again she saw the white South Africans who had shared her minibus from the airport.

She hated them.


The air conditioning buzzed in the background as she went to bed and put out the light. She sobbed herself to sleep, like a child. In her dreams she was transported from the burnt African terrain to the white plains of Härjedalen, the endless forests, the silence, and her father who observed her with an expression that combined pride and surprise.


The next morning a young woman in reception informed Louise that one of the hotel's closest neighbours was the Swedish Embassy. If she walked past the street vendors and a petrol station, she would find herself outside the brownish-yellow building that contained the embassy.

'I was mugged yesterday when I went in the opposite direction and turned off into a side street.'

The girl at the desk shook her head in sympathy.

'I'm sorry to say that such things happen all too often. People are poor, they lie in wait for our guests.'

'I don't want to be mugged again.'

'Nothing will happen, it's not far to the embassy. Were you injured?'

'They didn't beat me up. But they did stab me, under my eye.'

'I can see. I'm very sorry.'

'That doesn't help much.'

'What did they take?'

'My handbag. But I'd left most things here at the hotel. They got a bit of money, but no passport, no mobile phone, no credit cards. They took my brown comb – I wonder if they can make use of that?'


Louise had breakfast on the terrace, and experienced a short if somewhat bewildering few minutes of well-being. It was as if nothing had happened.


On the way to the embassy, she kept looking over her shoulder. A lump of iron ore featured as a sculpture outside the green-painted fence. A uniformed guard opened the gate for her.

The usual official portraits of the king and queen were hanging in reception. Two men were sitting on a sofa and discussing in Swedish 'the shortage of water and the input we need to make in Niassa Province as soon as the funding comes through'. She was reminded that, sadly, she had lost contact with what was happening in Argolis. What had she thought would ensue when she stood there in the middle of the night and smoked a cigarette while Mitsos's dogs were barking? The horrors in store had left no warning.

The person who had stood there in the darkness with a cigarette in her hand no longer existed.


At the reception desk she asked to speak to Lars Håkansson. The woman on duty asked why she wanted to see him.

'He knew my son. Just tell him that Henrik's mother is here. That will do.'

The woman set in motion a complicated sequence of key-pressing before eventually getting through to Håkansson.

'He's coming down.'

The two men who had been discussing water had moved on. Louise sat down on the dark blue sofa and waited.

A short man with thin hair and a face suffering from too much exposure to the sun, wearing a suit, came out through the glass door. She could see that he was on his guard even as he approached.

'So you are Henrik Cantor's mother, are you?'

'Yes.'

'I'm sorry, but I shall have to ask you for an ID. We have to be very careful nowadays. I very much doubt if terrorists are planning to blow up the embassy and us with it, but the Foreign Office has tightened up safety restrictions. I'm not allowed to take anybody through that glass door unless I'm 100 per cent certain who they are.'

Louise had left her passport and ID card in the safe in her hotel room.

'I don't have my passport with me.'

'Then I'm afraid we shall have to stay down here in reception.'

They sat down. She was still curious about his guarded approach. It offended her.

'For simplicity's sake can we assume that I really am who I say I am?'

'Of course. I'm sorry the world is in the state it's in.'

'Henrik is dead.'

He said nothing. She waited.

'What happened?'

'I found him dead in his bed in Stockholm.'

'I thought he lived in Barcelona?'

Steady now, Louise thought. He knows what you didn't know.

'Until he died I hadn't the slightest idea that he had a flat in Barcelona.

157

I've come here to try to find out what it was all about. Did you meet Henrik while he was here?'

'We got to know each other. He must have told you about me.'

'Never. On the other hand, he did tell a black woman called Lucinda about you.'

'Lucinda?'

'She works at a bar called Malocura.'

Louise produced the photograph of her and showed it to him.

'I know her. But her name's not Lucinda, she's called Julieta.'

'Perhaps she has two names.'

Lars Håkansson stood up.

'I'm about to break all the safety regulations. Let's go up to my office. It's no nicer up there, but it's not quite so hot.'


His office had windows overlooking the Indian Ocean. A few fishing boats with triangular sails were making their way into the bay. He had asked her if she would like a cup of coffee, and she had accepted.

He came back with two cups in his hand. The cups were white with blue and yellow flags on them.

'It occurs to me that I haven't expressed my condolences. It was a horrific piece of news for me as well. I had a high regard for Henrik. I often used to think that I wish I'd had a son like him.'

'Do you not have any children?'

'Four daughters from a previous marriage. A bunch of young ladies who will do well in the world. But no son.'

Pensively, he dropped a lump of sugar into his cup and stirred it with a pencil.

'What happened?'

'The post-mortem showed a high concentration of barbiturates in his blood, which would suggest that he committed suicide.'

He looked at her in astonishment.

'Can that really be true?'

'No. That's why I'm searching for the real cause. And I believe that whatever happened had its origins here.'

'In Maputo?'

'I don't know. In this country, in this continent. I hope you can help me to find an answer.'

Lars Håkansson put down his cup and glanced at his watch.

'Where are you staying?'

'At the moment, next door to the embassy.'

'Polana is a good hotel. But expensive. During the Second World War it was crawling with German and Japanese spies. Nowadays it's crawling with South Africans who have nothing better to do.'

'I'm thinking of changing hotels.'

'I live alone and have plenty of room. You're welcome to stay with me. Just as Henrik did.'

She decided on the spot to accept the offer.

He stood up.

'I have a meeting with the ambassador and some aid workers. It's about money which has disappeared from one of our accounts in mysterious circumstances. It's down to corruption, of course, light-fingered ministers who need money to build houses for their children. We spend an incredible amount of time on such matters.'

He accompanied her down to reception.

'Henrik left a tote bag behind when he was here last. I don't know what's in it, but when I put it into a wardrobe I noticed that it was heavy.'

'So it couldn't have contained clothes?'

'No, probably books and papers. I can drop it off at your hotel this evening. Unfortunately I have a dinner appointment with a French colleague that I can't get out of. I would have preferred to be on my own. I'm very distressed by the thought that Henrik is no longer with us. I suppose it hasn't sunk in yet.'


They said goodbye in the little courtyard in front of the embassy.

'I arrived yesterday and was mugged almost immediately.'

'You weren't injured, I hope?'

'It was my own fault. I know you should never walk down empty streets, but always stick to where there are other people around.'

'The most cunning muggers have an impressive ability to pick out people who have only just arrived in this country. But you can hardly call the people here criminals. The poverty you come across is hair-raising. What do you do if you have five children and no work? If I'd been one of the poor wretches in this city I'd have mugged somebody like me. I'll drop off the bag for you at around seven.'

She went back to the hotel. In an attempt to shake off her uneasiness, she bought a bathing costume that was far too expensive, in a shop inside the hotel. Then she went down to the large swimming pool and tired herself out by swimming lengths. She was the only person in the water.

*I'm floating on Röstjärn*, she thought. *That's the little lake where my father and I used to swim when I was a child. He used to frighten me by saying that the lake was bottomless. We would swim there in the evening in summer when the mosquitoes were whining, and I loved him because his strokes were so powerful.*

She returned to her room and lay naked on top of the bed. Her mind wandered.

*Lucinda and Nazrin? The flat in Barcelona and the flat in Stockholm. Why the smokescreens? And why was he wearing pyjamas when he died?*

She fell asleep and was woken up by the telephone.

'It's Lars Håkansson. I'm in reception with Henrik's bag.'

'Is it seven o'clock already? I'm in the shower.'

'I can wait. I came earlier than I'd thought. It's only four o'clock.'

She dressed rapidly and hurried downstairs. Håkansson stood up as she approached. He was holding a black sports bag with the logo Adidas in red letters.

'I'll pick you up at eleven tomorrow morning.'

'I hope I'm not going to put you to any trouble?'

'Not at all.'

She returned to her room and opened the bag. On top was a pair of trousers and a light khaki jacket. She had never seen Henrik wearing anything like that. Underneath were plastic envelopes with documents, and some files similar to those she had found in both Stockholm and Barcelona. She emptied the bag onto her bed. There was some soil at the bottom that also ran onto the bed. She picked some up. *Once again, red soil.*

She started going through his papers. A shrivelled insect, some sort of butterfly, fell out of a bundle of photocopies. It was an article in English written by Professor Ronald Witterman of Oxford University. The title was: 'Death's Waiting Room: A Journey Through the Third World'. The article oozed fury. There was no trace of the calm, disciplined style that was usual when professors were arguing cases. Witterman was bristling with anger.

Never before have we had such enormous resources at our disposal, enabling us to make the world bearable for more and more people. Instead, we betray all our awareness, our intellectual power and our material resources by allowing untold misery to increase. We have long since sold out our responsibilities by sponsoring institutions such as the World Bank, whose political activities more often than not result merely in sacrificing human suffering at the altar of arrogant economic advice. We offloaded our consciences long ago.

Here was a man whose anger knew no bounds, she thought. Witterman's fury had captured Henrik's attention.

The plastic envelopes also contained pages torn off a notepad. Henrik had started translating Professor Witterman's article into Swedish. She could see that he had found it difficult to find the right words, difficult to recapture the rhythm of the long sentences. She put the article to one side and opened the next folder. Kennedy's brain suddenly turned up again in what appeared to be a transcript. She arranged them in order and started reading.

On 21 January 1967, the American Prosecutor-General Ramsey Clark made a telephone call. He was worried, and unsure of what the reaction would be. When his call was answered, he spoke to a secretary who asked him to wait. A sullen-sounding voice asked him what he wanted. President Lyndon Baines Johnson could be a pleasant and jovial person, but just as often he could be surly when things did not go the way he wanted.

'Good morning, Mr President.'

'What's going on? I thought it was all done and dusted when the post-mortem on Jack was completed at the naval base?'

'We asked the three pathologists involved to come to Washington. We were also forced to bring Fink back from Vietnam.'

'I couldn't give a damn about Fink! I have a delegation from Arkansas chewing at the bit outside my office door. They've come to discuss oats and wheat. I don't have time for all this crap.'

'I'm sorry, Mr President. I'll be as brief as I can. They were going through the archive yesterday – one of them was Dr Humes, who testified to the Warren Commission, about a photo of the right lung. It was important for establishing the cause of Kennedy's death.'

'I've read about that in the Commission's report. What exactly do you want?'

'We seem to have a problem. The photograph is missing.'

'What do you mean, the photograph's missing?'

'It's vanished. And as far as we can see, another picture has disappeared as well, showing the entry hole for the bullet that was the direct cause of death.'

'How the hell can photographs of Kennedy's post-mortem disappear?'

'How could his brain disappear?'

'What do we do now?'

'Obviously, the medical guys are worried because they've testified under oath that the photographs exist. But now they don't. One of them, at least.'

'Is the press going to get hold of this?'

'Most probably. Everything will be dug up again. The conspiracy theories, Oswald wasn't acting alone, everything we thought we'd put to bed is going to be resurrected.'

'I don't have time to fuck around with Jack any more. He's dead. I'm trying to do what a president has to do, I'm trying to sort out a lunatic war in Vietnam, and blacks running amok in the streets if we can't solve this civil rights business pdq. Make sure those medics don't shoot their mouths off too much. And send Fink back to Vietnam by yesterday.'

Henrik concluded by noting that the material came from the 'Justice Department, recently opened archives'. He also made some comments of his own.

Louise thought over what she had read. *Everything is buried. Awkward facts are swept under the carpet. The truth is being disguised. We live in a world where it is more important to conceal facts than to reveal them. Anybody who makes secret moves to shine a light into the darkest corners can never be sure of what he or she might find. I must continue to shine lights. I shall soon put away all these documents about Kennedy and his accursed brain. But they seem to be a sort of handbook mapping out the world of lies, and hence lead us to the truth.*

Louise continued sorting through the papers. There was map of the southern part of Mozambique. Henrik had drawn a ring round a town called Xai-Xai and a district to the north-west of the town.

Louise put the map to one side. At the very bottom of the sports bag was a brown envelope. She opened it. It contained five silhouettes cut out of black paper. Two of them were geometric patterns. The other three were profiles of people.

She saw right away that one depicted Henrik. It was his profile, no doubt about it. She could feel uneasiness rising up inside her. The silhouette was skilfully made, but Henrik was merely a shadow: the black paper somehow seemed to presage what was to follow.

She examined the other two silhouettes. One depicted a man, the other a woman. The woman's profile made it clear that she was African.

There was nothing written on the reverse. All the silhouettes were pasted onto sheets of white paper. There was no signature, nothing to suggest who had made them. Could it have been Henrik himself?

She sorted through the contents of the bag one more time, but in the end she found herself staring at the silhouettes yet again. What did they mean?

She went down to reception, and out into the grounds. The wind off the sea was mild, laden with perfumes from mysterious spices.

She sat down on a bench and stared out over the dark sea. A light was flashing, and on the far horizon ships could be seen sailing southwards.

She was startled when Lucinda suddenly appeared behind her.

*Why does everybody here move without a sound? Why don't I hear them creeping up on me?*

Lucinda sat down beside her.

'What did you find in the bag?'

Louise gave a start.

'How come you know about that?'

'I met Håkansson. This is a big city, but at the same time it's very small. I happened to bump into him, and he told me.'

'He said your name was Julieta, and that he didn't know anybody called Lucinda.'

Lucinda's face remained in the shadows.

'Men sometimes give women whatever name they fancy.'

'Why should the women go along with that?'

As she spoke, but too late, Louise realised what Lucinda was saying.

'He thought that I looked like a woman who ought to be called Julieta. For three months we used to meet twice a week, always at specified times in the evening, nearly always in discreet rooms rented out specifically for meetings like ours. Then he found somebody else, or perhaps his wife turned up. I don't remember.'

'Am I supposed to believe this?'

The response came like a punch on the jaw.

'That I was his mistress? That I was his little black toy that he could play with in return for cash, always in dollars or South African rands?'

Lucinda stood up.

'I can't help you if you if you refuse to accept what happens in a country as poor as this.'

'I didn't mean to offend you.'

'You'll never understand, you'll never have to consider opening your legs in order to afford food for yourself, or for your children, or your parents.'

'Perhaps you can explain it to me.'

'That's why I've come. I'd like you to come with me tomorrow afternoon. There's something I want to show you. Something that Henrik saw as well. Nothing will happen to you, you don't need to be afraid.'

'I'm frightened of everything that happens here, of the darkness, of being mugged by people I can neither see nor hear. I'm frightened because I don't understand.'

'Henrik was frightened as well. But he tried to shake off his fear. He tried to understand.'

Lucinda left. The wind was still no more than a gentle breeze. Louise could picture her, walking along dark streets to the bar where she worked.

She looked around the extensive hotel grounds. Everywhere, she suspected she could see shadows in the darkness.

# CHAPTER 14

She stood by the window and watched the sun leap out of the sea. Once, when she was a child, her father had told her the world was like an enormous library stocked with sunrises and dusks. She had never really understood what he meant, how the movements of the sun could be like the pages of books. Not even now, as she watched light spreading over the water, could she fathom his thoughts.

She wondered whether to phone him and ask. But she let it pass.

Instead she sat down on the little balcony and dialled the number of her hotel in Barcelona. It was Xavier who answered. Mr Cantor had not been in touch, nor had the police. Mr Castells would have told him if there had been any news about Mr Cantor.

'But at least we haven't heard any bad news,' he shouted, as if the distance between Barcelona and southern Africa was too far for a normal tone of voice to be used.

The connection was lost. She did not try again, she had already received confirmation of what she knew already: Aron was still missing.

She got dressed and went down to the dining room. A fresh breeze was blowing in from the sea. She had just finished eating when somebody addressed her by name. 'Mrs Cantor', with the stress on the second syllable. When she turned round she found herself looking into a bearded face, a man of mixed race, just as much European as African. His eyes were bright. When he spoke she could see that his teeth were bad. He was short, corpulent and impatient.

'Louise Cantor?'

'That's me.'

His English had a strong Portuguese accent, but was easy to understand. Without waiting for an invitation, he pulled out the chair opposite her and sat down. He waved away the waitress who came up to the table.

'I'm Nuno, a friend of Lucinda's. I heard that you were here and that Henrik's dead.'

'I've no idea who you are.'

'Of course you don't. I haven't been here for a minute yet.'

'Nuno who? Did you know my son?'

'Nuno da Silva. I'm a journalist. Henrik sought me out a few months ago. He wanted to ask me some questions, important questions. I'm used to people seeking me out, but they don't always ask questions that interest me.'

Louise tried to remember if there had been any mention of the man's name in Henrik's notes, but she could not recall a Nuno da Silva.

'What kind of questions did he ask?'

'Tell me first what happened. Lucinda said that he died in his bed. Where was his bed?'

'Why do you ask such an odd question?'

'Because he seemed to be the sort of man who often slept in different places, a young man on the move. When I met him I thought immediately that he reminded me of myself twenty-five years ago.'

'He died in Stockholm.'

'I've been there. It was in 1974. The Portuguese were beginning to lose the war in their African colonies. It was not long before the captains started their revolt in Lisbon. There was a conference, I still don't know who paid my fare or fixed a visa for me. But it was encouraging to meet those young Swedes, none of them with the slightest experience of the horrors of war or colonial oppression, offering their support so wholeheartedly. But I also thought that it was a strange country.'

'In what way?'

'We spent day after day talking about freedom, but it was impossible to find a place where you could drink a beer or two after ten o'clock at night. Everywhere was either closed, or did not sell alcohol. Nobody could explain to me why. The Swedes understood us, but not themselves. What happened to Henrik?'

'The doctors said that his body was full of barbiturates.'

'He would never have committed suicide! Was he ill?'

'No, he wasn't ill.'

*Why am I lying? Why don't I say it's possible that what killed him was his fear of the infection he was carrying? Perhaps it's because I still can't believe that really was the case. He was ill, but he would have fought it. And he would have told me about it.*

'When did it happen?'

'On 17 September.'

The little dark-haired man's response to Louise's answer came with full force.

'He phoned me a few days before then.'

'Are you sure?'

'I'm a journalist, but also a newspaper publisher. My little faxed newspaper comes out every day except Sunday. I have a calendar built into my brain. He rang me on the Tuesday, and you say you found him on the Friday.'

'What did he want?'

'He had a few questions that couldn't wait.'

The dining room began to fill up with breakfasters. Most of them were loud-voiced South Africans with large beer bellies. Louise could see that Nuno was becoming increasingly irritated.

'I never usually come here. There's nothing here that tells the truth about this country. It could be a hotel in France or England, or why not in Lisbon. In here, poverty has been swept away and forbidden to show itself.'

'I'm moving out today.'

'Henrik would never have set foot in this place unless he had an important errand.'

'What would that have been?'

'To meet his mother and tell her that she should leave this hotel. Can't we sit outside?'

He stood up without waiting for an answer, and marched off over the terrace.

'He's a very good man,' said the waitress to Louise. 'He says what others are afraid to say. But he lives dangerously.'

'In what way?'

'The truth is always dangerous. But Nuno da Silva is not afraid. He's very brave.'


Nuno was leaning on the railings, staring pensively out to sea. She stood next to him. They were shielded from the sun by an awning that swayed slightly in the breeze.

'He came to me with his questions, but they were statements as much as questions. I realised immediately that he was onto something.'

'What?'

Nuno da Silva shook his head impatiently. He did not want to be interrupted.

'Our first meeting began with a minor catastrophe. He turned up at the newspaper office and asked if I wanted to be his Virgil. I could hardly hear what he said, but I had heard of Virgil and Dante. I thought he was an overgrown student who wanted to draw attention to himself for some incomprehensible reason. So I answered him the way I usually do; I told him to go to hell and stop bothering me. Then he apologised, said he wasn't looking for a Virgil, he was not Dante, but he just wanted to talk. I asked why he had come to me of all people. He said that Lucinda had told him to get in touch with me. But most of all because everybody he spoke to came up with my name sooner or later. I am proof of how hopeless the situation is here nowadays. I'm almost the only person who questions the current state of affairs, why the abuse of power, why the corruption. I asked him to wait as I needed to finish an article. He sat on a chair, said nothing, waited. Then we went outside – my newspaper is located in a garage on a farm. We sat on some oil drums that we have joined together to make a couple of uncomfortable benches. They make a good place to sit because resting in comfort makes you tired. You get back pain from idleness.'

'Not my father. He used to be a lumberjack. His back has given way, but not because he's been idle.'

Nuno da Silva appeared not to have heard what she said.

'He had read some articles I'd written about Aids. He was convinced I was right.'

'About what?'

'About the causes of the epidemic. I have no doubt that dead chimpanzees and people who have eaten their meat have something to do with the illness. But a virus that is so skilful at concealing itself, going into hiding, manipulating itself and constantly reappearing in new forms – I refuse to believe that it hasn't had some kind of assistance. Nobody is going to convince me that this virus didn't originate in some secret laboratory or other, the kind of place the Americans looked for in vain in Iraq.'

'Do you have any proof of this?'

Nuno da Silva's impatience progressed into open irritation.

'You don't always need proof for things that are so self-evident. You find them sooner or later. What the old colonialists used to say still holds true. "Africa would be heaven on earth if it weren't for all those damned Africans who live there." Aids is a means of killing off all the black men in this continent. The fact that it's rife among homosexuals and promiscuous people in America is just a blip. You find that cynical attitude among the people who consider it their right to dominate the world. Henrik had had similar thoughts himself. But he had added a rider of his own. I can remember it word for word. *Men in Africa are busy exterminating the women.*'

'What did he mean by that?'

'Women have very few possibilities of protecting themselves. The way men are dominant in this continent is horrifying. We have patriarchal traditions that I'm the last person to defend. But I'll be damned if that gives laboratories in the Western world the right to kill us off.'

'What happened next?'

'We sat talking for an hour or so. I liked him. I suggested that he should write articles for European newspapers, but he said it was too soon. *Not yet.* I remember that clearly.'

'Why did he say that?'

'He had a line of investigation that he wanted to follow up, but he never said precisely what it was. He was reluctant to talk about it.

170

Maybe he didn't know enough about it. Then we went our different ways. I invited him to visit me again. But he never did.'

He glanced at his watch.

'I have to go.'

She tried to hold him back.

'Somebody killed him. I have to know who, and why.'

'He didn't say anything to me, as I've said. I don't know what he was looking for. Even if I have my suspicions.'

'What do you suspect?'

He shook his head.

'Suspicions. That's all. Perhaps what he knew became too difficult for him to bear. People can die because they know too much about other people's suffering.'

'You said that he was on to something?'

'I think it was inside him. A clue that was a thought. I never understood properly what he meant. The link he was looking for was very unclear. He talked about drug smuggling. Big cargoes of heroin from the poppy fields of Afghanistan. Vessels anchored off Mozambique's ports at night, fast motorboats collecting goods, lorries taking stuff through unmanned border crossings into South Africa in the dark, and then on to the rest of the world. Even if fat bribes had to be paid to police officers, customs officers, prosecutors, judges, civil servants and not least the ministers responsible, the profits are astronomic. In this day and age the turnover in drug smuggling is as high as that of the tourist industry. More than arms manufacturing. Henrik spoke in guarded fashion about a link between all that and the Aids epidemic. I don't know where he got his information from. I have to go now.'

They said their goodbyes outside the hotel.

'I'll be staying with an official at the Swedish Embassy by the name of Lars Håkansson.'

Nuno da Silva pulled a face.

'An interesting person.'

'Do you know him?'

'I'm a journalist. It's my job to know everything that's worth knowing. About what goes on, and about people as well.'

He shook hands, turned on his heel and headed for the street. She could see that he was in a hurry.

The intense heat was upsetting her. She returned to her room. There had been no mistaking Nuno da Silva's facial expression. He had no time at all for Lars Håkansson.

She gazed up at the ceiling and wondered what she ought to do next. Perhaps she ought to give Lars Håkansson a wide berth. Then again, Henrik had stayed at his place. *I have to go to the places where Henrik might have left some traces behind,* she thought.

It was a quarter past nine. She phoned Artur. She could tell from his voice that he'd been waiting for her to ring. That brought a lump into her throat. Perhaps he'd been awake all night yet again. *It's just him and me now. There's nobody else.*

She thought he would feel better if she told him that all was well, and that she was going to stay with a man employed by the Swedish Embassy. He informed her that it was snowing now, harder than ever, over ten centimetres during the night. Moreover, he'd found a dead dog on the road when he'd gone to buy a newspaper.

'What had happened?'

'It didn't look to me as if it had been run over. It looked as if somebody had shot its head to pieces and thrown it onto the road.'

'Did you recognise it?'

'No. It wasn't from round here. But how can anybody hate a dog as much as that?'


After the call she lay down on the bed. *How can anybody hate a dog as much as that?* She thought about what Nuno da Silva had said. Could he really be right in thinking that the Aids epidemic was caused by a conspiracy with the aim of exterminating the population of Africa? Could Henrik have been a part of the 'drop in the ocean' he'd spoken about? It seemed utter madness to her. Surely Henrik could not have believed that either. He would never have believed in a conspiracy theory that could not withstand detailed examination.

She sat up in bed and pulled the blanket around her. The air conditioning made her shiver, she was getting goose pimples on her arms.

What was it that da Silva thought Henrik was on to? A clue that was a thought? What had Henrik discovered? Where ought she to be looking? She did not know, but nevertheless, she had the feeling she was getting warm.

She swore out loud. Then she got up, took a long, cold shower, packed her case and had paid her bill by the time Håkansson turned up.

'I was just thinking that if I'd been a boy, I'm sure my father would have called me Lars.'

'An excellent name. Easy to pronounce in any language you care to name, with the possible exception of Mandarin speakers in China. Lars Herman Olof Håkansson. Lars after my paternal grandfather, Herman after my maternal grandfather who was a naval officer, and Olof after the first king of Sweden in the eleventh century. I sail through life with those characters as my patron saints.'

*But you wanted to call Lucinda Julieta. Why did changing her name turn you on?*

She asked him to write down his address, and handed it over to reception with the request that they should pass it on to a woman by the name of Lucinda if she should come to the hotel and ask for Louise.

Håkansson stood some way away, lost in thought. Louise spoke in a low voice so that he would not hear.

His house was in Kaunda Street. A diplomatic district, with lots of national flags flying. Mansions behind high walls, uniformed guards, barking dogs. They went through an iron gate and a man working in the garden insisted on carrying her bags, although she tried to carry them herself.

'The house was built by a Portuguese doctor,' Håkansson explained. 'In 1974, when it finally dawned on the Portuguese that the blacks

173

would very soon be declaring independence, he went home. They say he left a yacht in the marina, and a piano that slowly rotted away on the quay because it was never loaded onto the cargo ship bound for Lisbon. The state took over the empty house. Now it's rented by the Swedish government – the taxpayers pay my rent.'

The house was surrounded by a garden, with several tall trees at the back. A German shepherd on a chain eyed her suspiciously. There were two maids inside the house, one old, the other young.

'Graça,' Håkansson said when Louise introduced herself to the older woman and shook hands. 'She does the cleaning. She's too old, of course, but she wants to stay on. I'm the nineteenth Swede she's worked for.'

Graça picked up Louise's bags and carried them up the stairs. Louise stared in horror at the old woman's emaciated body.

'Celina,' said Håkansson. Louise shook hands with the younger woman. 'She's bright and a good cook. If you need anything, talk to her. There's always somebody here during the day. I'll be home late this evening. Just say when you're hungry, and they'll provide you with some food. Celina will show you to your room.'

He was halfway out of the door when Louise caught up with him.

'Is it the same room as Henrik stayed in?'

'I thought that's what you would want. But if you don't like the idea you can always change. The house is big. They say that Dr Sa Pinto had a very large family. All the children had to have their own room.'

'I just wanted to know.'

'Well, now you do.'

Louise went back inside the house. Celina was waiting at the bottom of the stairs. Graça had come down and was busy doing something in the kitchen. Louise followed Celina up the stairs in this totally white house.

They came to a room where patches of damp had turned the plaster yellow. She detected a faint smell of mould. So this is where Henrik had slept. It was not a large room, most of the space was taken up by the bed. There were bars outside the window, as in a prison. Her suitcase was lying on the bed. She opened the wardrobe door. It was empty, apart from a golf club.

She stood motionless beside the bed and tried to imagine Henrik in this room. But he wasn't there. She could not find him.

She unpacked, then found a bathroom after taking a look at Håkansson's large bedroom. Had Lucinda, or Julieta as he paid to call her, slept in that bed?

Her distaste kicked in with full force. She went back downstairs, took the cork out of a half-empty bottle of wine and drunk directly from the bottle. Too late she noticed that Graça was standing in the half-open kitchen door, watching her.

At noon she was served an omelette. A table had been laid for her, as if she had been in a restaurant. She merely toyed with the food.

This is the empty feeling one has before a decision is made, she thought, I know really that I ought to get away from here, the sooner the better.

She drank coffee at the back of the house where the heat was less intense. The chained dog was lying down, watching her intently. She eventually dozed off. She was woken up by Celina tapping her on the shoulder.

'You have a visitor,' she said.

Louise stood up, half asleep. She had been dreaming about Artur, something that had happened when she was a child. Once again they had been swimming in that dark tarn. But that was all she could remember.

When she entered the living room she found Lucinda waiting for her.

'Were you asleep?'

'My grief and my sleep are intermingling. I've never slept so much nor so little as I have since Henrik's death.'

Celina came into the room and asked something in an African language. Lucinda replied. Celina went out again. It seemed to Louise that Celina was so light on her feet that it was impossible to imagine them actually touching the dark brown wooden floor.

'What were you talking about? I couldn't understand a word.'

'She asked me if I wanted something to drink. I said no thank you.'

Lucinda was dressed in white. Her shoes had very high heels. Her hair was in plaits and clung to the crown of her head. Louise was struck by Lucinda's beauty. *She has shared Henrik's bed, and Lars Håkansson's as well.*

She found the thought distasteful.

'I want to take you on a car trip,' Lucinda said.

'Where to?'

'Somewhere out of town. To a place that meant a lot to Henrik. We'll be back here by evening.'

Lucinda's car was parked in the shade of a flowering jacaranda tree. Lavender-blue petals had fluttered down onto its red bonnet. The car was old and battered. When Louise sat down in the passenger seat she could smell fruit.

They drove through the city. It was very hot in the car. Louise turned towards the open window in order to catch some of the slipstream. The traffic was chaotic, with vehicles overtaking haphazardly. Nearly all these cars would have been ordered off the roads immediately in Sweden, she thought. But they were not in Sweden, they were in a country on the east coast of Africa, and Henrik had been here a short time before he died.

They approached the outskirts of the city, shabby warehouses, pavements smashed up, rusty abandoned cars and an endless stream of pedestrians wherever you looked. When they stopped at a red light Louise watched a woman carrying a large basket on her head, and another woman balancing a pair of red high-heeled shoes on her head. *Everywhere, women carrying burdens on their heads. And they are bearing other burdens inside themselves, burdens I can only guess at.*

Lucinda turned off at a chaotic crossroads where the traffic lights were not functioning. She piloted her way forcefully through the confusion. Louise saw a signpost saying Xai-Xai.

'We're heading north,' said Lucinda. 'You'd end up in your own country if we carried on driving in this direction.'

They passed a large cemetery. Several funeral processions were assembled round the entrance gates. Then, suddenly, they had left the city, there was less traffic, fewer low houses built of mud and corrugated iron, the countryside took over, high grass, and a range of mountains in the distance, everything in various shades of green. Lucinda concentrated on her driving. Overloaded lorries and buses coughing out clouds of black exhaust fumes blocked the lanes of traffic, and there were few places where one could overtake. Louise observed the people in the fields. She could see a few men but they were mostly women; mattocks were being raised and lowered, backs bent, and along the verges a constant stream of pedestrians.

'This is Henrik's car,' Lucinda said out of the blue.

She had just overtaken one of the buses spitting out fumes, and the road ahead was straight and clear.

'He bought it for 4,000 dollars,' she added. 'That was far too much to pay. When he left he asked me to look after it until he came back. I suppose it's your car now.'

'No, it's not mine. Why did he need a car?'

'He liked driving. Not least since he started visiting the place we're going to now.'

'I still don't know where we're going.'

Lucinda did not answer, and Louise did not ask again.

'He bought it from a Dane who's lived here for many years and runs a little repair workshop. Everybody knows who Carsten is. A friendly man with a big stomach who's married to a thin little black woman from Quelimane. They're always quarrelling, especially on Sundays when they go for walks on the beach. Everybody loves it when they quarrel because you can see how much they like each other.'

They drove for just over an hour, most of the time in silence. Louise took in the changing countryside. She sometimes thought it reminded her of a winter landscape in Härjedalen, if you replaced the greens and browns with white. There was also a hint of the Greek countryside on

Peloponnisos. Everything seemed to be part of a whole. You can build all kinds of landscapes from nature's fragments.

Lucinda changed down and turned off the road. There was a bus stop and a little market. The ground along the side of the road had been trampled down and a row of little kiosks sold beer, fizzy drinks and bananas. Some boys carrying cool boxes came rushing towards the car. Lucinda bought two bottles of soda water and gave one to Louise before shooing away the boys. They obeyed immediately, without trying to sell their packets of South African biscuits.

'We always used to stop here,' Lucinda said.

'You and Henrik?'

'Sometimes I don't understand your questions. Who else would I have come here with? Some of my customers from the past?'

'I know nothing about what Henrik did in this country. What did he want? Where are we going to?'

Lucinda was watching some children playing with a puppy.

'The last time we were here he said he loved this place. This is where the world ended, or started. Nobody would be able to find him.'

'He said that?'

'I remember the exact words. I asked what he meant, because I didn't understand. He could be so dramatic sometimes. But when he talked about the beginning and the end of the world he was completely calm. It was as if the fear that always troubled him had suddenly gone away, for one brief, passing moment at least.'

'What was his answer?'

'Nothing. He sat in silence. Then we drove off. That was all. As far as I know he never came here again. I don't know why he left Maputo. I didn't even know he was going. Suddenly he was no longer there. Nobody knew anything.'

*Just like Aron. The same way of vanishing, without a word, without any explanation. Just like Aron.*

'Let's go and sit in the shade,' said Lucinda, opening the car door. Louise followed her to a tree whose trunk had twisted to form a somewhat lumpy bench big enough for both of them.

'Shade and water,' said Lucinda. 'Two things we always share in hot countries. What do you share in a country where it's cold?'

'Heat. There was a famous man in Greece who once asked a powerful emperor, who had promised to grant him the thing he wanted more than anything else, if he would kindly move because he was preventing the sun shining on him.'

'You are similar, you and Henrik. You have the same sort of . . . helplessness.'

'Thank you.'

'I didn't mean to offend you.'

'It was a genuine expression of thanks, because you think I take after my son.'

'Isn't it the other way round? That he took after you? If not, that's where you and I are different. I don't think your origins are based in the future. You can't approach the unknown lying in wait for you unless you know what happened before.'

'I've been an archaeologist all my life for that very reason. Without fragments and whispers from the past there is no present, no future, nothing. Perhaps we are more alike than you think after all?'

The children playing with the skinny puppy came running past. Dust rose up in clouds from the dry earth.

Lucinda drew with her foot something that looked like a cross inside a circle.

'We're on our way to a place where Henrik experienced great happiness. Perhaps he even encountered something there that he considered to be a state of bliss. He had bought his car without saying why he needed it. Sometimes he would vanish for several weeks without saying a word. One night he turned up at the bar, it was well past midnight, and he stayed there until I finished work and he drove me home. He told me about a man called Christian Holloway, who had built some villages where Aids suffering could get treatment. The place Henrik had visited didn't have a name because Holloway preached humility. Even having a name was presumptuous. The people being nursed there paid nothing. Those who worked there were volunteers, many of them Europeans, but there were also some Americans and Asians. Their input was exclusively charitable, and they lived simply. It wasn't a religious sect. Henrik said that no gods were needed because what the volunteers were doing was divine. That morning I saw something in Henrik that I'd never seen before. He had forced his way through that wall of despair he had fought so hard against.'

'What happened next?'

'He drove back there the very next day. Perhaps he only came to Maputo to tell me about how happy he was. Now he'd found something to balance the scales, to prevent a total victory for misery and suffering. Those were his own words – he could sometimes sound a bit high-flown, but he really meant it. Henrik was Henrik. He had seen the injustice, he'd seen that Aids was a plague that nobody wanted to come into contact with. I don't know the significance of Henrik himself carrying the infection. Nor do I know how it happened. Or when. But every time we met up, he said he wanted to show me Holloway's village where benevolence and consideration for others had conquered. And eventually, he did take me there. Only once.'

'Why did he leave the village and travel back to Europe?'

'Perhaps you'll find the answer to your questions when you get there.' Louise stood up.

'I can't wait, How far have we still to go?'

'We're about halfway there.'


The countryside alternated between green and brown. They came to a plain with a wide river, crossed over a bridge and drove through the town Xai-Xai. Shortly afterwards Lucinda turned off along a road that seemed to lead into endless bush. The car creaked and clattered along the potholed road.

After twenty minutes they came to a village made up of white mud huts. There were also some larger buildings, all of them clustered around an open stretch of sand. Lucinda parked the car in the shadow of a tree and switched off the engine.

'This is it. Christian Holloway's village.'

*I'm close to Henrik. He was here only a couple of months ago.*

'Henrik said that visitors were always welcome,' Lucinda said. '*Benevolence should not be kept secret.*'

'Is that what he said?'

'I think he had heard Holloway or one of his helpers use those words.'

'Who is this Holloway exactly?'

'According to Henrik he's a very rich man. He wasn't sure, but he thought Holloway had made his money from various technical patents that have made it easier to search for oil under the seabed. He's rich and extremely shy.'

'That hardly sounds like the kind of man who is starting to devote his life to people suffering from Aids.'

'Why not? I've made a clean break with the life I used to lead. I know a lot of others who have done the same thing.'

Lucinda closed the conversation by getting out of the car. Louise stayed put. Heat and sweat were making her feel sticky all over. But eventually she got out and stood beside Lucinda. The place seemed to be enveloped by an oppressive silence. Louise shuddered despite the heat. She was feeling increasingly uncomfortable. Although there was no sign of any people, she felt as if she were being watched.

Lucinda pointed to a pond surrounded by a fence.

'Henrik spoke about that pond, and the old crocodile.'

They went closer. The pond was full of slow-moving slimy water. On the muddy bank was a large crocodile. Both Lucinda and Louise gave a start. It was at least four metres long. The remains of a blood-soaked rabbit or monkey were hanging from the beast's jaws.

'Henrik said it was over seventy years old. Christian Holloway maintained it was their guardian angel.'

'A crocodile with white wings?'

'There have been crocodiles on the earth for 200 million years. Crocodiles scare us because of their ferocity. But nobody can deny them the right to exist, nor can anybody ignore their fantastic ability to survive.'

Louise shook her head.

'I still don't know what he meant. I'd like to ask him in person. Is he here?'

'I don't know. Henrik said that Holloway seldom put in an appearance. He was always surrounded by darkness.'

'Is that what Henrik said? *Surrounded by darkness?*'

'Yes. I remember his words clearly.'

A door opened in one of the large buildings. A white woman in light-coloured hospital uniform came out and walked towards them. Louise noticed that she was barefoot. Her hair was cut short, she was thin and her face full of freckles. She seemed to be about the same age as Henrik.

'Welcome,' she said in bad Portuguese.

Louise replied in English.

The girl changed languages immediately and introduced herself as Laura.

Three Ls, Louise thought. Lucinda and me and now a Laura.

'My son, Henrik Cantor, worked here,' she said. 'Do you remember him?'

'I only got here from the USA a month ago.'

'He said that you allowed visitors.'

'Everybody is welcome. I'll show you round. Just let me warn you that Aids is not a pretty illness. Not only does it kill people and ruin their appearance, it also creates horror that can be difficult to cope with.'

Lucinda and Louise exchanged looks.

'I can tolerate the sight of blood and frightened people,' said Lucinda. 'Can you?'

'I was one of the first to arrive at the scene of a road accident. There was blood everywhere, one person had had his nose cut off and blood was pouring out. I coped with that. Or at least, I managed to block out the horror.'

Laura led them out of the bright sunshine and into the buildings and huts. It seemed to Louise that she was entering a church-like darkness in which the small windows helped to create a strange sort of mystery. *Christian Holloway was a man surrounded by darkness.* In the huts they were hit by the stifling smell of urine and excrement: patients were lying about on stretchers and raffia mats on the ground. Louise had trouble in making out faces. All she registered was glinting eyes, groans and the smell. Relief came only during the few moments they emerged into the bright sunshine on their way to the next building. It was like sinking down through the centuries and entering a room full of slaves waiting to be transported. She whispered a question to Laura who told her that all the people hidden in the darkness were dying and would never see the sun again, they were beyond help, they were in the final stages where the only possible treatment was to ameliorate the pain. Lucinda kept to herself, at a distance from the other two. Laura said very little, merely led them in silence through the darkness and suffering. Louise thought of the classical cultures, not least that of Greece whose graves she spent much of her time excavating, and how they had clear ideas about dying and death, about the waiting rooms both before and after the departure from life. *Now I am wandering with Virgil and Dante through the kingdom of death.*

The journey felt endless. They went from building to building. Everywhere groans, rattles, whispers, words bubbling up from invisible cauldrons, desperate, resigned. It cut her to the quick when she heard a child crying, that was the worst of all, the invisible children who lay there dying.

She could just make out in the darkness young white people leaning over the patients, with glasses of water, tablets, whispering consoling words. Louise saw a very young girl with a shiny ring through her nose holding an emaciated hand in her own.

She tried to imagine Henrik in the middle of this hell. Perhaps she could just about make him out in there, and she had no doubt that he would have had the strength to assist these people.

When they left the last of the buildings and Laura had taken them to an air-conditioned room where there was a refrigerator with iced water, Louise asked if she could speak to somebody who had known Henrik. Laura left to see if she could find anybody.

Lucinda was still silent, declined to drink the water that was standing on the table. Suddenly she opened a door leading to another, inner room. She turned and looked at Louise.

The room was full of dead bodies. They were lying on the floor, on raffia mats, dirty sheets, an enormous number of dead people. Louise took a step back. Lucinda closed the door again.

'Why didn't she show us this room?' Lucinda asked.

'Why should she?'

Louise felt sick. At the same time she had the feeling that Lucinda knew about the room. She had opened that door before.

Laura came back with a man in his thirties. His face was spotty, his hand limp when he shook hands. His name was Wim, he came from England and remembered Henrik very well. Louise made up her mind on the spot not to say that Henrik was dead. She could not cope with any more dead bodies just now. Henrik did not belong here, the thought of him being in that room with all the other corpses was too horrific to bear.

'Were you close friends?' Louise asked.

'He kept himself to himself. A lot do that in order to cope.'

'Was there anybody especially close to him?'

'We are all good friends.'

*Good God. Answer my questions. You are not standing before the Good Lord, you are standing before Henrik's mother.*

'You can't have been working all the time?'

'Almost.'

'What do you remember about him?'

'He was nice.'

'Is that all?'

'He didn't say very much. I hardly noticed that he was Swedish.'

Wim seemed to realise at last that something must have happened. 'Why do you ask?'

'In the hope of receiving answers. But I see that there aren't any. Thank you for talking to me.'

Louise suddenly felt furious at the fact that this pale, limp person was still alive while Henrik was dead. That was an injustice that she would never be able to accept. God's mysterious ways were as crude as the cawing of a crow above her head.

She left the room, emerged into the crippling heat. Laura showed them the living quarters for those who had volunteered to help the dying patients, the dormitories, the neatly assembled mosquito nets, the communal dining-room that smelled of soft soap.

'Why have you come here?' Lucinda asked, turning to Laura.

'To help, to do some good. I couldn't accept my passivity.'

'Have you ever met Christian Holloway?'

'No.'

'Have you ever seen him, at least?'

'Only in a photograph.'

Laura pointed at one of the dining-room walls. There was a framed photograph hanging there. Louise went up to it and examined it. A man in profile, grey hair, narrow lips, pointed nose.

Something demanded her attention, but she could not decide what it was. She held her breath and contemplated the picture. A fly was buzzing in front of the glass.

'We must go back now,' said Lucinda. 'I don't want to have to drive through the dark.'

They thanked Laura and returned to the car. Laura waved to them, then went back inside. The place was empty once more. Lucinda started the engine and was about to drive off when Louise asked her to wait. She ran through the heat, back to the dining room.

She looked again at the photograph of Christian Holloway. Then the penny dropped.

Christian Holloway's profile.

One of the black silhouettes in Henrik's bag was a reproduction of the photograph she was now looking at.

# PART 3

# The Silhouettist

'You are also affected
when your neighbour's house is on fire.'

*Horace*

# CHAPTER 15

On the way back, during the short African sunset, Louise kept repeating the same thoughts to herself, like a mantra.

*Henrik has gone forever. But perhaps I can get close to what he felt, and what he was determined to achieve. In order to find out why he died I must find out what made him want to live.*

They stopped at the the kiosks near the bus stop. Fires were burning. Lucinda bought some water and a packet of biscuits. Only then did Louise realise that she was hungry.

'Can you imagine Henrik there?' Louise asked.

Lucinda's face was lit up by the glow from the fires.

'I didn't like it. I didn't the last time either. Something about it scares me.'

'Surely everything about it was horrific? All those dead bodies, all those people waiting to die?'

'That's not what I mean. There's something about the place that can't be seen or heard, but it's there even so. I tried to find out what Henrik had suddenly discovered, and was scared of.'

Louise looked attentively at Lucinda.

'He was frightened to death on the last occasions I saw him. I haven't told you that before. All the joy had suddenly vanished. Something that came from deep down had turned him as pale as a sheet. He became so silent. Before that he'd always been talkative. Sometimes he would go on and on and tire me out. But then came the silence, as if from nowhere, and then he disappeared without trace.'

'He must have said something. You made love together, you went to sleep and woke up together. Didn't he have any dreams? Did he really not say anything at all?'

'He slept badly towards the end, often woke up sweating, long before

189

dawn. I asked what he'd been dreaming about. "About the darkness," he said. "About all the things that are hidden." When I asked what he meant by that, he didn't reply. And when I persisted he would bellow and jump out of bed. He was stricken by fear asleep and awake.'

'*Darkness and all the things that are hidden*? Did he never speak about people?'

'He spoke about himself. He said that the most difficult thing of all was learning how to put up with yourself.'

'What did he mean by that?'

'I don't know.'

Lucinda looked away. Louise was confident that sooner or later she would find the right question to ask. But just now she was searching in vain for the appropriate key.

They returned to the car and continued their journey. Headlights were dazzling in the darkness. Louise called Aron's number. She heard it ringing, but there was no answer.

*I could have done with you here. You would have been able to see what I can't see.*

They stopped outside Lars Håkansson's house. The guards at the entrance stood up.

'I came here a few times,' Lucinda said, 'but only when he was drunk.'

'With Henrik?'

'Not Henrik. Lars Håkansson, the do-gooder from Sweden. He could only bring himself to take me home to his own bed when he was drunk. He was ashamed that the security guards would know what he was doing, afraid that somebody would see him. European men run after whores, but they do it in such a way that nobody notices. To prevent the guards from seeing that I was in the car I had to lie down and he would cover me with a blanket. Naturally, they saw me even so. Sometimes I used to stick my hand out from underneath the blanket and wave to them. The most remarkable thing was that all the friend-liness he usually paraded fell off him the moment we entered his house. He would carry on drinking, but never drank so much that he was incapable of having sex. That's the expression he always used, "having sex". I think it turned him on to keep any emotions at bay. What was going to happen would be crude and clinical, a piece of meat was going to be cut up. I had to get undressed and pretend that I didn't know he was there, that he was merely a peeping Tom. But then another game started. I had to take off all his clothes but not his underpants. Then I had to take his cock in my mouth while he still had his underpants on. Then he would come into me from behind. Afterwards it was one big rush, I got my money, he threw me out and I didn't need to be Julieta any more. And he didn't care if the guards saw me or not.'

'Why are you telling me this?'

'So that you know who I am.'

'Or who Lars Håkansson is?'

Lucinda nodded.

'I must go to work. I'm late already.'

Lucinda kissed her quickly on the cheek. Louise got out of the car and the guards opened the squeaky gate.

When she entered the house she found Håkansson sitting waiting for her.

'I got worried when you didn't appear and hadn't left a message.'

'I ought to have thought of that.'

'Have you eaten? I've saved some dinner.'

She went with him to the kitchen. He dished up some food and poured her a glass of wine. Lucinda's story was echoing eerily inside her head.

'I've been to visit Christian Holloway's village for sick people near a town whose name I can't pronounce.'

'Xai-Xai. Think Shy-Shy. So you've been to one of *the missions*? That's what Christian Holloway calls them, even though he doesn't have any religious beliefs.'

'Who is he?'

'My colleagues and I often wonder if he really exists, or if he's just some kind of an elusive phantom. Nobody knows very much about him. Apart from the fact that he holds an American passport and has an inconceivably vast fortune that he's now pouring over Aids victims in this country.

'Only in Mozambique?'

'In Malawi and Zambia as well. He's said to have two of his *missions* near Lilongwe, and another one or possibly more than one up in Zambia, near the border with Angola. Rumour has it that Holloway once went on a pilgrimage to the sources of the River Zambezi. It starts off as a trickle in the Angolan mountains before it becomes a stream and eventually a river. They say he put his foot over the hole where the trickle of water comes out of the ground, and thereby stopped the flow of the mighty River Zambezi.'

'Why would anybody want to do that?'

'It's not impossible to combine charitable visions with megalomania. Perhaps also with even worse things.'

'Who spreads stories like that?'

'It's probably the same as with the river. A few drops trickle out, then more and more until it becomes a rumour that can't be stopped. But the source remains unknown.'

He offered her more food, but she declined. Nor did she have any more wine.

'What did you mean when you said *even worse things*?'

'It's a well-known fact that many a crime hides behind a large fortune. You only need to look around Africa. Corrupt tyrants sweating among their wealth in the middle of the most catastrophic poverty. Even Christian Holloway seems not to be as pure as the driven snow. Oxfam made an investigation into him and his activities a year or so ago. Oxfam is a superb organisation that uses its limited resources to bring great bene-fits to the poor people of this world. When Holloway was a young man everything was very clear and transparent. Everything he undertook was clear and could be checked. There were no stains, no grey areas. He was the only son among lots of daughters in a family that was one of the biggest producer of eggs in the USA. He had a colossal fortune behind him based not only on eggs but also various other products such as wheelchairs and perfumes. He was bright, and was awarded a first-class degree by Harvard University. He had a doctorate before his twenty-fifth birthday. Then he started experimenting with advanced oil pumps that he patented and sold. Up to that point, everything is clear. Then Christian Holloway vanishes. It was cleverly done, because nobody seems to have noticed. Not even the press, usually so good at spotting such things, started to ask questions.'

'What happened?' Louise asked.

'He reappeared, three years later. It was only then that anybody noticed he'd been missing. He claimed to have been travelling around the world, and realised that he felt the need to change his life dramatically. He was going to create *missions*.'

'How do you know all this?'

'Part of my job is to know about people who turn up in poor countries with ambitious plans. In all probability they will eventually come knocking at the door of aid organisations, asking for money they once claimed to possess, but might have exaggerated slightly. Or we might find ourselves standing in the middle of ruined enterprises and having to pick up the pieces after people who came here to swindle the poor and line their own pockets.'

'But surely Holloway was rich from the very start?'

'It's hard to get insight into the lives of wealthy men. They have the necessary resources to create sophisticated smokescreens. You can never be certain if there really is anything inside the shell, if the ample resources they claim to have in fact conceal imminent bankruptcy. It happens every day. Gigantic oil companies or concerns such as Enron suddenly collapse, as if a series of invisible explosions has taken place. Nobody knows what's about to happen apart from those most deeply involved. Either they run away, hang themselves, or they just sit there apathetically and wait for the handcuffs to be clipped on. There was a lot of speculation when Holloway suddenly decided to become a Good Man and help those afflicted with Aids. There were millions of egg-laying hens clucking away in Christian Holloway's background, but there were also rumours, as usual.'

'Saying what?'

'I assume you are who you say you are. Henrik's grieving mother, and not somebody else?'

'What else could I be?'

'An investigative journalist, for instance. I've learned to prefer the journalists who bury things others try to dig up.'

'Are you suggesting that the truth should be suppressed?'

'Perhaps rather that lies shouldn't always be exposed for what they are.'

'And what have you heard about Christian Holloway?'

'Things you should never talk about openly. Even a whisper can sometimes have the same effect as a shout. There are things I know that mean I would be dead within twenty-four hours if I made them public. In a world where a human life is worth no more than a few packets of cigarettes, you have to be careful.'

Lars Håkansson recharged his glass. Louise shook her head when he held out the bottle of South African red wine.

'Henrik surprised me many times. One of the first occasions was when he tried to establish how much a human life was actually worth. He got fed up with me and my friends, thought we spoke in far too generalised terms about the value of a human life. He set out to pin down the real price in the current market. I've no idea how he went about it. He found it easy to make friends. He must have ventured into circles he shouldn't really have had anything to do with. Illegal bars, dark corners, of which there are so many in this city. But that's where you find the people who trade in death. He told me that for thirty American dollars, you could hire somebody who was prepared to kill anybody you cared to name, without asking why.'

'Thirty dollars?'

'May be forty dollars today. But no more. Henrik could never get over that. I asked him why he'd bothered to find out. *It shouldn't be brushed under the carpet*, was all he would say.'

He broke off, as if he had already said too much. Louise waited for what was coming next, but didn't.

'I suspect there is more you could tell me.'

Håkansson screwed up his eyes and looked hard at her. His eyes were red and shiny. He was tipsy.

'You should be aware that in a country like Mozambique people are always talking about the greatest of all dreams. The modern version of King Solomon's Mines. Every day people are lowered down into mines with lanterns in their hands. What do they find? Most probably nothing. They come back to the surface, freezing cold, bitter, furious over the fact that the dream has collapsed. The next day they allow themselves to be lowered down again.'

'I don't understand what you're getting at. What is it that they don't find?'

'The cures.'

'The cures?'

'The remedies. Medicines. Rumour has it that Christian Holloway has secret laboratories where researchers from all over the world are looking for the new penicillin, the cure for Aids. That's what they're hoping to find in the new version of Solomon's Mines. Who cares about precious stones when you can search instead for a cure for the insignificant, weak virus that's well on its way to wiping out the whole of this continent?'

'Where are these laboratories of his?'

'Nobody knows, they don't even know if the accusation is true. At the moment Holloway is merely a Good Man investing his money in helping the people nobody else cares about.'

'Did Henrik know about this?'

'Of course not.'

'Did he suspect it?'

'It's often very difficult to know for certain what people think. I don't base judgements on guesses.'

'But did you tell him what you've just told me?'

'No, we never spoke about that. Henrik might well have looked for information about Christian Holloway on the Internet. Henrik used to use my computer. If you'd like to borrow it, be my guest. It's always best to look for oneself.'

Louise was convinced that the man opposite her was lying. He had told Henrik. Why was he denying it?

She felt a sudden hatred of him, his self-assurance, his red eyes and bloated face. Did he humiliate the whole of the Third World in the same way as he trampled all over Lucinda? The man who chased women with his diplomatic passport in his pocket?

She emptied her glass and stood up.

'I need to get some sleep.'

'If you like I can show you round town tomorrow. We can drive to the beach and have a decent lunch, then continue our conversation.'

'Let's decide on that tomorrow. By the way, should I be taking something to avoid catching malaria?'

'You should have started on that a week ago.'

'A week ago I didn't know I would be here. What do you take?'

'Nothing at all. I've had my attacks, I've had malaria parasites in my blood for over twenty years. There wouldn't be much point in my starting to take preventative medicine now. But I'm very careful to make sure that I always sleep under a mosquito net.'

She paused in the doorway.

'Did Henrik ever speak to you about Kennedy?'

'The president? Or his wife? John F or Jackie?'

'About his brain that disappeared?'

'I didn't know that. That his brain had disappeared.'

'He never mentioned it?'

'Never. That's something I would have remembered. I remember that November day in 1963. I was a university student in Uppsala. A rainy day, and deadly boring lectures on law. And then the news broke. Details emerged bit by bit from the wireless, then everything went strangely quiet. What do you remember?'

'Very little. My father frowned and was even quieter than usual. That's about all.'


She took a shower, then settled down in bed and lowered the mosquito net. The air conditioning hummed away, the room was dark. She thought she heard his footsteps on the stairs, and shortly afterwards the corridor light went out. The patch of light under the door disappeared. She listened into the darkness.

She went over in her mind everything that had happened that day. The hellish walk through the dark rooms full of dying people. Everything she had heard about Christian Holloway, the clean exterior and the dirty contents. What had Henrik seen that produced such a change in him? Something that had been hidden was revealed. She tried to link the loose ends together, but failed.

She fell asleep but woke up with a start. Everything was very quiet. Too quiet. She opened her eyes in the darkness. It took her a few seconds to realise that the air conditioning had stopped. She fumbled for the bedside lamp. Nothing. There must be a power cut, she thought. Somewhere in the distance she heard a generator whirr into life. Down at street level somebody laughed, perhaps one of the security guards. She got out of bed and walked over to the window. The street lights had gone out as well. The only light came from the fire the guards had lit. She could just make out their faces.

She was scared. The dark frightened her. With no torch or candle for comfort, Louise got back into bed.

*Henrik had been afraid of the dark when he was little. Aron was always afraid of the night. He couldn't sleep without a light.*

The electricity returned. The air conditioning started to whine. She switched on her bedside lamp and settled down to sleep again. But she started thinking about the conversation with Håkansson in the kitchen. Why would he have lied about not having said anything to Henrik? She could think of no plausible explanation.

She recalled his words: *If you'd like to borrow it, be my guest.* Henrik had sat at that computer. Perhaps she would be able to find some trace of him?

Suddenly she was wide awake again. She got out of bed, dressed quickly and opened the door to the corridor. She stood completely still until her eyes had grown used to the light. The door to Lars Håkansson's bedroom was closed. The study was at the other end of the corridor, overlooking the garden. She groped her way to the door that was standing ajar, closed it and located the light switch. She sat down at the desk and switched on the computer. A flashing message told her that the computer had not been switched off properly. Presumably it had been in sleep mode when the electricity supply was interrupted. She opened an Internet link and typed Holloway into a search engine. There were many hits, including the addresses of a chain of restaur-ants, the Holloway Inn in Canada and a little airline in Mexico,

Holloway-Air. But Christian Holloway's missions were there as well. She was just about to open the link when a flashing light indicated an incoming email message. She had no intention of examining Håkansson's correspondence, but perhaps Henrik might have left traces on Håkansson's email.

Håkansson had not used a password to prevent others from gaining access to his emails. She immediately found two messages sent by Henrik. Her heart started beating faster. The first had been sent four months ago, the other just before Henrik must have left Maputo for the last time.

She opened the first message. It had been sent to Nazrin.

First I scratch my fingernail over the hard surface of the wall, but it makes no impression. Then I take a piece of stone and scrape the wall with that. It only makes a faint mark, but what I have done is there, no matter what. So I can continue to scratch and scrape and make the impression I've made on the wall deeper and deeper until it falls down. That's the way I think about my life here. I'm in Africa, it's very hot, I lie awake at night, naked and sweaty because I can't put up with the buzzing of the air conditioning. I think the main point of my life is that I shall not give in until the walls I want to pull down really do fall. Henrik.

She read the email again.

The second one had been sent to himself at his own Hotmail address.

I'm writing this as dawn starts to break, when the cicadas have fallen silent and the cocks have started to crow, despite the fact that I'm living at the very heart of the city. Soon I must write to Aron and tell him that I'm going to break off all contact with him unless he accepts his responsibilities and becomes a father to me. Becomes a man I can associate with, feel devotion to, see myself in. If he does that I shall tell him about the remarkable man I still haven't met in person, Christian Holloway, who has shown that, despite everything, there are examples of goodness

198

in this world. I am writing these lines in Lars Håkansson's house, on his computer, and I can't imagine that I could have asked for anything more out of life than it is giving me at the moment. I shall soon be going back to the village with all those sick people, and once again I shall feel that I am doing something useful. Henrik, to myself.

Louise frowned and shook her head. She read the letter again, slowly. There was something that did not add up. Henrik writing a letter to himself need not be of any significance. She had also done that when she was his age. She had even posted letters to herself. There was something else that worried her.

She read it again. Then the penny dropped. It was the language used, the way the letter was constructed. Henrik never wrote like that. He wrote in a straightforward fashion. He would not use a word like 'devotion'. That was not him speaking, it was not a word used by his generation.

She shut down the computer, switched off the light and opened the door to the corridor. Just before the computer screen went dead, it flared up for a few seconds. In the light it gave off she thought she could see the handle of the door to Håkansson's bedroom move slowly. The light went out, the corridor was dark. Håkansson must have been out in the corridor and returned quickly to his room when he heard that she had switched off the computer.

She felt a brief moment of panic. Should she get out of here, leave the house in the middle of the night? But she had nowhere she could go to. She went back to her room and placed a chair behind the door in such a way that nobody would be able to enter. Then she went back to bed, switched off the air conditioning but left the bedside lamp on.

A solitary mosquito was dancing outside the white net. She listened for sounds, her heart pounding. Was that his footsteps she could hear? Was he listening outside her door?

She tried to think completely calmly. Why had Håkansson written a letter in Henrik's name and kept it on his computer. There was no answer, only a creeping sense of unreality. It was like entering Henrik's flat in Stockholm again and finding him dead.

I'm scared, she thought. I'm surrounded by something that frightened Henrik, an invisible but dangerous membrane that enveloped him as well.

The night was stiflingly hot and damp. She could hear a thunderstorm in the distance. It drifted away in what she imagined was the direction of Swaziland's distant mountains.

# CHAPTER 16

She lay awake until dawn. She could no longer remember how many sleepless nights she had endured since Henrik died. Her existence now was characterised by a permanent lack of sleep. Only when the pale morning light seeped through the curtains and she heard Celina talking to one of the security guards who was getting washed under the tap in the garden did she feel sufficiently calm to doze off.

She was woken up by a dog barking. She had slept for three hours, it was nine o'clock. She stayed in bed, listening to Celina or Graça sweeping the corridor floor. She was no longer afraid; instead she felt helpless anger at having been insulted. Did Lars Håkansson really believe that she was incapable of seeing through what he had written in Henrik's name? Why had he done it?

She now thought she no longer needed to be considerate towards him. He had intruded brutally into her life, he had lied and had planted a forged letter in his computer. Moreover, he had scared her and robbed her of sleep. Now she would ransack his computer, his cupboards and his drawers to find out if there was anything Henrik really had left behind. Not least, she wanted to know why Henrik had trusted Håkansson.

By the time she went to the kitchen she found that Graça had made breakfast for her. Louise felt embarrassed at being served by this old lady who had severe pains in both her back and her hands. Graça's smile was made by a mouth almost totally bereft of teeth, and her Portuguese, mixed with a few English words, was almost incomprehensible. Graça fell silent when Celina joined them. Celina asked if it was convenient for her to clean Louise's room.

'I can make the bed myself.'

Celina laughed hollowly and shook her head. When Celina left the room, Louise followed her.

'I'm used to making my own bed.'

'Not here. That's my job.'

'Are you happy here?'

'Yes.'

'How much are you paid per month for the work you do here?'

Celina hesitated and wondered if she ought to reply. But Louise was white, she was her superior even if she was only a guest.

'I get fifty dollars a month, and a similar amount in Mozambique meticais.'

Louise did the sums in her head. Seven hundred kronor per month. Was that a lot or a little? What was its purchasing power? She asked about the price of cooking oil and rice and bread, and was surprised by Celina's answers.

'How many children do you have?'

'Six.'

'And your husband?'

'I suppose he's in South Africa, working in the mines.'

'Suppose?'

'I haven't heard from him for two years.'

'Do you love him?'

Celina looked at her in astonishment.

'He's the father of my children.'

Louise regretted asking that question when she saw how upset Celina was.

She followed her upstairs and went to Håkansson's study. The heat was already oppressive. She switched on the air conditioning and sat still until she could feel it becoming cooler.

Somebody had been in the room since she left it. But it could not have been Celina or Graça, the floor had not been swept this morning. And the chair in front of the computer was not tucked under the desk. But it had been when she left it.

*That was one of King Artur's most important commandments from her childhood. When you had finished eating, you should always tuck your chair back under the table before leaving the room.*

She looked around the study. Shelves with files, official documents, reports, presentations. Several shelves containing documents from the World Bank. She selected a file at random: 'Strategy for Sub-Saharan Development of Water Resources 1997'. She replaced it after noting that it had hardly been opened or read. Several shelves were stacked with journals in Swedish, English and Portuguese, the rest were packed with books. Håkansson's library was disorganised, haphazard. Well-thumbed editions of Agatha Christie stood alongside factual reports and vast numbers of books on Africa. She found tomes on the most dangerous snakes in Africa and Australasia, well-tried recipes for traditional Swedish dishes, and a collection of faded sepia pornographic photographs from the middle of the nineteenth century. In one of them, dated 1856, two girls sat on a wooden bench with carrots inserted between their legs.

She replaced the book and recalled stories about chefs who spat or peed onto plates before they were placed before aristocratic diners. *If only I could vomit onto his hard drive. Every time he switched on he would smell something unpleasant without realising what it was.*

An envelope from a Swedish bank was sticking out from between two books on one of the shelves. It had been opened. She took out the contents and found that it was a confirmation of payment of Håkansson's monthly wages. On the basis of her current wage, it would take Celina nearly four years to earn as much as Håkansson was paid per month. How was it possible to build bridges over a gulf that wide? How could a man like Lars Håkansson even begin to understand the life that Celina lived?

Louise noticed that in her mind she was conversing with Artur. She raised her voice because his hearing was defective. After a while she changed her choice of discussion partner to Aron. They were sitting at the table where the red parrots used to assemble and eat bread-crumbs. But Aron was on edge, he did not want to listen. In the end she found herself talking to Henrik. He was near by. She had tears in her eyes, closed them, and imagined that when she opened them again, he would be sitting next to her. But, of course, she was alone in the room. She drew a curtain in order to keep out the sunlight. Down in the street she could hear dogs barking, security guards laughing. All this laughter, she thought. I noticed it the day I landed here. Why do poor people laugh so much more than somebody like me? She asked the question of Artur, Aron and Henrik in turn. But none of her three knights answered, they were all silent.

She switched on the computer, determined to erase Henrik's two messages. She also wrote a message to Lars Håkansson in which she had Julieta speaking Swedish and telling him what she thought of him. Was he not somebody posted to Africa to help the poor?

Then she tried systematically to open various files on the computer, but met barriers wherever she turned. Håkansson's computer was now riddled with reinforced doors. She was also convinced that she was leaving a trail behind her. He would be able to follow all her clicks, and her attempts to break open the doors. Wherever she turned she was confronted by a raised hand that demanded a password. She tried all the obvious ones at random: his name spelled correctly, his name spelled backwards, various possible abbreviations, Needless to say, no doors opened. All she succeeded in doing was to leave evidence of her own failed attempts to hack into the computer.


Louise jumped when Celina suddenly asked her if she wanted tea.

'I didn't hear you,' Louise said. 'How can you move so quietly?'

'Senhor doesn't like noise,' explained Celina. 'He likes a silence that doesn't really exist here in Africa. But he creates it himself. He wants Graça and me to move silently, barefoot.'

She declined the tea. Celina left on her soundless feet. Louise stared at the computer screen that stubbornly refused to open its doors. Underground tunnels, she thought, with no lights, no maps. I can't get to him.

She was about to switch off when she started to think again about Henrik and his obsession with Kennedy's brain. What was the significance? Did Henrik seriously believe it would be possible to find imprints of thoughts, of memories, of what other people had said to the world's most powerful man before a rifle bullet made his head explode? Were there already instruments in advanced military laboratories to extract material from dead tissue, just as technicians can retrieve data from emptied hard drives?

Her thoughts came to a stop in mid-stride. Had Henrik found something he had been intending to look for? Or had he stumbled upon something by chance?

Working at the computer had made her hot and sweaty, even though the air conditioning was switched on. Celina had cleaned Louise's room and taken away her dirty linen. She changed into cotton underwear. As she was changing she heard Celina talking to somebody downstairs. Could it be Håkansson who had come back home? Celina came up the stairs.

'You have a visitor. The same person as yesterday.'

Lucinda was tired. Celina had given her a glass of water.

'I didn't get home last night. A group of Italian navvies occupied the Malocura. For once the bar was able to live up to its name. They drank vast amounts and didn't stagger away until dawn.'

'What does "Malocura" mean?'

'It means "madness". The bar was started by a woman called Dolores Abreu. It must have been in the early 1960s, before I was even born. She was big and fat, one of the powerful whores of those days who made sure that her professional duties never interfered with her family life. Dolores was married to a considerate little man called Nathaniel. He played the trumpet and is said to have been one of the creators of the popular dance called "marrabenta" here in Maputo, in the 1950s. Dolores had regular customers from Johannesburg and Pretoria. It was during the golden age of hypocrisy. White South African men were not allowed to buy black prostitutes because of the race laws. So they had to take to their cars or the train and come here to get a taste of black pussy.'

Lucinda paused and looked at Louise with a smile.

'I hope you'll excuse my language.'

'A woman's sex is called "pussy" in many languages. I might have been shocked when I was young, but not nowadays.'

'Dolores was thrifty and saved a lot of money – not really what you might call a fortune, but enough to invest in this bar. They say it was her husband who invented the name. He thought she would lose all her money in this hopeless venture, but it went well.'

'Where is she now?'

'She's in the cemetery at Lhanguene with Nathaniel. Their children inherited the bar, started squabbling from day one, and sold it to a Chinese doctor who lost it through some complicated loan transaction to a Portuguese fabric trader. A few years ago it was bought by the daughter of our Finance Minister. But she's never actually been there. That would be beneath her dignity. She spends most of her time buying expensive clothes in Paris. What's the name of the poshest brand?'

'Dior?'

'That's it, Dior. Her two little daughters are said to wear Dior dresses. Meanwhile the country starves. She sends one of her underlings to the bar every other day, to collect the cash.'

Lucinda shouted for Celina, who brought her some more water.

'I came here because I had an idea last night. When the Italians were close to legless, and started groping me I went outside for a cigarette. I looked up at the stars. Then I remembered that Henrik once said that the starry sky over Inhaca was just as clear as the one he used to see up in the north of Sweden.'

'Where?'

'Inhaca. An island in the Indian Ocean. He often used to talk about it. Perhaps he'd been there a few times. The island seemed to mean something special to him. I suddenly remembered something I think might be important. He said: *I can always hide away on Inhaca*. Those were his exact words. Sometimes he had prepared what he was going to say very carefully. That was one of those moments.'

'What did he do on Inhaca?'

'I don't know. People go there to swim, walk along the beaches, go diving, fishing, or to get drunk at the hotel.'

'Henrik was too impatient to lead that sort of life.'

'Exactly. That's why I think there was something else that attracted him to the place.'

'Do you think he was looking for somewhere to hide?'

'I think he met somebody there.'

'What kind of people live on the island?'

'Mainly farmers and fishermen. There's a marine biology research station that belongs to Mondlane University. A few shops and the hotel. That's all. Apart from masses of snakes, they say. Inhaca is paradise for snakes.'

'Henrik hated snakes. But on the other hand he was fascinated by spiders. Once when he was a child he ate one.'

Lucinda did not seem to hear what Louise said.

'He said something I never understood. He spoke of a painting and an artist who lived on the island. I can't remember properly.'

'Where were you when he told you this?'

'In a hotel bed. For once he hadn't been able to find an empty house where we could be. I can see him in front of me now. It was in the morning. He was standing by the window with his back to me. I could not see his face as he spoke.'

'What had you been talking about previously?'

'Nothing. We'd been asleep. When I opened my eyes I saw him there by the window.'

'Why did he speak about an artist?'

'I've no idea. Perhaps he'd dreamt something.'

'What happened afterwards?'

'Nothing. He came back to bed.'

'Was that the only time he spoke about this artist and a painting?'

'He never mentioned either again.'

'Are you sure?'

'Yes. But I realised afterwards that the meeting on Inhaca had been very important for him.'

'How can you be so sure?'

'His tone of voice as he stood there by the window. I think he really wanted to tell me something. But he couldn't bring himself to do it.'

'I must find that artist. How do you get to Inhaca? By boat?'

'That takes ages. It's best to fly. It will only take ten minutes.'

'Can you come with me?'

Lucinda shook her head.

'I have a family to look after. But I can help you to book a room at the hotel, and drive you to the airport. I think there are flights to Inhaca twice a day.'

Louise hesitated. It was too vague. But she had to follow up every possibility, she had no choice. She tried to imagine what Aron would have done. But Aron had nothing to say. He had vanished.

She gathered together a few clothes in a plastic bag, dug out her passport and some money, and she was ready to leave. She told Celina she'd be away until the next day, but did not mention where she was going to.

Lucinda drove her to the airport. The heat lay over Maputo like a stifling blanket.

'Ask for help at the hotel. There's a receptionist with a limp. He's called Zé. Pass on greetings from me, and he'll do what he can for you,' said Lucinda.

'Does he speak English?'

'Not very well. Never assume that he's understood what you say to him. Always ask again, to be on the safe side.'

When they reached the airport they were immediately besieged by boys who wanted to wash or guard the car. Lucinda declined their offers, patiently and without raising her voice.

Before long she had established that the next flight to Inhaca would leave in just over an hour, and after a quick telephone call she was able to inform Louise that a room had been booked for her.

'I took it for just the one night, but you can extend that if you want. It's not high season at the moment.'

'You mean it can get hotter than it is now?'

'It can get cooler. That's what those who can afford holidays are interested in.'

There was a café over the terminal. They drank soda water and ate a few sandwiches. Lucinda pointed out the rather battered-looking propeller-driven aeroplane that would take Louise to Inhaca.

'You mean I'm going to fly in that wreck?'

'The pilots used to fly fighter planes. They're very good.'

'How do you know? Are you acquainted with them?'

Lucinda laughed.

'I don't think you need to worry.'

Lucinda went with her to the check-in. Besides Louise there were two other passengers: an African woman with a baby in a carrier on her back, and a European man with a book in his hand.

'Perhaps this trip will be a complete waste of time.'

'At least you'll be completely safe on Inhaca. Nobody will mug you. You can walk along the beaches without feeling frightened.'

'I'll be back tomorrow.'

'Unless you decide to stay longer.'

'Why should I do that?'

'Who knows?'


The passengers walked to the aircraft through the extreme heat. Louise felt dizzy and was afraid of fainting. She took a deep breath and clung tightly onto the rail by the stairs. She sat as far back as possible. Diagonally in front of her was the man with the book.

Had she seen him before? His face was unfamiliar, but she seemed to recognise his back. Her fear came out of nowhere. She told herself that she was imagining things. She had no reason to be afraid of him. He was merely a delusion deep down in her brain.

The plane took off and circled round the white city before heading out to sea. Far down below she could see fishing boats with triangular sails, moving unsteadily through the waves. The aeroplane began its descent almost immediately, and five minutes after taking off its wheels thudded down on the runway at Inhaca. It was very short, and weeds were growing through cracks in the tarmac.

Louise emerged into the heat. She and the man with the book sat in a trailer and were towed by a tractor to their hotel. The woman with the child disappeared on foot into the tall grass. The man looked up from his book and smiled at her. She smiled back.

\*　\*　\*

When they arrived at the hotel she asked the young man in reception if his name was Zé.

'He's off today. He'll be back on duty tomorrow.'

She felt frustrated, but thrust any such thoughts aside. She had no desire to waste energy on getting annoyed.

She was shown to her room, emptied her plastic bag and stretched out on the bed. But lying there was not an attractive option. She walked down to the beach. It was low tide. A few decrepit-looking fishing boats lay on their sides on the sand like beached whales. She waded into the water, and gazed out into the heat haze where a group of men were pulling in nets.

She spent several hours paddling in the warm water. Her head was a vacuum.

As dusk fell she took dinner in the hotel dining room. She had fish, drank wine and was tipsy by the time she got back to her room. She lay on the bed and called Aron's mobile. The phone rang, but nobody answered. She texted him: *I could do with your help now.* It was like sending a message out into the void, without having the slightest idea if anybody would ever receive it.

She fell asleep, but woke up with a start. A sound had disturbed her. She listened into the darkness. Had the sound come from her? Had she been awakened by her own snoring? She switched on the bedside light. Eleven o'clock. She left the light on, adjusted the pillows, and established the fact that she was wide awake. She no longer felt the slightest bit drunk.

A memory forced its way into her head. It was a drawing Henrik had made when his teenage problems had been at their worst. He had been unapproachable, hidden away in an invisible cave to which she had no access. She had hated being a teenager, a time of freckles and complexes, of suicidal thoughts and a maudlin fury at the injustices of this world. Henrik was her opposite. He suppressed everything. But one day he had emerged from his cave and without saying a word had placed a drawing on the kitchen table. The whole page was coloured blood red, with a black shadow starting to spread from the bottom part of the drawing. That was all. He had never elaborated on the drawing, nor explained why he had given it to her. But she thought she had understood the point.

*Passion and despair, constantly at war, a duel to the bitter end, and when life was over, neither triumphant.*

She still had the drawing. It was in an old clothes chest in Artur's house.

Had Henrik ever sent drawings to Aron? That was another of the questions she would have liked to ask him.

The air conditioning hummed faintly, an insect with many legs crawled slowly and methodically, upside down, over the ceiling.

Once again she tried to think through everything that had happened. She retraced her steps, with all her senses on the alert, to see if she could now detect a context and an explanation for why Henrik was dead. She moved gingerly, and it seemed to her as if Aron was lying by her side. He was close to her now, as close as the period at the beginning of their marriage when they had been in love, and always been careful to ensure that they never strayed too far apart from each other.

It was to Aron that she tried to formulate her thoughts, as if in a conversation or a letter. If he was still alive he would gather that she was trying to understand, and he would help her to interpret what as yet she had only vague suspicions about.

*Henrik died in his bed in Stockholm with barbiturates in his body. He was wearing pyjamas, and the sheet had been pulled up to his chin. That was the end for Henrik. But did the story continue? Was his death nothing more than a link in a long chain? He discovered something here in Africa, among the dying at Xai-Xai. Something that made his brief joy, or rather the vanished depression as Nazrin put it, change into fear. But there was also an element of fury, a desire on Henrik's part to stir up a revolt. A revolt against what? Something inside himself? The thought that his ideas, his brain were being stolen or hidden away just like Kennedy's brain after the murder in Dallas? Or was he the one trying to force his way into somebody else's brain?*

Louise plodded on. It was like forcing one's way through the forests around Sveg, where fallen branches and saplings sometimes made it impossible to make progress.

*He had a flat in Barcelona that nobody knew about, and access to a lot of money. He collected articles about the blackmailing of people afflicted with Aids. He felt more and more frightened. Why was he frightened? Because he had realised too late that he had strayed into dangerous territory? Had he seen something he ought not to have seen? Had somebody noticed him, or managed to read his intentions?*

*Something was missing. Henrik was always on his own, despite having a lot of people around him: Nazrin, Lucinda, Nuno da Silva, his incomprehensible friendship with Lars Håkansson. But he is on his own even so. These people rarely occur in his notes, he hardly ever mentions them.*

*There must have been more people. Henrik was not a loner. Who were these other people? Were they in Barcelona or Africa? He often used to talk to me about the amazing electronic world that enabled people to create networks and alliances with people from all over the real world.*

She was not convinced, the ice was too thin, she kept on falling through. I'm too impatient. I speak before having listened properly. I must keep on searching for new fragments. There's still time to start piecing them together and to try and find a pattern.

She drank some water from a bottle she had taken with her from the restaurant. The insect on the ceiling was no longer there. She closed her eyes.


She was woken up by the telephone ringing. There was a flashing of lights and vibrations on her bedside table. She answered half asleep. There was a crackling noise from the static, somebody was listening. Then the connection was broken off.

It was shortly after midnight. She sat up. *Who had called her? The silence had no identity.* She could hear faint music coming from the hotel bar. She decided to go there. If she had a glass or two of wine she would be able to go back to sleep.

The bar was almost deserted. An elderly European man sat in a corner with a young African woman. Louise felt uncomfortable. She pictured the overweight man lying naked on top of the black woman who could hardly have been more than seventeen or eighteen years old. Was this the kind of thing Lucinda had been forced to endure? Had Henrik seen the same kind of thing that she was observing now?

She drank two glasses of wine without a pause, signed the bill and left the bar. The night breeze was mild. She passed the swimming pool and left the area illuminated by lights from the hotel windows. She had never seen a sky like the one that confronted her now. She thought she had eventually pinned down the Southern Cross. Aron had once described it as 'the saviour of seafarers in the southern hemisphere'. He was always surprising her with unsuspected knowledge. Henrik sometimes also took a whimsical interest in the unexpected. At the age of nine he had talked about running away from school to the wild horses of the Kirghistan steppes. But then decided to stay at home after all as he did not want to leave his mother on her own. Another time he had stated loud and clear that he wanted to go to sea and learn how to sail a boat all by himself. Not in order to sail round the world in record time nor to demonstrate that he could survive such a journey. His dream was to be alone on a boat for ten, perhaps twenty years without ever landing anywhere.

Her grief returned. Henrik never became a sailor, nor did he ever go looking for wild horses on the steppes of Kirghistan. But he was on the way to becoming a Good Man when somebody dressed him in pyjamas instead of a funeral shroud.

She was on the sands now. It was high tide, breakers were rolling in towards the shore. Darkness swallowed the contours of the beached fishing boats. She took off her sandals and walked to the water's edge. The heat took her back in her mind to Peloponnisos. She was overwhelmed by a tidal wave, a longing to return to her work in the dusty graves, to her colleagues, the eager but careless students, her Greek friends. She felt the urge to stand in the shadows outside Mitsos's house and smoke one of her nocturnal cigarettes while the dogs barked and the gramophone churned out its melancholy Greek music.

A crab crawled over her foot. In the distance she could see the lights from Maputo. Once again Aron came to haunt her: *Light can travel long distances over dark water. Imagine light as a wanderer who could be fleeing from you, or coming closer and closer. In the light you discover both your friends and your enemies.*

Aron had said something more, but she couldn't remember what.

She held her breath. There was somebody there in the night, somebody watching her. She turned round, lights from the bar in the far distance puncturing the darkness. She was scared stiff, her heart was pounding.

She started screaming, shrieking into the dark until she saw torches coming from the hotel. When she was pinned down in the beam from one of them, she froze like an animal caught in headlights.

Two men had come to investigate, the very young man from reception and one of the bartenders. They asked why she had screamed: was she injured? Had she been bitten by a snake?

She merely shook her head, took the receptionist's torch and shone it round the beach. Nobody. But there had been somebody there. She had felt it.

They walked back to the hotel. The young man from reception accompanied her to her room. She lay down on the bed, prepared to lie awake all night. But she managed to fall asleep. The red parrots from Apollo Bay came flying into her dreams. There were masses of them, a huge flock, and their wingbeats were totally silent.

# CHAPTER 17

The sky was hidden behind damp mist when she went down to the dining room for breakfast. The man on duty in reception was somebody she had not seen before. She asked if he was Zé.

'José,' he said. 'Shortened to Zé.'

Louise mentioned Lucinda, and asked him if there was anybody on the island who painted pictures.

'That can only be Adelinho. Nobody else here on the island paints, nobody else orders parcels of paint from Maputo. Many years ago he used to mix his own paints, from roots, leaves and soil. They are remarkable pictures – dolphins, dancing girls, sometimes distorted faces that can make you feel sick.'

'Where does he live?'

'It's too far to walk, but Ricardo, who collected you from the airport, will drive you there for a small fee.'

'I'd like to pay a visit to Adelo.'

'Adelinho. Learn his name. He's become vain since his paintings have been in demand. I'll ask Ricardo to pick you up here an hour from now.'

'Half an hour will be long enough for my breakfast.'

'But not for Ricardo. He insists that his old jeep should be thoroughly cleaned before he can undertake a journey with a beautiful woman. He'll be waiting for you outside the entrance in an hour's time.'


Louise had her breakfast outside, at a table in the shade of a tree. In the swimming pool a man was swimming slowly, length after length. A shaggy dog came to lie down at her feet. *An African elkhound. A reminder of the dogs I used to play with as a child. Now I have a father who's just as hairy as you.*

The man who had been swimming in the pool clambered out. Louise discovered that one of his legs had been amputated at the knee. He hopped to a lounger, beside which lay an artificial leg. The waiter, who was barefoot, asked if Louise would like more coffee. He nodded at the man who had just left the pool.

'He swims every day, all year round. Even when it's cold.'

'Can it ever be cold in this country?'

The waiter looked worried.

'In July it can be five degrees at night. We all freeze then.'

'Minus five degrees?'

She regretted asking that question the moment she saw the waiter's expression.

He refilled her cup and brushed a few crumbs off the table. The dog immediately licked them up. The man on the lounger had finished strapping on his leg.

'Colonel Ricardo is a remarkable man. He's our chauffeur. He's taken part in many wars,' said the waiter. 'But nobody knows anything about him for certain. Some say that he got drunk and trespassed on the railway line and that's where he lost his leg. But you can never be completely sure. Colonel Ricardo is a one-off.'

'I've heard that he keeps his jeep very clean and tidy.'

The waiter leaned towards her and said confidentially: 'Colonel Ricardo is very keen on keeping himself clean and tidy. But he often gets complaints about his jeep being dirty.'

Louise signed the bill and watched the colonel walk away towards the hotel exit. Now that he was dressed she could see no sign that one of his legs was artificial.


He picked her up outside the hotel. Colonel Ricardo was about seventy. He was trim, sunburnt, and his grey hair was neatly combed. A European with more than a few drops of black blood in him, Louise thought. No doubt there's a fascinating story hidden within his family history. The colonel spoke English with a British accent.

'I gather Mrs Cantor would like to pay a visit to our famous

Raphael. He will appreciate that. He is especially pleased to receive female visitors.'

She sat in the front passenger seat. The colonel used his artificial foot on the accelerator. They drove along a dirt road that wound its way through the metre-high grass towards the southern part of the island. The colonel drove jerkily and seldom bothered to slow down when the road turned into a mudbath. Louise held on tightly with both hands to avoid being thrown out. The dashboard instruments either pointed to zero or vibrated around incomprehensible speeds and temperatures. It was like being in an armoured car.

After half an hour the colonel slowed down. They had reached a wooded part of the island. She could glimpse low cabins through the trees. Colonel Ricardo pointed.

'Our dear old Raphael lives over there. How long do you intend staying? When shall I collect you?'

'So you're not going to wait?'

'I'm too old to have time to wait. I'll come back here and fetch you in a few hours' time.'

Louise looked round but could see no sign of life.

'Are you sure he's at home?'

'Our dear old Raphael came to Inhaca at the end of the 1950s. He had fled from the country known in those days as the Belgian Congo. Since then he has never left the island, and hardly ever leaves his home.'

Louise got out of the jeep. Colonel Ricardo raised his cap and disappeared in a cloud of dust. The sound of the engine faded away. Louise was enveloped by remarkable tranquillity. No birds, no croaking frogs, not even any wind. She had a vague feeling of recognition, and then she realised that it was like being in the depths of a forest in northern Sweden, where both distance and sound can cease to exist.

Being surrounded by total silence is to experience severe loneliness. Those were Aron's words when they had been hiking in the Norwegian mountains. Early autumn, rusty brown colours, and she had begun to suspect that she was pregnant. They were walking in the Rjukan mountains. One evening they had pitched their tent by a mountain tarn.

Aron spoke about silence being able to convey extreme, almost unbearable loneliness. She had not paid much attention at the time, the thought that she might be pregnant had dominated her mind. But she could remember what he said.

A few goats were grazing and ignored her. She walked along the path to the huts hidden among the trees. There was a patch of open, sandy ground surrounded by a circle of huts. The embers of a dying fire were glowing. Still no sign of people. Then she noticed a pair of eyes observing her. Somebody was sitting on a veranda, only his head was visible. The man stood up and beckoned to her. She had never seen a man as black as that before. His skin was so black that it gave the impression of being dark blue. He stepped down from the veranda, a giant bare-chested man.

He spoke hesitantly, searching for words in English. His first question was if she could speak French.

'It flows more fluently over my tongue. I take it you don't speak Portuguese?'

'My French isn't very good either.'

'In that case we'll speak English. You are very welcome, Mrs Cantor. I like your name. Louise. It sounds like a sudden movement over the water, a reflection of the sun, a hint of turquoise.'

'How do you know my name? How did you know I was going to come?'

He smiled and led her to a chair on the veranda.

'On islands, only a fool tries to keep a secret.'

She sat down on the chair. He remained standing, and eyed her up and down.

'I boil all my water as I don't want my guests to suffer from stomach bugs. So it's not dangerous to drink anything I offer you. Or perhaps you would like a drop of Roman schnapps? A good friend of mine is Italian, Giuseppe Lenate. A friendly man who comes to visit me now and then. He seeks out the solitude that this island has to offer when he can't take any more of all the navvies he's responsible for, busy building roads on the mainland. He brings Roman schnapps with him. We both get so drunk that we pass out. Colonel Ricardo drives him to the airport, he flies back to Maputo and a month later he's back here again.'

'I don't drink schnapps.'

Adelinho the giant vanished into his dark little house. Louise thought about the Italian navvy. Was he one of the men who had spent the night in Lucinda's bar? Maputo was evidently a very small world.

Adelinho returned with two glasses of water.

'I take it you've come to see my paintings?'

On the spur of the moment Louise decided not to mention Henrik yet.

'I heard about your paintings from a woman I met in Maputo.'

'Does that woman have a name?'

Yet again she avoided giving a straight answer.

'Julieta.'

'I don't know anybody called that. A Mozambique woman, a black woman?'

Louise nodded.

'Who are you? Let me guess your nationality. Are you German?'

'Swedish.'

'One or two people from there have come to see me. Not many, and not often.'

It started raining. Louise had failed to notice that the morning mist had developed into cloud cover that had closed in on Inhaca. It was a serious rainstorm from the very first drop. Adelinho frowned as he eyed the veranda roof, and shook his head.

'One of these days the roof will collapse. The corrugated-iron sheets are rusting away, the beams are rotting. Africa has never been well disposed towards houses built to last.'

He stood up and beckoned her to follow him indoors. The house comprised just one large room. There was a bed, bookshelves, rows of paintings along the walls, a few carved chairs, wooden sculptures, carpets.

Adelinho started displaying paintings, standing them on the floor and leaning them against the table, the bed and the chairs. They were oil paintings on sheets of hardboard. The form and motifs expressed an enthusiastically naive style, giving the impression of having been painted by a child trying to reproduce reality. Dolphins, birds, women's faces, just as Zé had said.

She immediately classified Adelinho as the Dolphin Painter, somebody who could strike a chord with her father up in the forests of northern Sweden, and his carved gallery that was growing more extensive by the day. They were leaving dolphins and faces for future generations to cherish, but her father had artistic talent that the Dolphin Painter lacked.

'Is there anything you like?'

'The dolphins.'

'I'm a rotten painter, I don't have any talent. Don't think that I'm not aware of that. I can't even get the perspective right. But nobody can force me to stop painting.'

The rain was clattering down on the corrugated-iron roof. Neither of them spoke. After a while the rain eased off, and it became possible to talk again.

'The man who drove me here said that you came from Congo?'

'Ricardo? He always talks too much. But on this occasion he's right. I left the country when all hell broke loose. When that Swede by the name of Hammarskjöld was shot down over northern Zambia near Ndola – it was called Northern Rhodesia in those days – I was already here in Mozambique. It was absolute chaos. The Belgians were very brutal, they'd been cutting off our hands for several generations, but when we were about to become independent the conflict that broke out was just as brutal.'

'Why did you flee the country?'

'I had to. I was twenty years old. It was too early to die.'

'But you were politically involved even so? At that age?'

He eyed her up and down. The rain had plunged the room into semi-darkness. She sensed rather than saw his eyes.

'Who said I was politically involved? I was an ordinary young man with no education who captured chimpanzees and sold them to a Belgian laboratory. It was in the outskirts of the city known then as Leopoldville: now it's been renamed Kinshasa. There was something secretive about that gigantic building. It was off the beaten track, and surrounded by a high fence. Men and women in white coats worked there. Sometimes they wore masks. And they wanted chimpanzees. They paid well. My father had taught me how to capture apes alive. The white men thought I was good. One day I was offered a job inside the big building. They asked me if I was afraid of butchering animals, cutting up their meat, seeing blood. I was a trapper, a hunter, I could kill animals without blinking, and I got the job. I'll never forget how I felt, the first time I put on a white coat. It was like putting on a regal robe, or the leopard skin that African rulers often wear. That white coat signified that I had entered into a magic world of power and knowledge. I was young. I didn't realise that the white coat would soon become so drenched in blood.'

He paused and leaned forward on his chair.

'I'm an old man who talks far too much. I've had no company for several days. My wives live in a house of their own, they come and make my meals, but we don't talk as we have nothing more to say to one another. This silence makes me hungry. Just say if I'm boring you.'

'I'm not bored. Tell me more.'

'About when my coat was drenched in blood? There was a doctor there called Levansky. He took me to a big room where all the chimpanzees I and others had caught were kept in cages. He showed me how to cut the animals up and extract their livers and kidneys. The rest of the cadaver should be thrown away, it was of no value. He taught me how to write down in a book what I had done and when. Then he gave me a chimpanzee, I remember that it was a young one, screeching loudly for its mother. I can still hear that screech to this day. Dr Levansky was pleased with me. But I hated it. I couldn't understand why it had to be done in that way. It could well be said that I did not like the way in which my white coat became drenched in blood.

'I don't quite understand what you mean.'

'Is it so difficult? My father had taught me that you killed animals for food, or for their pelts, or to protect yourself, your livestock or your crops. Torture was not involved. If you tortured, the gods would strike you down. They would send out their invisible hounds who would hunt you down and gnaw all the flesh from your bones. I couldn't understand why I had to remove the liver and kidneys from an animal that was still alive. They would pull and yank at the straps holding them down on the table, and scream like human beings. I learned that animals and people sound just the same when they're being tortured.'

'Why was it necessary?'

'In order to make the special preparation the laboratory manufactured, the body parts had to be taken from living animals. They said I would lose my job if I mentioned what I did outside the laboratory. Dr Levansky said that people who wore the white coat always kept their secrets. Later I felt as if I'd been caught in a trap, as if I were one of the chimpanzees and the whole laboratory was my cage.'

The rain drummed more heavily against the corrugated-iron roof. A wind was getting up. They waited until the rain eased off again.

'A trap?'

'Yes, a trap. It didn't crash down onto my hand or my foot. It wound itself silently round my neck. I didn't notice anything at first. I grew accustomed to killing my screaming chimpanzees, I removed their body parts and placed them in buckets of ice and took them to the laboratory itself, where I was never allowed in. Some days none of the apes were to be killed. Then it was my job to see that they were in good condition, that none of them were sick. It was like visiting prisoners on death row and pretending everything was normal. But the days grew very long. I started exploring, even though I had no right to be anywhere except among the ape cages. One day, after a few months, I went down into the basement.'

Adelinho fell silent. The drumming of rain on the roof had almost ceased.

'What did you find there?'

'More chimpanzees. But with a difference in genetic material of less than 3 per cent. At the time I didn't know what genetic material was. But I do now. I've learned about it.'

'I don't understand. More apes?'

'Not in cages. On stretchers.'

'Dead apes?'

'People. But not dead. Not quite dead. I found myself in a room where they were crammed closely together. Children, old people, women, men. They were all ill. There was an awful stench in the room. I ran away. But I couldn't resist going back again later. Why were they lying there? It was then that I realised I'd landed in the worst trap a human being could possibly get caught in. A trap in which you are not supposed to see what you see, not to react to what you do. I went back to try to discover why sick people were being hidden in a basement room. As I got close I heard horrible screams coming from an adjacent room. I didn't know what to do. What was going on? I had never heard such screams in all my life. Then, suddenly, they stopped. There was the sound of a door closing. I hid underneath a table. I glimpsed white legs and white coats walking past. When they'd gone I went to the room where I'd heard the screams coming from. There was a dead person lying on a table. A woman, she must have been about twenty. She had been cut open in the same way as I cut my chimpanzees. I realised immediately that her liver and kidneys had been removed while she was still alive. I got out of there as fast as I could, and didn't return to the laboratory for a week. One day a man came with a letter from Dr Levansky, who threatened me with retribution if I didn't return. I didn't dare to stay away any longer. Dr Levansky wasn't angry, he was friendly, which confused me. He wondered why I'd stayed away so I told him I'd seen all the sick people and the woman who had been cut open while she was still alive. Dr Levansky explained that she had been anaesthetised and not felt any pain. But I had heard her. He was sitting there and lying through his teeth, his friendly attitude was not genuine. He told me that with the aid of these sick people, they were discovering new medicines. Everything that happened in the laboratory had to remain secret because there were so many people trying to get hold of these drugs. When I asked what illnesses they were trying to cure, and what the sick people were suffering from, he said that they all had the same sort of diseases, a fever caused by an infection in their stomachs. Again I knew he was lying. I had noticed when I was in the room full of stretchers that they all had different illnesses. I think they had been deliberately infected, poisoned. That they had been made ill in order to see if they could be cured. I think they were being used as chimpanzees.'

'What happened to you afterwards?'

'Nothing. Dr Levansky continued to be friendly. Even so, I knew that I was being kept under constant observation. I had seen something I ought not to have seen. Then a rumour spread to the effect that people living in the vicinity of Leopoldville were being kidnapped, and that they ended up in the laboratory. That was in 1957, when nobody really knew what was going to happen to the country. Without having planned it, I woke up one morning and just knew that I had to get away. I was sure that one day I would end up in that basement room myself, be tied down with leather straps on a table and be cut open while I was still alive. I fled. I went to South Africa first, and then here. But I know now that I was right. The laboratory used both chimpanzees and living human beings for their tests. There is only a 3 per cent difference in the genetic material of a chimpanzee and a human being. But even then, in the middle of the 1950s, they wanted to go one step further; they wanted to erase that 3 per cent.'

Adelinho paused. Gusts of wind tore at the roofing sheets. There was a smell of decay coming from the damp earth.

'I came here. For many years I worked at the little cottage hospital here. Now I have my field, my wives, my children. And I paint. But I've kept abreast of what is happening: my friend, the Cuban doctor, Raul, keeps all his medical journals for me. I read them, and I can see that even today, human beings are used in experiments. It happens in this country as well. A lot of people would deny that, of course. But I know what I know. Though I'm a simple man, I have educated myself.'

The rain clouds had moved on, the sunlight was stronger. Louise looked at Adelinho. She shuddered.

'Are you cold?'

'I was thinking about what you said.'

'Medicines are raw materials that can be just as valuable as rare metals or jewels. That's why there is no limit to what people are prepared to do, in the name of greed.'

'I want to know what you have heard.'

'I don't know any more than I've told you. But there are rumours.'

*He doesn't trust me. He's still afraid of that trap that was on the*

*point of capturing him, way back in the 1950s, when he was still a young*
*man.*

Adelinho stood up. He pulled a face when he stretched his legs.

'Age brings pains. Your blood hesitates to flow through your arteries, you suddenly find that your dreams are in black and white. Would you like to see some more paintings? I also paint people who come to visit me, just like the group photos I used to take in the old days. Am I right in guessing that you are a teacher?'

'I'm an archaeologist.'

'Do you find what you're looking for?'

'Sometimes. Sometimes I find things I didn't know I was looking for.'

She took a few paintings to the veranda door and examined them in the sunlight.

She found him immediately. His face, in the back row. It was not a very good likeness, but there was no doubt about it. It was Henrik. He had been here and had heard Adelinho's story. She continued examining the picture. Were there other faces here she recognised? Young people, Europeans, a few Asians. Young men, but also some of young women.

She put the painting back on the floor and tried to gather her thoughts. Discovering Henrik's face had been a shock.

'My son Henrik has been here. Do you remember him?'

She held the painting up for Adelinho and pointed. He screwed up his eyes, then nodded.

'I remember him. A friendly young man. How is he?'

'He's dead.'

She made up her mind. Here, on Inhaca, in the house of a man she did not know, she could allow herself to say what she really thought.

'He was murdered in his flat.'

'In Barcelona?'

Jealousy struck her once again. Why did everybody know more than she did? After all, she was his mother and had brought him up until he had weighed anchor and sailed off to lead his own life.

A thought suddenly struck her. He had always said he would protect her, no matter what happened. Is that what he was doing by not telling her about the little flat in Christ's Cul-de-sac?

'Nobody knows what happened. I'm trying to find out by retracing his footsteps.'

'And they've led you here?'

'Yes. You have painted his face, and I think you told him the same story as you've told me.'

'He asked me about it.'

'How could he know that you knew anything?'

'Rumours.'

'Somebody must have talked about you. And you in turn must have talked to somebody. Spreading rumours is a human art form that requires patience and daring.'

As he did not respond, she continued. She had no need to think up questions, they presented themselves.

'When did he come here?'

'Not all that long ago. I painted the picture shortly afterwards. Before the rains came, if I remember rightly.'

'How did he get here?'

'The same way as you. With the colonel in his jeep.'

'Was he alone?'

'He came alone.'

Was that true? Was there not another, invisible person by Henrik's side?

Adelinho seemed to understand why Louise had paused.

'He came alone. Why should I not tell you the truth about that? You don't honour the memory of the dead by lying at their graves.'

'How did he know where to come?'

'He'd heard from my friend Dr Raul. Raul is proud of his name. His father was also called Raul, and he was on board the ship, whatever it's called, that took Fidel and his friends to Cuba and started the freedom struggle.'

'*Granma.*'

He nodded.

'That was the boat. It was leaking and seemed likely to sink, the young men were stricken with seasickness, it must have been a distressing sight. But misleading. A few years later they had driven out Batista and the Americans. But they didn't say Americans, they said Yankees. *Yankees go home.* That became a war cry that echoed all round the world. Today our country bows before the Americans, but one of these days we'll force out the truth. About how they helped the Belgians and the Portuguese to grind us into the ground.'

'How had Henrik found Raul?'

'Dr Raul is not only a skilful gynaecologist but is much loved by our women because he treats them with great respect. He's also a fiery spirit who hates the big pharmaceutical companies and their research laboratories. Not all of them, not everywhere. Even in that world there is the brutal contrast between goodwill and greed. The battle is going on all the time. But Dr Raul maintains that greed is gaining ground. Every minute, every second, round-the-clock greed is on the march and pressing forward. In an age where millions and millions of dollars and meticais are allowed to run amok, always seeking out the greenest grass, greed is well on the way to achieving world hegemony. That's a difficult word I didn't know until I reached old age. And now greed is homing in on the little virus that is spreading all over the world like the plague. Nobody knows even now where it originated, even if one can assume that it was an ape virus that somehow managed to scale the mountain peaks of immunity and enter into humans. Not in order to destroy them, but to do the same as you and I want to do.'

'What's that?'

'To survive. That's all this weak little virus wants to do, nothing more. A virus is not a conscious being, it can hardly be blamed for not understanding the difference between life and death: it merely does what it's programmed to do. To survive, to create a new generation of viruses with the same aim: survival. Dr Raul says that, really, this little virus and the human race ought to stand on opposite banks of the river of life and wave to each other. The banners fluttering in the wind should be speaking the same language. Survival. But that's not what happens, the virus causes chaos like a driverless car on a busy road. Dr Raul says that this is because there is another virus. He calls it "The Greed virus, type 1". It spreads just as quickly and is just as deadly as the insidious disease. Dr Raul tries to whip up resistance to greed, to attack the virus that is infecting the bloodstream of an ever increasing number of people. He sends the people he trusts here to me. He wants them to know that there is 'A History of Cruelty'. People come here and I tell them how organs were being cut out of living people as long ago as the 1950s. People who were snatched from their homes, injected with various illnesses and then used as guinea pigs or monkeys. It didn't only happen under a sick political regime such as Hitler's. It happened after the war, and it's still happening today.'

'In Xai-Xai?'

'Nobody knows.'

'Can Henrik have been on to something?'

'I think so. I told him to be careful. There are people prepared to do absolutely anything in order to conceal the truth.'

'Did he ever talk to you about Kennedy?'

'The American president whose brain disappeared? He had read widely on the subject.'

'Did he explain why he was obsessed by that incident?'

'It wasn't the incident itself. Presidents have been assasinated before, and they'll be murdered again. Every American president is aware that a large number of invisible guns are aimed at him. Henrik wasn't interested in the brain as such. He wanted to know how and why it had happened. He was trying to understand how you go about concealing something. He was walking backwards in order to find out how you move forwards. If he could understand how you go about concealing something at the highest possible political level, he would be able to discover how to expose it.'

'I know that he saw something in Xai-Xai that changed him.'

'He never came back here even though he had promised to do so. Raul didn't know what had happened to him either.'

'He fled because he was afraid.'

'He could have written, he could have used the electronic magic we have access to now, in order to whisper something in Raul's ear.'

'He was murdered.'

It was now clear to both Louise and the man on the chair opposite her what that meant. There was no need to wonder any more. Louise felt that she was reaching a point where an explanation for Henrik's death might be found.

'He must have found out. He must also have realised that they knew that he knew, and so he fled.'

'Who is "they"?' Louise asked.

He shook his head.

'I don't know.'

'Xai-Xai. Christian Holloway?'

'I don't know.'

They could hear the sound of a vehicle approaching. Colonel Ricardo drove his jeep into the courtyard. Just as they were about to go onto the veranda, Adelinho placed his hand on Louise's shoulder.

'How many people know that you are Henrik's mother?'

'Here in Mozambique? Not many.'

'Perhaps it's best that it stays that way.'

'Are you warning me?'

'I don't think I need to.'

Colonel Ricardo sounded his horn aggressively. As they drove away she turned round to look at Adelinho standing on the veranda.

She missed him already because she suspected she would never see him again.


She flew back to Maputo soon after two in the afternoon, in the same aircraft with the same pilots. The passenger with the book was not around, but a young man was helped aboard. He was so weak that he could hardly stand up. Perhaps it was his mother and sister helping him. Although she could not be certain, she suspected that the man had Aids. He was not only infected by the virus: the illness was now full-blown and was syphoning his life away.

She was upset by the experience. If Henrik had lived, he might have ended up in a similar state himself. She would have supported him. But who would have supported her? She felt her grief building up.

When the plane took off, she hoped it would crash and allow her to escape into oblivion. But she could already see the turquoise water down below. She could not go backwards.

By the time the aircraft landed on the hot tarmac, she thought she knew. *It was in Xai-Xai that Henrik had been most tangible. That is where she had felt his presence.* She did not even bother to go to Lars Håkansson's house to change her clothes. Nor did she phone Lucinda. Just now she needed to be alone. She went to one of the car hire offices at the airport, signed a contract and was told that the car would be ready for her in half an hour. If she left Maputo by three o'clock, she should reach Xai-Xai before dark. While she was waiting she thumbed through the telephone directory. She found several doctors by the name of Raul, but could not tell which was the right one as none of them was listed as a gynaecologist.

On the way to Xai-Xai she very nearly ran over a goat that suddenly appeared in front of the car. She swerved violently and almost lost control. At the last moment one of the rear wheels got a grip on a rut in the tarmac and kept the car on the road. She was forced to stop and get her breath back.

Death had almost claimed her.

She found her way to the turn-off leading to the beach in Xai-Xai and checked into the hotel. She was given a room on the first floor. She spent ages with the shower before persuading it to produce a jet of water. All her clothes smelled of sweat. She went to the beach and bought a *capulana*, a length of fabric that African women wrapped round themselves. Then she walked along the sand and thought over what the man in the rain, the Dolphin Painter, had said.

The sun vanished. The shadows lengthened. She went back to the hotel and ate in the dining room. An albino sat in a corner playing an instrument that looked like a sort of xylophone. She drank red wine but it tasted musty, watery. She abandoned the bottle and drank beer instead. The moon was shining over the sea. She felt an urge to wade out along the beam of light it cast. When she went up to her room she barricaded the door with a table, then fell asleep with her feet entangled in the torn mosquito net.

In her dreams horses galloped through a wintry landscape. Everything was white with snow. Artur stood and pointed at the horizon. A lump of snot had frozen to his upper lip. She never caught on to what he wanted her to see.


She woke early and went down to the beach. The sun was rising up out of the sea. For a brief moment she felt that Aron and Henrik were standing by her side, and all three were gazing straight at the sun before the light became too strong.

She went back to Christian Holloway's village. Everything was as quiet and still as last time. She had the feeling that she was visiting a cemetery. She remained seated in the car for ages, waiting for somebody to appear. A lone dog with a shaggy black coat was wandering around on the gravel. Something that might have been a large rat scuttled alongside one of the buildings.

But no people. Completely still. Like a prison. She got out of the car, walked over to one of the buildings and opened the door. Immediately she found herself in a different world, the world of the sick and the dying.

Even more strongly than last time she noticed the pungent smell. *Death smells like bitter acid. A cadaverous odour, the fermentation comes later.*

The rooms were filled with dirt, uncleanliness, angst. Most of the sick people lay curled up in the foetal position in bunk beds on the floor; only the very youngest children lay stretched out on their backs. She moved slowly among the afflicted, peering at them through the gloom. Who were they? Why were they lying there? They had been infected with HIV and were going to die. This is what it must have looked like in the classical opium dens. But why did Holloway allow them to live in such squalor? Did he think it was enough to give them a roof over their heads? It struck her that she had no idea about his motives behind a village for the poverty-stricken sufferers.

She paused to contemplate a man lying in front of her. He was looking at her, his eyes gleaming. She bent down and put her hand on his forehead. He did not have a temperature. The feeling of being in an opium den rather than in death's waiting room increased. The man suddenly started moving his lips. She leaned forward to hear what he said. His breath was poisonous, but she forced herself to bear it. He was repeating the same phrases, time after time. She could not understand what he said, over and over again, like a mantra, just something that started with 'In . . .' and perhaps also the word 'them'.

She heard a door opening. Then the man in the bunk bed reacted as if he had been punched. He turned his face away and curled up. When she touched his shoulder he gave a start and drew away.

Louise sensed somebody standing behind her. She turned round, as if afraid of being attacked. It was a woman, of about her own age, grey-haired. She peered short-sightedly at Louise.

'I didn't know we had visitors?'

The woman's accent reminded Louise of when she visited Scotland, and met Aron for the first time.

'I've been here before, and was told that everybody is welcome.'

'And everybody *is* welcome. It's simply that we prefer to open doors ourselves for visitors. The rooms are dark, there are thresholds, people can stumble. We show our guests round.'

'I had a son who used to work here, Henrik. Did you know him?'

'I wasn't here then. But everybody speaks highly of him.'

'I'm trying to understand what Henrik did here.'

'We look after sick people. We take care of patients that nobody else bothers about. The helpless.'

The woman who had yet to introduce herself, took Louise by the arm and led her to the exit. She is being gentle with me, but the claws are there, Louise thought.

They emerged into the bright sunshine. The black dog was lying in the shade of a tree, panting.

'I'd like to meet Christian Holloway. My son spoke about him with great respect. He adored him.'

Louise felt uneasy about lying in Henrik's name, but she felt obliged to do so if she was going to get any further.

'I'm sure he will get in touch with you.'

'When? I can't stay here for ever, doesn't he have a telephone?'

'I've never heard of anybody speaking to him on the telephone. I have to go now.'

'Can't I stay and watch you at work?'

The woman shook her head.

'Today's not a good day. It's treatment day.'

'That would be an especially good time.'

'We are responsible for seriously ill people, and we can't just let anybody wander around when we're busy.'

Louise could see that she was wasting her time.

'Would I be wrong in thinking you come from Scotland?'

'From the Highlands.'

'What brought you here?'

The woman smiled.

'Roads don't always lead to where you think.'

She shook hands and said goodbye. The conversation was over. Louise went back to the car. The black dog watched her longingly, as if it would also have liked to leave. Louise could see the grey-haired woman in the rear-view mirror. She was waiting for Louise to drive off.


She returned to the hotel. The albino sat in the empty dining room playing his xylophone. Children were playing in the sand with the remains of a dustbin. They were beating the bin as if giving it a good hiding. The man in reception smiled. He was reading a well-thumbed Bible. She felt dizzy, everything was so unreal. She went up to her room and lay down on the bed.

Her stomach was in uproar. She could feel it coming and managed to get to the toilet before it came gushing out of her. She had barely returned to bed before she was forced to hasten up again. An hour later, she was running a temperature. When the cleaner came, Louise managed to explain that she was ill, and needed bottled water and would then like to be left in peace. An hour later a waiter from the dining room appeared with a small bottle of mineral water. She gave him some money and asked him to return with a large bottle.

She spent the rest of the day running backwards and forwards between the bed and the toilet. By dusk she had no strength left. But the attacks seemed to be receding. She managed to get up on shaky legs and go down to the dining room to drink tea.

She was about to leave when the whispering man in the dark room came back into her consciousness.

*He wanted to speak to me. He wanted me to listen. He was ill, but much more than that, he was scared. He turned away from me as if to emphasise that he hadn't made contact.*

*He wanted to talk to me. Behind those glittering eyes of his was something different.*

It suddenly dawned on her what he had been trying to say.

Injections. That was the word he had been trying to whisper. *Injections.* But surely injections were part of their treatment?

*He was scared. He wanted to tell me it was the injections that scared him.*

The man had been seeking help. His whispers had been a cry for help.

She went to the window and looked down at the sea. The strip of light reflected from the moon had gone. The sea lay in darkness. The gravelled area in front of the hotel was lit up by a single bulb in a lamp post.

She peered into the shadows. Henrik had done the same. What had he discovered?

Perhaps a whispering man in death's waiting room?

# CHAPTER 18

The next day, early morning again.

Louise wrapped the length of fabric round her body and went down to the beach. Some of the small fishing boats came in with their catches. Women and children helped to sort the fish, pack them into plastic buckets filled with ice, then carry them off balanced on their heads. A boy grinned broadly as he showed her a large crab. Louise smiled back.

She waded out into the water. The fabric clung to her body. She swam a few strokes, then dived. When she came up to the surface again she had decided to go back to the dying man on the bunk at Xai-Xai. She would not give up until she had understood what he had wanted to tell her.

She rinsed away the salt under the dripping shower in her bathroom. The albino was still playing his xylophone. The sound drifted in through the window. He always seemed to be there, playing his instrument. She had noticed that the bright sun had scarred his forehead and cheeks.

She went down to the dining room. The waiter smiled and served her coffee. She nodded towards the man playing the instrument.

'Is he always here?'

'He likes to play. He goes home late and comes back early. His wife wakes him up.'

'So he has a family?'

The waiter looked at her in surprise.

'Why not? He has nine children and more grandchildren than he can keep count of.'

*I don't. I don't have a family. There's nothing after Henrik.*

She experienced a feeling of helpless fury over the fact that Henrik no longer existed.

She left the breakfast table. The relentless monotony of the music resounded inside her head.

She went to the car and drove to Christian Holloway's village. It was even hotter now than the day before. The thumping inside her head replaced the monotonous music.

When she pulled up it seemed as if everything was repeating itself in the heat haze. The air was dancing before her eyes. The black dog was panting underneath a tree. There was no sign of any people. A plastic bag was being blown back and forth over the sands. Louise sat behind the wheel and fanned herself with her hand. Her fury had faded away, to be replaced by resignation.

That night she had dreamt about Aron. It had been a painful nightmare. She had been busy with one of her digs at Angolis. They had exposed a skeleton, and it had suddenly dawned on her that it was Aron's bones they had discovered. She had tried desperately to break free from the dream, but it had clung on to her and pulled her down. She had not woken up until she had been on the point of suffocating.

A white man dressed in light-coloured clothes came out of one building and entered another. Louise continued fanning herself as she watched him. Then she left the car and headed for the building she had been in the previous day. The dog watched her.

She stepped into the darkness, stood motionless until her eyes had grown used to the dark. The stench was even more potent than last time. She started breathing through her mouth so as not to be sick.

The bunk was empty. The man was no longer there. Had she lost her bearings? There had been a woman next to him, lying under a batik cover with a flamingo motif. She was still there. Louise had not become disorientated. She wandered around the room, being careful not to stand on any of the emaciated bodies. There was no sign of him. Had he been moved? Could he be dead? Something inside her rebelled at that thought. Death could come quickly to anybody suffering from Aids, but even so, something did not seem right.

She was about to leave the room when she had the feeling that she was being watched. All around her was a circle of slowly moving arms and legs. Many of the afflicted had covered their heads with sheets and quilts, as if keeping their misery to themselves. Louise looked round. Somebody was watching her. In one corner of the room she observed a man leaning against the stone wall looking at her. She approached him cautiously. He was a young man, about Henrik's age, though emaciated, his face covered in sores, and patches of his head without hair. He was looking at her without blinking. A slight movement of one hand suggested that she was welcome to come closer.

'Moises has gone.'

His English had a South African accent, she had picked that up after listening to her white fellow passengers on the bus from the airport to her hotel. She knelt down in order to hear his weak voice.

'Where is he?' she asked.

'In the ground.'

'Is he dead?'

The man grasped her wrist. It was as if a little girl had taken hold of her. His fingers were thin, weak.

'They fetched him.'

'What do you mean?'

His face moved closer to hers.

'You killed him. He tried to appeal to you.'

'I couldn't understand what he said.'

'They gave him an injection and took him away. He was asleep when they came.'

'What happened?'

'I can't speak here. They'll see us. They'll fetch me in the same way. Where are you staying?'

'I'm in the hotel on the beach.'

'If I can make it, I'll go there. Leave now.'

The man lay down and curled up under a blanket. *The same fear. He's hiding.* She went back through the room. When she emerged into the sunshine it was like being hit hard in the face. She kept in the shade.

*Henrik had told her once about his experiences of hot countries.*

237

*People didn't only share water with their brothers and sisters, but also shade.*

Had she understood the man in the darkness rightly? Would he really be able to visit her? How would he get to the beach outside her hotel?

She was about to go back when she noticed that there was somebody standing in the shade of the tree where she had parked her car. It was a man in his sixties, perhaps older. He smiled as she approached. He came towards her and stretched out his hand.

She knew immediately who he was. His English was unabrasive. His American accent had disappeared almost completely.

'My name's Christian Holloway. As I understand it, you are Henrik Cantor's mother, and he has died under tragic circumstances.'

Louise was confused. Who had told him that?

He sensed her confusion immediately.

'News, especially tragic news, spreads very quickly. What happened?'

'He was murdered.'

'Can that really be true? Who would want to harm a young man who had dreams of a better world?'

'That's what I'm trying to find out.'

Holloway touched her lightly on the arm.

'Let's go to my office. It's much cooler than out here.'

They walked over the gravel towards a white house some way away from the rest. The black dog watched their progress intently.

'When I was a child I used to spend my winter holidays with an uncle in Alaska. It was my far-sighted father who sent me there, to toughen me up. The whole of my childhood and youth was really a sort of continuous toughening-up process. Learning things, knowledge, was not considered to be any more important than acquiring "an iron skin", as my father called it. It was very cold where my uncle lived and worked, drilling for oil. But getting used to extreme cold has made me better equipped than many to withstand extreme heat as well.'

They entered a house which comprised just one large room. It was built like an African rondavel, intended for a chieftain. Holloway kicked off his shoes outside the door, as if he were about to enter a holy place. But he shook his head when Louise bent down to unfasten her laces.

She looked round, taking in details of the room as if she were visiting a newly excavated tomb in which reality had remained untouched for thousands of years.

The room was furnished in what she imagined was classical colonial style. In one corner was a computer with two screens. On the stone floor was an antique carpet, Persian or Afghan, expensive.

Her attention was attracted to one of the walls. There was a picture of the Madonna hanging on it. She saw immediately that it was very old, originating from the Byzantine age, presumably early. It was far too valuable to be hanging on the wall of a private house somewhere in Africa.

Holloway saw what she was looking at.

'Madonna and child. For me they are constant companions. Religions have always imitated life, the divine always stems from the human. You can find a beautiful child in the most horrific slum in Dhaka or Medellín, a mathematical genius can be born in Harlem as the son or daughter of a crack addict. The thought that Mozart was buried in a pauper's grave in Vienna is really not so much shocking as uplifting. Everything is possible. We can learn from the Tibetans that every religion ought to place its gods in our midst, and let us find out about them. It's among human beings that we should find divine inspiration.'

He never took his eyes off her as he talked. They were blue, bright and cool. He invited her to sit down. A door opened without a sound. An African dressed in white entered and served tea.

The door closed. It was as if a white shadow had flitted through the room.

'Henrik made himself well liked in no time at all,' said Holloway. 'He was clever, and managed to shake off the distaste that affects everybody who is young and healthy when they are forced to come into contact with death. Nobody likes to be reminded of what lies in store for us just round the corner that is closer than we think. Life is an incredibly short journey, it's only in one's youth that it is eternal. But

Henrik got used to it. Then all of a sudden, he disappeared. We never understood why he left.'

'I found him dead in his flat. He had his pyjamas on. That's how I knew he had been murdered.'

'Because of the pyjamas?'

'He always slept naked.'

Christian Holloway nodded thoughtfully. He was watching her all the time. Louise had the impression that he was conducting a conversation with himself about what he saw and heard.

'I could never have imagined that such an outstanding young man with so much lively energy inside him would die before his time.'

'Isn't energy always lively?'

'No. A lot of people drag around burdens comprising unused energy, and that weighs heavily on their lives.'

Louise decided not to beat about the bush.

'Something happened here that changed his life.'

'Nobody who comes here can avoid being affected. Most people are shocked, some run away, others decide to be strong and stay.'

'I don't think it was the sick and dying people that changed him.'

'What else could it have been? We look after people who would have died alone in ramshackle huts, in the gutter, among the trees. Animals would have started eating their bodies before they even had time to die.'

'It was something different.'

'One can never fully understand a person, be it oneself or somebody else. That no doubt applies to Henrik as well. The inner being of a person is a landscape reminiscent of what this continent looked like 150 years ago. Only the areas along the coasts and rivers had been explored, the rest was endless blank patches where it was thought there were cities made of gold and creatures with two heads.'

'I know that something happened. But I don't know what.'

'Something is always happening here. New people are carried in, others are buried. There is a cemetery here. We have the priests we need. No dogs will come to chew dead people's bones before we have them interred.'

'A man I spoke to yesterday is no longer there. He must have died during the night.'

'For some reason, most of them die at dawn. It's as if they want to be able to see where they are going as they die.'

'How often did you meet Henrik while he was here?'

'I never meet people very often. Twice, perhaps three times. No more.'

'What did you talk about?'

'As I have learned to remember only things of note, I very seldom remember afterwards what was said. People are often boring and uninteresting. I don't think we ever talked about important things. A few words about the heat, the weariness that affects us all.'

'Did he never ask any questions?'

'Not of me. He didn't seem to be that sort of person.'

Louise shook her head.

'He was one of the most inquisitive and curious people I have ever met. I can say that despite the fact that he was my son.'

'The questions one asks here are on a different, inner plane. When you are surrounded on all sides by death, questions are always concerned with the meaning of everything. And they are questions you ask yourself, in silence. Living means having the will to resist. In the end the hunter ants will find their way into your body even so.'

'Hunter ants?'

'Many years ago I spent some months in a remote village up in north-western Zambia. There had been Franciscan monks there earlier, but they had left in the mid-1950s and established themselves further south, between Solwezi and Kitwe. What was left of their buildings had been taken over by a couple from Arkansas who wanted to create a spiritual oasis, unconnected to any particular religion. That was where I came into contact with hunter ants. What do you know about them?'

'Nothing.'

'Not many people do. We imagine that beasts of prey are powerful. Perhaps not always especially big, but rarely as small as ants. One night I was alone with the guards when I was woken up by shouts in the darkness outside, and a belting on my door. The guards had torches they had used to set fire to the grass. I had nothing on my feet when I went outside. Immediately I felt shooting pains in my feet. I didn't understand what it was. The guards shouted that there were ants, armies of hunter ants were on the march. They eat everything in their path and there is no stopping them, but by setting fire to the grass you can force them to change direction. I put my boots on, fetched a flashlight and saw angry little ants in perfect formation marching by. Suddenly there was a deafening cackling from the henhouse. The guards tried to catch the hens and chase them out, but it was already too late, it went incredibly quickly. The hens tried to defend themselves by eating the ants, but they were still alive in the hens' stomachs and started eating their insides. Not a single hen survived. They were running around in agony as their guts were being eaten by the ants. I've often thought about that. The hens put up resistance, and by doing so ensured that they would suffer an agonising death.'

'I can imagine what it must be like to be bitten by hundreds of ants.'

'I wonder if you really can. I certainly can't. One of the guards got a stray ant inside his ear. It was biting away at his eardrum. The guard was screaming with pain until I poured whisky into his ear and killed the ant. One single ant, less than half a centimetre long.'

'Do you get those ants here in Mozambique?'

'They exist all over the African continent. They appear after heavy rain, never at other times.'

'I find it hard to understand the comparison between life and having ants crawling inside your body.'

'It's the same as it was for the hens. The tragedy of life is brought to its culmination by the human being him or herself. It doesn't come from the outside.'

'I don't agree.'

'I know that there are gods for sale or for borrowing when the pain becomes too great, but that way has never brought me any consolation.'

'Instead, you try to divert the ants? Drive them as far away as possible?'

Holloway nodded.

'You're following my train of thought. Naturally, that doesn't mean that I delude myself into thinking that I shall succeed in resisting the final tragedy. Death is always by our side. The real waiting rooms of death are the wards where women give birth to children.'

'Did you ever tell Henrik about the ants?'

'No. He was too weak. The story could have given him nightmares.'

'Henrik was not weak.'

'Children don't always act for their parents in the same way as they do when they meet people they don't know. I know that because I have children myself. Despite everything they stretch a thin film of meaning over life.'

'Are they here?'

'No. Three are in North America and one is dead. Like your son. I also have a son who died before his time.'

'In that case you know how painful it is.'

Holloway looked at her long and hard. He rarely blinked. Like a lizard, she thought. A reptile.

She shuddered.

'Are you cold? Shall I turn down the air con?'

'I'm tired.'

'The world is tired. We live in an old, rheumatic world, despite the fact that it's teeming with children wherever we turn. Children everywhere while we two sit here and mourn those who chose to give their lives away.'

It took a moment or two for her to realise the implication of what he had said.

'Did your son take his own life?'

'He lived with his mother in Los Angeles. One day when he was on his own, he emptied the swimming pool, climbed up to the highest of the diving boards and threw himself off it. One of the security guards heard him screaming. He didn't die right away, but it was all over before the ambulance came.'

The waiter in white appeared in the doorway. He gave a signal. Holloway stood up.

'Somebody needs my advice. That is in fact the only thing I think is important: supporting people by listening and perhaps being able to offer advice. I'll be back in a moment.'

Louise walked over to the wall and studied the Madonna. It was an original. She realised that it must have been painted by a Byzantine master in Greece during the twelfth or early thirteenth century. No matter how Christian Holloway got hold of it, it must have cost a vast amount of money.

She wandered round the room. The computer screens were glowing. Both screen savers depicted dolphins jumping out of a turquoise sea. One of the desk drawers was half open.

She could not resist the temptation. She opened it fully. At first she could not make out what was in it.

Then it dawned on her that it was a dried brain. Small, shrivelled, probably human.

She closed the drawer. Her heart was pounding. A dried brain. *Kennedy's missing brain.*

She went back to her chair. Her hand was shaking when she lifted her teacup.

Was there a connection between Henrik's obsession with what had happened in 1963 in Dallas, and what she had discovered in the drawer of Christian Holloway's desk? She forced herself to back off. Her conclusion was too simple. Imagined pieces of pot fell into place in imagined patterns. She did not want to be a drunken archaeologist who had gone berserk. The shrivelled brain in the drawer had nothing to do with Henrik. At least, she had no grounds for assuming that it had, until she knew more.

The door opened, Holloway came back.

'I apologise for keeping you waiting.'

He looked her in the eye and smiled. At that moment Louise was convinced that somehow or other he had watched her exploring his office – perhaps there was a peephole in the wall? Or a camera she had failed to notice? He had watched her examining the painting and opening the desk drawer. It had been halfway open, in order to tempt her. No doubt he had left the room to see how she reacted.

'Perhaps you could give me some advice, too,' she said, forcing herself to keep calm.

'I can always try.'

'It's about Henrik and your son. We share an experience that all parents are terrified of.'

'Steve did something in a moment of fury and desperation. Henrik fell asleep in his bed, if I understand the situation rightly. Steve turned outwards. Henrik turned inwards. Those are two different ways.'

'Even so, they both led in the same direction.'

*Steve.* The name brought a vague memory to life. She had stumbled upon it previously, but could not remember when or where. Steve Holloway?

She thought hard but came up with nothing.

She changed tack. Perhaps it was the other way round. Perhaps Holloway knew no more than he said he did, but was trying to prise information out of her, through her questions?

You ask questions about what you do not know. You do not ask about what you do know.

She had no desire to stay there any longer. Christian Holloway and his secret peephole scared her. She stood up.

'I won't disturb you any longer.'

'I'm sorry I haven't been able to be of help.'

'You've tried, at least.'

He accompanied her to her car in the scorching heat.

'Drive carefully. Drink plenty of water. Are you going back to Maputo?'

'I might stay here until tomorrow.'

'The beach hotel in Xai-Xai is simple, but usually clean. Don't leave anything valuable in your room. Don't hide anything in the mattress.'

'I've already been robbed once, in Maputo. I'm careful. The first thing I was forced to acquire here was eyes in the back of my head.'

'Were you hurt?'

'I gave them what they wanted.'

'This is a poor country. People rob and steal in order to survive. We'd have done the same in their situation.'

She shook hands and sat down behind the wheel. The black dog was still lying in the shade.

She watched in the rear-view mirror as Holloway turned round and went back to his house.

When she got back to her hotel room, she fell asleep. It was already dark by the time she woke up.

Where had she seen the name Steve before? She knew she had come across it somewhere. But Steve was a common name, like Erik in Sweden or Kostas in Greece.

She went down to the dining room to eat. The albino was still sitting by the wall, playing his xylophone. The waiter was the same one as had served her breakfast that morning. In answer to her question he informed her that the instrument was called a timbila.

When she had finished her dinner she remained seated. Insects were buzzing around the light over her table. There were not many people in the dining room. Some men were drinking beer, a woman with three children was eating in total silence. Louise slid the coffee cup to one side and ordered a glass of red wine instead. It was ten o'clock by now. The albino stopped playing, slung his instrument over his shoulder and disappeared into the darkness. The woman with the three children paid her bill then waddled off like a ship with three lifeboats tied to its stern. The men carried on talking. In the end they left as well. The waiter started clearing up. She paid and went out into the night air. The water was glistening in the beam of a single light.

The whistle was very faint, but she heard it immediately. She looked hard into the shadows beyond the circle of light. The whistle was repeated, just as softly. Then she saw him. He was sitting on an upturned fishing boat. She thought of the silhouettes in Henrik's bag. The man waiting for her could have been cut out of the darkness in similar fashion.

He slid down from the boat and beckoned her to follow him. He walked towards the remains of a building that had once been a beach kiosk. Louise had noticed it earlier in the day. The name was still legible in the crumbling concrete: *Lisboa*.

When they came closer she saw that a fire was burning inside the ruined building. The man knelt down by the fire and added some twigs. She sat opposite him. In the glow she could see how thin he was. His skin seemed to be stretched tightly over his cheekbones. He had wounds on his forehead which had not healed.

'You don't need to worry. Nobody's followed you.'

'How can you be so sure?'

'I was watching you for ages.'

He gestured into the darkness.

'There are others keeping a look out as well.'

'Who?'

'Friends.'

'What do you want to tell me? I don't even know your name.'

'I know that you are called Louise Cantor.'

She wanted to ask how he knew her name, but realised she was hardly likely to get a reply, just a vague gesture into the darkness.

'I find it hard to listen to people whose names I don't know.'

'I'm called Umbi. My father named me after his brother who died when he was young, working in the South African mines. A shaft collapsed. His body was never found. I shall also be dead shortly. I want to talk to you because the only thing left for me in this life, the only thing that might be meaningful, is to prevent others from dying in the same way as me.'

'I gather you have Aids?'

'I have the poison in my blood. Even if all my blood were to be drained away the poison would remain.'

'But aren't you getting help? Drugs that delay the onset of the illness?'

'I get help from those who don't know anything.'

'I don't follow you.'

Umbi did not reply. He added more wood to the fire. Then he whistled quietly into the darkness. The faint whistle that followed in response seemed to reassure him. Louise began to feel uncomfortable. The man sitting on the other side of the fire was dying. For the first time she realised the significance of someone being on the way out. Umbi was on the way out from life. His stretched skin would soon split.

'Moises, the man you talked to, shouldn't have spoken to you. Even if you think you're alone in the room with the sick, there's always somebody keeping an eye on what happens. The people who are going to die shortly aren't allowed to have any secrets.'

'Why is a watch kept on the sick people? And on visitors like me? What do they think I'm going to steal from poverty-stricken, dying people who are in Christian Holloway's care because they own nothing?'

'They took Moises at dawn. They came in, gave him an injection, waited until he was dead and carried him away in a blanket.'

'Gave him an injection in order to kill him?'

'All I'm saying is what happened. Nothing else. I want you to tell people about this.'

'Who was it that gave him the injection? One of the pale little girls from Europe?'

'They don't know what goes on.'

'Neither do I.'

'That's why I've come here. In order to tell you.'

'I'm here because my son used to work here among the sick and dying. Now he's dead. He was called Henrik. Do you remember him?'

'What did he look like?'

Grief welled up inside her as she described his face.

'I don't remember him. Perhaps I hadn't been visited by the archangel then.'

'The archangel?'

'That's what we called him. I don't know where he came from, but he must be very close to Christian Holloway. A friendly man with a bald head who spoke to us in our own language and offered us what we lacked above all else.'

'What was that?'

'A way out of poverty. People like you think that really poor people don't realise how badly off they are. I can assure you that this assumption is wrong. The archangel said he had come to us because our suffering was the greatest and most bitter. He asked the village elder to pick out twenty people. Three days later he came in a lorry and fetched them. I wasn't chosen that time, so when he came again I made sure I was standing right at the front, and I was selected.'

'What had happened to the first batch he had taken?'

'He explained that they were still there, and would be staying on for a while longer. Naturally many of their relatives were worried because they hadn't heard anything for such a long time. When he had finished talking he gave the elder a large sum of money. There had never been as much money as that in our village. It was as if a thousand miners had come back after working for many years in South Africa, and now they were spreading out all their savings on a rush mat in front of us. A few days later the other lorry came. This time I was one of those who climbed into the back of it. I felt as if I were one of the chosen people who would be able to extract myself from the poverty that tarnished me even in my dreams.'

He paused and listened into the dark. All Louise could hear was the surging of the ocean and the call of a nocturnal bird. She thought he seemed worried, but she could not be certain why.

He whistled softly and listened. There was no answer. It suddenly seemed to Louise that the situation was surreal. Why was she sitting here by a fire with a man who kept whistling into the darkness? A pitch black that she could not penetrate. It was not merely the darkness of the African continent, it was also the dense darkness inside her, containing Henrik's grave and Aron's disappearance. She wanted to scream out loud at everything that was happening all around her, that she did not understand and that nobody else seemed to understand either.

*One evening I was standing outside my house in Argolis, smoking. I could hear dogs barking, and music coming from my neighbour's. The starry sky up above was completely clear. I would soon be leaving for Sweden where I was due to give a lecture on ceramics and the importance of ferrous oxides in determining the black and red colours. I stood there in the dark and had decided to put an end to my relationship with Vassilis, my beloved accountant. I was looking forward to meeting Henrik shortly, it was a mild night and the cigarette smoke rose straight up in the calm air. Now, a few months later, my life is in ruins. All I can feel is emptiness, and fear of what is in store for me. In order to survive I try to accept my fury at what has happened. Deep down, perhaps, without ever having said it aloud to myself, I am looking for whoever is or are responsible for Henrik's death, in order to kill them. Whoever killed Henrik is condemned to death. He is responsible not only for Henrik's death, but mine as well.*

Umbi stood up, with great difficulty. He was close to collapsing. Louise made to support him but he shook his head.

He whistled once more, without receiving a reply.

'I'll be back shortly.'

He vanished into the darkness. Louise leaned forward and put more wood on the fire. Artur had taught her how to light a fire and keep it going. It was an art learned only by those who had been really cold in their lives. Artur had also coached Henrik in the art of making fires. It was as if she had always had a fire burning in her life. Even Aron had occasionally rushed off into the forest with a coffee kettle and a rucksack, and forced her to accompany him, whenever he had decided he was going to smash up his computer and escape to a new life in the wilds.

Fires burned all the way through her life. Without firewood and love she would be unable to carry on living.

There was still no sign of Umbi. Worry crept up on her. A whistle had failed to receive a reply.

She suddenly felt convinced that danger threatened. She stood up and withdrew quickly from the firelight. Something had happened. She held her breath and listened. All she could hear was her own heart beating. She continued to back away. The darkness surrounding her was a sea. She started to grope her way towards the hotel.

She stumbled against something soft lying on the ground. An animal, she thought as she gave a start. She fumbled in her pockets for a box of matches. When the match flared up she saw that it was Umbi. He was dead. His throat had been cut, his head almost severed from his body.

Louise ran away. Twice she stumbled and fell.

When she unlocked the door of her room she saw straight away that somebody had been there. A pair of socks were lying where she had not put them. The door to the bathroom was ajar, although she was almost certain that she had closed it. Was there somebody in there? She opened the door to the corridor and made herself ready to flee before plucking up the courage to kick the bathroom door open. There was nobody there.

But somebody was watching her. Umbi and his friends had not seen what was hiding in the darkness. That was why Umbi was dead.

Her fear was like a paralysing chill. She flung her belongings into her bag and left the room. The night porter was asleep on a mattress behind the counter. He jumped up with a startled roar when she shouted at him to wake up. She paid her bill, unlocked the car and drove off. Not until she had left Xai-Xai and made sure that no car was visible in the rear-view mirror did she regain her self-control.

She now knew where she had seen the name Steve.

Aron had been sitting at Henrik's computer, and she had been leaning over his shoulder. It was an article from the *New York Times* about a man called Steve Nichols who had committed suicide after being blackmailed. Steve Nichols. Not Steve Holloway. But he had been living with his mother. She might have been called Nichols.

The fragments she had gathered began to take shape in a way she had not expected.

Could Henrik have been murdered because he had driven Steve Nichols to his death? Had the murder been disguised as suicide as a grim message from whoever had taken revenge?

She hammered at the steering wheel and shouted into the darkness for Aron. Now she needed him more than ever. But he was silent, he did not answer.

When she realised that she was driving far too fast, she slowed down.

She was fleeing in order to survive. Not to kill herself on a dark country road in the endless African continent.

# CHAPTER 19

The engine died without warning. She stamped and kicked at the accelerator in an attempt to make the car move. The petrol indicator showed that the tank was half full, the temperature gauge was in the green.

Cause of death unknown, she thought in a mixture of anger and fear. The accursed car has died when I need it most.

She remained in darkness. There was no sign of a light anywhere. She did not dare open the window, never mind the door. She was trapped in the dead car, she would be forced to stay there until somebody came past who could help her.

She concentrated on the rear-view mirror, looking for any sign of movement, of somebody approaching through the darkness. The danger was behind her, not in front of her. Time after time she tried to resuscitate the car. The starter's efforts were in vain. In the end she switched on the headlights and forced herself out of the car.

The silence enveloped her. It was as if somebody had thrown a blanket over her head. She was surrounded by unlimited and silent nothingness. The only thing she could hear was her own breathing. She took a deep breath, as if she had been drained of all air.

*I'm running. I'm being chased by fear. Whoever cut Umbi's throat is here, right next to me.*

She gave a start and turned round. There was nobody there. She managed to open the car bonnet and stared down into an unknown world.

She remembered what Aron had said, in the most sneering tone of voice he could muster, at the very beginning of their marriage. 'If you don't learn the basic essentials of how an engine works, and what you can repair yourself, you're not fit to hold a driving licence.'

She had never learned. She hated getting oil on her hands. But what motivated her most of all was her refusal to respond to Aron's arrogant challenge.

She closed the bonnet again. The noise it made was deafening and rolled away into the darkness.

What had Shakespeare written? 'As cannons overcharged with double cracks.' That's how Aron described himself. He was the man who produced double cracks, nobody could match what he could do. What would he have said if he'd seen her in a car that had given up the ghost in the African darkness? Would he have delivered one of his condescending lectures about how incompetent she was? That's what he usually did when he was in a bad mood, and it usually led to long drawn-out trials of strength which frequently ended up with them throwing cups and glasses at each other.

I love him even so, she thought as she squatted down and peed next to the car. I have tried to replace him with other men, but have always failed. Like Portia, I have waited for my wooers. They have danced and pranced around and performed their tricks, but when the last act begins they have all been rejected. Is this my last act, perhaps? I thought I would have at least another twenty years to go. When Henrik died, in the course of just a few seconds I raced through the whole play and now only the epilogue remains.

She continued to keep an eye on the rear-view mirror. No headlight beams pierced the darkness. She took out her mobile and dialled Aron's number. *The number you have called is unavailable at the moment.*

Then she dialled the number of Henrik's flat. *You know what to do.* She started crying, and her sobs became a message on his answering machine. Then she rang Artur. The connection was good, with no delay. His voice made him seem close by.

'Where are you? Why are you ringing in the middle of the night? Are you crying?'

'My car's broken down on a deserted country road.'

'Are you on your own?'

'Yes.'

'You must be out of your mind! In a car on your own in the middle of the night in Africa? Anything at all could happen.'

'Anything at all has happened. The car has stopped. I have petrol, the engine hasn't overheated, there are no warning lights flashing. Having a breakdown here isn't really any worse than breaking down in the Härjedalen mountains.'

'Can't somebody come to help you? Is it a hire car? If so there must be an emergency number you can call.'

'I want you to help me. You've taught me everything; from how to cook, to mending a broken record player. Even to stuff birds.'

'I'm worried about you. What are you afraid of?'

'I'm not afraid. I'm not crying.'

He bellowed at her. The noise hit her like a heavy blow.

'Don't tell me barefaced lies! Not even when you can hide inside a telephone.'

'Don't shout at me! Help me instead.'

'Is the starter working?'

She put the phone on her knee, turned the key and made the starter turn.

'That sounds like it should,' said Artur.

'So why doesn't the engine start?'

'I don't know. Is the road potholed?'

'It's like driving on a dirt road in the north of Sweden in the spring thaw.'

'Maybe a cable has been shaken loose.'

She switched on the headlights, opened the bonnet for the second time and followed his instructions. When she tried to start the car again, the result was the same.

She was cut off. She shouted into the darkness, but Artur's voice was no longer there. She dialled his number again. A woman's voice said something that sounded apologetic in Portuguese. She hung up and hoped that Artur would be able to get through to her.

Nothing happened. She tried the number given in the rental contract. No answer, there was neither an answering machine nor any recorded instructions.

She saw the distant gleam of headlights in the rear-view mirror. Fear cut deep into her. Should she get out of the car and hide in the darkness? She was incapable of moving. The headlights came closer. She was convinced the oncoming vehicle would crash into her. It swerved away at the last moment. A battered lorry rattled past.

It was as if she had been overtaken by a riderless horse.

It developed into one of the longest nights of her life. She listened through the half-open window and kept her eyes skinned for lights. She occasionally tried to ring Artur again, but failed to get through.

Shortly before dawn she tried the starter again. The engine spluttered into life. She held her breath. The engine continued turning.

It was broad daylight when she arrived at the outskirts of Maputo, everywhere there were women with backs as straight as ramrods walking out of the sun and the red dust, with gigantic loads balanced on their heads and children in slings on their backs.

She edged her way through the chaotic traffic, through the black smoke oozing out of buses and lorries.

She needed a wash, a change of clothes, a few hours of sleep. But she had no desire to see Lars Håkansson. She found her way to the house where Lucinda lived. No doubt she would be asleep after a long night's work in the bar. Too bad. Lucinda was the only person who could help her now.

She parked the car and tried Artur's number one more time. She thought of something he'd said once.

*Neither the devil nor God wants competition. That's why we humans end up in our lonely no-man's-land.*

She could hear that he was tired. No doubt he'd been up all night. But he would never admit as much. Even if she was not allowed to tell lies, he had granted that privilege to himself.

'What happened? Where are you?'

'Nothing's happened, except that the car started again for no obvious reason. I'm back in Maputo.'

'These damned telephones!'

'They are fantastic.'

'Isn't it time for you to leave there?'

'Soon, but not yet. We can talk about that later. My battery's nearly flat.'

She hung up, and at the same time noticed that Lucinda was standing by the house wall with a towel wrapped round her head. She got out of the car thinking that the long night was over at last.

Lucinda was surprised to see her.

'A bit early, isn't it?'

'That's what I ought to ask you. When did you get to bed?'

'I never get much sleep. Perhaps I'm permanently tired? Without noticing it?'

Lucinda patiently shooed away some children who might have been her brothers and sisters or cousins or nieces and nephews. She shouted to a teenager who was sprucing up some plastic chairs standing in the shadow cast by the house, and shortly afterwards appeared with two glasses of water.

She noticed that Louise was uneasy.

'Something's happened. That's why you've come here so early.'

Louise decided to tell Lucinda the truth. She told her about Christian Holloway and Umbi, the darkness on the beach and the long night in the car.

'They must have seen me,' Louise said. 'They must have heard what we were talking about at the village. They followed him, and when they realised that he was going to spill the beans, they killed him.'

It was obvious that Lucinda believed her, every word, every detail. When she had finished, Lucinda sat there for ages without speaking. A man started hammering away at a roofing sheet in order to bend it and make a ridge. Lucinda shouted at him. He stopped immediately and sat down in the shade of a tree, waiting.

'Are you convinced that Henrik was involved in the blackmailing of Christian Holloway's son?'

'I don't know anything for certain. I try to think calmly and clearly and logically, but everything is so elusive. I can't imagine Henrik as a blackmailer, not even in my wildest dreams. Can you?'

'Of course not.'

'I need a computer and a link to the Internet. I might be able to find those articles, and it might be possible to see if it really was Christian Holloway's son. If so, at least I'll have found something that hangs together.'

'What?'

'I don't know yet. Something fits, but I don't know how yet. I have to start somewhere. I keep on starting, over and over again.'

Lucinda stood up.

'There's an Internet café not far from here. I went there with Henrik once. Just let me get dressed and I'll take you there.'

Lucinda disappeared into the house. The children were lined up, looking at Louise. She smiled. The children smiled back. Tears started to run down Louise's cheek. The children continued smiling.


Louise had dried her eyes by the time Lucinda reappeared. They crossed over the long street; its name was Lenin Street. Lucinda paused outside a bakery that was in the same building as a theatre.

'I ought to have given you breakfast.'

'I'm not hungry.'

'Of course you're hungry, but you don't want to admit it. I've never understood why white people find it so hard to tell the truth about the little things in life. If you've slept well, if you've eaten, if you're longing to change into clean clothes.'

Lucinda went into the bakery and emerged with a paper bag containing a couple of bread rolls. She took one herself and gave the other to Louise.

'Let's hope that everything is explained and rounded off in the end.'

'Umbi was the second dead person I've seen in my life. Henrik was the first. Don't people have a conscience?'

'People hardly ever have a conscience. Poor people don't because they can't afford it. Rich people don't because they think that if they do, it will cost them money.'

'Henrik had a conscience. He inherited it from me.'

'Henrik was no doubt the same as everybody else!'

Louise raised her voice.

'Henrik wasn't like everybody else!'

'Henrik was a good human being.'

'He was much more than that.'

'Can you be more than a good human being?'

'He wished other people well.'

Lucinda gritted her teeth with a loud clicking noise. Then she ushered Louise into the shade of an awning over the window of a shoe shop.

'He was like everybody else. He didn't always behave well. Why did he do what he did to me? You tell me that.'

'I don't know what you're talking about.'

'He made me HIV-positive. I got it off him. I denied it the first time you asked. I thought you had enough to cope with already. But I can't let it pass any longer. Now I'm going to tell you it as it is. If you haven't caught on already, that is.'

Lucinda hurled the words into Louise's face. Louise made no attempt to resist, because she knew that Lucinda was right. Louise had suspected the truth from the moment she landed in Maputo. Henrik had kept his illness a secret from his mother, he had never told her about his flat in Barcelona. After his death, now when she also felt that she was dead, she had been forced to admit that she had hardly known him at all. She had no idea when the change had taken place, she had noticed nothing. Henrik had not wanted her to know that he was becoming a different person.

Lucinda started walking. She didn't expect a reply from Louise. The security guard outside the shoe shop eyed the two women with a degree of curiosity. Louise was so upset that she marched up to him and addressed him in Swedish.

'I don't know what you're staring at, but we like each other very much. We're friends. We're upset but we like each other very much.'

She caught up with Lucinda and took her hand.

'I didn't know.'

'You thought it was me who'd infected him. You assumed that it was the black whore who'd passed the infection on to him.'

'I've never regarded you as a prostitute.'

'White men nearly always regard black women as permanently

258

available, whenever, wherever. If a pretty young black woman tells a fat white man that she loves him, he believes her. He assumes that his power is unlimited when he comes to a poor country in Africa. Henrik told me that the same applies to Asia.'

'Surely Henrik never regarded you as a prostitute?'

'To tell you the truth, I don't know.'

'Did he offer you money?'

'That's not necessary. A lot of white men think that we should be grateful for the opportunity to open our legs.'

'That's disgusting,'

'It can get even more disgusting. I could tell you stories about young girls aged eight or nine.'

'I don't want to hear.'

'Henrik did. No matter how unpleasant it was, he wanted to hear. "I want to know so that I understand why I don't want to know." That's what he said. At first I thought he was just trying to make himself important. But later I realised that he really meant what he said.'

Lucinda stopped. They had come to an Internet café in a newly renovated stone building. Women were sitting on small raffia mats on the pavement and displayed a range of goods they had for sale. Lucinda bought a few oranges before they entered the café. Louise tried to keep her outside on the pavement.

'Not now. We'll talk about it later. I had to tell you the truth.'

'How had Henrik discovered that he was infected?'

'I asked him, but he never answered. I can't tell you about something I don't know. But once it dawned on him that I had caught the virus from him he was absolutely devastated. He talked about committing suicide. I tried to convince him that if he didn't know about it, he wasn't guilty. The only thing I wanted to be sure about was if he ought to have known that he was infected. He denied that he did. Then he promised to ensure that I would receive all the antiretroviral drugs in existence, in order to delay the onset of full-blown Aids. I received five hundred dollars every month. I still do.'

'Where does the money come from?'

'I don't know. It's paid into a bank account. He promised that even if anything were to happen to him, I should still receive the money for twenty-five years. It arrives on time on the twenty-eighth of the month in a bank account he opened for me. It's the same as if he were still alive. In any case, it can't be his spirit that is continuing to ensure that the money is paid every month.'

Louise made a quick calculation in her head. Six thousand dollars a year for twenty-five years equals a staggering amount, 150,000 dollars, or about a million kronor. Henrik died a rich man.

She looked through the window of the Internet café. Had he taken his own life after all?'

'You must have hated him.'

'I don't have the strength to hate anybody. Whatever happens might well be preordained.'

'Henrik's death wasn't preordained.'

They went inside and were allocated a vacant computer. Young people in school uniforms were sitting at other tables, studying their screens in intense silence. Despite the air conditioning the place was suffused with damp heat. Lucinda was annoyed by the fact that her computer screen was dirty. When the manager came to wipe it, she snatched the cloth from his hand and did it herself.

'During all our years under colonial rule we learned to do no more than we were instructed to do. Now we're slowly learning how to think for ourselves. But there's still a lot that we daren't do. Wipe a computer screen off our own back, for instance.'

'You said that you came here once with Henrik?'

'He was looking for something. It had to do with China.'

'Do you think you could find it again?'

'Possibly. If I think about it. Carry on and do what you have to do first. I'll be back shortly. Malocura doesn't look after itself. I have an electricity bill that needs paying.'

Lucinda went out into the bright sunlight. Sweat was pouring off Louise under her thin jumper. She could smell the sweat from her armpits. When had she last had a wash? She made the Internet connection while ransacking her mind for details of what she and Aron had done in Barcelona. She could remember the newspapers, but not what she had read in which. She was quite sure that the articles had appeared in 1999 and 2000. She started with the *Washington Post* archive, but there was nothing there about either a Steve Nichols or a Steve Holloway. She wiped the sweat from her brow and found her way into the *New York Times* archive. It took her half an hour to check all articles published in 1999. She moved on to 2000. Almost immediately she stumbled upon the article they had found in Henrik's Spanish computer. '*A man by the name of Steve Nichols has taken his own life after being subjected to blackmail. The blackmailers threatened to expose the fact that he was HIV-positive, and to reveal how he had become infected.*' Louise read the article carefully, followed up various links, but found nothing that suggested a connection between Steve Nichols and Christian Holloway.

She went to the counter and bought a bottle of water. Flies buzzed persistently around her sweaty face. She drained the bottle and returned to the computer. She ran a search for Christian Holloway, found her way into various organisations working with Aids patients. She was about to give up when the name Steve Nichols cropped up again. There was a photograph of a young man with glasses, a little mouth and a timid smile, perhaps a couple of years older than Henrik. She could see no similarity at all with Christian Holloway.

Steve Nichols described the charitable organisation he worked for, A for Assistance, which was active in the USA and Canada, and helped those suffering from Aids to lead a decent life. But he did not reveal that he was suffering from Aids himself. There was nothing about blackmail. It said merely that he was dedicated to working on behalf of the afflicted.

She was about to give up in despair when she came across a little window with biographical details.

*Steve Nichols. Born in Los Angeles, May 10, 1970, mother Mary-Ann Nichols, father Christian Holloway.*

She slammed her hand down on the desk. The supervisor, a young black man wearing a suit and tie, looked at her with eyebrows raised. She made a reassuring gesture and explained that she had just found what she had been looking for. He nodded, and returned to his newspaper.

She was shaken by her discovery. It was still not clear what the implications were. Christian Holloway mourned the death of his son, but what was concealed behind his grief? A desire for revenge and a determination to find out who was behind the blackmail and his son's suicide?

Lucinda reappeared, drew up a chair and sat down. Louise told her about what she had discovered.

'But I'm sceptical. If it had been twenty years ago it would have been different. But not now. Would a person really commit suicide now, for fear that he was about to be exposed as being HIV-positive?'

'Maybe he was afraid it would emerge that he'd been infected by a male or female prostitute?'

Louise could see that Lucinda might be right.

'I'd like you to try and find out what Henrik was looking for when you were here. Are you familiar with computers?'

'Even if I'm just a waitress in a bar and have occasionally made a living as a woman for sale, that doesn't mean that I'm computer illiterate. If you must know, it was Henrik who taught me.'

'That's not how I meant it.'

'You know best what you meant.'

It was obvious to Louise that she had offended Lucinda yet again. She apologised. Lucinda nodded curtly without saying anything. They changed places. Lucinda's hand hovered over the keyboard.

'He said he wanted to read about something that had happened in China. Let me see, what was the home page called?'

She thought hard.

'Yes, "Aids Report",' she said. 'That's what it was called.'

She started searching. Her fingers tripped fast and lightly over the keyboard.

Louise was reminded of the time when Henrik was a young boy and she had tried to teach him how to play the piano. His hands were transformed in a flash into hammers that thumped down on the keys with gay abandon. After three lessons, Henrik's piano teacher suggested that he should become a drummer instead.

'It was in May,' Lucinda said. 'It was windy, the sand was being whipped up all over the place. Henrik got something in his left eye. I helped to remove it. Then we came in here and sat over there.'

She pointed to a corner of the room.

'This place had only just opened. We sat at a window table. The computers were brand new. The owner himself was here, a Pakistani or Indian, or he might even have been from Dubai. He was walking round nervously, yelling at customers to be careful with the computers. A month after opening he fled the country. The money he'd invested in the café had come from a major drug-smuggling scandal via Ilha de Mozambique. I don't know who owns this café now. Perhaps nobody knows. Which usually means that the owner is some government minister or other.'

Lucinda ran a search through the archive of articles, and scored the hit she was hoping for almost immediately. She moved her chair to one side and let Louise read the article for herself.

It was clear and unambiguous. In the late autumn of 1995 some men came to Henan province in China to buy blood. For the peasants in the squalid villages, this was a once-in-a-lifetime opportunity to earn quick money. The only way they had ever been able to earn money before was by means of hard labour. Now all they needed to do was to lie down on a bunk and let somebody syphon off half a litre of blood. The purchasers of the blood were only interested in the plasma, and pumped the blood back into the peasants' bodies. But they failed to sterilise the needles. Among the peasants was a man who, some years previously, had made a journey into a province bordering on Thailand. While there he had sold his blood in a similar fashion, and as a result had picked up the Aids virus. And now it found its way into the bloodstream of all his fellow peasants. When a health inspection took place in 1997, doctors discovered that a large proportion of the population of several villages were now HIV-positive. A lot of them had already died, or were chronically ill.

Then phase two of what Aids Report called 'The Catastrophe in Henan' came into operation. A team of doctors turned up in one of the villages. They offered the afflicted a new type of drug called BGB-2, a treatment patented by Cresco, a company in Arizona that was developing various forms of antiviral drugs. The doctors offered the poor peasants this drug free of charge, and promised that they would be restored to health. But BGB-2 had not been approved by the Chinese health authorities. They did not even know about its existence, nor did they know anything about the doctors and nurses who had travelled to Henan province. In fact, nobody knew if BGB-2 was effective or not, or what the side effects might be.

A few months later the peasants who had been treated began to deteriorate. Some had a very high temperature, lost all their strength, started bleeding from the eyes and acquired rashes that refused to go away. More and more of them died. All the doctors and nurses suddenly disappeared. The company in Arizona denied knowing anything about what had happened, changed its name and rose phoenix-like from the ashes in England. The only person to be arrested and punished was a man who had travelled from village to village, buying blood. He was convicted of serious tax fraud and was executed after a people's court condemned him to death.

Louise stretched.

'Have you finished reading? Henrik was most upset. We both had the same thought.'

'That it could happen here as well?'

Lucinda nodded.

'Desperate people always react in the same way. Why shouldn't they?'

Louise tried to gather her thoughts. She was tired, hungry, thirsty and, most of all, confused. All the time she found herself trying to block out Umbi's head, almost severed from his body.

'Had Henrik been in contact with Christian Holloway in Xai-Xai when you came to the café?'

'No, that was a long time afterwards.'

'Was it before he started to change?'

'It was at about the same time. He came to my house one morning – he was staying at Lars Håkansson's place – and asked me to take him to an Internet café. It was urgent. Just for once he was impatient.'

'Why didn't he use Lars Håkansson's computer?'

'He didn't say. But I do remember asking him that.'

'What did he say?'

'He just shook his head and urged me to hurry up.'

'Is that all he said? Think carefully! It's important.'

'We came to this café which had only just opened. I remember that it was drizzling. We could hear thunder in the distance. I remember saying that there might be a power cut if the thunderstorm drifted in over Maputo.'

Lucinda paused. Louise could see that she was thinking hard. For her part, she was plagued by the image of Umbi, a poverty-stricken peasant in the midst of all those patients dying of Aids, who had something important to say to her. Louise shuddered, despite the heat and dampness of the Internet café. It seemed to her that she stank of impurity.

'He kept checking his back as we walked down the street. I remember now. Twice he stopped dead and looked round. I was so surprised that I forgot to ask him what was the matter.'

'Did he say anything?'

'I don't know. We just resumed walking. He stopped and turned round one more time. That was all.'

'Was he afraid?'

'Hard to say. He might have been worried without my noticing it.'

'Do you remember anything else?'

'He spent less than an hour on the computer. He seemed to know exactly what he was doing.'

Louise tried to picture what had happened. The pair of them had been sitting at a table in a corner. From there, if he had looked up, Henrik would have been able to see what was going on in the street. But he was hidden behind the computer.

*He had chosen an Internet café because he didn't want to leave any trace in Lars Håkansson's computer.*

'Can you remember if anybody came into the café while he was working at the computer?'

'I was tired and hungry. I drank something and ate a sticky sandwich. Of course people kept coming and going. I don't recall any particular faces.'

'What happened next?'

'He copied the article. We left. It started raining just as we got to my house.'

'Did he turn round at all as you were walking home?'

'I don't remember.'

'Think!'

'I am thinking! I don't remember. We ran most of the way in the hope of beating the rain. It poured down for several hours, once it started. The streets were flooded. Naturally, there was a power cut that lasted until the afternoon.'

'Did he stay at your place?'

'I don't think you understand what pouring rain means in Africa. It's like hosepipes aimed onto our heads. Nobody goes out if they don't have to.'

'Did he say anything about the article? Why did he want to read it? How had he heard about it? What did it have to do with Christian Holloway?'

'When we got to my place he asked if I minded if he had a nap. He lay down on my bed. I told my brothers and sisters to be quiet. They weren't, of course, but he did get some sleep. I thought he must be ill. He slept as if he'd been deprived of sleep for a very long time. It was afternoon before he woke up, just after it stopped raining. We went out after the clouds moved on. The air was nice and fresh. We went for a walk along the beach.'

'Did he still not say anything?'

'He told me about something he'd heard once. A story he'd never been able to forget. I think it took place in Greece, or maybe Turkey. It had happened a very long time ago. A group of people hid from enemy insurgents by withdrawing into a cave. They had enough food with them to last for several months, and they had access to water from the dripping roof. But they were discovered. The enemy bricked up the cave opening. Some years later the cave was found and the wall broken down, but they were long dead of course. But the most remark-able thing was a ceramic jug standing on the ground. It had been used to collect water dripping from the roof. As the years went by, the dripping water crystallised and was transformed into a stalagmite that included the jug. Henrik said that was how he imagined patience to be. The jug and the water coalescing into each other. I don't know who told him the story in the first place.'

'It was me. It was a sensation when the cave was discovered on Peloponnisos in Greece. I was actually there when the discovery was made.'

'What were you doing in Greece?'

'I was working there as an archaeologist.'

'I don't know what that is.'

'I search for the past. Traces of people. Graves, caves, ancient palaces, manuscripts. I dig down looking for things that existed a long time ago.'

'I've never heard about any archaeologists existing in this country.'

'Maybe not very many, but there are some. Did Henrik really not tell you where he got the story from?'

'No.'

'Did he never say anything about me?'

'Never.'

'Did he never say anything about his family at all?'

'He said he had a grandfather on his mother's side who was a very well-known artist. World-famous. And he spoke quite a lot about his sister Felicia.'

'He doesn't have a sister. He was my only child.'

'I know that. He said he had a sister on his father's side.'

Just for a moment Louise thought that could be right. Aron could have had a child with another woman without mentioning it. In that case it would have been the most awful insult possible, telling Henrik about it but not her.

But it could not be true. Henrik would never have been able to keep a secret like that, even if Aron had begged him to be discreet about it.

There was no sister. Henrik had invented her. She had no memory of Henrik complaining about not having any brothers or sisters. She would have remembered if he had.

'Did he ever show you a photograph of his sister?'

'Yes. I still have it.'

Louise thought she was going out of her mind. There was no sister, no such person as Felicia. Why had Henrik made her up?

She stood up.

'I can't stay here a moment longer. I need something to eat, I need some sleep.'

They left the Internet café and walked through the streets in the stifling heat.

'Could Henrik cope with the heat?'

'He loved it, but I don't know if he could cope with it.'


Lucinda invited Louise into the cramped house. Louise shook hands with Lucinda's mother, an elderly woman with a stoop, strong hands, a wrinkled face and friendly eyes. There were children everywhere, of all ages. Lucinda said something and they all ran off immediately through the open door, where a curtain was flapping in the breeze.

Lucinda disappeared behind another curtain. A crackly radio could be heard from inside the room. She reappeared, carrying a photograph.

'I was given this by Henrik. Him and his sister, Felicia.'

Louise took the photograph to one of the windows. It was a picture of Henrik and Nazrin. She tried to understand what Henrik had said. Thoughts were buzzing round her head, but nothing stuck. Why had he done that? Why had he fooled Lucinda into thinking that he had a sister?

She gave the photograph back.

'That's not his sister. It's a good friend of his.'

'I don't believe you.'

'He didn't have a sister.'

'Why should he tell me a lie?'

'I don't know. But you mark my words. This is a good friend of his, by the name of Nazrin.'

Lucinda had stopped protesting. She put the photograph on a table.

'I don't like people who tell lies.'

'I can't understand why he told you he had a sister called Felicia.'

'My mother has never told a single lie in all her life. For her there is nothing but the truth. My father has always told her lies, about other women he claimed didn't exist, about money he'd earned but lost. He's lied about everything apart from the fact that he would never have survived if she hadn't been there by his side. Men tell lies.'

'So do women.'

'They do it in self-defence. Men have declared war on women in so many ways. One of their most common weapons is lies. Lars Håkansson even wanted me to change my name, to become a Julieta instead of a Lucinda. I still wonder about what the difference is. Does Julieta open her legs in a different way from me?'

'I don't like the way you talk about yourself.'

Lucinda withdrew into her shell. Louise stood up. Lucinda accompanied her to the car. They made no arrangements for a next meeting.

Louise got lost several times before eventually finding her way to Lars Håkansson's house. The guard at the gate was half asleep in the heat. He leapt to his feet, saluted and let her in. Celina was busy hanging up washing. Louise said she was hungry. An hour later, shortly before eleven in the morning, she had washed and eaten. She lay down on the bed in the cool breeze from the air conditioning, and fell asleep.

It was dusk by the time she woke up. Six o'clock. She had slept for many hours. The sheet beneath her was damp. She had been dreaming.

Aron had stood on the peak of a distant mountain. She had been trudging around some never-ending swamp somewhere in Härjedalen. In her dream they had been very far apart. Henrik had been sitting on a rocky outcrop next to a tall fir tree, reading a book. When she asked what he was reading, he explained that it was a photo album. She failed to recognise any of the people in the pictures.

Louise gathered together her dirty linen. She felt a distinct twinge of bad conscience as she left them on the floor for washing. Then she opened the door slightly, and listened. Not a sound from the kitchen. The house seemed to be empty.

She took a shower, got dressed and went downstairs. On all sides she could hear the whining noise from the air conditioning. There was a half-full bottle of wine on the table. She poured herself a glass and sat down in the living room. The security guards were conversing loudly outside. The curtains were drawn. She took a sip of wine and wondered what had happened after she had left Xai-Xai. Who had found Umbi? Had anybody associated her with what had happened? Who had been hiding in the darkness?

It was only now, after she had caught up on sleep, that panic seized her. *A man who wanted to tell me something in secret is murdered in bestial fashion.* It could have been Aron lying there with his throat cut.

She felt sick, ran to the toilet and threw up. Then she collapsed in a heap on the bathroom floor. She felt as if she was being dragged down by a whirlpool. Perhaps now, at last, she was on her way down into Artur's bottomless tarn with its black water?

She remained lying on the floor and paid no attention to the cockroaches that scuttled past and disappeared down a hole in the tiles behind the water pipes.

*I must start piecing together the fragments. There are several patterns that I ought to be able to make out. I must do what I usually do with old vases: feel my way forward with stalagmite-like patience.*

The picture she pieced together was unbearable. First of all Henrik discovers that he is HIV-positive. Then he discovers that ruthless experiments are being carried out on human beings in order to find a vaccine or some kind of cure for the virus. In addition, he is involved in some way or other in blackmailing Christian Holloway's son, who commits suicide.

She tried fitting the fragments together in various different ways, leaving gaps where shards as yet undiscovered might be able to fall into place. But the pieces simply refused to interlock.

She tried another approach. A blackmailer would hardly assume that his victim would commit suicide. The whole point is that the money paid is a guarantee for the victim that everything will be kept secret.

If Henrik had not anticipated that the blackmail would lead to Steve Nichols' death, how did he react when he heard what had happened? Was he resigned? Or ashamed?

The fragments were silent. They offered no answer.

She tried to take a step further. Could Henrik have been black-mailing a blackmailer? Had Steve Nichols been his friend? Was it through him that Henrik had heard about Christian Holloway's activities in Africa? Did Nichols know what really went on in Xai-Xai, behind the façade of loving charity?

Everything ground to a halt when she came to the final link in the chain: was Umbi's death a sign of something that could be compared with what had happened in distant Henan?

She was half lying on the bathroom floor, her head leaning against the lavatory. The sound of the air conditioning drowned out all other noise, but she suddenly had the feeling that somebody was standing behind her. She turned her head sharply.

Lars Håkansson was watching her.

'Are you ill?'

'No.'

'Then what the hell are you doing lying on a lavatory floor? If you'll allow me to ask?'

'I was sick. I didn't have the strength to stand up.'

She stood up and closed the door in his face. Her heart was pounding with fear.


When she emerged he was sitting with a glass of beer in his hand.

'Do you feel better?'

'I'm fine. I suppose I might have eaten something I shouldn't.'

'If you'd been here for a few weeks I'd have asked questions about headaches and high temperatures.'

'I haven't got malaria.'

'Not yet. But if I remember rightly you haven't been taking any preventative medicines?'

'You are right.'

'How was the trip to Inhaca?'

'How do you know I've been there?'

'Somebody saw you.'

'Who knew who I was?'

'Who knew who you were'

'I ate and slept and swam. And I also met a man who paints pictures.'

'Dolphins? Big-breasted women dancing in rows? He's a strange fellow who's been washed up on Inhaca. Fascinating life story.'

'I liked him. He'd painted a picture with Henrik in it, his face among many other faces.'

'The pictures I've seen in which he tries to depict living people have seldom been up to much. He's not a genuine artist, he doesn't have a shred of talent.'

Louise was annoyed by his dismissive tone.

'I've seen worse. And I've met a lot of artists who have been applauded for their pretensions rather than the talent they don't possess.'

'Naturally, my judgements on what is good art can't compare with those of a classically trained archaeologist. As an adviser to the country's Ministry of Health, what I normally discuss is anything but art.'

'What do you talk about?'

'The fact that there aren't any clean sheets in Mozambique hospitals, if indeed there are any sheets at all. It's very regrettable. Even more regrettable is that year after year we provide them with money to buy sheets, but it all disappears, both the money and the sheets, into the bottomless pockets of corrupt officials and politicians.'

'Why don't you protest?'

'I'd lose my job and be sent home. I try to make sure that the wages paid to officials are raised – they are unbelievably low – so that the motivation for corruption is no longer there.'

'Aren't two pairs of hands needed for corruption to take place?'

'Of course. There are many hands keen to dig into the millions paid out in the form of aid. Both givers and takers.'

His mobile rang. He answered abruptly in Portuguese and switched it off.

'I'm afraid I shall have to leave you on your own this evening. I am required to attend a reception at the German Embassy. Germany pays for a large part of health care in Mozambique.'

'I can manage.'

'Make sure you lock yourself in. It will probably be very late when I get back home.'

'Why are you so cynical? As you make no effort to conceal it, I don't hesitate to ask.'

'Cynicism is a defence mechanism. Reality appears in a slightly milder light through the filter of cynicism. Otherwise it would be easy to lose one's grip and let everything sink to the bottom.'

'What bottom?'

'There is no bottom. There are a lot of people who maintain in dead earnest that the future of the African continent is already in the past. All there is in store is an endless series of painful experiences for those who have the misfortune to be born here. Who really cares about the future of Africa? Apart from those with special interests, be they South African diamonds, Angolan oil or Nigerian football players.'

'Is that what you think?'

'Yes and no. Yes, when it comes to the continent itself. Africa is a place you would prefer not to have to deal with because it's obvious it's in such a mess. No, because it simply isn't possible to banish a whole continent to stand in the punishment corner. The best-case scenario is that international aid can keep the continent's head above water until they themselves can find some way of standing on their own feet. Here, if anywhere in the world, the wheel needs to be invented all over again.'

He stood up.

'I must get changed. But I'd be pleased to continue our conversation later. Have you found anything or anybody who can help you with your quest?'

'I keep finding something new all the time.'

He eyed her thoughtfully, nodded and headed upstairs. She could hear him taking a shower. After a quarter of an hour he came back down again.

'Perhaps I said too much? I'm not really cynical, but I am honest. There's nothing that can discourage people as much as honesty. We live in an age of mendacity.'

'Perhaps that means that the image one has of this continent isn't true?'

'Let's hope you're right.'

'I found two emails that Henrik had sent from your computer. Although I think in fact that you had written one of them. Why did you do that?'

Håkansson eyed her non-committally.

'Why should I have faked a letter from Henrik?'

'I don't know. To confuse me, perhaps.'

'Why should I do that?'

'I don't know.'

'You're mistaken. If it weren't for the fact that Henrik is dead, I'd throw you out.'

'I'm only trying to understand.'

'There's nothing to understand. I don't fake other people's letters. Let's forget about it.'

Håkansson went into the kitchen. She heard a clicking sound, then a door being closed and locked. He came back, left the house and closed the front door. His car started, the gate was opened and closed again. She was alone. She went upstairs and sat down in front of the computer, but she did not switch it on. She could not face it.

The door to Håkansson's bedroom was ajar. She opened it wider with her foot. His clothes lay in a heap on the floor. There was a television set in front of the king-sized bed, a chair overladen with books and magazines, a bureau with a fall front and a large wall mirror. She sat down on the edge of the bed and tried to imagine that she was Lucinda. Then she stood up and walked over to the bureau. She could remember a similar one from her childhood. Artur had shown it to her when they were visiting one of his elderly relatives, a lumberjack who had celebrated his ninetieth birthday when she was very small. She could picture it in her mind's eye. She picked up some of the books lying on Lars Håkansson's bureau. Most of them were about health care in Third World countries. Perhaps she had been unfair to Håkansson. What did she really know about him? Perhaps he was a hard-working aid worker and not a cynical observer?

She went to her own room and lay down. As soon as she felt up to it she would prepare a meal. Africa tired her out.

All the time, Umbi's face came gliding towards her through the darkness.

She woke up with a start. She'd dreamt she had been in the old people's home where the ninety-year-old with the shaking hands lived, a human wreck after a long, hard life as a lumberjack.

She could see the whole scene clearly. She had been six or seven at the time.

The bureau was standing by one of the walls in his room. Standing on top of it was a framed photograph of people from a different age. They could have been his parents.

Artur had opened the fall front and pulled out one of the drawers. Then he had turned it round and showed her the secret compartment, a drawer that could be opened from the other direction.

She stood up and went back to Håkansson's bedroom. It had been the drawer highest up on the left-hand side. She pulled it out and turned it round: nothing. She felt embarrassed at the fact that her dream had fooled her. Even so, she took out the other drawers as well.

The last one had the hidden compartment. Inside the compartment were some notebooks. She leafed through until she reached a page dated yesterday. She stared incredulously at what was written there. An 'L', and then 'XX'. It could hardly mean anything other than the fact that she had been to Xai-Xai. But he had not known that she was going to go there.

She leafed back a few pages and found another note. 'CH Maputo'. That could mean that Christian Holloway had been in Maputo. But Lars Håkansson had maintained that he was unacquainted with him.

She put the notebook back in and replaced the drawer. The guards in the street outside had fallen silent. She started walking round the house, checking that doors and windows were closed and the bars in place.

There was a little room behind the kitchen where the laundry was dried and ironed. She tried the window. The catch was off. And the bars were not closed. She slid the bars into the closed position, and recognised the noise they made. She opened them again. The same noise. At first she failed to remember why she recognised the sound. But then the penny dropped. She had heard it when Håkansson had gone into the kitchen just before leaving.

He told me to lock up, she thought, but the last thing he did was leave a window open. So that somebody could climb in?'

She panicked. Perhaps because she was so agitated, she could no longer distinguish between reality and her imagination. But even if she was misinterpreting everything that happened and was exaggerating the danger, she did not dare to stay. She switched on every light in the house and gathered up her clothes. Hands shaking, she unlocked all the locks on the front door, and then the wrought-iron gate. It was like breaking out of prison using a warder's keys. The security guard was asleep when she emerged into the street. He woke up with a start and helped her to put her bags onto the back seat of her hired car.

She drove straight to the Hotel Polana where she had stayed the first couple of nights in Maputo. She carried her bags upstairs herself, despite the friendly protests from the receptionist. Once installed in her room, she sat down on the edge of her bed, trembling.

Perhaps she was wrong, seeing shadows where she ought to have seen people, links that were really coincidences. But it had all become too much.

She remained sitting on the bed until she had calmed down. She went back to reception and established that the first flight to Johannesburg left Mozambique at seven o'clock the next morning. The receptionist helped her to book a seat. After eating she returned to her room and stood by the window, gazing down at the empty swimming pool. I don't know what it is I'm seeing, she thought. I'm in the middle of something, but I don't know what it is. Only when I get away from here will I start to understand what it was that drove Henrik to his death.

She hoped desperately that Aron was still alive. One day he would turn up again.

She drove to the airport shortly before five in the morning. She put her keys in the box provided for rented cars, collected her ticket and was just about to pass through security when she noticed a woman standing outside the terminal entrance, smoking. It was the girl who worked in the bar with Lucinda. Louise had never heard the girl's name, but was certain it was her.

She had been going to leave the country without first speaking to Lucinda. She felt ashamed.

Louise went up to the girl, who recognised her. Louise asked in English if she could take a message to Lucinda for her. The girl nodded. Louise tore a page out of her diary and wrote: *I'm leaving. But I'm not one of those who just disappear. You'll be hearing from me.*

She folded the paper and gave it to the girl, who was examining her nails.

'Where are you going?'

'To Johannesburg.'

'I wish it was me. But it isn't. Lucinda will get the message this evening.'

She passed through the security checks. Through a window she could see the enormous aircraft waiting for boarding.

*I think I'm beginning to sense something about the reality of this continent. Brutal forces grow out of all the poverty and spread without meeting any opposition. Poor Chinese peasants and their equally poor brothers and sisters in Africa are treated like rats. Was that what Henrik had realised? I still don't know what happens in the secret world that Christian Holloway has created. But I have a few pieces. I shall find more. As long as I don't give up. As long as I don't lose heart.*

She was one of the last passengers to board the flight. The aircraft thundered down the runway and took off. The last thing she saw before they were engulfed by the thin clouds was small fishing boats with bulging sails heading for land.

# CHAPTER 20

Twenty-three hours later Louise landed at Venizelos airport just outside Athens. The approach was over the sea. Pireus and Athens and all the chaotic jumble of streets and houses rose up to greet her.

When she left there, she had felt very happy. Now she was returning with her life in ruins, haunted by events she did not understand. Inside her head was a teeming mass of details that had so far eluded her ability to link together and interpret.

What was she returning to? An excavation of graves that she no longer had any responsibility for. She would pay whatever she owed in rent to Mitsos, pack her few belongings, and bid farewell to whoever was still around before the dig closed down for the winter.

Perhaps she should also pay a visit to Vassilis in his accountant's office? But then again, what did she have to say to him? What did she have to say to anybody?

She had flown with Olympic Airways, and treated herself to business class. During the long flight through the night she had enjoyed two seats to herself. When she had flown south, she thought she could see fires burning far below in the darkness. One of them was Umbi's fire, the last one he ever lit. Also hidden in the darkness were the people who had silenced him.

She knew now, she was certain of it: Umbi died because he had spoken to her. She would never be able to accept sole responsibility for what had happened, but if he had not come to see her he might well still have been alive.

Could she be sure of that? It was a question that haunted her dreams as she tried to sleep in the comfortable Olympic Airways seat. Umbi was dead. His eyes were staring out into the unknown, past her own.

She would never be able to see that look again. Nor would she ever know what he wanted to tell her.

At the airport she suddenly felt an urge to let the dig at Argolis wait, book herself in to a hotel, perhaps the Grande Bretagne at Syntagma, and just disappear into the teeming crowds of people. Spend a day or two there, force time to stand still so that she could find her way back to herself.

But she rented a car and drove along the newly-built motorway towards Peloponnisos and Argolis. It was still warm, autumn was no nearer now than when she had left. The road meandered through the dry hills, the white rocks protruded like pieces of bone between tufts of brown grass and stunted trees.

As she approached Argolis it struck her that she was no longer scared. She had managed to shake off her pursuers and leave them behind in the African darkness.

She wondered if Lucinda had received her message, and what she thought. And Lars Håkansson? She put her foot down and increased speed. She hated the man, even if she could not accuse him, naturally, of being involved in the events that had led to Henrik's death. He was a man she had no desire to have in her vicinity.

She turned off at a service station that also had a restaurant. She had been there before, with Vassilis, her patient but somewhat nonchalant lover. He had collected her from the airport. She had been in Rome to participate in a dreary conference on the discovery of ancient books and manuscripts in the desert sands of Mali. The discoveries had been sensational, but the seminars sleep-inducing, with far too many speakers and hopeless organisation. Vassilis had met her plane, and they had drunk coffee here together.

She had spent that night with him. It now seemed just as distant as anything she had experienced in her childhood.

Lorry drivers were half asleep over their coffee cups. She had a salad, water and a cup of coffee. All the scents and tastes told her that she was back in Greece now. Nothing seemed foreign, as had been the case in Africa.

\* \* \*

279

It was about eleven when she arrived in Argolis. She turned off towards the house she rented, but changed her mind and headed for the excavation site. She assumed that most of her colleagues would have left for home but that a few would still be there, putting the finishing touches to the necessary precautions as winter approached. But there was nobody there at all. The place was deserted. Everything that could be closed down was closed. Not even the security guards were there any more.

It was one of the loneliest moments in her life. Nothing could compare with the shock of finding Henrik dead in his bed, of course. This was a different kind of loneliness, like finding oneself abandoned in a landscape that went on for ever.

She recalled the game that she and Aron sometimes played. What would you do if you were the last person alive on earth? Or the first? But she could not remember any of the suggestions and answers they had given each other. Now it was not a game any more.

An old man was approaching, walking his dog. He had been a regular visitor to the dig. She had forgotten his name, but remembered that the dog was called Alice. Politely, he took off his cap and shook hands. He spoke rather complicated and slow English and was only too pleased to have an opportunity to practise it.

'I thought everyone had returned to their homes?'

'I'm just paying a fleeting visit. Nothing will happen here until next spring.'

'The last ones departed a week ago. But you were not here then, Mrs Cantor.'

'I've been in Africa.'

'So far away. Is it not frightening?'

'What do you mean?'

'All that . . . wildness. What is it called? The wilderness?'

'It's not so different from here. We forget too easily that people all belong to the same family. And that every landscape has something that reminds you of other landscapes. If it's true that we all came originally from Africa, that must mean that we all had a black mother long, long ago.'

'That can be true.'

He gave his dog a worried look. It was lying down with its head resting on its paws.

'She will probably not live beyond the winter.'

'Is she ill?'

'She is very old. At least a thousand years, I would think. A classic dog, a remnant from antiquity. Every morning I see with what difficulty she stands up. It is I who take her for walks now, not vice versa as it was before.'

'I hope she survives.'

'We shall meet again in the spring.'

He raised his cap again and continued his walk. The dog followed him, stiff-legged. She decided to visit Vassilis in his office. It was time now to draw a line under everything. It was clear to her that she would never come back here. Somebody else would have to take over as director of the excavations.

Her life had turned off in a different direction, but she had no idea which.

She stopped outside his office in the town centre. She could see Vassilis through the window. He was on the telephone, making notes, laughing.

*He has forgotten me. I've gone as far as he's concerned. I was no more than a casual acquaintance to sleep with and share his pain. Just like he was for me.*

She drove off before he noticed her.

When she came to her house, it took her some considerable time to find the keys. She could see that Mitsos had been in. No taps were dripping, no light was switched on unnecessarily. There were several letters on the kitchen table, two from the Swedish Institute in Athens, one from the Friends of Kavalla House. She left them unopened.

There was a bottle of wine on the bench next to the little refrigerator. She opened it and poured herself a glass. She had never drunk as much as she had been doing these last few weeks.

There was no rest for her. She was in a state of constant inner turmoil which was not always in step with the hustle and bustle around her.

She drank her wine and sat down in Leandros's creaking rocking chair. She gazed and gazed at her CD player without being able to make up her mind what she wanted to listen to.

When the bottle was half empty she moved to the desk, took out some writing paper and a fountain pen and started to write a letter to Uppsala University. She explained her situation and asked for a year's unpaid leave.

My pain and confusion are such that it would be presumptuous of me to believe that I could carry out responsibly the tasks the director of the excavations would need to undertake. Right now I am using up all my resources – if I have any left? – in an attempt to look after myself.

The letter turned out to be longer than she had intended. A request for leave ought to be brief. What she had written was a prayer, or perhaps a confused confession.

She wanted them to know what it felt like to lose your only child.

She found an envelope in a box, inserted the letter and sealed it. Mitsos's dog was barking. She took the car and drove to a nearby taverna where she often used to eat. The owner was blind. He sat motionless on a chair, as if he were slowly turning into a statue. His daughter-in-law did the cooking and his wife acted as waitress. None of them understood English, but Louise used to go into the cramped, steam-filled kitchen and point out what she wanted.

She had stuffed cabbage rolls and salad, a glass of wine and a cup of coffee. There were not many other diners. She recognised nearly all of them.

When she returned to her house, Mitsos suddenly loomed up in the darkness. She gave a start.

'Did I scare you?'

'I didn't know who it was.'

'Who could it have been, apart from me? Panayiotis perhaps. But he's gone to a football match, Panathinaikos are playing tonight.'

'Will they win?'

'They're bound to. Panayiotis reckons it will be three–one. He's usually right.'

She opened the door and let him in.

'I've been away longer than I thought.'

Mitsos had sat down on one of the kitchen chairs. He eyed her seriously.

'I've heard what has happened. I'm very sorry to hear about the boy's death. All of us are. Panayiotis has cried. The dogs have kept quiet for once.'

'It was so unexpected.'

'Nobody expects a young man to die. Except in wartime.'

'I've come to pack my things and pay you the rest of the rent.'

Mitsos flung his arms out wide.

'You don't owe me anything.'

He said it so forcefully that she did not insist. Mitsos was obviously embarrassed and was searching for something to talk about. She reminded herself that she used to think he was like Artur. There was something about their inability to handle emotions that touched her.

'Leandros is ill. The old security guard. What is it you call him? He was your *phylakes anghelos*.'

'Our guardian angel. What's the matter with him?'

'He started stumbling when he walked. Then he kept falling over. At first they thought it was his blood pressure. Last week they found a big *ongos* in his head. I think it's called a "tumour".'

'Is he in hospital?'

'He refuses to go. He won't allow them to open up his skull. He'd prefer to die.'

'Poor Leandros.'

'He's had a long life. He thinks that it's time for him to die. *Oti prepi na teleiossi, tha teleiossi*, as we say. "What has to come to an end will end".'

Mitsos stood up to go.

'I intend leaving tomorrow. I'll be flying to Sweden.'

'Will you be coming back next year?'

'I'll be back.'

She could not stop herself. The bird flew away without her managing to catch hold of its wing.

Mitsos was on his way out when he paused and turned round.

'There was somebody here looking for you.'

She was on her guard immediately. Mitsos had touched the tripwire that surrounded her.

'Who was it?'

'I don't know.'

'Was he a Greek?'

'No. He spoke English. He was tall, with thin hair, slim. He had a high-pitched voice. He asked after you. Then he paid a visit to your excavation. He seemed to know what had happened.'

Louise was horrified to think that it could be Aron that Mitsos was describing.

'Did he say what his name was?'

'Murray. I don't know if that is a first name or a surname.'

'Could be either. Tell me exactly what happened. When did he come? What did he want? How did he come? by car? on foot? Had he parked his car so that it couldn't be seen from here?'

'Why on earth should he want to do that?'

Louise felt she no longer had the strength to beat about the bush.

'Because he might have been dangerous. Because he might have been the person who killed Henrik, and maybe also my husband. Because he might have wanted to kill me.'

Mitsos stared at her in astonishment, and looked as if he was going to protest. She raised her hand to prevent him speaking.

'I want you to believe me. That's all. When did he come?'

'Last week. On Thursday. In the evening. He knocked on the door. I hadn't heard a car. The dogs hadn't started to bark. He asked about you.'

'Do you remember what his exact words were?'

'He asked if I knew whether Mrs Cantor was at home.'

'He didn't say Louise?'

'No. Mrs Cantor.'

'Had you ever seen him before?'

'No.'

'Did you have the feeling that he knew me?'

Mitsos hesitated before replying.

'No, I don't think he knew you.'

'What did you tell him?'

'That you'd gone to Sweden, and I didn't know when you'd be back.'

'You said he'd paid a visit to the dig?'

'That was the following day.'

'What happened next?'

'He asked if I was sure I didn't know when you were coming back. I felt he was asking too many questions. I told him I had nothing else to say and that I was in the middle of dinner.'

'How did he react to that?'

'He apologised for disturbing me. But he didn't mean it.'

'What makes you think that?'

'You notice that sort of thing. He was friendly, but I didn't like him.'

'Then what happened?'

'He went off into the darkness. I shut the door.'

'Did you hear a car starting?'

'Not as far as I can remember. And the dogs still didn't bark.'

'And he never came back?'

'I haven't seen him again.'

'And nobody else has been asking for me?'

'No, nobody.'

Louise could see that she was not going to get any further. She thanked Mitsos, who left. As soon as she heard his front door close, she locked up and drove away. There was a hotel on the way to Athens, Nemea, where she had stayed when she'd had a burst pipe. She was almost the only guest at the hotel and was given a double room overlooking extensive olive groves. She sat on the balcony, felt the cool autumn breeze and went to fetch a blanket. She could hear music in the distance, and people laughing.

She thought about what Mitsos had said. She had no idea about the identity of the man who had been looking for her, but whoever it was was close by. She had not succeeded in throwing them off.

*They think that I know something, or won't give up until I have found what I'm looking for. The only way I can shake them off is by ceasing to search. I thought I had got rid of them when I left Africa, but I was wrong.*

She made up her mind in the darkness on the balcony. She would not remain in Greece. She could choose between returning to Barcelona, or going back to Sweden. That was not a difficult choice to make. She needed Artur now.

The following day she packed up her belongings and moved out of the house. She left the keys in Mitsos's letter box and hoped that one of these days she would be able to come and collect the rocking chair that had been given to her by Leandros. She left an envelope addressed to Mitsos, containing money and asking him to buy flowers or cigarettes for Leandros, and wishing him all the best.

She drove back to Athens. It was foggy, the traffic was dense and impatient. She drove far too quickly, despite the fact that that she was not really in a hurry. Time was an alien concept, something beyond her control. In the chaos in which she found herself, timelessness ruled.

That evening she took an SAS flight to Copenhagen with a connection to Stockholm. She arrived around midnight and booked herself into the airport hotel. She still had enough of Aron's money to cover her flights and hotel bills. After studying the next day's departures she phoned Artur from her room and asked him to pick her up at Östersund airport. She would be arriving in the evening as she first wanted to go to Henrik's flat again. She could tell that Artur was relieved she was back in Sweden.

'How are you?'

'I'm too tired to talk about that just now.'

'It's snowing here,' he said. 'A light, gentle snowfall. It's four degrees below zero, and you haven't even asked me how the elk hunt went.'

'I'm sorry. How did the elk hunt go?'

'It went well. But it didn't last long enough.'

'Did you shoot one yourself?'

'No elks appeared in my patch. But it only took us two days to shoot our quota. Let me know your arrival time and I'll collect you from the airport.'


That night, for the first time in ages, she slept without being dragged up into consciousness by dreams at frequent intervals. She left her bags at the left-luggage office and took the train into Stockholm. It was cold and raining, with squally winds blowing in from the Baltic. She ducked into the wind as she started walking towards Slussen, but it was too cold. She changed her mind and flagged down a taxi. As she sat down on the back seat, she suddenly saw Umbi's face again in her mind's eye.

*Nothing is finished. Louise Cantor is still surrounded by shadows.*

She paused in the street to gather strength before entering the building in Tavasgatan and unlocking the door to Henrik's flat.

There was some junk mail and local news-sheets on the floor behind the door. She took them into the kitchen with her. She sat down at the table and listened. She could hear music coming from somewhere or other. She had a vague memory of having heard the same music previously when she had been in Henrik's flat.

Her mind wandered back to the moment when she had found Henrik lying dead.

*He always slept naked. But now he was wearing pyjamas.*

She suddenly realised that there was an explanation for the pyjamas that had never occurred to her before, because she had refused to believe that he had taken his own life. But what if he had done so, in fact? He knew that he would be dead when somebody found him. He did not want to be naked in those circumstances, and hence had put on his neatly pressed pyjamas.

She went into the bedroom and looked at the bed. Perhaps Göran Wrath and the pathologist had been right after all. Henrik had taken his own life. He had been unable to reconcile himself to the idea of his illness; perhaps also the realisation of how ruthless and deeply unjust the world was had become too great a burden for him to bear. Aron had disappeared because he was what he had always been, a man incapable of accepting responsibility for anything. The murder of Umbi was inexplicable, but need not have anything to do with either Henrik or Aron.

I've been hiding myself away in a nightmare, she thought. Instead of accepting the facts of what happened.

But she did not succeed in convincing herself. There was too much pointing in the opposite direction. She did not even know what had happened to the sheets on Henrik's bed. Perhaps they had simply been taken away when Henrik's body was removed? There was always irregular imperfections in the vases she pieced together from fragments dug out of the Greek soil. Reality never released all its secrets. When she left the flat she was still full of doubts.

She walked as far as Slussen and hailed a taxi that took her to Arlanda airport. The countryside was grey and misty. It was late autumn, soon winter. She bought a ticket for the 16.10 flight to Östersund. Artur was in the forest when he answered her call and assured her that he would be there to meet her.

She had three hours to fill before the flight left. She found a café table with a view of incoming aircraft taxiing to the terminal building, and phoned Nazrin. No answer. Louise left a message on the answering machine, and asked Nazrin to call her in Härjedalen.

That was her greatest worry at the moment. She needed to talk to Nazrin about Henrik's illness. Had he infected her? Nazrin, who had been his sister, Felicia.

Louise contemplated the forest beyond the airport. How would Nazrin cope if it turned out to be true?

In that case, Henrik would have passed the illness on to the sister who did not exist.

While she waited she pondered on what the future held for her.

*I'm still only fifty-four. Will I be keen and enthusiastic about all the things lying hidden in the ground, waiting for my attention? Or is that all in the past? Do I have any future at all?*

She still had a long way to go before she came to terms with Henrik's death.

*What's killing me off is not knowing. I must force the fragments to fall into place and tell me their story. Perhaps the only archaeological investigation I have left to solve is the one inside me.*

She dialled Aron's number. Unavailable.

Aircraft took off and headed into the grey sky or appeared like glittering birds from out of the clouds. She made her way to left luggage, collected her bags, checked in and sat down on a blue sofa to await her flight. The plane was only half full, and took off on time.

It was dark, calm and snowing lightly as she walked towards the terminal building in Östersund.

Artur was waiting for her by the luggage carousel. He had shaved and put on his best suit to celebrate her arrival.

As they sat down in the car she burst into tears. He patted her on the cheek, then headed for the bridge over Storsjön and the road leading south towards Sveg. As they approached Svenstavik she started telling him about her visit to Africa.

'I'm feeling my way,' she said. 'I think I need to do that in order to find out what happened. I have to grope my way forward in order to find the right words to tell the real story.'

'Take as long as you need.'

'I have the feeling it's urgent.'

'You've always lived your life in a hurry. I've never understood why. Nobody ever manages to do more than a tiny proportion of what they'd like to achieve. Long lives are also short lives. People aged ninety can have dreams just as impatient as those of a teenager.'

'I still know nothing about Aron. I don't even know if he's alive.'

'You have to look for him. I didn't want to do anything until I'd talked to you about it, but I did look into whether or not he'd returned to Apollo Bay. He hasn't.'

They drove through the darkness. The headlights illuminated the dense forest on both sides of the road. It was still snowing gently.

Somewhere between Ytterdal and Sveg she fell asleep, her head resting on the only shoulder she had left to lean on.

The next day she went to the police station in the civic centre and reported Aron missing. The officer who dealt with her submission was somebody she had known since she was a little girl. He had been a few classes ahead of her at school. He'd had a moped, and she had been head over heels in love with him – or perhaps with the moped. He expressed his condolences without asking questions.

Then she went to the cemetery. There was a thin layer of snow over the grave. Still no headstone. But Artur had told her that it had been ordered from a stonemason in Östersund.

As she approached the cemetery, she was afraid that she might not be able to cope with what was in store. But when she stood by the grave she was composed, almost cold.

*This is not where Henrik is. He is inside me, not down there under the ground, covered by a thin layer of snow. He had made a long journey, despite being so young when he died. We are both alike in that respect. We both take life extremely seriously.*

A woman walked past on one of the paths among the graves. She greeted Louise, but did not stop. Louise had the impression that she knew the woman, but could not remember her name.

It started snowing. Louise was about to leave the cemetery when her mobile rang in her pocket. It was Nazrin. At first interference made it difficult to understand what she was saying.

'Can you hear me?' Nazrin was shouting.

'Hardly. Where are you?'

'How times change! In the old days the first question was always "How are you?" Nowadays, the first thing you do is fix a geographical location – "Where are you?" – before you ask about a person's health.'

'I can hardly hear what you're saying.'

'I'm at Central Station. Trains are coming and going. People are dashing back and forth.'

'Are you going away?'

'I've just come back, from Katrineholm of all places. Where are you?'

'I'm standing beside Henrik's grave.'

Nazrin's voice faded away, but returned almost immediately.

'Are you up north?'

'I'm standing by his grave. It's snowing. It's white everywhere.'

'I wish I was there with you. I'll go to the ticket office. It's quieter in there.'

Louise heard the background noise fade away, to be replaced by individual voices that boomed forth and then fell silent.'

'Can you hear me better now?'

Nazrin's voice seemed very close. Louise could almost hear her breathing.

'I can hear you loud and clear.'

'You just vanished. I wondered what was going on.'

'I've been on a long journey. It's been shattering, frightening. I need to see you. Can you come here?'

'Can't we meet halfway? I've got my brother's car on loan while he's abroad. I like driving.'

Louise remembered that she and Artur had once taken a break in Järvsö on a journey to Stockholm. Maybe that was about halfway? She suggested that they should meet there.

'I've no idea where Järvsö is. But I'll find it. I can be there tomorrow. How about meeting at the church? Two o'clock?'

'Why at the church?'

'Surely there must be a church in Järvsö? Can you think of a better place? You can always find a church.'

When they'd finished talking Louise went to the church in Sveg. She remembered having been there as a child, all by herself, to look at the big altarpiece and imagine the Roman soldiers striding out of the picture and capturing her. She'd called it the *terror* game. She'd toyed with her own fear in that church.


Louise left early the next morning. It had stopped snowing, but the road could well be icy. She wanted to have plenty of time. Artur stood outside the door, naked from the waist up despite the temperatures below freezing, to wave goodbye.

They met at the church, which was on an island in the middle of the River Ljusnan, at the agreed time. Nazrin arrived in an expensive Mercedes. The clouds had receded, the sun had broken through, early winter had taken a step backwards and it was autumn once more.

Louise asked if Nazrin was in a hurry to go back home.

'I can stay until tomorrow.'

'There's a fine traditional hotel here called Järvsöbaden. I don't think it's exactly high season now.'

They were allocated two rooms in one of the wings. Louise asked Nazrin if she'd like to go for a walk, but she shook her head. Not yet. What she wanted to do now was talk.

They sat in one of the drawing rooms. An old grandfather clock was ticking away in a corner. Nazrin was absent-mindedly fingering some spots on her cheek. Louise decided to take the bull by the horns.

'It's not easy for me to say this. But I have to do it. Henrik was HIV-positive. Ever since I discovered that I've gone through agonies, thinking about you.'

Louise had been worrying about how Nazrin would react to the news. What would she have felt in Nazrin's place? But she had not expected what actually happened.

'I know.'

'Did he tell you?'

'He said nothing about it. Not until after he was dead.'

Nazrin opened her handbag and took out a letter.

'Read this.'

'What is it?'

'Read it!'

The letter was from Henrik. It was short. He explained how he had discovered that he was HIV-positive, but he hoped that he had been sufficiently careful to ensure that he had not passed the infection on to her.

'I received this a few weeks ago. It came from Barcelona. Somebody must have posted it after they'd heard that he was dead. I'm sure that's how he'd arranged it. He was always going on about what to do *if something happened*. I always used to think he was going over the top. I know different now, of course, when it's too late.'

Blanca must have had that letter hidden away somewhere when Louise and Aron visited her. He must have given her strict instructions: *Only send this if and when I die.*

'I was never worried. We always took precautions. I went for tests, of course. No problem.'

'Can you imagine how much I was dreading this conversation?'

'Perhaps. But Henrik would never have exposed me to danger.'

'But if he didn't know he was infected?'

'He knew.'

'But even so, he said nothing to you.'

'Perhaps he was afraid that I might have left him. Maybe I would. I don't know.'

A woman came in and asked if they were intending to have dinner in the hotel. They said they would. Nazrin wanted to go out now. They went for a walk beside the river. Louise told Nazrin about her long trip to Africa and all that had happened. Nazrin did not ask many questions. They clambered up a hill and enjoyed the view.

'I still can't believe it,' Nazrin said. 'That Henrik could have been killed because of what he knew. And that your husband disappeared for the same reason.'

'I don't ask you to believe me. I just wonder if the thought brings any memories to life. Something Henrik said or did. Maybe a name you thought you'd heard before?'

'No, nothing.'

They continued talking until late. When Louise left the next morning, Nazrin was still in bed. Louise left a message, paid the bill for both of them, and drove back northwards through the forest.


During the weeks that followed Louise submersed herself into the stillness and expectations of early winter. She slept late most mornings, and finished her report for the university on the year's excavations.

She spoke to her friends and colleagues, all of whom expressed their condolences and looked forward to welcoming her back to the fold once her grief had subsided. But Louise knew that it would not go away: her grief would persist and grow worse.

She occasionally went to see the solitary policeman in his little office. But he had no news for her. There was no sign of Aron, despite the fact that he was now being looked for all over the world. He had vanished, as so often before, and left not a trace behind.

During this time Louise did not contemplate her future. It did not exist as yet. She was still managing to stand upright, but often felt as if she might collapse at any moment. The future was blank, an empty space. She took long walks, over the old railway bridge and then back over the new one. She sometimes got up early in the morning, borrowed one of Artur's old rucksacks and wandered off into the forest, returning only when it started to get dark.

Louise tried to reconcile herself to the fact that she might never understand what had caused Henrik's death. She was still trying to juggle with the pieces and search for a connection, but her hopes of success were diminishing as time went by. All the time Artur was there, ready to listen, ready to help her.

They would occasionally have long talks in the evenings. They were mostly about everyday events, about the weather, or memories from her childhood. Now and then she would try out various hypotheses on him. Is this what might have happened? He listened, but she knew even as she spoke that once again she had entered into a cul-de-sac.

One afternoon at the beginning of December, the telephone rang. The man wanting to speak to her was called Jan Lagergren. She had not heard his voice for many years. They had been students together in Uppsala, but their career paths lay in different directions. At one time there had been a mutual attraction between them, but it never led to anything. All she knew about him was that his ambition was to find a job in the civil service which would take him abroad.

Despite all the years that had passed, his voice had hardly changed.

'Something unexpected has happened. I had a letter from one of my numerous aunts who happens to live in Härjedalen. She claimed that she had seen you in the cemetery in Sveg one day. God only knows how she knew that we were acquainted. She told me that your son had died recently. I just wanted to ring and pass on my sincere condolences.'

'How nice to hear your voice again. You sound just the same as you always did.'

'But everything has changed even so. I still have my voice, and a few tufts of hair; but everything else has changed.'

'Thank you for ringing. Henrik was my only child.'

'Was it an accident?'

'The doctors say it was suicide. I refuse to believe that, but perhaps I'm deceiving myself.'

'What can I say?'

'You've already done everything you can do, you phoned me. Don't go yet. We haven't spoken to each other for twenty-five years. What happened to you? Did you join the foreign service?'

'Very nearly. I have occasionally been issued with a diplomatic passport. I've been posted abroad, but not with the Foreign Office. I worked for the aid organisation Sida.'

'I've just come back from Africa. Mozambique. '

'I've never set foot there. I did one tour of Addis Ababa and another in Nairobi. That first time I was in charge of agricultural aid, the second time I was in charge of all Swedish aid going to Kenya. At the moment I'm head of department at our office in Sveavägen here in Stockholm. And you became an archaeologist?'

'Yes, in Greece. Have you ever come across a man working for Sida called Lars Håkansson?'

'I've bumped into him once or twice, and we've exchanged a few words. But our paths have never really crossed. Why do you ask?'

'He works in Maputo. For the Ministry of Health.'

'I hope he's a decent fellow.'

'To tell you the truth, I don't like him.'

'Then it's a good job I didn't tell you he was my best friend.'

'Could I ask you something? What sort of a reputation does he have? Are there any rumours about him? I have to know because he knew my son. I'm embarrassed to have asked you this.'

'I'll see what I can dig out. Without mentioning who wants to know, of course.'

'Has your life in general turned out as you'd planned?'

'Hardly. But does it ever? I'll get back to you when I've got something to tell you.'


Two days later, when Louise was thumbing through one of her old archaeology textbooks, the phone rang.

Every time it happened she hoped it was Aron. But it was Jan Lagergren.

'Your intuition seems to have been right. I talked to a few people here who can usually be relied on to distinguish between malicious insinuation and envy on the one hand, and what is true on the other. Lars Håkansson is evidently not a man with many friends. He is considered to be haughty and arrogant. Nobody doubts that he is competent and does his job well, but it seems that his hands are not clean even so.'

'What has he done?'

'Rumour has it that he has taken advantage of his diplomatic immunity to smuggle home rare skins of big game and reptiles, all of which are classified as endangered species. That kind of thing can be a big earner for unscrupulous people. It's not all that difficult either. A python's skin doesn't weigh very much. Other rumours attached to Mr Håkansson's CV suggest that he is involved in illegal car trading. The most significant thing, no doubt, is that he has a mansion in Sörmland which ought to be beyond his means. "Toppman's Manor" sounds almost too appropriate a name for it. To sum up, I think I would characterise Lars Håkansson as a competent but ruthless person who looks after number one in every conceivable situation. But then he's hardly the only one in that category.'

'Did you find anything more?'

'Don't you think that's enough? Lars Håkansson appears to be a dodgy character who operates in murky backwaters. But he's clever. He walks a tightrope but nobody has found a way of knocking him off it.'

'Have you ever heard of a man called Christian Holloway?'

'Does he also work for Sida?'

'He runs private hospital villages for Aids sufferers.'

'That sounds very praiseworthy. But I don't recall ever having heard the name.'

'And it didn't crop up in connection with Lars Håkansson? I think Håkansson was working for that man in some way or other.'

'I'll keep the name tucked away in the back of my mind. I promise to let you know the moment I hear anything about him. I'll give you my phone number. And I'm very keen to hear why you're so interested in Lars Håkansson.'

She noted the phone number down on the cover of her old archaeology textbook.


Another ceramic fragment had been dug up out of the dry African soil. Lars Håkansson, a ruthless person prepared to do more or less anything. She placed the shard alongside the others, and felt how cripplingly heavy her weariness was.

It was getting dark earlier, both inside her and out.

But there were days when her strength returned, and she managed to keep despondency at bay. Then she would spread out her fragments on the old dining table, symbolically speaking, and try once again to fit them together so as to form the beautiful urn they had once been. Artur would shuffle around silently, pipe in mouth, serving her a cup of coffee at regular intervals. She started sorting the pieces into two sections: a periphery and a centre. Africa was in the centre of the urn, and the very hub was the town of Xai-Xai. She found details on the Internet about the floods that had devastated the town some years previously. Pictures of a little girl had been transmitted all round the world. What made her famous was the fact that she had been born in the crown of a tree: her mother had climbed up there to avoid the rising mass of water.

But Louise's fragments did not breathe birth and life. They were dark, and spoke of death, of Aids, of Dr Levansky and his experiments in the Belgian Congo. She shuddered every time she thought about the screaming apes, strapped down onto a table and cut up alive.

It was like a freezing cold draught constantly by her side. Is that what Henrik had felt as well? Had he also felt the cold? Had he taken his own life when his insight into the fact that human beings were being treated like apes became too hard to bear?

She started again from the beginning, rearranged the pieces and tried to interpret what she saw in front of her.

All around her autumn slipped away, and winter tightened its grip.


Thursday 16 December was a bright, cold day. Louise was woken early by Artur, clearing snow from the drive. The telephone rang. When she answered, she could not make out who the caller was at first. There was a loud crackling noise in the receiver, the call was evidently a long-distance one. Could it be Aron, sitting among his red parrots in Australia?

Then she recognised Lucinda's voice, faint, forced.

'I'm ill. I'm dying.'

'Can I do anything for you?'

'Come here.'

Lucinda's voice sounded very distant now. Louise felt as if Lucinda was slipping out of her grip.

'I think I can see it all now. All that Henrik discovered. Come before it's too late.'

The line went dead. Louise sat up in bed. Artur was still shovelling snow. She was completely motionless.


On Saturday 18 December Artur drove her to Arlanda airport. In the morning of 19 December she disembarked in Maputo.

The heat struck her like a red-hot fist.

# CHAPTER 21

Louise found her way to Lucinda's house with the help of a taxi driver who spoke no English. When she finally reached there, Lucinda was nowhere to be found. Her mother burst into tears when she saw Louise, who thought she must have come too late. One of Lucinda's sisters stepped forward and spoke broken but understandable English.

'Lucinda is no dead. She came suddenly sick, had not strong to get out from bed. In only few weeks she went down a lot in weighing.'

Louise was not certain she had understood. The sister's bad English grew even worse, the longer she talked; it was as if the little power that remained in a battery was running out.

'Lucinda say Donna Louise come very much yes and ask for her. We must say Donna Louise that she gone to Xai-Xai for getting aid.'

'Did she say that? That I would come?'

The conversation took place outside the house. The sun was directly overhead. The heat was making Louise feel ill, the Swedish winter was still inside her. *Lucinda gone to Xai-Xai for getting aid.* Louise had no doubt that what Lucinda had said on the phone was true – that she had very little time left.

The taxi that had brought her from the airport was waiting. The driver was sitting on the ground in the shadow thrown by his car, listening to the radio, which was very loud. Louise took Lucinda's sister with her and asked her to explain to the driver that she wanted to go to Xai-Xai. When the driver understood, he sighed and looked worried. But Louise insisted. She wanted to go to Xai-Xai and she wanted to go right now. He gave a price, Louise asked for a translation and gathered he wanted to charge several million meticais. She suggested that she should pay in dollars, which immediately made the driver more interested. They eventually agreed on a price, plus petrol charges, plus everything else that seemed to be necessary for a trip to Xai-Xai. It was 190 kilometres, Louise seemed to recall. The taxi driver gave the impression that he was preparing for an expedition to a far distant and unexplored land.

'Ask him if he's been to Xai-Xai before.'

The driver shook his head.

'Tell him I've been there before. I know the way. Ask him his name.'

Besides discovering that his name was Gilberto, Louise was informed that he had a wife and six children and believed in the Catholic God. She had noticed a faded colour photograph, pinned to the sun visor in his cab, of the increasingly ill Polish Pope.

'Tell him I need to rest. He must not talk all the time during the journey.'

Gilberto reacted to the instruction as if he had been given an extra sum of money, and closed the back door quietly after her. The last Louise saw of Lucinda's family was her mother's desperate face.


They arrived in Xai-Xai late in the afternoon, after a puncture in a front tyre and a temporary repair tying the exhaust pipe to the chassis with a piece of string. Gilberto had not uttered a word during the journey, but had repeatedly turned the music from the radio up louder and louder. Louise tried to rest. She had no idea what was in store for her, but knew she would need all her strength.

The memory of what had happened to Umbi would not go away. Several times during the journey she considered telling Gilberto to stop and go back. Panic was only just under the surface. She had the feeling that she was on her way into a trap that would slam shut and never release her again. But all the time she could hear Lucinda's voice in the telephone. *I'm dying.*

Just before they came to the bridge over the river, the photograph of the Pope came loose and fell onto the floor between the seats. Gilberto stopped to pin it back up again. Louise became increasingly irritated. Did he not realise that time was short?

They drove through the dusty town. Louise had still not made up her mind what to do. Should she continue to Christian Holloway's village and leave the taxi there? Or should she go to the beach hotel first, and find somebody else to take her to the village? She opted for the hotel. When she got out of the taxi the first thing she heard was the melancholy and monotonous sound of the albino's timbila. She paid Gilberto, shook hands with him and carried her bag into the hotel. As usual there were plenty of empty rooms. The keys were hanging in neat rows behind the reception desk, hardly any were missing. She noticed that the receptionist did not recognise her, or pretended not to. He asked for neither her passport nor a credit card. She felt both invisible and trusted at the same time.

The receptionist spoke good English. Yes, of course he could call her a taxi; but it would be better if he had a word with one of his brothers who had an excellent car. Louise asked for it to pick her up as soon as possible. She went up to her room, stood in the window and gazed at the remains of the beach kiosk. That was where Umbi had had his throat cut after talking to her. She almost vomited at the thought. Her fear had acquired claws. She managed to wash despite the fact that the bathroom tap only produced a thin trickle of water, then forced some food down her: grilled fish and a small salad that she toyed with on her plate extremely hesitantly. The timbila sounded more doleful than ever, the fish was full of bones. She sat for some time with her mobile in her hand, wondering whether to phone Artur. But she decided not to. The only thing that mattered at the moment was to respond to Lucinda's cry for help. Always assuming it was a cry for help? Perhaps it was more of a battle cry, Louise thought.

The albino stopped playing his timbila. She could hear the sea now, roaring, wild. The breakers came rolling in from India, from the distant coast of Goa. The heat was not as extreme here by the sea as it had been in Maputo. She paid her bill and left the dining room. A man in shorts and an overwashed shirt with a Stars and Stripes motif was waiting by the side of a rusty old lorry. He greeted her with a smile, and said that his name was Roberto, but for some reason Louise found impossible to understand, he was always known as Warren. She climbed into the passenger seat and explained where she wanted to go. Warren spoke English with the same South African accent as his brother in reception.

'To Christian Holloway's village,' he said. 'He's a good man. He does a lot for the sick people. Before long we'll all be ill and die,' he said offhandedly. 'We Africans will no longer exist in a few years' time. Nothing but bones in the sand and empty fields. Who will eat all the cassavas when we've gone?'

Louise was intrigued by the evident enthusiasm with which he spoke about the painful death which was common around here. Was he ill himself? Or was it merely a disguised expression of his own fear?


They arrived at the village. The first thing she noticed was that the black dog that had always been lying in the shade was no longer there. Warren asked if she wanted him to wait, or come back later and collect her. He showed her his mobile telephone and gave her his number. They made a test call, and she got through at the second attempt. He did not want to be paid, that could wait, there was no hurry, not when it was as hot as it was today. She clambered out of the lorry. Warren turned round and drove away. She stood in the shade where the dog used to lie. The heat was motionless around her and the white-painted buildings. There was not a sound to be heard. Five o'clock. She wondered if Artur had needed to clear away snow that morning. A bird flew past close to the ground, its wings flapping at an incredible rate, and disappeared in the direction of the sea. *Was it a cry for help or a battle cry?* Perhaps Lucinda had sent out both messages at the same time? Louise eyed the row of houses that formed a semicircle.

*Lucinda knows that she needs to give me accurate instructions. Which of the buildings is she in? Naturally, in the one we visited when we came here together.*

She set off over the gravel with the feeling that although the place seemed deserted, people were watching her without her being able to see them. She opened the door and stepped into the darkness. She was hit by the stench of unwashed, sweaty bodies. Nothing had changed since she was last there. There were sick people lying everywhere. Hardly any of them moved.

*The beach of death. These people have come ashore here in the hope of finding help. Alas, there is nothing here but death. Like on the beaches at Lampedusa in the Mediterranean, where the dead refugees come ashore but never find the life they have dreamed of.*

She stood still until her eyes grew accustomed to the dim light. She listened to the chorus of breathing. Some were short, intense, strained; others so thin that they could barely be heard. There was a rattling and groaning and hissing and shrieking that subsided into whispers. She glanced round the overcrowded room, looking in vain for Lucinda. She took a handkerchief out of her pocket and held it over her mouth. Soon she would no longer be able to suppress the vomit rising in her throat. She started moving round the room, moving her feet carefully so as not to stand on a leg or an outstretched arm. Human roots, she thought, waiting to trip me up. She banished the thought, it was pointless, she had no need to transform reality into imagery. It was sufficiently incomprehensible as it was. She continued searching.

She found Lucinda in a corner. She was lying on a mat behind a wall projecting slightly into the room, formed by one of the pillars supporting the roof. Louise caught her eye. Lucinda really was very ill; almost naked, her chest was rising and falling with short, sudden breaths. It was clear to Louise that Lucinda had chosen her position carefully. The pillar created a blind spot. Nobody would be able to see her face when Louise was standing in front of her. Lucinda pointed at the floor. There was a matchbox lying there. Louise pretended to drop her handkerchief, bent down to pick it up and hid the matchbox in her hand. Lucinda shook her head, almost imperceptively. Louise turned round and left the building, as if she had failed to find what she was looking for.

She flinched when she emerged into the bright light, then started to walk along the dusty road leading away from the village. When she was out of sight she rang Warren. Ten minutes later he picked her up. She apologised for not realising that her visit would turn out to be so brief, but she might well need to fly back home, possibly even today.

When they reached the hotel Warren still refused to accept any payment. If she wanted him, all she needed to do was ring. He was now going to have a nap in the shadow of his lorry, then go down to the sea for a swim.

'I swim with whales and dolphins. Then I can forget that I am a human being.'

'Do you want to forget that?'

'I think that sometimes all humans have wished that they had not only arms and legs, but fins as well.'


She went up to her room, and washed her hands and face under the tap that had now suddenly acquired a new lease of life and produced a strong jet of water. She sat down on the edge of her bed and opened the matchbox. Lucinda had torn a scrap from the margin of a newspaper, and written a message in tiny handwriting. *Listen for the timbila in the dark.* That was all.

*Listen for the timbila in the dark.*

She waited for dusk after succeeding in bringing the air conditioning to life by thumping it with a shoe.

Warren rang and roused her from her slumbers. Did she need him now? Or would it be all right if he drove into Xai-Xai to see his wife, who was due to have a baby any day now? She told him to go.

She had bought a swimming costume at the airport before leaving Stockholm. She felt embarrassed, because her reason for going to Mozambique was to meet a young woman who was dying. She made several attempts to persuade herself that it would be acceptable to go to the beach. But she could not bring herself to do it. She needed to conserve her strength, even though she did not know what lay in store. Lucinda and her laboured breathing made her both upset and afraid.

In this oppressive heat everything smacked of death and decay. But on the other hand, there was nothing so life-giving as hot sunshine. Henrik would have protested vehemently at the designation of Africa as the continent of death. He would have argued that it is our own inability to dig out the truth that is responsible for the idea that '*we know all about how Africans die, but hardly anything about how they live*'.

Who had said that? She could not remember, but the words had been in one of the documents she had read when she went through his papers in the flat in Stockholm. She suddenly remembered something he had written on the front of one of the vast number of files containing material about Kennedy's brain. Henrik had been furious. He had asked the question: *How would we Europeans react if the world only knew about how we die, but nothing at all about how we live our lives?*

As the brief dusk approached, she stood in the window, looking down at the sea. What remained of the beach kiosk was in shadow. The lorry had gone. Some children were playing with what appeared to be a dead bird. Women carrying baskets on their heads were walking along the beach. A man was trying to avoid falling off his bicycle as he rode through the deep sand. He failed, fell over, and stood up again, laughing copiously. Louise admired him for his genuine amusement at having failed.

Darkness fell, spreading a dark cloak over the earth. She went down to the dining room. The albino with his timbila was in his usual place. But he was not playing, he was eating rice and salad from a red plastic bowl. There was a bottle of beer by his side. He ate slowly, like someone who was not really hungry. She went to the bar. Several men were sitting at a table, half asleep over their beer glasses. The woman behind the bar was so like Lucinda that she gave a start. But when the woman smiled it became obvious that she was toothless. Louise felt the need to drink something strong. Artur would have produced a bottle of aquavit, and plonked it down on the table. *Here, drink up, fortify yourself!* She ordered a whisky, something she did not really like, and a bottle of the local beer, Laurentina. The albino started playing his timbila again. *Listen for the timbila in the dark.* Some more guests came into the dining room, an elderly Portuguese man with a very young African girl. Louise estimated about forty years between them. She felt an urge to march over and punch him on the nose. He embodied the way in which love and contempt combined to embody the way in which colonial oppression was still going strong.

*I know too little. With my knowledge of Bronze Age graves, or the importance of ferrous oxides for the colour of Greek ceramics, I'm a match for almost anybody. But when it comes to life beyond burial grounds and museums I know nothing compared with what Henrik knew. I am a very ignorant person, and I've only just realised that, after I've turned fifty.*

She emptied her glass and felt herself breaking into a sweat. A thin fog descended over her consciousness. The albino was still playing. The woman behind the bar was biting her fingernails. Louise listened out into the darkness. After a few moments' hesitation, she ordered another glass of whisky.

It was twenty minutes to seven now. What time was it in Sweden? Was the time difference one hour or two? In which direction? Earlier or later? She was not at all sure.

Her questions were unanswered because the timbila suddenly stopped playing. She emptied her glass and paid. The albino wound his way slowly through the tables in the empty dining room, heading for the toilets. Louise went to the front of the hotel. Warren's lorry had not yet returned. She could hear the sighing of the sea, somebody passed by in the darkness, invisible, whistling. A flickering bicycle light staggered past, then vanished. She waited.

The albino started playing his timbila again. The sound was different now, more distant. It suddenly dawned on her that what she was hearing was another timbila. The instrument in the dining room had been abandoned, the albino had not returned.

She took a few steps forward into the darkness. The vibrating sounds of the timbila were coming from somewhere closer to the sea, but not from the ramshackle beach kiosk, in the other direction, where the fishermen used to hang up their nets. Once more Louise was gripped by fear, she was afraid of what was about to happen, but she forced herself to think of Henrik. She felt closer to him now than at any other time since his death.

She listened for other noises besides the timbila, but there was only the ocean, and her own isolation, like an icily cold winter night.

She walked towards the source of the music. It came closer, but she could see no fire, nothing. Now she was very close, the invisible timbila almost next to her. It stopped playing abruptly, between two notes.

Then she felt a hand on her ankle. She gave a start, but nobody was pinning her down. She stopped dead when she heard Lucinda's voice in the darkness.

'It's me.'

Louise squatted down and groped into the blackness. Lucinda was sitting on the ground, leaning against a withered tree that had been blown over in a storm. Louise could feel her feverish, sweaty face against her hand, which Lucinda took hold of and pulled her down to the ground beside her.

'Nobody saw me. Everybody thinks I'm so weak that I can't stand up. But I can. Not for much longer, though. But I knew you would come.'

'I'd never have believed that you could become so ill so quickly.'

'Nobody believes that death is just round the corner. For some, it all happens very quickly. I'm one of those.'

'I can take you away from here and make sure you get the necessary drugs.'

'It's too late. Besides, I have all Henrik's money. It doesn't help. The illness is spreading through my body like a fire in dry grass. I'm ready. I'm only occasionally afraid, at dawn, on certain days, when the sunrise is more beautiful than usual and I know that soon I shall never be able to experience it again. Something inside me has already laid itself to rest. A human being dies one step at a time, like when you wade out into the shallows on a very gently sloping beach, and it's only after several kilometres that the water comes up to your neck. I thought I would stay and die at my mother's place. But I didn't want to die pointlessly, I didn't want my life to pass by without leaving something behind. I thought about you and how you were searching for Henrik's soul in everything he had done or tried to do. I came here to see if things really were as Henrik suspected they were, that behind all the goodwill there was a different reality, that behind all the young idealists lurked people with black wings who were exploiting the dying for their own ends.'

'What have you seen?'

Lucinda's faint voice trembled as she spoke.

'Terrible things. But let me tell you the whole story. How I got to

307

Xai-Xai is neither here nor there, it doesn't matter if I was taken there in a wheelbarrow or on the back of a lorry. I have a lot of friends, I'm never alone. I had put on the shabbiest clothes I could find, and then they left me in the dirt and sand outside the buildings in Christian Holloway's village. I lay there, waiting for dawn. The first one to see me was an old man with white hair. Then all the others came, all of them wearing rubber boots, big aprons and rubber gloves. They were white South Africans, one might have been a mulatto. They asked me if I had Aids, where I'd come from, it was as if they were cross-questioning me. In the end they decided to let me stay. They put me in one of the buildings, but when night fell I moved to the place where you found me.'

'How were you able to ring me?'

'I still have a mobile phone. The man who drove me here recharges my battery every other day and passes it to me in secret at night. I phone my mother and listen to her terror-stricken appeals to keep death at bay. I try to console her although I know that's not possible.'

Lucinda started coughing, hard and long. Louise changed her position and noticed that there was a little cassette recorder standing by the tree. *Listen for the timbila in the dark.* It had not been a spectre playing. The sound came from a cassette. Lucinda stopped coughing. Louise could hear her panting with the strain. I can't leave her here, she thought. Henrik would never have abandoned her. There must be something that can ease her pain, perhaps she can be saved.

Lucinda grasped hold of her hand as if seeking support, but she made no attempt to stand up. She carried on speaking.

'I listen as I lie there on the floor. Not to the sickly, but to the healthy people in the room. In the night, when most of the white angels are asleep and only the night security guards are awake, the underworld comes to life. There are rooms under the floor, dug out of the ground.'

'What's in them?'

'The terrible things.'

Her voice was so weak that Louise was forced to lean forward in order to hear it. Lucinda had another coughing attack that threatened to choke her. When she tried to draw air into her lungs there was a gurgling noise. It was a long time after the end of the coughing attack before Lucinda could speak again. Louise heard the albino starting to play his timbila again after his break.

'You don't need to continue if you don't feel up to it.'

'I must. I might be dead tomorrow. I don't want you to have made this journey for nothing. Or Henrik.'

'What did you see?'

'The men in boots, aprons and rubber gloves giving people injections. But it's not only the sick who are injected. A lot of the people who come here are healthy, just as Umbi said. They are used as guinea pigs to try out untested vaccines. Then they are injected with infected blood. They're infected with the HIV virus to see if the vaccine works. Most of those lying in the room where you found me have been infected here. They were healthy when they arrived. But there are others as well, people like me who have been infected in some other way. We get drugs that haven't even been tested on animals, in an attempt to find a cure for people with full-blown Aids. For those carrying out the tests, it doesn't matter if the patients are humans or rats or chimpanzees. The animals are only a means to an end, really. They are not the ones the experimenters are trying to cure, after all. Who cares if some Africans are sacrificed if the outcome is drugs and vaccines that people in the Western world can benefit from?'

'How can you know that?'

'I just know.'

Lucinda's voice had suddenly become stronger.

'I don't understand.'

'You ought to do.'

'How have you found out about all this? Just by listening?'

'I learned it from Henrik.'

'Did he see what you've seen?'

'He never said he had in so many words. I think he wanted to spare me that. But he taught me about the virus, how they try out various substances to see if they have a positive reaction and if there are any side effects. He'd taught himself, he'd never studied medicine. But he wanted to know. He started work here as a volunteer in order to find

309

out the truth. I think that what he experienced here was worse than anything he'd imagined.'

Louise felt for Lucinda's hand in the darkness.

'Do you think that's why he died? Because he'd discovered what went on in the underworld?'

'The people who work here are strictly forbidden to go down to the basement where all the virus samples and drugs are kept. Henrik disobeyed that order. He needed to find out, he dared to enter the forbidden area and he went down those stairs.'

Louise tried to let what Lucinda had said sink in. Henrik had descended into another world and discovered a secret that had cost him his life.

She'd been right. Henrik had been murdered. Somebody had forced those sleeping pills down him. But there was still a doubt gnawing inside her. Could the truth really be that simple?

'I can tell you more tomorrow,' said Lucinda, and now her voice was once more a whisper, barely audible. 'I don't have the strength to speak any more now.'

'You can't stay here. I'll take you away.'

'If you try to take me away they'll never leave my family in peace. I'm staying here. I have to die somewhere.'

Louise realised that it was pointless trying to persuade her to allow Warren to lift her into his lorry and carry her away.

'How will you manage to get back here?'

'It's as well that you don't know. But you don't need to worry. Can you stay here until tomorrow?'

'I have a room in the hotel.'

'Come back when you hear the timbila in the darkness. I might be in a slightly different place, but I'll be back, unless I've stopped breathing. It's never good to die before you've finished saying what you have to say.'

'You're not going to die.'

'I am going to die. Neither you nor I can doubt that fact. Do you know what I'm most afraid of? Not that it might hurt, not because my heart will resist until the very last moment. I'm afraid because I shall be dead for such an incredibly long time. I see no end to my death. Go now.'

Louise made no reply. There was nothing she could say.

The sound of the timbila rose and sank in the darkness and the breezes off the sea.

Louise stood up and walked to the illuminated hotel entrance. There was no sound from the darkness where Lucinda was concealed.

A party of South Africans were eating at a table in the dining room. Louise discovered Warren in the bar. He beckoned to her. She could see from his eyes that he was drunk.

'I've been trying to call you, but you didn't answer. I thought you must have walked out into the sea and disappeared.'

'My mobile has been switched off.'

'I've been very worried. Do you need me any more tonight?'

'No.'

'What about tomorrow? I usually have a bet with the sun, about who'll be up first, her or me.'

'Can I pay you for what you've done so far?'

'Not now. Tomorrow, or another day. Sit down here and tell me all about the country you come from. About all that cold and snow.'

'I'm too tired. Maybe tomorrow.'

She went up to her room. She was completely exhausted. Her thoughts were spinning round inside her head. She ought to go to the dining room and have something to eat, despite the fact that she was not hungry in the least. She also needed to sit down and write out everything that Lucinda had said. It would be the first step towards a deposition. But all that happened in fact was that she stood at the window.

There were three vehicles parked outside the hotel, two white 4x4 people carriers and Warren's lorry. She frowned. Who was Warren, in fact? Why had his brother, the receptionist, not recognised her? He ought to have done. Had he concealed the fact that he knew who she was? Why did Warren not want to be paid? The questions were racing through her head. Had he been commissioned to keep an eye on her?

She shook her head, drew the curtains, checked that the door was locked, jammed a chair between the door and a chest of drawers and got ready for bed. She heard the two South African cars starting up and driving away. When she had finished washing she went back to the window and peeped out between the curtains. Warren's lorry was still there. The timbila had fallen silent.

She snuggled down in bed. The air conditioning was clattering, and coughing out short bursts of cool air. In her mind she filtered through what Lucinda had said, searching for anything important that she had overlooked.

When she woke up it was already morning. At first she had no idea where she was. She leapt out of bed and opened the curtains. Warren's lorry was no longer there. A black woman naked from the waist up was getting washed under the tap outside the hotel entrance. Louise looked at the clock and realised that she must have slept solidly for eight hours. She looked at the place where she had met Lucinda. The tree was still lying there. A few hens were scratching and pecking in the grass. She remembered what she had thought about Warren, and felt ashamed.

I see things that are not there, she thought. I must search where it's dark, not where it's light.

The sea was glistening. She could resist no longer. She put on her bathing costume, wrapped a bath towel around her, and walked down to the beach. It was almost deserted. A few small boys were playing on the sands, a group of women were paddling around in the shallows with backs bent, gathering something or other from the water, possibly mussels. Louise waded out until she was able to start swimming. There was a current, but nothing she was unable to cope with.

Artur was by her side. They were swimming in the dark tarn, and between strokes he kept telling her that it was bottomless.

She speeded up. Swimming always made her feel more relaxed. At times when she and Aron were having major problems, she had sometimes gone off to swim, in the sea or a lake or a pool, whatever was nearest to hand. She lay on her back and gazed up at the blue sky. The meeting with Lucinda had been a dream hard to pin down.

When she finally left the water and dried herself, she felt more relaxed than she had done for ages. She went back to the hotel. Warren's lorry was not parked under any of the shady trees. She could smell the aroma of newly grilled fish from the nearby camping site. The albino had not yet arrived with his timbila. She was the only person in the dining room. A waitress she had never seen before came to take her order. She ordered not only coffee and rolls, but also an omelette. There was an air of unreal calm over the dining room. Apart from herself, the waitress and somebody busy out of sight in the kitchen, the world was empty.

*Henrik must have been in this dining room at some point, eating. Perhaps it was like now, having breakfast in total isolation, waiting for the albino to start playing his timbila.*

She had another cup of coffee. There was no sign of the waitress when she wanted to pay. She put the money under her saucer and left the dining room. Warren had not arrived yet. She went back to her room and unlocked the door.

Only when she had closed the door behind her did she notice that there was a man sitting on one of the two chairs in front of the window. Christian Holloway rose to his feet. He smiled and stretched out his arms apologetically.

'I know that one ought not to enter the rooms of people one doesn't know without being invited. If you like I'll be happy to leave and then knock on your door, like honest men do.'

'How did you get in? Wasn't the door locked?'

'I've always had a penchant for what one might call unusual accomplishments. I found it a challenge to learn how to pick locks. I must say that this door wasn't the most difficult one I've managed to negotiate. In Shanghai I once succeeded in forcing a triple lock on the door of a temple. But I also devote myself to other skills. For instance, I have acquired the ancient skill of cutting out silhouettes. It's difficult, demands a lot of practice, but is an excellent way of relaxing.'

'Why did Henrik have a silhouette of you?'

'I gave it to him. He had seen Chinese silhouettists, and was keen

313

to learn the art. There's something fascinating about the process of reducing people to shadows and profiles.'

'Why have you come here?'

'You have displayed an interest in the work I do here. The least I can do is to devote some time to a conversation which might enable me to give you something in return.'

'I would like to get dressed in private.'

'When would you like me to return?'

'I would prefer to meet you downstairs.'

He frowned.

'There's too much noise, too many distractions in the restaurant and the bar. Instruments playing out of tune, pots and pans clattering in the kitchen, people talking about nothing.'

'I don't share that attitude. But I'll be ready in half an hour.'

'Then I'll come back here then.'

He left the room without a sound. He had evidently learned something from the Africans he held in such contempt. He had learned how to move across a floor in total silence.

She got dressed and at the same time tried to prepare herself for his return. How would she be able to confront him with all her questions? Would she be able to tell him outright that she thought he was responsible for the death of her only son? I ought to be afraid, she told herself. I ought to be terrified. If I'm right he could easily kill me in the same way as he's killed Henrik and Umbi. Even if he's alone when he enters this room, he has bodyguards everywhere. They are invisible, but they're there.

His knock on the door was so quiet that she hardly heard it. When she opened it there stood Christian Holloway, alone. He smiled and came in.

'Once upon a time this hotel is said to have been a favourite haunt of South African tourists. During the era of Portuguese colonialism Mozambique was a paradise on earth. It could offer beaches, fishing, heat, and not least lots of young girls who cost next to nothing to bed. Now all that is a memory that has almost faded away.'

'Despite everything, the world sometimes becomes a better place.'

'That depends on who you ask.'

'I'm asking. I wonder who you are, what drives you to do what you do.'

'Is that why you keep coming back here?'

'My son Henrik came here once. You know that. Then he went back to Sweden and died. You know that as well.'

'I've already expressed my condolences. Unfortunately, I don't believe it's possible to share one's grief with anybody else. One is alone with one's grief, just as one is alone when one dies.'

'Why did my son have to die?'

He did not lose his composure. His expression was sincere, his eyes looked straight into hers.

'Why do you think I'd be able to answer that question?'

'I think you're the only one who can answer that question.'

'What do you think I know?'

'Why he died. And who killed him.'

'You said yourself that the police concluded it was suicide.'

'But it wasn't. Somebody forced those sleeping tablets down him.'

'I know from experience how difficult it is to accept the facts when one's child takes his own life.'

'I know that your son committed suicide because he was HIV-positive.'

She detected a glint of surprise in Holloway's eyes, but he quickly regained his composure.

'I'm not surprised that you know about that. Your son obviously knew. It's not possible to keep anything secret in these times.'

'Henrik was convinced it was possible to cover anything up. Hence his interest in the conspiracy theory behind Kennedy's brain.'

'I remember that. The Warren commission failed to unearth anything. I expect there is a very simple explanation that nobody bothered to look into.'

'Henrik said that what is typical of the modern world is that the truth is always suppressed by those who have an interest in allowing untruths to hold sway. Or in using them as a means of encouraging wild speculation that is difficult to counter.'

'I wouldn't have thought that was typical only of our age. I can't think of any epoch when exactly the same criteria didn't apply.'

'But isn't it our mission to expose lies and fight injustice?'

Christian Holloway spread his arms out wide.

'I oppose injustice in my own way, by fighting ignorance and fear. I demonstrate that one can make a contribution. You ask what drives me. I'll tell you. It's the desire to know why an uneducated man like Genghis Khan could defeat sophisticated military organisations and civilised high nations far away from the steppes of Mongolia and establish an empire, the likes of which the world had never seen. What was the weapon that nobody could cope with? I think I have the answer.'

'And that is?'

'Their longbows. The way in which they learned to become as one with their horses. Their ability to define that magic moment when an arrow could be dispatched with great accuracy, despite the fact that their horses were galloping at breakneck speed. Like all important solutions, that one was simple. Nowadays I can only blush when I think how long it took me to reach that conclusion. The answer was, of course, that the cavalrymen learned how to shoot their arrows when their horses hooves were in the air. For a brief moment there was perfect balance. A cavalryman who could shoot at that split second was certain to hit his target. The main point about Genghis Khan was not that he and his hordes advanced thirsting for blood: he had calculated the exact moment when chaos can be transformed into calm. I use that as my inspiration, and I try to live my life in accordance with that.'

'By building these complexes?'

'By trying to attain a balance that has not been achieved hitherto. The people in Africa who become HIV-positive die. Unless you happen to have been born into one of the few rich families. But if you are infected in the Western world, you can count on receiving the treatment and the drugs that you need irrespective of the status of your parents.'

'There's an underworld out there in your village. It's like a slave ship.

The well-to-do passengers pace back and forth on deck; but down below, the rest are huddled together in chains, the slaves.'

'I don't understand what you're talking about.'

'There is an underworld. Where experiments are taking place on both sick and healthy people. I know about it, even if I can't prove it.'

'Who says so?'

'There was a man there who tried to talk to me about it. The next day, he had vanished. Another man tried to tell me about what goes on. He had his throat cut.'

'I know nothing about this.'

'But you are responsible for what goes on out there?'

'Of course.'

'In that case you are responsible for the opposite of what you say happens in your *missions*.'

'Let me explain something to you. There is no such thing as a world without combat, no civilisation which doesn't start off by laying down the rules for relations between people. But the rules are there for the weak. The strong man experiments to find out how far they can be stretched, he creates his own rules. You would like everything to be based on the goodwill and charity of one's fellow men. But if there is no private profit to be made, there will be no progress. Drug patents guarantee the profits that make research and the development of new drugs possible. Just let's suppose that what you allege about our villages is true – I'm not saying that it is, but let's suppose it. Surely some good would come out of what appears to be a brutal activity? Remember how urgent it is to find a cure for Aids. Southern Africa in particular is faced with a catastrophe of gigantic proportions – the only possible comparison is the plague. Which governments do you imagine are prepared to invest the billions needed to find a vaccine? The kind of money that is needed for more important ventures, such as the war in Iraq.'

Christian Holloway stood up.

'My time is precious. I have to go now. Please do come back here, whenever you like.'

'I shall not give up until I find out what happened to Henrik.'

He opened the door without a sound.

'I apologise for having picked the lock on your door. The temptation was irresistible.'

He vanished down the corridor. Louise watched through the window as he left the hotel and was picked up by a car.

Her whole body was shaking. He had eluded her. She had not succeeded in confronting him and breaking down his defences. She had asked her questions, but he was the one who had received the answers. She realised *now* that he had come in order to find out how much she knew. He had left her because he no longer needed to be afraid of her.

Now her big hope was Lucinda. She was the only one who could throw light on what had actually happened.


That evening she heard the timbila playing in the darkness. This time the music was coming from a spot closer to the sea. She followed the sound, being careful where she placed her feet and peering into the night. The moon was new, the night sky covered by a thin mist.

When the music stopped she listened for Lucinda's breathing, but heard nothing. For a moment she wondered if she had fallen into a trap. There was no Lucinda there in the darkness, there were different shadows lying in wait for her, just as they had waited for Umbi, for Henrik, and perhaps also for Aron.

Then she heard Lucinda calling to her, close by. A match flared up, a lantern was lit. Louise sat down on the ground beside her. She felt Lucinda's forehead: she must have a very high temperature.

'You shouldn't have come. You're too ill.'

'I know. But you have to die somewhere. The soil is just as good here as it is anywhere else. Besides, I shan't die alone. I shan't lie under the ground without company. There are more people in the land of the dead than in the land of the living. It's just a question of choosing to die where other dead people are waiting.'

'Christian Holloway came to visit me today.'

'I gathered he was going to. Did you watch your back when you came here? Was there anybody following you?'

'I didn't see anybody.'

'I didn't ask what you saw. I asked if anybody followed you.'

'I neither heard nor saw anything.'

Louise noticed that Lucinda moved further away from her.

'I need space around me. My fever is burning all the oxygen away.'

'What did you want to tell me?'

'The continuation. The end. If there is an end.'

But Lucinda was unable to say any more. A gun shot shattered the silence. Lucinda gave a start, then fell to the side, and lay there totally still.

Louise suddenly saw before her all the pictures in Henrik's files. Lucinda had been hit in the head in exactly the same place as the bullet had entered John F. Kennedy's brain. But nobody would bother to hide the brain that was now oozing out of Lucinda's head.

Louise screamed. She had reached the end of her journey, but nothing had turned out as she had hoped. She now had the truth before her. She knew who had fired the shot. It was a man who cut out silhouettes, an elusive shadow, who maintained to the world that he only meant well. But who would believe her? Lucinda's death was the inexorable end of the story.

Louise wanted to stay with Lucinda, but she did not dare. In all her confusion and fear she hoped that one of Lucinda's invisible friends was in the darkness outside the circle of light surrounding the lantern, and that they would take care of her.

Yet another sleepless night filled with terror. She did not have the strength to think. Everything was an infinite, frozen vacuum.

In the morning she heard Warren's lorry approaching the hotel. She went down to reception and paid her bill. When she left the hotel she found Warren waiting outside, smoking. There was no sign of anything at the spot where Lucinda had died. No people, no corpse, nothing. Warren threw away his cigarette when he saw Louise, and frowned at her.

'There was shooting here last night,' he said. 'We Africans have far too many ownerless weapons in our hands. We shoot one another far too often.'

Warren opened the lorry door for her.

'Where do you want to go today? It's a lovely day. I can show you lagoons where the water runs through your hands like pearls. In South Africa I used to dig for treasure in deep mines. Here, diamonds run through my fingers in the form of valuable drops of water.'

'Another time. Not now. I have to return to Maputo.'

'So far?'

'So far! I'll pay you whatever you ask.'

He did not mention a price, merely climbed into the driver's seat, started the engine and engaged first gear. Louise turned round and took one last look at the beach where she had been forced to endure all the terrible happenings, and which she would never see again.


They drove through the morning, creating clouds of red dust. The sun was soon high in the sky, and heat sank down over the countryside.

Louise sat in silence all the long journey to Maputo, and paid without saying a word when they arrived. Warren asked no questions, merely said goodbye. She took a room in a hotel called Terminus, closed the door behind her and found herself diving headlong into an abyss. She spent two days at the hotel, spoke to nobody except the waiters who occasionally brought her meals which she hardly touched. She did not even phone Artur, to ask for help.

On the third day she forced herself to get out of bed and left both the hotel and Mozambique. She came to Madrid via Johannesburg in the afternoon of 23 December. All flights to Barcelona were fully booked by people wanting to celebrate Christmas there. She toyed with the idea of taking a train, but decided to stay when she found a seat on a flight leaving the following morning.

It was raining in Madrid. Glittering Christmas decorations were hanging over the streets and in shop windows, and she glimpsed strange-looking Father Christmases through the window of her taxi. She had booked a room in the most expensive hotel she knew, the Ritz, with its fine old traditions.

She and Aron had passed by there once, on their way to the Prado Museum. She could still remember how they had considered splashing out on a suite for the night. Now her room was being paid for by Aron's money, but he himself had vanished. His absence was causing her constant pain. It was only now she began to realise that when she found him among the red parrots, something of her original love for him had been reawakened.

She visited the museum on the other side of the street. She could still remember the way to the collections of Goya's paintings and etchings.

She and Aron had spent ages gazing at the painting of an old woman, he had taken hold of her hand, and they realised afterwards that they had both been thinking about inevitable old age.

She spent the whole afternoon at the museum, trying to forget for a while everything that had happened.


It was raining the next day when she left for Barcelona. When she disembarked she felt dizzy and had to lean against the wall of the ramp leading into the terminal building. A stewardess asked if she needed help. Louise shook her head, and continued walking. She felt as if she had been travelling constantly since the day she left Argolis and boarded the early Lufthansa flight for Stockholm via Frankfurt. In her mind, mainly to keep the dizzy feeling at bay, she counted up all the departures and arrivals: Athens–Frankfurt–Stockholm–Visby–Stockholm–Östersund–Stockholm–Frankfurt–Singapore–Sydney–Melbourne–Bangkok–Frankfurt–Barcelona–Madrid–Johannesburg–Maputo–Johannesburg–Frankfurt–Athens–Frankfurt–Stockholm–Östersund–Stockholm–Frankfurt–Johannesburg–Maputo–Johannesburg–Madrid–Barcelona.

They had been stations on a nightmarish journey. All around her people had kept disappearing or dying. She would never be able to forget the sight of Umbi and Lucinda, even if the images would perhaps begin to fade and resemble pale old photographs in which eventually it would be impossible to distinguish facial features any more. Christian Holloway would also remain in her memory. A cut-out silhouette of a totally ruthless person who would never submit.

And behind these faces were all the shadows, the faceless ones.


She went to Henrik's flat. Blanca was scrubbing the stairs when she arrived.

They sat for a long time in Blanca's flat, talking. Afterwards, Louise could not remember much of what had been said. But she asked who it was that had visited Henrik's flat, shortly after he had died. Blanca looked uncomprehendingly at her.

'I had the distinct impression that you were not telling the truth, that somebody had been here in fact.'

'Why would I have lied?'

'I don't know. That's why I'm asking.'

'You must have been mistaken. Nobody came here. I held nothing back from you.'

'OK, I got it wrong.'

'Has Aron come back?'

'No.'

'I don't understand it.'

'Perhaps it was all too much for him. People can be fragile. Maybe he simply ran off to Apollo Bay.'

'Haven't you been there to look for him?'

'I mean a different Apollo Bay, one whose location I don't know. The only reason I've come back here is to take one last look at Henrik's flat. I'd like to be alone there.'

She went up to the flat, and it struck her that just now the room she was standing in was at the very centre of her life. It was Christmas Eve, grey, raining, and she still had no idea of what course her life would take in future.

When she left, Blanca came to her with a letter in her hand.

'I forgot to give you this. It arrived a couple of days ago.'

There was no sender's address. The postmark showed that it had been posted in Spain. It was addressed to her at the hotel she had stayed in previously.

'How did you get hold of this?'

'Somebody from the hotel brought it. You must have given them Henrik's address.'

'Perhaps I did. I can't remember.'

Louise put it into her pocket.

'Are you sure there aren't any more letters that you've forgotten about?'

'I haven't got any more, no.'

'No more letters that Henrik asked you to send? In a year's time? Ten years'?'

Blanca understood what Louise meant. She shook her head. There were no more letters like the one she had sent to Nazrin.


It had stopped raining. Louise decided to go for a long walk, tire herself out, and then have dinner at her hotel. Before going to sleep she would phone Artur and wish him a Merry Christmas. Perhaps she would go back home in time for Boxing Day? At the very least she would assure him that she would be home for New Year.

It was late in the evening that she remembered the letter. She read it in her room. With a sense of increasing horror, she realised that nothing was over, the pain that was afflicting her had not yet reached its culmination.

The text was in English. All references to names, countries, towns were crossed out in black Indian ink.


Personal particulars correspond to the data on the identification tag attached to the corpse. The overall skin colour is pale, livor mortis bluish-red on the back of the corpse. Rigor mortis is still present. There are petechiae in the conjunctivae and around the eyes. No foreign bodies are present in the auditory meatus, the nasal cavities, the oral cavity or the rectal orifice. Visible mucous membranes are pale with no sign of haemorrhage. There are no signs of injury on the body, apart from an old scar on the back. The external sexual organs are uninjured and free from extraneous content.

Louise still had no idea what the letter was about. But she had a vague feeling of anxiety. She read on:

The internal examination shows that the scalp displays no sign of haemorrhage. The skull is uninjured, the cranium pale on the inside. No haemorrhage is visible outside or underneath the hard membrane of the brain. The surface of the brain appears to be normal. The tentorium and occipital cavity have not been exposed to pressure. The medial line has not been distorted. The soft membranes are glossy and smooth. There is no trace of haemorrhage or pathological change between the membranes. The brain cells are normal in size. The border between grey and white fluid is clearly marked. The grey cells are normal in colour. The brain tissue is normal in consistency. There is no trace of deposits in the arteries at the base of the brain.

She continued reading about circulatory organs, breathing organs, digestive organs, urinary organs. The list was long, and concluded with an examination of the skeleton. The conclusions came at the end.

The deceased was found dead lying face down on the tarmac. No specific objects have been found at the site. The occurrence of petechiae indicates that the cause of death was strangulation. The conclusion is that the cause of death was probably intentional action by another party.

What she had in her hand was a forensic report of a post-mortem examination, conducted at an unknown hospital by an unknown pathologist. It was only when she read the details of height and weight that she realised to her horror that the corpse being subjected to the autopsy was that of Aron.

*Intentional action by another party.* When Aron left the church, some-body had attacked him, strangled him and left him lying in the street. But who had found him? Why had the Spanish police not contacted her? Who were the doctors who had conducted the post-mortem examination?

She felt a desperate need to speak to Artur. She phoned him but made no mention of Lucinda or the post-mortem report, merely said that Aron was dead and she was unable to say any more at this moment. He was too sensible to ask any questions. Apart from wondering when she was coming home.

'Soon,' she said.

She emptied the minibar and wondered how she would be able to cope with all the grief she was being forced to bear. She felt that the last of the columns propping up her inner resistance was about to give way. That night in her hotel room in Barcelona, with the post-mortem report lying on the floor beside her bed, she had the feeling that she no longer had the strength to keep going.

The next day she returned to Henrik's flat. While she was trying to make up her mind about what to do with his belongings, it suddenly dawned on her what she had to do in order to continue living.

There was only one way, and it started here, in Henrik's flat. Her mission would be to finish the story he had been unable to tell. She would dig down, and piece together the fragments she found.

What was it that Lucinda had said? *It's never good to die before you've finished saying what you have to say.* Her own story. And Henrik's. And Aron's.

Three stories that had now combined to form one.

She had to take over, now that nobody else could.

She felt that it was urgent. Time was shrinking wherever she looked. But first of all she would go home, to Artur. They would go together to Henrik's grave, and also light a candle for Aron.

\*  \*  \*

On 27 December Louise left her hotel and took a taxi to the airport. It was foggy. She paid the taxi driver and made her way to the Iberia check-in desk before boarding the flight that would take her to Stockholm.

For the first time for ages she felt strong. Her compass had ceased to spin wildly.

When she had checked in her bag she paused to buy a newspaper before proceeding to the security barrier.

She never noticed the man observing her from a distance.

It was only when she had passed through security that he left the departure lounge and headed for the city.

# EPILOGUE

Twenty years ago, close to Zambia's western border with Angola, I watched a young African man die of Aids.

It was the first time I had witnessed such a thing, but not the last.

The memory of that man's face has been in my mind's eye all the time I spent planning and writing this book.

It is a novel, it is fiction. But the borderline between what has really happened and what might well have happened is often almost non-existent. Naturally, I dig down in a different way from a journalist; but we both illuminate the darkest corners of people, society and the world around us. The result is not infrequently identical.

I have taken the liberties that fiction allows me. To give just one example: as far as I am aware, no member of the past or present embassy staff or Sida delegation in Maputo, or anywhere else come to that, is called Lars Håkansson. In the unlikely event of my assumption being wrong, I hereby declare once and for all that he is not the person portrayed in this book!

One seldom comes across the values I have attributed to him. I wish I could write 'never', but alas, I cannot.

I have received help from many people in what can be described as this descent into an abyss. I would like to mention two of them by name. First and foremost Robert Johnsson, in Gothenburg, who dug out everything I asked him for, and in addition added extra spice by way of his own discoveries. Also Dr Anastazia Lazaridou at the Byzantine Museum in Athens, who piloted me through the complicated world of archaeology.

Many thanks to them, and to all the others.

In conclusion, a novel can end on page 185 or page 326, but reality continues apace. What is written in this book is exclusively the result of my own choices and decisions, of course. Just as the anger is also mine, the anger that was my driving force.

Henning Mankell
Fårö, May 2005